Light in the Shadow

A Romance Novel

by

Annetta Hobson

Light in the Shadow

Cover Art: Dana Queen, DonnaInk Publications.

Editors: Philip Bartholomew, Tracey Street.

Published by: DonnaInk Publications.

Copyright © 2013.

ISBN: 978-1-939425-18-8

Published in the United States of America.

First Edition 2013.

All Rights Reserved. Safe Harbor as Appropriate.

No part of this publication may be reproduced, stored in or introduced into a retrieval system or transmitted, in any form or by any means (electronic, mechanical, photocopying, recording or otherwise) without prior written permission of DonnaInk Publications (www.donnaink.org). For more information contact the Special Markets Division at DonnaInk Publications (special_markets@donnaink.org).

Library of Congress Cataloging-in-Publication Data

Hobson, Annetta – Author, 2013.

Light in the Shadow / Annetta Hobson.

358 p. cm.

ISBN – 13 – 978-1-939425-18-8 (alk. paper)

1-Fiction, 2-Romance, 3-Thriller, 4-Drama, 5-Relationships, 6-Psychological Thriller, 7-Mystery, 8-Sexting, 9-Murder Mystery, 10-Other.

First Edition 10 9 8 7 6 5 4 3 2 1; March 2013.

Other Annetta Hobson Works
Soon to be released by DonnaInk Publications!

Chronicles of a Betrothed

Love's Therapy

Reverse Seduction Prequel

Reverse Seduction

The Flame

Weather Vane

Table of Contents

Other Annetta Hobson Works i
Dedication v
Acknowledgements vii
Chapter 1 1
Chapter 2 25
Chapter 3 49
Chapter 4 71
Chapter 5 91
Chapter 6 115
Chapter 7 137
Chapter 8 159
Chapter 9 183
Chapter 10 203
Chapter 11 219
Chapter 12 245
Chapter 13 269
Chapter 14 287
Chapter 15 303
Chapter 16 321
About the Author 345
Connect With Annetta! 347

Dedication

I would like to dedicate this novel to my wonderful husband Lindsay Hobson, who believed in me when I did not believe in myself. Also for giving me the inspiration to put my steamy imagination in writing. I thank him for his understanding, while I continue to burn the midnight oils typing away on my laptop. I love you with all of my heart.

~Annetta~

Acknowledgements

First, I would like to thank my sister Anetris Norman-Williams who has been writing since the age of thirteen. I would have never started this novel, if it was not for her. Although I am living a dream she once desired, she has remained my biggest supporter. Growing up without her would have been very lonely. "Light in the Shadow," is our baby. Rayen Vasu was created during a three way conversation with Vivian about Mother's Day dinner. I pray you will get the time to finish what you have started.

Second, I would like to thank my best friend Vivian McClendon who stayed up many nights helping me with character development. Laughing and joking at some of the names she suggested, my list was finally completed. Also, for listening to all of my steamy scenes, even though we were both totally embarrassed. I love you!

I would like to thank Donna Quesinberry and DonnaInk Publications for taking a chance with my titles, I am eternally grateful. This company has been an absolute delight. I have never met anyone like them and I hope to continue working with you guys for years to come. As long as she publishes my work, I will continue writing.

Last, but not least, I would like to thank my little and big one's for annoying me into working with headphones blasting in my ears; I would have never learned music inspires novels if it were not for them. I love my children to pieces!

I hope everyone enjoys this, my debut, novel. I promise there is much more to come, including a sequel!

Chapter 1

Sunday, May 12th, Rayen enters the penthouse. The decorations are beautiful. She is happy her fifteenth birthday has finally arrived. *Today is going to be awesome!* She looks up at the banner overhead, which says. . . *Happy Birthday, Rayen.*

I can't wait! This is going to be my greatest birthday ever, Mom promised! Rayen spies the perfectly wrapped gift boxes and cannot help smile – she glances at the equally decorative box in her hands.

Mom's going to love her Mother's Day gift!

The dining room table is covered in elegantly wrapped boxes and as Rayen enters the kitchen her three-tiered birthday cake designed in red, pink and baby blue (her favorite colors) commands the room. Overwhelmed with excitement, she picks up the cordless from the kitchen wall.

"Aunt Margie, what time are you and Angie coming to my party? It's already three o'clock!" Rayen's racing pulse explodes into the phone.

"Well, dear, doesn't your party start at five? A little anxious aren't you?"

"Yes it does, and yes I am."

"We'll be there shortly, sweetie, we have some surprises you're going to like." Margaret speaks in a calming tone. . . "Don't worry Rayen – we wouldn't miss your special day!"

"May I speak with Angie, please?"

"Sure, hold on, sweetie."

"Hey Birthday Girl!" Angie says courteously.

Annetta Hobson

"Hi, Ang, I'm super psyched. You know Connor Worthy is coming. And, I'm so nervous, I want to pass out!" Rayen blushes as her cousin Angie begins to laugh.

"Rayen, you are so silly. What are you wearing?"

"You will see. Bye!" Rayen hangs up the phone and runs to her room.

"Mom! Where are you? Are you here?"

She steps into her bathroom and showers, when she's finished she walks back toward her room to dress. Lifting her dress in the air she looks it over. *I just love this dress. The pink satin, the flares at my knees, mom's so cool – it is just perfect!*

Stepping into the dress, Rayen zips the back and takes a look at herself in her mirror.

"Mom!" *Why hasn't she come to help me get ready? What could she be doing?*

Rayen walks into the hallway. *Why it is so quiet?* "Mom! Dad! Where are you guys?"

Running up the second flight of stairs, Rayen heads to her parents' room and hollers for them again.

"Mom! Dad! Are you guys here? My party starts in an hour."

At the corner of her parents' room, she spots the heel of the blue shoe her mother was wearing earlier in the morning. Then she rounds the corner into her folks bathroom to find her mom lying in the middle of the floor.

Her mother's long black hair covers her face; Rayen's heart starts to beat.

"Mom!" She screams.

Light in the Shadow

Rayen races to her mother's side and uncovering her face she gently pulls her mom's hair back.

"Mom?" Crying in a whimper, Rayen spots the thick pool of red blood surrounding her mother's head.

"Mommy! Mommy!"

Rayen lays her mother's head back down on the floor and rests her own head on her mother's back and begins to sob uncontrollably.

"Help me! Somebody, help me!" She screams wildly as the front door creeks open.

"Rayen! Rayen! Where are you dear? What's going on? What are you screaming about?"

"Aunt Margie? Is that you?" Lifting her head and sobbing relentlessly, Rayen asks. . . "Help me! It's momma – something's wrong!"

Margaret bolts up the stairs to the sounds of Rayen's voice.

"Oh my God!" Margaret covers her mouth seeing Kalena lying in a pool of blood and rushes to stop her daughter Angie from entering the room and seeing the gruesome scene.

"Angie, go - call the police! Hurry – do it now!"

Running down to the kitchen Angie dials 911.

"Rayen, what happened? Who did this? Where you here?" Aunt Margie's questions pulse through a sea of tears.

"I don't know, Aunt Margie. I just found her before you got here."

Margaret lifts Rayen from the floor and pulls her away from her parents' room.

***

Annetta Hobson

What seems like only moments later - police knock at the door. In a short time, a full force of men and women bombard the normally quiet penthouse suite.

Margaret, Rayen and Angie sit in the living room on the sofa in shock and disbelieving silence.

All Rayen can do is think. Why is *everyone speaking so loudly? Why do all these cameras keep snapping?*

Angie sits next to her with arms wrapped around Rayen's neck. *Who would do this?* Burying her head in Rayen's shoulder, Angie's tears soak the sleeve of her satin party dress.

Staring at the police Rayen continues to think, *When will they tell me mom is okay? Where is my dad?*

No one approaches her for what seems like hours passing in silence. Finally, an African American woman with a short haircut walks over to talk with Rayen, her aunt and cousin.

"Hello, Rayen. I am Detective Joanna Shaw. We are with the homicide division of the NYPD. Do you understand what has happened here?"

"No ma'am. Is my mom okay? And, where is my dad?" Rayen chokes - her voice cracks.

Detective Shaw sits down next to her while Angie and Aunt Margie get up to stand nearby.

"Well, honey, your dad was in the bathroom a few feet away from your mom."

"Can I see him? Where is he at?"

Detective Shaw bows her head, *God, I don't want to traumatize this child more than she has already been today...*

"Rayen you can't talk with your father, we need to go to the police station and discuss this where it is quieter."

Light in the Shadow

The detective helps Rayen up from the couch and signals to her aunt to join them. Margaret wraps her arm around Rayen's shoulder and they head to the police station with the detective.

***

Exhausted after hours in the stationhouse, Rayen begins pleading to return home. . ."I just want to go home!"

"I know you are tired, but we have questions, which have to be answered. I'm sorry – we'll get you out of here as soon as possible." Detective Shaw tries to be empathetic.

"Can you tell me about my parents first?"

"Well, Rayen, Mr. and Mrs. Vasu are both dead. We are trying to learn what happened, so far we can't tell. We are hoping you may have details from today to help us."

"No! You're lying! No!" Rayen shrieks while shaking her head from side to side hysterically. She tries to dismiss all thoughts. . . *They are wrong – that cannot be true. It just can't be true.*

"I wish I could say I'm lying Rayen, but it is true we're very sorry."

Positioning her head on the cold table over her hands, Rayen's tears stream down her face over the tan fleshiness of her hands onto the silver metal table where they form a pool of liquid.

"Why? Why?"

"I was hoping you could tell us, Rayen. Can you give us all the details from the time you woke this morning till you found your mom?"

"I don't know. We were getting ready for my birthday party. It was a normal morning. Nothing strange happened, but yes, I'll try." An incoherently detailed expose of her day ensues as Rayen explains how her mother woke her for a big birthday breakfast. She then rambles in disjointed fashion as to how her father gave her mom a platinum pendant and necklace because it happened to also be Mother's Day. She mumbles further regarding her mother's need for her to visit with her friend Evelyn Drake so the party and decorations could be handled without her supposedly knowing... *If only I hadn't gone, maybe...*

"Evelyn and I went on 5th Avenue to shop for mom's day gifts. Then, I returned home." Rayen begins to slur unintelligibly as shock and exhaustion seize her mind, she mutters to the detective... "This is all I can say about today – other than – than finding my mom..." Tears again course her face to the table and the room grows silent.

"Well, thank you, Rayen. I think it is time for you to leave and get some rest. We are doing everything we can to find out what happened to your mom and dad. We'll discover who did this to your parents.

Here take my card and call me for anything and if you remember something else let me know." The detective motions to Margaret who grabs Rayen's arm and to lead her out of the stationhouse.

"I will Detective Shaw." Rayen mutters...

Aunt Margie responds, "Yes, we'll call if we learn anything else."

"One more thing, do you know of anyone who would want to hurt Rayen's parents Margaret, Rayen?" The detective asks probingly.

"No ma'am. Everyone loves my mom and dad. They are the best." Margaret nods her head in agreement.

Light in the Shadow

With her face planted in her palms, Rayen is ushered out of the lobby by her Aunt Margret and Cousin Angie.

***

"Come on, baby. You have Angie and me. We'll get you home and take care of this. Don't you worry." Margaret smiles with tears in her eyes while hugging Rayen as they leave the police department.

***

The following morning, Rayen wakes disoriented, not quite remembering where she was and the reality of her situation.

"Rayen, how are you?" Angie asks concerned. Rayen stares blankly, realizing once again the events of the day prior were not a dream.

Her parents are dead – she is alone in the world.

"I wish I were dead too; why am I still here? It's not fair!"

"Rayen! What are you saying?" Angie barks at her cousin, "I'm appalled you'd say something like this – your mother and father would not want you to die."

Rayen blinks and pulls the covers over her head.

Margaret enters the room, her bloodshot eyes are red and her mocha colored skin is flushed from crying all night. "Rayen, baby, are you hungry?"

There's no answer.

***

Margaret had met Kalena when Rayen was a baby. She wanted to work for her as a nanny. Kalena felt a connection to her because they were both new mothers. They were best friends. And, their girls were inseparable. She did not know how she would stay strong for them. Her dear friends were dead.

Rayen's head continues shaking frenziedly under her covers while nothing is said. They are all numb.

"Honey, I know that this is the most horrific experience that could ever happen to you, but you need to be well. Your mom and dad would. . ."

Rayen lifts up her head from under the covers looking into Margaret's eyes with a grave sadness. Not knowing what else to say, Margaret leaves the room, Angie follows.

The next day is the same – questions about eating – no response. Rayen only gets up to use the restroom.

"Ma, if Rayen doesn't eat, will she die too?" Angie inquires with worry.

"Angie, I would never let that happen! Now, you eat your food, honey. Rayen will eat when she is ready. We cannot even imagine how hard this must be for her."

***

Days pass. Rayen's reddish brown skin begins to appear pekid. Her face becomes sunken in. Her Native American features seem more and more evident as the baby fatty cheeks reveal more definition in her cheek bones.

Her mother's Hawaiian heritage shows only in Rayen's beautiful hair.

***

Angie and Margaret sit in the kitchen hoping for a change in Rayen's composure.

Light in the Shadow

"Kalena had such beautiful hair." Margaret shares better times with her daughter.

"She was just beautiful, period, Mommy," Angie responds trying to make some sense of their plight.

"And, Rayen is a wonderful mixture of them both."

"Yes, her father Alec was a handsome man."

Rayen peeks around the corner and Margaret attempts to hide her tears. "Finally, you are up and walking around!"

"Who could have done this to my mom and dad, Aunt Margie? Who?"

"I wish I knew honey." Margie reaches out and hugs her as Rayen hums with discomfort. "Sorry, love. I'm just so happy you decided to get up again and to have you stay here with us.

Are you hungry?"

"Yes. I am."

Finally, Rayen consumes a full meal. She scarfs it down as if she's never eaten before.

"What day is this?" Rayen asks pausing from her assault on her plate.

"Umm, it's Thursday," Angie replies.

"Everyone at school sends condolences Rayen, especially Connor."

"I'm not ready to see anyone."

"It's fine Rayen, you'll go back to school when you are ready to speak to people. *That reminds me I need to contact Rayen's grandfather to ask for formal custody and find out what he is intending for funeral arrangements.*

Annetta Hobson

Rayen, your father's business partners have been calling for days. I have to get in touch with your grandfather, is this okay with you?

"I don't know my grandfather, Aunt Margie. Why do you have to talk with him?" Rayen sounds irritated.

"Well, he is your only living relative. He has to be contacted." Margaret sets a parental tone.

"Oh, okay. I guess so. Go ahead."

***

After a couple more days, Rayen talks more and begins to feel a little better interspersed with depression, but living with her Aunt Margie and Cousin Angie gives her a sense of normality.

The following Sunday morning, her Aunt Margaret tells Rayen her grandfather has been in touch and does not want a funeral for Kalena or Alec.

"Why not, Aunt Margie?"

"I don't know. Your parents never spoke of your grandfather, Len Chevey Vasu. I don't know or even understand his motives, but he has not mentioned his intentions for you. So, for now, we will rejoice you are here with us!" Margaret jumps in relief.

"Okay. Should I go to school now Aunt Margie?"

"If you want to, sweetie, but you can take your time."

"I will."

And, for the first time in a week, Rayen smiles.

***

Light in the Shadow

Monday morning is bleak. The rain is pouring outside. It is a dreary day. The memorial service for Rayen's parents is sweet and sad. It was finally arranged by Alec's business partners. Rayen holds up surprisingly well as everyone hugs her and gives their condolences. She nods and sobs all day.

Weeks pass quickly, and Rayen misses her parents dearly.

Through it all, she begins to shine a little more every day, which is a delight for Margaret to see. Aunt Margie is able to clean out the Vasu penthouse but doesn't tell Rayen.

Margaret knows she is not ready for that. Kalena was very organized, which made it possible for Margaret to gather everything Rayen needed to be cared for with a great ease.

By the first of July, Rayen is doing great - almost back to her bubbly self. The weight she had lost returned and her skin regained a beautiful red tone once again.

Rayen's beauty is evident. Her gorgeous hair flows in the wind as she runs around outside in the yard chasing Angela.

Life is almost normal for her again.

***

On Thursday, July 4th Rayen wakes up smiling.

Margaret promised to take her and Angela to the fireworks show.

It is something her and her parents did every year.

Around 2:00 in the afternoon, there is a stern knock at the front door.

Angela opens it.

"Hi," she says as she peers at the elderly man standing squarely in their doorway with a stone cold stare.

"I am Len Vasu. I am looking for my granddaughter."

"Umm, yes. Hold on a moment please." Angela runs and informs her mother. Margaret returns to the door.

"Yes, Mr. Vasu. May I help you?"

"Yes, by fetching my granddaughter. All the arrangements are set. I will take care of her now." Mr. Vasu speaks very rudely to Margaret.

"Mr. Vasu, I was under the impression Rayen would be staying here with me. You did not respond to any of my letters or phone calls," she returns meekly but with courage.

"You thought wrong, Miss Taylor. Your services are no longer needed." He stares, his eyes black as coal, at Margaret to let her know the conversation is over.

Len Chevey Vasu is a handsome man to be sixty-five with his rustic dark skin and long grey braid. He exudes power and is very scary!

Margaret turns away slowly.

"I'll get Rayen."

"I will send for her things. I have my own staff, so say your goodbyes," he resounds in a whisper of thunder.

She gasps, "We are all she has left! Surely, there is a way I can remain at least as her tutor or something. Please!"

"That will be all, Miss Taylor! Get my granddaughter."

Margaret goes to the bedroom. Rayen is bobbing her head to the music playing through headphones. She is on her stomach sprawled across the bed with her feet up behind her.

"Rayen, honey?" Margaret gently pulls the headphones away from her head.

Light in the Shadow

"Yes, Aunt Margie?"

"Your grandfather is here. He's going to take you to live with him. He has come to collect you." Margie cannot hide the tears in her eyes.

"Grab what you can. He does not want to wait."

"What? But...."

"Just get up, baby, and get what you can. You are leaving."

Puzzled, Rayen sits up. She grabs a duffle bag and stuffs some clothes in it and walks to the door.

"Grandfather, I would like to stay here with Aunt Margie and Angie."

He replies resoundingly, "This is not a request nor will it be debated."

A slim woman with large breasts, curly dirty blonde hair, and an expensively tailored navy blue suit walks up and grabs Rayen by the arm. She literally drags her off the porch without any introduction.

Margaret yells after the woman with fearlessness.

"Stop it! You don't have to do that to her!"

The woman pushes Rayen in the black limousine without a response and sits next to Rayen behind Len Chevey as the limo driver closes the door behind them.

Margaret and Angela stand in the doorway, hugging and crying as they watch the limousine pull off.

***

The airplane ride is silent. Rayen's grandfather and his aide don't speak. Tears stream down her face as she watches clouds from the window.

"Grandfather, where are we going? Will I ever see Aunt Margie or Angie again?"

Her grandfather doesn't answer; instead he drinks his scotch from his glass. Finally, the plane descends, and Rayen sees McCarran International Airport.

"Where are we, miss?" Rayen is curious where they've flown to.

"We are home!" The woman answers her fiercely.

Rayen hangs her head as they proceed to exit the plane.

The ride from the airport remains even more uncomfortable. There is a lot of desert land, which Rayen has never seen before. She stares at the dreary scenery in silence.

At last, the car pulls up to a glorious mansion surrounded by beautiful mountaintops. It has rust exterior with a lot of windows. The stairs spiral around the front to a grand porch.

There is no grass but lots of little pebbles. On the side, there is a manmade waterfall. The sight of it is breathtaking.

How could a mean old man live in such a dazzling place? They enter the foyer, and the inside is somehow not the sight the outside portrays. The hall leading toward the living room is draped in paisley fabric, making it dark. None of the windows allow the sun to shine through. The dining room is mostly the same; dark fabric covers the windows. When the woman turns on the light, the dining table looks as if it belongs in a castle hundreds of years old. All of the chairs are so tall they would swallow Rayen up.

"You are never to enter this area of the house unless you are summoned!" her grandfather belts without raising his voice.

"Yes, sir," Rayen says in a very small tone.

Light in the Shadow

"Vera, show the child where she will reside."

"Yes, Mr. Vasu," says the woman now known as Vera.

"Come girl." She waves at Rayen.

Traveling up a never-ending staircase, they finally reach a floor with many mahogany doors.

"This will be your room," Vera snaps.

"Thank you...Ms. Vera," Rayen answers timidly.

But, she just shoots Rayen a foul look and slams the door behind her.

Rayen is tired. It has been an exhausting time for her. She does not like her new home, but she decides to sleep since there is nothing she can do for now.

The next day, she wakes up very early to explore her new surroundings ever so cautiously. Everything is so dark. *It is so gloomy here.* As she enters one of the rooms, she hears a footstep behind her.

"Breakfast is ready!" Rayen spins around, startled by Vera.

"Yes Ma'am."

"Stay in your room, you little cunt!"

Rayen's mouth flies open. "I...I apologize."

"Just get your ass down stairs to eat."

Rayen is horrified.

At the table, Rayen looks at her grandfather as he robotically eats his breakfast. She just stabs at the eggs as if she is spearing fish. "Is there something wrong with the meal?"

"Umm, no, Grandfather...I just miss everyone."

"Well, since you are not grateful for a meal, return to your room. Vera?"

"Come," says Vera.

"But…" Rayen tries to protest.

"Close your fucking mouth, girl!" Vera Scolds. Rayen's eyes are so wide they look like they will pop out of her head.

"One thing you will learn: I am not the spineless man your father was. I will not coddle you!" Rayen's terror is evident.

Every passing day is torture for Rayen. She is not allowed to go anywhere, see or talk to anyone. She misses home terribly. There would be nothing better than being able to crawl up in bed with her mom and wake up to Aunt Margie's chocolate chip pancakes. Rayen wonders what Angela is doing and if they are thinking of her, too. "I hate who ever took my mom and dad from me!" Rayen screams in her pillow.

It has been weeks since Rayen has seen outside of this awful house. And, she tries to steer clear of that disgusting woman. One morning, Rayen awakes and lifts her head from under the covers, and Vera is standing over her.

"Oh my God! You frightened me." She clenches her chest. Vera smiles a devilish smile.

"Oh, child, it has only just begun. Rayen sits up and cocks her head to one side. "Get up and put this on!" She tosses a red nightgown to her.

"But, it is morning Ver…ma'am." Out of nowhere Vera slaps Rayen so hard she bites her lip.

"Shut up bitch and put it on!" Rayen begins to cry.

"I am sorry," she weeps. Vera just stands there and watches Rayen undress.

Light in the Shadow

"Hurry up!" She slips out of her t-shirt and night pants and puts on the gown. When she is dressed in the gown, Vera grabs her arm and whisks her down the hall and up some back stairs. Rayen is so frightened. She just keeps quiet. She doesn't want Vera to hit her again.

Vera lets go of Rayen's arm when they come to a door. It has a plate on it that says 'Library'. Vera knocks on the door, and her grandfather opens it. "What took so long?"

"She got testy. I had to silence her."

"Is that why her lip is bleeding?"

"Uh, yes, Chevey. Are you angry?"

"No. I am just anxious," he chuckles.

Rayen is confused. Her breathing is so rapid; they turn and look at her. Calm down girl. I am about to make you a woman. I hope you are as fine as you mother was under that gown.

Rayen gulps a big chunk of air. Then she lets out a gasp. "No! Grandfather! Please!"

"Say one more thing, and I am going to knock all those teeth out of that beautiful mouth!" Vera threatens. Before Rayen can say another word, Vera slams her on the chaise in the middle of the room. Her grandfather takes a step towards her.

The next day, Rayen awakes. She is sore and morbidly disgusted. Her body is covered with bruises. "Ooowww," she says silently. She rubs her arm. Sobbing, she looks up to the sky. "Mom, dad why? Why did you leave me? Please come get me. I want to be with you…" Just then, the door opens and Vera steps in.

She says, smirking, "Feel like a woman?" Rayen turns away. "Oh no bitch! Look at me!" Rayen turns slowly.

"What did I do...to deserve this?"

"You are breathing," Vera laughs. As she closes the door, she says, "Get dressed. Breakfast is ready."

Rayen comes down the stairs and slowly sits at the table. She is alone today. No one will be eating with her today. As the days drag by, Vera only yells in the door when it is time to eat. For a moment, Rayen thinks the worst is over.

About a week later, Vera shows up early at her bedside. "Get up, little whore!" Tears stream down Rayen's cheeks. "Oh, come on with the faucet! Let's go!" This time it goes on forever. Rayen cries and cries.

"I can't concentrate! Shut her up, Vera!"

"Look, little girl. Be quiet and still, or I will kill you!"

Rayen immediately stops her tears. Before Vera takes Rayen back to her room, she stops in the hall. "I hate you and I will never be rid of you because you are his granddaughter. So from now on, I will beat your ass every day to make myself feel better. Looking at your young beautiful face makes me want to vomit!" And suddenly, she punches Rayen in her face. When she falls she begins to kick her.

Every night Rayen goes to bed, she wishes she was dead. When Vera comes to her door for her daily beating, she would not make a sound. And then when she is summoned for her grandfather, she just takes a deep breath and does not breathe until she is back in her bed. Rayen does not know how much time she has spent in the mansion of horror, but she just lies in bed and waits for the day she could leave that wretched place. "Maybe I will die here," she thinks. She just doesn't care anymore.

One day, she is going to the restroom, and she hears Vera on the phone. "Maybe I will put antifreeze in her juice," she says

Light in the Shadow

chuckling. "No one would know nor would anyone care. It is totally undetectable. I keep it on hand in the room next to hers. I got to go. He will be back, so I'll talk to you later."

A light goes off in Rayen's brain. She hashes a plan and looks out the door to see if Vera is there. She enters the room next to hers to look around. Sure enough, like Vera said, there were bottles of antifreeze and some other things. It was supposed to be a storage room, she guessed. Rayen grabs a bottle and hurries to her room.

Rayen waits days and days to pass for her chance. She knows the day has come one morning Vera comes to her room for her weekly duties, but her grandfather yells, "Vera! We have business in the city. I need you now! Professional!"

"Lucky girl. I'll be back later. Don't even think about leaving. This place is a fortress," Vera scowls.

As soon as the big door closes, Rayen runs from her room with the antifreeze. Looking through the fridge she thinks, "How do I even know if it will work?" She doesn't care. She has nothing to lose. Finally she sees the fancy dark colored glass bottle her grandfather keeps his brown drink in. She quickly pours as much as she can in the bottle. She pours a little out so it will have the same amount in it as before. She quickly discards the antifreeze bottle so no one will find it. Then she goes in her room to patiently see if her nightmare will end.

Rayen opens her eyes, and the house is darker than usual, completely somber. She does not know the time, but she knows it is very late. Suddenly, she hears voices.

"Damn it, Vera! What were you thinking?"

"I'm sorry, Chevey. I…I thought I could help."

"I needed you to just sit there and display your body as usual!

"You are to be seen and not heard! Now get me a drink! I'll need several."

"Yes, right away."

"I need this deal. I am almost broke! And, Alec made sure I could not touch his little bitch's money ever! Shit!"

"Well, we could wait for the little whore to turn 18 and make her sign it over to you."

"Don't state the obvious. I don't keep you around for your brains."

"Yes, Chevey. Here is your drink."

"Get lost, stupid bitch."

"Yes."

Rayen runs quietly back to her room. Vera comes right to her door. "Well, well, you didn't escape? Get up and come here!" Rayen stands and walks to her. As soon as she reaches her, she slaps her. She stays on the floor. "Get up, little bitch!"

Before Rayen could stand, "Vera!" Chevey calls.

"Lucky again." She shakes her head and laughs. Vera doesn't return and Rayen finally falls asleep.

The next morning, Rayen wakes to a loud noise. "Chevey! Chevey!" She peeks down the stairs, and Vera is running around. "Go back in your room, bitch!" Rayen closes her door, and a sly smile touches her lips. About an hour later an ambulance is outside and paramedics are entering the big door. Rayen steps out. Vera is talking to them. She is crying uncontrollably. They all leave out the door and forget Rayen exists.

Rayen leaves out of her room and searches for what looks like could be Vera's room. She comes across a door slightly

Light in the Shadow

different from the rest. It has a silk scarf hanging from the top. She steps in and sees a white oak bedroom suit. The armoire has makeup and perfume bottles atop it. The bed has beautiful white oak posts that stretch toward the ceiling. The linen is the finest she has ever seen. Egyptian cotton is what it looks like.

As she walks toward the closet, she sees a collection of designer shoes enough to change into every day for months. This room is the most elegant in the entire mansion! Finally, she gets to the walk-in closet with all Vera's clothes. Quickly, Rayen searches for something that fits her. She finds a white sundress with thick elastic straps and blue flowers along the bottom. It looks about her size. She showers and brushes her hair. When she is ready, she put on her black flats she wore when she arrived. She dashes down the stairs and pours the liquid out of the dark bottle and rinses it out. After she leaves, no trace of her crime will be found. She opens the big door. The light hurts her eyes at first. When her eyes focus, she heads in any direction away from the hellhole she has called home.

Walking up the road, Rayen spots the faint shape of a vehicle. She has been walking for hours, and she doesn't know where she is. As the vehicle approaches, she starts to wave her hands. The car slows.

"Hi, baby. What are you doing out here alone?"

"Umm…" Rayen clears her throat. She hasn't spoken in a long time.

"I think my grandfather has died, and I don't know where to go."

"Oh, no! Sweetheart, hop in. I'll take you to the authorities. By the way, sugar, I am Donna."

"Rayen," she says clipped. She rides in silence never giving the woman eye contact.

"Well, here we go. This is the police station." Rayen steps out of the car, and Donna waves as she pulls off. Rayen steps in the station, and it is practically deserted.

"Yes, little lady, can I help you?" The man smiles from behind a desk. "Yes. My grandfather is Len Chevey Vasu, and he was taken to the hospital. No one has called or returned back to our home."

"Okay, let me check. Give me a second." He starts to make calls, and Rayen has a seat in the lobby. Moments pass, and he stands. "Come here, little lady." Rayen walks to him. "Do you have any other relatives here?"

"No, I do not."

"Well I…um, see, your grandfather passed away. I am so sorry. Can I call someone for you? What is your name?"

"Rayen, Rayen Vasu. Call Margret Taylor in Manhattan, New York."

"Okay, young lady. Hold tight. By the way, I am Officer Matthew Brennan." After what seems to be forever, he calls to her. "Ms. Vasu, come here." He hands her the phone. She hears a familiar voice, but for some reason, there is no comfort.

"Rayen, honey! Are you okay? It's been four months, no calls or no letters."

"Grandfather is dead."

Margret gasps. "No, Rayen, no!"

I need you to come get me."

"Rayen, baby, I am so sorry. I can't believe this is happening to you."

"Miss Margret, how soon can you get here?"

Light in the Shadow

Margaret is silenced by her abrasiveness. "I'll be there tomorrow. Where will you stay?"

"Can you get me a hotel room?"

"You don't know anyone there, honey?"

"No, Miss Margaret. I do not."

"Well, let me speak with Officer Brennan."

Rayen hands the phone to the officer. He speaks to Margaret and then looks at Rayen. "Well, Ms. Vasu, you will be sleeping here while I get some details about what is going on here."

"Okay." He takes Rayen to a room in the very back of the station, and there is a small television mounted on the wall. There is a humble cot in the corner with a prickly white blanket securely wrapped around the mattress military style.

"I knew your grandfather. I am sorry for your loss," he says. Rayen just plays with her hands. He walks away, closing the door. Rayen is left to her thoughts. "Lucky girl…lucky girl? You're the lucky one, Vera! Next time."

The next morning, Officer Brennan explains he could not get in touch with anyone at her grandfather's house, and the hospital was holding Len Chevey's body in the morgue. The woman that was with him left and no one could find her to get the final arrangements for him. Rayen's expression is mundane. "Miss Taylor will be arriving in an hour. I have volunteered to insure your delivery to her since my shift has ended. Let's go."

When Rayen boards the plane with Margret, she is just numb. Margret tries to ask how it was living in Vegas, but Rayen is not speaking. She concedes, and the plane ride is very quiet.

Chapter 2

"The clouds are especially fluffy today," Angela says as she lies on the grass.

"I guess," Rayen shrugs. Her legs are folded. She holds her laptop in place, typing.

"All you ever do is work. You never have any fun or just lie back and enjoy the scenery," Angela adds.

Rayen looks at the clouds. "Nothing fascinating to see." She continues typing on her computer. "I have deadlines and orders I have to complete."

"Well, later let's go have some fun!"

"And, what, pray tell, do you consider fun?"

"Rayen, you are the most serious person I have ever met."

"This is fun, an afternoon sitting in the grass at a park. And, really, Angela, I have serious things on my mind and serious things to do."

"I give up. Anyway, I have a date this evening. I thought maybe we could double date."

"Absolutely not!"

"Well, I wasn't finished, Rayen. I thought that, but as I've stated, I give up."

"Good. I don't have time to fraternize with juvenile, sex-crazed animals. I'll pass every time."

"Rayen, you are so beautiful. Will you ever want someone to cuddle with at night, make love to you, maybe one day marry, and have children with?

"Angela, not every woman wants a Cinderella fantasy like you. It just does not exist. There is no Prince Charming!"

"Oh my, dear, you are no Cinderella."

"You are right. Her stepsisters would have been toast!" A small smile crosses her lips.

"Anyway, I am looking forward to tonight. Justin is so cute. He has beautiful green eyes, curly brown hair, and body of a Greek god!"

Rayen pauses from typing. "Angela…never mind."

"What? Rayen, what is it?"

Rayen continues to type. "I have to leave New York Tomorrow. I haven't spent one night in my new condo in Michigan. I must go unpack and make it look like home."

"So soon? You just got here!" Angela pouts.

"I've been here three days. I have to go, and you need to go to school. Each time I visit, you miss class," Rayen says authoritatively.

Angela smiles, "At least we know you care about something. We never see you anymore."

"My father's company is struggling. We don't have the contracts we once had. I have to travel to make sure my colleagues are getting new clients. That's why I need to be in Michigan for a while. The buildings we are handling need hands on attention."

"Okay, but one day you need to have some fun," Angela says as she stands. They leave the park and return to Margaret's home.

Light in the Shadow

"My date was so nice, Mom," Angela says, glowing. "That's wonderful, Angie. But, take your time with this guy," Margaret scolds.

"Is Rayen up yet?"

"Don't know, honey. She was up working late on something. Why didn't you convince her to tag along?"

"Well, Mom, I tried, but she almost took my head off for suggesting it. She never has any fun."

"She is just trying to preserve her father's legacy. She will enjoy life one day."

"Really?"

Rayen stretches as she enters the kitchen. "You two always talk about folks while they sleep?"

"No, just you. What time is your flight?" Angie says chuckling.

"10:30."

"Rayen, when will you come back to see us? We really miss you," Margaret says with sad eyes.

"I think you should visit me in Michigan. I have so much work to do. I won't be free anytime soon."

"I graduate college in June. Maybe I could find a job there?" Angela eyes Rayen.

"Maybe," Rayen shrugs. Rayen eats breakfast and heads towards her bedroom she has had at the Taylor house since she came back from her grandfather's. Her room still remains the same with a white wicker chair in the corner. It is her favorite spot to think. There's one oak desk with a wooden chair to match, flower embroidery throughout her comforter, and a four-post wooden bed where she enjoys the best sleep she has ever had. She packs her suitcases, takes a shower, and gets dressed. A horn resounds. Margaret hugs Rayen so hard.

"Call me when your plane lands, Rayen. Please do not forget. I worry about you, honey," Margaret proclaims.

"I will," Rayen says. Angela hugs her from behind.

"Will you attend my graduation, Rayen?"

"I'll try. No promises."

"Well, if not, I'm coming to you as soon as I leave school."

Rayen gets in the black Cadillac, and the car pulls down the street.

The plane lands at James Clements Municipal Airport. The last time she was here, it was just to pick out her condo. She looks around, and the airport is really empty. She sees her driver holding a sign reading 'Ms. Rayen Vasu'.

"Hello. I'm Ms. Vasu."

"Ma'am, I'm Sterling Winters. I was hired by your colleagues to be your permanent driver while you are in Michigan. Welcome to Bay City."

Sterling is quite a handsome man. He has short cut blonde hair with a boy band spike. He has piercing grey eyes and is about 5'11, slim, but fits a suit well. Rayen is not impressed by his bright smile.

"Why is he smiling so big? He looks like a chess cat!" she says to herself.

"This way, Ms. Vasu," Sterling says. He is very professional, but he looks Rayen over very carefully. One cannot help but admire Rayen's beauty. Her long black hair touches the middle of her back. It has a slight wave to it. Her skin looks like smoothed sand on a sunny day. Her eyes have the perfect slant

Light in the Shadow

and are a beautiful brown that almost looks like hard blonde caramel. The cream colored slacks she is wearing fit just right. They hug her slender waist but curve with her hips. She is a total package. But, Sterling knows not to look too long because her perfectly arched eyebrow has been hitched since she spotted him at the doors of the Airport.

"Are you familiar with Bay City, Ms. Vasu?"

"No, but I will be."

The remainder of the ride is silent. Rayen takes in the scenery of Bay City. It is quaint like a hometown you see in the movies. Gorgeous green grass, nice buildings that are beautifully built, and children riding bikes just like a place she never imagined living. She can't help but think about Angela. "I see it, Angela!" she snorts to herself.

"We are here, Ms. Vasu."

The Escalade pulls up to a stretch of condominiums that resemble townhouses. The bricks are dark red. The windows are trimmed in cherry oak along with the door.

"Thank you, Sterling. I have to unpack, but I will need to go out to eat later. It is two now. Please, be back at eight."

"Yes ma'am."

"That will be all."

Sterling starts up the stairs and helps Rayen in the door with her bags, sets them in the front hall, and exits back out the door. Rayen continues to the stairway that leads up to her bedroom. She passes her bathroom at the top of the stairs and looks in her office. The furniture she ordered has been delivered, and it is exquisite. She continues to a spare bedroom. She admires the work the decorator she hired has performed. Finally, she arrives at her room, still the same as the day she moved in. She purchased the furniture for that room herself. She didn't want anyone picking out furniture she would sleep on, at least, not a stranger.

Rayen had clothes sent to her place before she arrived, so she just unpacks the clothes she has with her from Manhattan. She huffs as she realizes she will be spending the next few days unpacking the several boxes she lays eyes on in the dining room. "They will have to wait until tomorrow. I'm starving!" She stares at the clock. It is 7 p.m., and she knows Sterling will be there soon. "What to wear? Hmmmm." She lifts her eyebrow as she looks through the clothes beautifully and neatly color coordinated in her closet. She decides to wear a candy apple red, satin wrap dress with sleeves that barely touch over her shoulder. She wraps the dress around and ties a bow at her side. Then she slips into some black high heel shoes. As she bends to grab her black patent leather purse, she hears the doorbell.

"Ms. Vasu."

"Sterling."

"Where would you like to dine tonight?" Sterling asks as he helps her down the stairs and opens the door to the SUV.

"Where do you suggest? As you know, I am unfamiliar with this city," Rayen returns.

"World Café is very elegant."

"World Café it is, then."

The truck pulls up in front of the restaurant, and Sterling jumps out to open the door for Rayen. "Enjoy your meal, Ms. Vasu. Please call me when you are ready to leave."

"Thank you."

Light in the Shadow

Sterling takes her hand to help her out of the truck. Rayen enters the restaurant, and a lovely young lady greets her. "Good evening. Welcome to World Café. How many this evening?"

"One, please."

"Right this way."

Sipping her cosmopolitan, Rayen watches the glass door swirl while couples prance hand and hand through them. "I'll kill Sterling. I must look pathetic sitting here alone. But, who cares," she whispers. "I guess this is the date night spot." Her dinner arrives, salmon with steamed vegetables and mushroom risotto. It smells delectable. As she is finishing her meal, the waiter begins to clear the table.

"Dessert?"

"No, thank you. I would like my bill now." Rayen gives the waiter her Visa Infinite Diamond card. "Take 30% for your tip." The waiter returns with her card. She signs her receipt and collects her purse to leave. Walking towards the door, she bumps someone. "Pardon me."

"No, that was my fault. I'm sorry. Are you alright?" the man returns.

She hesitates. "Umm...I'm fine."

Rayen is very reserved. She has rarely given men the time of day over the years. Her horrid experience at the mansion of hell changed her to a cold, domineering being. She is not the bubbly young lady she was when she left for Vegas. Vera and Len Chevey made sure of that. The sexual and physical abuse she endured turned her into a shadow of her former self, and she vows to never be that helpless girl again. The few dates she has accepted in the past years were over very quickly. The men she dated were handsome, some rich, and successful, never held her attention. No man could ever crack the cement exterior she created to protect herself from ever being violated again. Mainly, she has to keep everyone at a distance because no one could or would ever find out her fatal secrets.

"Have a good evening." He turns to walk away. By the way, I'm Blake Pierce. And, you are?"

"Rayen Vasu," she says pursing her lips. She leaves out of the restaurant feeling unsettled.

Rayen walks to the curb totally perplexed. "What is wrong with me?" Her stomach is fluttering. "Maybe I should not have had a drink with the risotto." Sterling pulls up and comes to Rayen's side. He opens her door.

"Ms. Vasu."

"Sterling," she snaps. Rayen sits in the truck with her hands in her lap the whole ride. Her stomach is tossing and turning.

"Sterling, can you go to a pharmacy? I need something for an upset stomach."

"Yes, ma'am."

After she comes from the pharmacy, she returns to her home.

"Good evening, Ms. Vasu."

"Evening."

Rayen takes a bath. She steps in the whirlpool tub and turns on the jets. As she is soaking, she closes her eyes and reflects on her evening. Rayen steps out of the tub and looks around. The bathroom is very high-end with a walk-in shower directly next to the tub. She has vertical mirrors aligned on the adjacent wall with a dual sink beneath. Next to the sink is the porcelain comfort height toilet. She walks out of the master bathroom directly into her master bedroom. The bedroom is adorned in the most impeccable red and gold drapery. The bed is a king size

Light in the Shadow

Del Corto poster headboard with two dressers, night stands, and media chest to match. There is a 46" flat LED screen television mounted to the wall opposite the bed. Rayen climbs into her bed and snuggles under her baby blue comforter. She drifts into a somber.

***

Rayen kicks her instructor over and over as she yells "huh, huh!"

"You have a hell of a roundhouse."

Rayen purses her lips. Sweat is dripping from her hair down her face. She takes her hand and flattens her wet ponytail as she steadies her stance.

"Rayen, when you kick it this time, point your toes right before you land."

Rayen nods. "Huh, huh!"

"Good. You've come a long way in a year. The more you learn the art, you learn self-control." She bows to her.

"Sensei Sayuri Hikaru." She bows back.

"Rayen."

At sixteen, she has never felt more liberated, strong, and even invincible. "See you Friday after school." Sayuri locks the doors to the studio as she leaves. She bends down to tie her shoes and fastens her headphones tightly on her head. Looking around, she begins her journey down Mount Carmel towards 28th. She is only blocks away from home.

"I am so hungry. I hope Miss Margaret has prepared dinner," she says aloud. It is especially dark tonight. Practice ran longer than usual. Rayen glances at her watch. "10:30! No wonder the streets are deserted." Suddenly, she spots a dark figure crossing the street. Her heart begins to pump so loud, she can feel it in her ears. Slowly, she turns to see the martial art studio. It is dark and distant. She sticks her hands in her jacket pocket and picks up the pace. Looking out the corner of her eye, the shadow appears to be a tall brawny man matching her stride. He was wearing a baseball cap, a black shabby sweatshirt, and ripped jeans. Frantically, she searches for someone. She looks around to see if any of the businesses are open for a quick escape, but to no avail. Abruptly, the man snatches Rayen and drags her into the nearby alley.

He slams her on the ground. She tries to scream, but her sounds are choked by fear.

"Oh, no, not again! Sir, please, don't!"

"Oh, sugar, yes! You are a sweet piece of ass. Can't believe how lucky I was to see you alone." The man laughs, showing all his rotten teeth. He leans up and proceeds to unbutton his pants. He then yanks them down. Laughing the whole time, he reaches for Rayen's jogging pants. Right then calmness comes over her. She looks up at his face and smirks.

"What are you smiling at, bitch?"

She says nothing as she just grabs his sweatshirt and pushes him up. She uses her palm and hits him in the nose. It makes a breaking sound. She struck so hard it begins to bleed.

"You bitch! You broke my nose!"

She turns to walk away, but she thinks about him doing this to some other poor, unsuspecting girl. An infernal look washes over her face. She turns back. By the dumpster there is a glass bottle. She checks to see if the streets are still vacant. He is still moaning. "My nose," he cries. He hasn't paid any attention to her approaching him. He is still on his knees crying.

"Die, you motherfucker!"

Light in the Shadow

She breaks the bottle without shattering it. She takes the shard, grabs his forehead, and slits his throat in one clean cut. He falls to the ground gurgling. She cocks her head to one side and stares for a moment. Then, she takes off her jacket and wraps the weapon she made in it after wiping her hands.

The walk home, she is watching her surroundings. The streets are still empty. Finally, she reaches her building. She hurries up the stairs. When she gets to her apartment, she opens the door and scurries to the bathroom. "Rayen, honey, is that you?" yells Margaret.

"Yes! I'm going to take a shower."

"Okay, but next time, tell Sayuri you have to get home earlier. These streets are treacherous!"

A dangerous smile creeps across her lips.

***

Beep! Beep! Rayen opens her eyes and looks at the clock. It reads 'Monday, April 19th, 8:05 a.m.' "My meeting is at nine." She dials Sterling, but he is already en route. She runs to the bathroom to take a quick shower. She dashes to the closet, holding her towel around her, bunched between her fingers. She picks out a gray blazer, a silver camisole, and smoky gray slacks to wear. She matches some silver gray high heels to complete the look. After she pins her hair into a neat bun, there is a knock at the door.

She arrives at the office building on Wenona St. She is impressed with the architectural structure of the building. Evan Drake approaches her. "Hello, Rayen. How are you? Was your flight comfortable?"

"Yes, Mr. Drake, it was."

"Let's get straight to business then."

Annetta Hobson

They walk down a long hall with office doors on either side. At the end of the hall, there is an open door with an elaborate table with tall black chairs decorating it. They step in, and there are and three more older gentlemen seated. They all stand when she enters. In unison they say, "Ms. Vasu." Then they all sit in a rhythmic pattern. When everyone is seated, a woman enters. She begins to flip over cups that are placed in front of each person at the table. She has fiery red hair blown straight with a bang across her forehead. She is wearing a cream short sleeve dress with a navy blue belt and navy blue shoes. Rayen nods when she pours her coffee. Mr. Drake starts the meeting. He begins by showing plans for the buildings that are to be built in Bay City. Then he covers the buildings that they have accounts for overseas.

He catches her off guard when he says, "Rayen, we are doing our best to keep your father's vision for this company. We have been doing this for a long time, and everything is on schedule." Rayen unfastens her blazer.

"It must be frustrating having such a young woman in charge, but my father wanted me to know the inner workings of this company. Mr. Drake has mentored me in the dealings of all projects. We will continue to receive the large accounts that we were once flooded with. I am here to personally attend to those accounts because they are faithful clients old and dear. They worked with my father. I will be here in Michigan until the projects are completed. Also, as long as I am kept up to speed, I will allow the board to oversee the remaining projects. These clients stuck with our company even when things took a turn, so I want them to know my father appreciated them as do I." The meeting goes on for about two hours. They go over any and everything that has to do with the success and failures the company has endured over the last five years. "We break ground in three weeks from Thursday for the strip mall. So, we will fly

Light in the Shadow

down Tuesday to get everything started," Mr. Drake instructed. "I meet with D and D, INC. Friday to go over the final design plans. I have seen them before, but I just want to look them over again," she says with confidence. All of the men nod their heads. When she stands, the four men stand with her. Mr. Drake accompanies her out of the building.

"Rayen, would you like to have lunch?"

"No, thanks, Mr. Drake. I have to lease a car today and take care of some other things. I am just settling in here."

"Maybe we could do dinner then? I leave tomorrow. I would love to catch up. Evelyn asks about you all the time. You should call her."

She smiles, but it does not reach her eyes.

"Well, if not today, then next time."

Rayen nods.

They shake hands. At that moment, the other board members are exiting also. One of the men comes up.

"Drake."

"Fernando, I was just inviting Ms. Vasu to lunch. She declined, so how about you?" Mr. Drake returns.

"Sure. Ms. Vasu, how are you doing other than stepping successfully into your father's shoes?" says Mr. Fernando Alvarez, her father's other partner. He offered to have a funeral for her parents. Because he and his wife had no children at the time, they offered to take care of Rayen until family had come to claim her.

"Fine," she assures.

"You have grown to be quite the tycoon. Only three years you have been with us, and you are doing well. That scholarship your father left for your education must have been well deserved."

"I did alright. I learned everything my father wanted me to."

"Good. Let's do lunch sometime. Evan, lets go eat."

Sterling pulls up to the building. He gets out and opens her door. Before she gets in, she watches the gentlemen ride down the street. "Where to now, Ms. Vasu?" Sterling inquires. "I need a personal vehicle," she says.

"Is there a particular car you would prefer?"

"Just something new."

Finally, Rayen chooses a deep silver Lincoln Lacrosse to lease. It is so radiant, and the new car smell is intoxicating. The interior is white with black trimming. It has satellite radio and GPS. She wants to drive it now even though she does not know her way around town yet. But anyway, that is what a GPS is for. Sterling gives her a list of all the local restaurants and nightclubs.

"Be careful Ms. Vasu." She turns to look at him before she drives away.

"I'm always careful."

"Okay. Good evening." Sterling gets in the Escalade and drives in the opposite direction.

She looks at her watch. "6 p.m. What can I do? I need to eat." She looks at the list from Sterling. "Let' see…Ambrosia's sounds good. I'll go home and change first."

When she arrives at her condo, she showers and gets dressed. She slips into a white fitted skirt that stops two inches short of her knee and reveals a peek of her thigh. She matches it with a pink long sleeve blouse that hugs her waist. It has a

Light in the Shadow

ruffled line that trails up her cleavage and around her neck with ties that hang at her side. She completes the look in a pair of soft pink stilettos with geometric patterns of white mixed in. She glances in the mirror and dashes out the door.

The soft purr of the engine gives Rayen a sense of ease. She moves in and out of traffic, testing her new carriage. Her GPS sounds, "Turn left at Baldwin Ave." She takes the turn. The restaurant will be a nice change from the other place she dined at the night before. It is not a candle lit lovers' den. It is somewhere you can have a professional meeting or a first date.

The tall African American man steps towards her.

"Welcome to Ambrosia's. Do you have a reservation?"

"No, I do not. But, surely you have a table for one."

"As a matter of fact, I do."

"Hello. Would you like to start with wine?" the waiter politely asks.

"Yes, white wine."

The waiter leaves. He then returns with a bottle and a crystal wineglass. As he pours, he says, "Would you like to start with one of our signature soups?" Rayen's eyes sweep over the menu. "No. Actually, I would like the grilled lamb chops with potatoes."

"Excellent choice! Coming up." The waiter collects the menu and walks to another table diagonal to hers to talk to a couple of men sitting together. When he leaves, one of the men looks up.

"Well, hello, darling. You are so beautiful. Are you alone?" Rayen's eyes cut quickly to the man, but she says nothing.

"Oh, baby, don't be so mean."

Annetta Hobson

She just looks away and slowly sips from the crystal wine glass. The other guy nudges him. "Leave her alone, man. She is out of your league."

"Okay, okay. But, we will see each other again, sweetheart," he states darkly. Rayen smiles, and it is not a friendly one. The waiter burst through the double doors with a tray of delectable meals. He stops at her table first.

"Here is your lamb, miss." It smells absolutely heavenly. She starts to eat. A short time passes, and the gentlemen stand to retire for the evening. As they pass, the pushy guy touches her shoulder.

"See you around, gorgeous," he laughs. Rayen wipes her mouth with her napkin.

"Get your filthy hands off me!" she scolds with a death glance. "You just may lose them," she whispers. The smirk is completely snatched from his face. Before he can return a word, his friend whisks him out of the restaurant. She goes back to eating without missing a beat.

"Would you like dessert?" the waiter asks.

"No. Give me the check, please." She pays her bill, tips the waiter, and leaves the restaurant.

When she arrives at her home, she is extremely relaxed. She goes in the kitchen and unpacks the wine glasses Angela gave her for a housewarming gift for her first apartment in New York. She pours herself a glass of champagne. Soon, she is feeling the effects of the wine and champagne. She heads up to her room, climbs in her bed, and drifts off.

Rayen's first week in Bay City is a whirlwind. The town is quaint. Everyone goes about their way with not a care in the world. Secretly, she wishes she grew up in a place like this, but she didn't. Life in the big city is dangerous, and dangerous

Light in the Shadow

things happen. She keeps herself busy with details from her client's building plans. She wants to make sure Davidson and Davidson, INC. will have the most architecturally sound building in Michigan. By Thursday, she has special plans. She wants to meet with the general contractor who will be handling this contract. "I want to make sure all of our affiliates are competent enough for the accounts we will be handling here." She explains internally. She picks up her phone and dials Evan Drake. "Mr. Drake, I spoke to you about my meeting with D and D tomorrow. What I failed to mention is that I will be meeting with our general contractor, Joshua Manning, today."

"That's fine, Rayen. Just pass along the details of the meeting. Joshua is the best at what he does. You will come to recognize that. Your father was very fond of Joshua Sr. He was the most valuable employee. Five years ago, he found out he had prostate cancer. He has been unable to continue traveling, so he has turned his duties over to Joshua Jr. He is working very hard and is proving to be even better than his father, if that is even possible."

"Well I am looking forward to working with him. I will forward all details to you when the meeting concludes."

"By the way, Evelyn is looking to get into the business. Like Alec, I would love for her to continue my legacy. These projects in Michigan are the perfect opportunity for you both. I don't want to impose, but she is going insane waiting to hear from other businesses. I was thinking of setting up a central office there, since opportunities are popping up throughout Michigan abroad, but we will discuss that. She will be accompanying me on my visit there next month for the ground breaking."

"See you then. I will email you," Rayen answers.

After Rayen ends her conversation with Evan Drake, she searches her closet for something to wear. She looks through all her suits and dresses. "I want to exude business but not in a tyrannical way." She decides to go with a black blouse that resembles a gentlemen's dress shirt but is tailored to fit her curves. She adds a blue pencil skirt and black high heels to compliment her ensemble.

Buzz, buzz. "Where is that phone?" She grabs her cellphone off the nightstand. "Rayen Vasu speaking."

"Yes, Ms. Vasu? This is Joshua, Joshua Manning."

"Yes, Mr. Manning. Where would you like to meet? I take it your trip here was trouble free?"

"Yes, ma'am. It was delightful. Would you mind meeting in the hotel restaurant? It is very nice."

"That's fine. Which hotel are you staying in?"

"The Doubletree on the river. It is two now. How does four sound?"

"Four is fine. Thank you, Mr. Manning."

"Ms. Vasu."

She presses end on the phone and dials Sterling.

The Escalade pulls up in front of the hotel at 3:50 p.m. Sterling rounds the SUV to open her door. "I will phone you just before my meeting ends," Rayen confirms.

"Yes ma'am." Sterling takes her hand and helps her out. She enters the hotel and asks for directions to the hotel restaurant. A woman in her late forties with a white dress shirt, a green vest that reads 'Double Tree', and a black skirt gives her directions. She begins to walk around the large pillars and heads down the main corridor to the restaurant. When she enters, she states to the greeter that she is meeting with Mr. Manning. The greeter informs her that he is already waiting and escorts her to his

Light in the Shadow

table. When she approaches the table, he stands. "Ms. Vasu?" he questions.

"Yes, Mr. Manning."

Joshua Manning is ruggedly handsome. His curly dark brown hair touches the nape of his neck with dark eyebrows and trimmed stubble rounding his face. To top it off, he has a sexy cleft chin. He is not very tall, but he leans slightly over her in heels. His body is very athletic. Little dark curly hairs peek out of his dress shirt that is unbuttoned at the top. He has on black dress slacks. It is as if he never dresses in a suit. His eyes rake her over, and he thinks, "She is not what I expected at all! She is young and beautiful. I mean really beautiful." She sits at the table. Joshua begins, "I ordered some coffee. Would you like something different?"

"Coffee is fine," she says. They start with the plans for the strip mall. Then, he goes into the plans he has for the penthouse apartments with commercial shops below it. Rayen is impressed with his work. He presents his plans and how they will execute them. He is precise and well organized. Mr. Drake was right about him. "Well, all is definitely on schedule. You have impeccable workmanship. I am happy to have you working on these projects," she praises.

"I do my best. Your company has put me through school and provided me with a life that I am forever grateful for," Joshua says.

"Well, my father wanted all his business partners to live well, and I intend to help that vision continue."

"Your father? I didn't know you were Alec's daughter."

"The name Vasu didn't hint at that?" Rayen sarcastically spouts. Joshua chuckles.

"Ms. Vasu, the name, definitely did, but a sister or other relative would have honored the name as well. You think?" Rayen is amused. He is very charming she notes.

"Well if that is all, I will be going." She stands to leave. He matches her and rises from his seat.

"I was hoping we could continue maybe over drinks. I want to see what nightlife in this town has to offer since I'll be staying here a while." She looks around.

"I don't..."

He cuts her off. "Just a drink Ms. Vasu. I would not dare ask my boss on a date. I am not that kind of guy," he states. Rayen purses her lips.

"I suppose a drink would be ok. Let me call my driver."

Sterling drives up to the hotel doors and steps around to open the door. "Sterling, this is Joshua," she introduces before she bends to enter the truck. Joshua extends his hand. Sterling firmly shakes his hand and nods.

"Sterling, can you takes us somewhere for drinks?"

"Yes, Ms. Vasu. The Latitude is perfect for drinks. It's exclusive."

"Thank you. Latitude, then."

Joshua looks at her and says, "Thank you, Ms. Vasu. I hope I'm not imposing."

"No, it's fine. I haven't unwound since I've been here. And, call me Rayen."

"Okay, Rayen," he says then looks forward.

The Latitude is elegant and exclusive, as Sterling stated. When you walk in, there is a bar that wraps and bends around a never-ending curve on the left wall. It is aligned with mirrors, so

Light in the Shadow

all the bottles look doubled. The shelves the bottles rest on are clear glass. The bar itself is black lacquer. The floor is black marble with white lines through it, resembling lightning. All of the tables are to the right of the wall. There are clear circle tables with black and clear chairs. They grab a table near the middle. It is not crowded but people are scattered throughout. The waitress approaches as they sit. "May I get you guys a drink?" Rayen orders first.

"Yes, a Mojito, blended."

Then, Joshua orders, "A brandy on the rocks please."

"Great! I'll be right back." The waitress smiles and leaves.

"So, Ms. Vasu, I mean, Rayen, can you tell me some things about you?"

"There is nothing to tell," she says.

"Okay. Well I'll tell you some things about me." He sits up straight. She rolls hers eyes, so he doesn't see. "I am 30 years old. I've been employed by Vista Corp, your father's company, for five years. I have a M. Arch. Degree. I studied at Cornell University. My dad turned over all his contracts to me when he was diagnosed with cancer. He and my mom live in Syracuse. I have two brothers and one sister. They are not interested in my dad's business ventures." Joshua looks at Rayen. "Am I boring you with my resume?" Rayen jerks.

"No, I am just listening. Impressive, though."

He continues, "My dad is a great man, and he really admired your father, too. I met Alec several times. He always encouraged my drive for architecture. He told me I would replace my father one day, and he was correct. I just wish it wasn't under these circumstances." Rayen softens her glare.

"I've never met Mr. Manning, but I have heard great things about him. And, my dad was a great man." She folds her hands in her lap but composes herself.

"I am so sorry someone took him away before you could know how great," he says sorrowfully.

"I knew how great. Just because I was young does not mean I did not recognize my father's wonderful attributes. He is the greatest man I have ever known," she returns with pride. They sit in silence for a while. Joshua waves for the waitress to get them refills. The air has gotten heavy. "Are you married, Joshua? Any children to extend your legacy?" Rayen regains her sternness.

"No. I haven't met a woman who can match my mother's kindness and the pure love that she has for my father," he says as he looks at his glass. "What about you?" She gazes at him, slightly touched.

"No. No man has ever gotten within an inch of this heart," she says coldly.

"Wow. You are one tough cookie," he says.

"I am just taking care of myself," she states. They converse for a while and enjoy drinks. It is the most relaxed Rayen has been in a while, but she is extremely careful. Joshua is easy to talk to, but she never lets her guard down. She peeks at her watch. It is 9 p.m "We both have to meet with D and D in the morning, so I think it is time to retire." She calls Sterling, and they exit the lounge.

Sterling enters the parking lot of the hotel. "Rayen, you are an impressive young woman," Joshua says as he grabs the door handle. "Some man will crack that cement around your heart one day. Mark my words." She just watches him without expression. She lifts her brow.

Light in the Shadow

"Good evening, Mr. Manning," she says to warn him. He knows he has said too much.

"Evening, Ms. Vasu. Drive safely, Sterling."

"Sir," Sterling says as the door closes. Rayen just watches Joshua enter the hotel door.

"What is this city doing to me?" she thinks to herself.

Chapter 3

"Good Morning, Ms. Vasu. I trust that you slept well?" Sterling says as he opens the door to let her in the truck.

"Yes, very well!" She says with an enlightened tone. He glances at her. Though she isn't smiling, he knows her mood has changed. Sterling heads down W. Center Road to the building site. The representatives from Davidson and Davidson are already there along with Joshua.

"Am I late?" She lifts her wrist. It's only 8:30. "I'm early." When the SUV parks Joshua emerges quickly to open the door.

"I'll get that, Sterling, if you don't mind," he says. He softly takes her hand to help her exit the vehicle. "Good morning, Ms. Vasu."

"Morning, Joshua," she utters. One of the gentlemen comes over to greet her.

"Thank you for coming to meet with us personally. The integrity of the company has always been admired. We are so delighted you have taken up your father's business sense."

"Thank you. You are too kind. I am just doing what my father wanted for the company he worked so hard for," she returns humbly. They take a narrated tour hosted by Joshua. He rolls out the plans as he points and describes where things will be. Rayen eyes Joshua as he walks ahead of her. He looks very good in the khaki slacks and tan Polo. He looks simply delicious! Just as her eyes reach his face, he turns and meets her gaze.

"What do you think, Ms. Vasu?" Her face is suddenly flushed.

"Perfect," she says almost too harshly. "What is wrong with me? This is not me. It is like I'm not myself," she thinks.

"Okay. We will see you guys May 13th for the ground breaking." Joshua smiles.

She can't help but get lost in his innocent farm boy grin. She imagines him sitting on a hill of hay with a string of wheat between his teeth, revealing his manly chin. Simply gorgeous is all she can think. "Angela is rubbing her childish fantasies off on me!" she says to herself.

"Are you okay, Rayen?" he asks.

"I'm fine," she snaps.

"Okay." He laughs. "I have a favor I must ask you, since I haven't met anyone else." She stares at him secretly hoping he stops smiling.

"What might that be?" She raises her brow. "I need to go apartment hunting, and I would love a woman's opinion. Please accompany me." She looks away to gather her thoughts. "If it's an inconvenience I could just hire someone," he responds to her silence.

"No, no, I will. When are you going?"

"I was thinking we could start today. The agent sent me some places, and I don't like staying in hotels. I'm ready to go now, since it is still early. Do you have other plans today?"

Rayen feels very uncomfortable. She has never felt anything but rage. She needs to have rage to deal with things properly. If she does not have it, how will she protect herself?

"I don't have any plans. Let's go. We can have Sterling drive us, or I could grab my car."

She tries to hide her reluctance.

Light in the Shadow

"Let's drive your car!"

Sterling drives them to her condo. "Come in while I get out of my business attire," she says a little shaky. They enter the condo, and she invites Joshua to sit on the sofa in the living room. He takes a seat.

"Your place is really upscale. Hopefully I find something equally as nice." She doesn't know what to say, so she says nothing. She exits the living room and goes upstairs to change. While she changes, she thinks very hard.

"Why do I have this man in my house? Am I losing everything I worked so hard to keep? I cannot lose all I have built inside to protect myself!" She puts on a sleeveless purple dress with a cream jacket and slips on her purple wedges to match. She loosens her hair from her business bun and brushes it, so the natural wave flows down her back. When she returns to Joshua, he stands. His eyes slightly enlarge while taking in her beauty. "Ready?" she asks.

"Yes, let's go." He follows her out the side into the garage.

"Nice car, Rayen."

"Thanks."

They get in the car. He gives her the address to the first place. She puts it in the GPS, and they drive out of the garage.

Rayen looks at her watch. It is 5:30 a.m. She decides to go for a run. She needs to think about her friendship with Joshua. It is something she has never allowed before. She really enjoys his company. They have been spending a lot of time together over these last weeks. She believes he feels the same way, but he would never cross that line. She slowly begins to jog. She feels the wind whip through her hair. Her strides are faster and shorter. The May air is a little warm for Michigan. It is the perfect release. As she runs through the park, she notices a man standing on the bridge. He doesn't see her right away. She passes him and he yells to her, "Hello, beautiful."

"Get lost!" she shouts. When he runs past her, he looks in her face.

"Well, hello again. This is a small town, baby. I knew I would see you again." She quickens her pace.

"Threaten me now. I dare you."

She tilts her head and runs faster.

"You cannot out run me. You made a big mistake jogging in this park!"

She looks around for others, but the park is empty, not even a dog walker. She is not afraid, but she doesn't want to handle this the way she knows how to. Finally he reaches her. He grabs her and spins her around. I am going to teach you how to take a compliment.

"Really?" she says as if she is bored.

"Oh, okay. I'll just show you." He reaches for her breasts, but his hand doesn't land. Before he makes contact, she grabs his hands and breaks it. Before he can scream, she spins him around and covers his mouth. Carefully but very quickly, she snaps his neck. She looks around once more. To make sure the task is completed, she snatches the narrow icicle shaped pendant on her necklace and flips it like switch blade. Then, she slits his throat. It is so sharp that he doesn't bleed right away. She quickly drops the limp body. Watching all directions, she drags the body in the thick shrubbery. She is careful not to step in his now pooling blood. She drags his right hand and foot. After he is hidden from anyone just passing, she views her body to spot blood. She is good enough to make it home. She casually jogs away and obscurely searches for surveillance cameras.

Light in the Shadow

When she gets home, she goes straight to her washroom and throws her t-shirt, stretch pants, and gyms shoes in the washer. She washes them several times, the last time with bleach. Then she soaks her necklace pendant and checks it for human skin. After the things are done, she dries them and cuts the clothes into shreds. She then destroys the shoes the same way. She has showered several times to wash away any unseen blood. She ties the shredded fabric in three garbage bags and runs it to her car trunk.

Later that day, she meets Joshua for lunch at World Café. "So, I love my new place. Thank you for helping me find it and pick out the furniture."

"Anytime." She smiles.

"Rayen, your smile is radiant. You should do it more often."

She looks down at her hands, cutting her smile short.

"You are only 25. You should not be so serious all the time."

"I have been through so much. I cannot go back," she whispers. She looks so sad. She is vulnerable for the first time since she left her grandfather's house.

"You have to give someone a chance to take care of you. It's okay," he whispers to her as he pulls her close within his arms and hugs her. The booth they are sitting at makes it easy for him to close the gap in between them. She inhales his fresh smell, and he holds her close.

"You sound like Margaret and Angela." She then explains who they are.

"You have been through a lot," he says, still holding her.

"He has no idea," she says to herself. The waiter comes with their food, and he releases her. She has never had a man but her father hold her in a loving way. It felt nice.

After they finish lunch, they walk down to the park she jogged that morning. The park is swarming with police, news cameras, and onlookers. "What happened here?" Joshua asks.

An elderly lady answers, "They found a young man dead. First gruesome murder in 15 years." Joshua looks at Rayen. She tries to look mortified. She is successful.

"Come on, let me take you home."

"I'm fine," she says. They watch as the CSI team combs the scene. The police start talking to the crowd.

One gentleman that is talking to people doesn't look like just a police officer. He has on a navy suit, a white dress shirt, and black shoes. He is extremely handsome. He has light brown hair with sun washed blonde tones. It has big waves that flows back but is cropped at the neck. He has deep lines in each cheek. His blue eyes sparkle in the afternoon sun. He is very tall, around 6'2". His body is so scrumptious; you can see his physique through the suit. He has an all-American innocence to him that makes him look even more attractive. He finally makes his way to Rayen and Joshua. "Hello, I am Detective Blake Pierce with Bay City Homicide Division. I am questioning everyone in the area. Have either of you seen anything suspicious this morning? Anyone lurking or in a hurry?"

"No," they both say.

"We were only here a short time having lunch," Joshua assures. Right then, Blake looks to Rayen.

"How are you? Ms. Vasu? We bumped into each other over there a couple of weeks ago." He motions his hand towards the restaurant.

"Yes, I remember, Detective," Rayen returns.

Light in the Shadow

"If you know or hear of anything, can you please contact Bay City Police Department?" he asks.

"She is so beautiful! I wonder if they are together. The first time I saw her, she was alone. Wrong time to find out," Blake thinks to himself.

Rayen recalls the night she bumped into Blake. "He is very attractive. He is a total package. When he touched me that night, I felt queasy. When did I begin feeling this way about anyone? I have seen his face in my mind often. I bump into him now." She frowns. "He was with someone, and…he is a homicide detective! This damned town!" she thinks. Joshua pats her hand.

"Let's get out of here. This is too much." He walks her to the car. "Are you okay, Rayen?"

"I'm fine, just thinking who could do this? Horrible. Just terrible!" she says as she shakes her head in disbelief. Joshua is acting strange. He has his head bowed.

"The groundbreaking is this Thursday. So, we won't be able to hang out as much." He says looking at his feet. "I have really enjoyed your company these two weeks. You are an amazing woman, Rayen. You have accomplished so much in your life, and you are just getting started. I admire you." Joshua creases his eyebrows. He is staring at her with an intense look. It's as if he is waiting for her permission for something.

"Thank you Joshua," she returns. "I have never opened up to anyone. You have become a great friend," she says and steps towards him. But, he drops his hands that are resting on her shoulders. His face relaxes. "Yes. We have become great friends," he says sarcastically. Rayen is suddenly confused. "

I swear he was about to kiss me. What happened?"

"I must go. I have final papers to go over for our meeting with Mr. Drake tomorrow."

"Tomorrow is May 12th," she says.

"Yes it is."

But, she does not respond.

"Anyway, tomorrow we should meet around six, right after the board arrives."

"That will be fine," Rayen states in a professional voice. Joshua opens her car door.

"Get in. There is a murderer on the loose."

"I'll be alright. Get in your car," she says with authority.

"Yes ma'am!" he says jokingly. But, she does not smile.

"Good day, Joshua."

"Tomorrow, Rayen."

She drives out of the parking lot and heads home.

When she steps in her condo, she feels tears pool in her lower lids. "What am I doing? I never cry! This is bullshit!" She storms up the stairs toward her bedroom. She flops on her bed. She grabs her phone.

She doesn't realize who she is dialing until a giggly voice answers, "Hello."

"Hi Angela," she says softly.

"Rayen? Hi. What's wrong? You sound weird. Oh, tomorrow. You want us to come down there?" Angela rambles.

"No. I'll deal with that tomorrow." She sniffs.

"Rayen, are you crying?"

"What's wrong?" Margaret interrupts from the background.

Light in the Shadow

"Angela, please! Not Miss Margaret," Rayen scolds. "Leave the room."

"Of course. Mom, she is fine. I thought I heard her sniffle, but she is fine. I'm going to my room to talk," Angela assures, but Margaret is not convinced.

"Does she need us for tomorrow?"

"No, mom! When does Rayen ever want us to make a fuss over her?" Angela is successful in deflecting her mom. Margaret leaves and returns to her daily chores. "Okay she is gone, Rayen," Angela states. She does not speak at first.

"Angela I...I don't know how to begin. I need to talk to someone..." Rayen does not know how to ask for help. She never had these kinds of problems before.

"Please tell me. Rayen, let me help you," Angela pleads. She has a long pause. "Are you there, Rayen?"

"Yes...I. Let me just start by saying you and Margaret are the only family I have." Angela is shocked. Rayen is not the sentimental type.

"My God! What is wrong?"

"Angela, I met this guy. He is funny, handsome, and respectful. I have never met anyone like him."

"Well, what's the problem?"

"I thought he felt the same way," and she explains the day's events to her. "Maybe it was the fact that a murder happened right there! Or, maybe it's the fact that you called him your friend?" Angela speculates.

"Murders happen every day. And, we were so close to kissing. So I thought. Then, I called him a great friend. That's it Angela!"

Annetta Hobson

"He probably thinks you were blowing him off. But, I am so glad you are dating. I am so happy for you." Angela beams.

"We are not dating, Angela!" she corrects. "We have a meeting tomorrow. Maybe I can clear things up," Rayen says hopefully.

"Do you need me to come down there Rayen?" Angela asks.

"No, I am okay, and you have to complete school. You will be here next month, right?"

"Yes, as soon as I walk across the stage. I'll be there. I love you, Rayen. And, so does mom."

"I know. Thank you for being there for me."

They end their call.

Angela just sits on the bed. Tears start to run down her face. She places her hands on her knees and prepares to stand. Margaret enters her room. "Angie, is everything ok with Rayen?" she says, alarmed by Angela's tears.

"I'm wonderful, Mom. These are tears of joy! She's human after all. She is human." Margaret laughs and Angela lets out a huge sigh of relief.

When Rayen wakes, the sun is shining through her window. She squints to shield her eyes. Sitting up, she remembers yesterday and rubs her eyes. "I cannot believe this is possible. I'd abandoned my emotions a long time ago. I haven't cared about any man except for my father." She rubs her face and slides out of the bed. She glances over at the clock. It's 8 a.m. "I guess I'll cook breakfast this morning. It is my birthday." She heads to her kitchen. She glares at the food in her refrigerator. "I guess I will be going out."

She takes a moment to think about her parents. She remembers Kalena. She was the greatest. She was pure. She was

Light in the Shadow

kind to any and every one. Although she had no family here, she treated Margaret and Angela like they were. Leaving Hawaii was the best decision her mother could have made. Rayen and Alec were her only priorities. She made sure they never needed anything. That's why Alec married her. He left his life in Vegas and his Father to make a life for them. Alec was such a businessman, but he never neglected his family. He perfectly balanced life. He would want Rayen to be happy. His lifelong dream was to be a better parent then his father was. And, he succeeded in the greatest way. Rayen adored her parents. But, she hated reliving that time in her life. Their death was the very beginning of her hell. She decides to go back to bed. She just was not hungry anymore. She wanted this day to pass.

"Oh God, I am going to be late. It's 5 p.m. I overslept! But, that nap felt so good. I never sleep during the day. Lately, I have been doing lots of things I don't do." She showers and gets dressed. She decides to wear a short black cocktail dress with thin shoulder straps and a silver bodice. She slides her feet into some shimmering silver high heels and grabs a silver clutch. She calls Sterling to make sure he is on his way. Sterling arrives at 5:50 p.m. She checks her phone to see if she still has the text Joshua sent her yesterday. The place they are supposed to meet at is called Oasis. It is an upscale lounge and restaurant.

When she arrives, she is very nervous for some reason. She enters Oasis, and it is very nice. The maître d asks her name. "Oh, yes, Ms. Vasu. Right this way," he says. He leads her to a table to the back of the lounge. It is in a private room. The room is decorated with balloons.

"Oh no!" she thinks.

Joshua emerges and he says, "Happy Birthday, Rayen!" Then he kisses her on the forehead. The kiss is so sensual. His lips feel so soft and wet. It sends a jolt down through her stomach. She has never experienced a feeling so enticing. She closes her eyes and leans into the kiss so it lasts longer. Then, he breaks away. She is so mesmerized, she doesn't notice the others waiting. Suddenly a young woman grabs her.

"Happy Birthday, Rayen," the woman says. She focuses and notices it is Evelyn Drake.

"Thanks," she says dryly. She quickly searches for a seat. She has not had a party since the day her parents died.

"Rayen, I am very sorry. Evelyn insisted on surprising you. She hasn't seen you in so long. She wanted to do something special, but I know how painful this all must be. Please forgive us," Evan Drake explains. Joshua walks over to where she is sitting.

"Sorry. I know this is uncomfortable."

"No, I'm fine," Rayen says.

"You always say that. You are so closed. I thought we passed this part," he jokes. She smiles a half smile. "That's better." He grabs her hand to caress it. It feels so nice when he touches her. His touch is comforting. Just as Rayen prepares to discuss yesterday with Joshua, Evelyn plops in the seat beside them.

"How have you been girl? We have got to catch up." Joshua interrupts.

"I'll go get some drinks. What will you have, Rayen?"

She answers, "Wine."

"Boring! I'll have some tequila shots," Evelyn blurts. Rayen looks at Joshua as if she doesn't want him to go. He exits the room. "We have to hang out. My dad tells me a central office is in the works here. I need work so bad. I felt that, since you would be here, I could work with you. I've been trying to get close to Joshua for five years. We are never in the same place,

Light in the Shadow

but since my dad said he will be hands on here in Michigan, I have to be too." Rayen eyes get large.

"You're into Joshua?"

"Yes ma'am! He is so gorgeous and so single. He travels so much. He doesn't have time to date, but now he'll be here for a while, and this is my chance," Evelyn proclaims. "Excuse me, Evelyn." She stands.

"Mr. Drake, this was very thoughtful, but if we don't have a meeting, I'd like to go," Rayen states. She gets her clutch from the table and strides toward the door of the private room. Joshua enters with the drinks.

"You are not leaving yet are you?"

"Yes, Joshua. I don't do the Birthday deal," she says.

"Thank you, Joshua! You are not leaving so soon, Rayen. Are you?" Evelyn jumps in.

"Oh my lord, not now! I finally am interested in someone and here comes the fucking vultures." Rayen thinks. "Yes, I'm leaving." She hitches her eyebrow.

"I'll walk you out." He places the drinks on a table nearby and scurries behind her. She is walking so fast he has to jog to keep up. She stands on the curb and dials Sterling. Joshua grabs her hand and presses end on her cell. She gives him a dangerous look. "I'm sorry Rayen. I really am sorry. I was just as surprised as you were. May I drive you home, please?"

"I suppose," she snaps.

"Come, let's go to my car. It is right down here." They walk to his car. Rayen calls and dismisses Sterling for the evening.

The drive to her condo is comforting. She is so happy he followed her out. Evelyn was getting ready to strike. When they

Annetta Hobson

get to her place, they enter. She drops her keys on the table. "You want a drink, Joshua?" she yells as she enters the kitchen.

"That would be nice, since I left mine on the table at Oasis," he says as he looks around, checking out the place. She reenters the living room with two glasses of brandy. She sits beside him on the sofa and hands him a drink. She looks him over. She had not noticed how finely dressed he was tonight. He has on dark brown slacks with a cream dress shirt and a tan blazer. They just sit there, sipping their drinks for a while.

She kicks off her shoes and begins to rub her feet.

"May I?" Joshua asks nervously. But, she doesn't speak. She just nods and stretches her feet towards him. She relaxes. "Rayen?"

"Hmmm?" she purrs with her eyes closed.

"I really like you. You are the most extraordinary woman I have ever met. You are very beautiful, enchanting. You are so smart and business orientated. You have a heart for the people you service. The first meeting we had, you talked about the clients like you were personally invested. I have never met anyone like you," Joshua says. She opens her eyes slowly and looks at him.

"Joshua thank you but…"

"But what? I know you are my boss, but I feel something between us. I know you feel it too. Or, did you mean it when you said we were just friends." Joshua asks frantically. "I know you are out of my league, but I can't help how I feel. You've captivated me. I can't think about anything else. I try not to think of you in that way, but no matter what I do, I see you. You are in my head, and I can't get you out." Rayen is surprised by his admissions. She is so inexperienced. She does not know how to respond.

Light in the Shadow

"Joshua, I have never been in anything but business relationships." Joshua looks down at his hand in disappointment. He pauses from her foot rub and reaches down to grab his glass from the floor. She continues, "I don't know how to voice what I feel. It is so foreign to me, but I really like you, too. I enjoy your company. I look forward to seeing you. You make me rethink everything I have ever felt. You make me want to fantasize. I need you to teach me how to open up. I'm afraid of how you have changed me in this short time."

He sets his glass on the floor, lifts her legs and lays her feet on the couch. He props a hand on the back of the couch to lift himself and moves closer. She gently sucks in a gulp of air. He reaches out to her. He takes the back of his hand and trails it down her bare arm. She lets the air out. He moves closer. Now he is sitting on the edge of the couch directly in front of her. First, he kisses her cheek. He kisses her brow and then the tip of her nose. Sporadic pangs of pleasure are rumbling in her belly. She has never felt this way before. She is so still. He looks in her eyes. "I have never seen a woman as sublime as you, Rayen." She looks down at his hands, which are creeping up her legs. "I want to caress every inch of you," he moans. He slides his nose against her face. "Your skin smells so good." He inhales. Finally his lips meet hers. His kiss is so delicate. Rayen relaxes her head and gives in to it. The kiss slowly escalates into passion. Her head is spinning. This feeling is so delicious! She wants more. She curls her fingers into his hair. He lets out a slow, drawn out moan. Suddenly, he scoops her off the couch, still kissing her, and carries her up the stairs.

Through their kiss, she mumbles, "End of the hall." He whisks her down the hall and lightly kicks open her bedroom door. He lifts his head from their lip lock and scans the room. A lamp on her nightstand is the only way he sees her bed. He lays his lips back on hers and begins their passion once more. Finally they reach the bed, and without breaking contact, he gently lays her on the bed. Her heart is pumping so fast and hard, it feels as if it will burst through. He lifts his lips from hers once more.

"I'm not moving too fast. Am I, Rayen? I want you to be sure you want this," he whispers.

"Yes, I'm sure," she says breathlessly.

"But, please, be gentle with me, Joshua."

"Baby, I will be as gentle as you want. I want to savor every inch of you." He rubs his hands down her arms and around her shoulders. When he gets to her back, he unzips her dress. She lifts her body as he slides it off and tosses it on the floor. She is left dressed in a black strapless bra and a pair of lacey black thongs. He sits up straight and his eyes caress her body from head to toe. "Rayen, your body is a work of fine art." She is so nervous! No man has ever gotten this far, but she really wants this. Joshua is a very gentle man, and she wants him to touch her like no man has ever been allowed. She lies back and scoots up to her pillow. She spreads her hair out with her hand and forearm.

"Oh, Rayen. I've dreamed about this moment so many nights. I want you so bad." He kisses her lips, trails down to her breast, and lightly kisses her nipple through her bra. She lets out a moan and tingles with excitement. He pulls at her bra to reveal her perky, hardened nipples. He kisses then sucks them gently. He is driving her mad with ecstasy. He then leaves her breast and trails kisses down to her stomach and licks her navel. Her body is lifting off the bed. He pauses so her body returns to the bed. When she relaxes he begins again. Slowly, he opens her legs, and he looks in her eyes to reassure her permission. When her legs are spread, he kisses her lips in the middle of her thighs. The feeling is so intense that she moans and twists her body. He gently presses her belly and begins to suck on her womanhood

Light in the Shadow

through her thongs. She slides her fingers in his hair and holds his head in place. She does not know what she is feeling, but she has never felt it before, ever. He slips off her thongs and continues to slurp up the lips and then moves up to her pleasure point. When he thinks she is near release, he makes his way back up to her face and begins kissing her passionately. Finally he removes his shirt to reveal his wonderfully chiseled chest. She rubs her hands along the ripples of his abs. He removes his pants and underwear in one sweeping plunge. He then leans back into her and kisses her with his tongue, invading her mouth. All she can do is welcome it there. "Rayen, are you ready for me? I promise I won't hurt you. I will never hurt you."

"Please, I beg you."

He kisses her again and grabs his erection. She glances at it but doesn't stare. He slowly enters her, and she lets out a shout of pleasure.

"Are you okay?"

"Oh, yes, Joshua!"

He slides in and out, in and out. The feeling is too much for her. She shouts loudly as she releases. All the pain and all of the fear leaves with her glorious conclusion. She is shaking and moaning. Then, he follows her lead with a growling moan. He plants soft kisses on her shoulder and lies beside her. He looks over at her, and she turns her head. He hears her sniffling. "What's wrong, Rayen? Did I hurt you?" He asks, alarmed. He leans up on his arm and gently grabs her shoulder to turn her towards him.

"No, Joshua. I am wonderful. I have never in my life experienced something so intimate, so wonderful. Thank you," she sniffs.

"Come on. Let me do something for you." He grabs her hand and leads her into her master bath. He turns on the shower and slides his hand in the stream to test it. He takes off her bra and leads her by her hand into the walk in shower. He slides in behind her and begins to kiss her shoulders and back. "Thank. You. Rayen. I appreciated every inch of your scrumptious body. I pray this is not my last time indulging in what you have bestowed upon me this evening." She smiles and leans into his kiss. He grabs a hand towel and begins to scrub her back. He lathers the soap and washes every inch of her. After their shower, they climb in bed, and he drifts off into a deep sleep. And, all Rayen can do is think about this major breakthrough in her existence.

The alarms beep. Joshua jumps up. "What time is it?"

"It's 7:30." Rayen answers. She turns toward him and leans into her pillow.

"What's wrong, Rayen? You look so intense," Joshua inquires.

"I can't believe the night we had. I feel like it was a dream. I am reveling in the thought of change."

"That's good, right?"

"Yes, of course. I had one way of thinking for so long. This, this has never been something I could have. I never knew I needed it."

"Were you a virgin?"

Rayen doesn't respond right away. She lies on her back and looks up at the ceiling. Finally she adds, "You are a gentle man. No one has ever gotten this close to me. No matter where this leads, I will be eternally grateful to you." Joshua beams.

Light in the Shadow

"Wow, Rayen, you are great for the ego. And, it was my pleasure. Your body is like none I've seen. Plus, you taste superb." She covers her eyes with her hands. He reaches for her hand and removes it from her face. "You have no need to hide. I see you, and I desire every inch of you." She looks into his eyes, and he leans up over her and kisses her lips softly. He takes his hand and smoothes her hair. As he caresses her hair, he leans in for another kiss. This one is more passionate than before. She pushes his chest very lightly.

"The groundbreaking is at 9 a.m., Josh."

"Well, that means we have time." He leans back in, kissing her, invading her mouth. He climbs atop her. He gently but excellently ravishes her one more time.

When Sterling arrives, he steps out of the car. He walks around and opens Rayen's door. He notices Joshua with her.

"Sterling, please stop at Mr. Manning's condo first."

"Yes, Ms. Vasu."

"Oh, I'm Mr. Manning now? I was Josh earlier," he jokes. She smirks. Joshua runs into his condo and quickly dresses. Tan polo, Khakis, and Rockport's are his construction site attire. He runs down to get in the truck, and they are off to the groundbreaking. When they arrive to the site, there are news cameras and townspeople gathered. Everyone is excited about the businesses coming to their small city. When Rayen and Joshua exit the vehicle, Evelyn runs to greet them.

"Here they are. The people we all have been waiting for!" Everyone turns and looks at them. Then a cameraman and woman greets them. "Fox 2 News. May we ask you some questions?"

"Sure," Joshua answers.

Annetta Hobson

"We know there are other projects in the works. Is Bay City going to be a lucrative site for your company?"

"Yes, we have Davidson and Davidson's strip mall and Jason Bartle's Condos. Hopefully we grab other companies wanting to move business here."

"Thank you, Mr...."

"Mr. Joshua Manning of Vista Corp International, lead architect, and general contractor."

"Thank you, Mr. Manning." He winks at Rayen and heads toward the spot where the ceremony will be held. Mr. Drake and Mr. Alvarez greet Rayen. All together, they walk over to the groundbreaking site.

Evan taps Rayen and asks if he could speak with her alone. "Rayen, you know I had mentioned creating a central office here. Well, I spoke with our other board members and everything is a go. All I need is your blessing to continue."

"That is certainly fine with me."

"Great. The other thing is would you mind running it, Rayen? I will have my daughter heading in operations handling the accounts. Will you oversee it?"

"I will be happy to run the central office, Mr. Drake."

"I trust that you will do great here. There are a lot of opportunities opening in Michigan. I already have the location. Your staff will be here Monday. You may want to hire an assistant. The staff that is transferring here is already Vista Corp employees and is up to speed on all current and future contracts. What do you think, Rayen?"

"I think that is the reason my father went into business with you and the reason you are the CEO. Email me the information."

Light in the Shadow

"I will. One thing: please keep an eye on Evelyn. She has never lived anywhere but in New York. I'm skeptical, but she wants the responsibility."

"No, what she wants is Joshua!" she thinks. "Oh, she'll be fine."

"Okay, Rayen. I'll be heading back tonight. The accounts in China need my attention."

Mr. Drake goes to his limo.

Joshua approaches Rayen as she heads for her ride. "Hello, gorgeous," he says.

She smiles a half smile. "Hi."

"What's wrong?"

"Nothing, Joshua."

"Are you hungry? Let's have lunch, since we missed breakfast," he smirks. "I mean, since you missed breakfast. I feasted on you this morning." Rayen's light brown skin flushes.

"Stop, before someone hears you," she snaps. He leans close and whispers in her ear.

"I can't help it, Rayen. You tasted so good…mmmm," he moans. A chill runs through her. He makes her feel like no man has ever been able to.

While they converse, Evelyn spots their intimate exchange. "Really? He likes Rayen? She will never return his advances. I hope…" she says scowling. Joshua opens the door for Rayen.

"Thank you," she says in her business voice.

They get into the Escalade and decide to go to the World Café for lunch. They arrive at the restaurant, and the waiter seats them. Joshua is in an excellent mood. He is smiling. He hasn't felt this good in years. He picks up his glass and sips his drink. "Rayen, may I be candid with you?"

"Sure," she responds.

"I haven't been with a woman in so long. Being with you is so intoxicating, even before last night. Being in your presence is like sipping expensive, vintage wine."

"Joshua, you are too kind. I know I am a handful. I am not very friendly. I do it on purpose to keep people at a distance. It has been a successful tactic to keep them out of my space. I don't know how you slipped through, but you did."

"It's because I see a wounded and abandoned woman beneath the strong one who will eat any man for lunch if he even thinks about getting over on her."

A dangerous smile crosses her lips. "You think you have me figured out. Don't you?"

"No, but I really want to. I want to know your every thought. Your every hurt unveiled. I really care for you Rayen." Just as he leans forward to kiss her, Evelyn interrupts. "Well, hello, you two. I was on my way to my hotel when I spotted your driver, Rayen." Rayen rolls her eyes secretly.

"Oh, great. Join us," she spouts sarcastically.

"I will, thank you." She sits next to Joshua. The waiter comes to the table carrying a large tray with their meals.

"I'll have what they are having."

Chapter 4

This is the most uncomfortable Rayen has ever been since she left her grandfather's house. The nice, intimate, afternoon lunch has become an unwelcomed threesome. Evelyn sips some wine and licks her lips seductively. "Mmm, Joshua, you should try the wine. It is absolutely titillating."

Joshua looks at Evelyn and says, "Wine is wine. What I've had today is so much sweeter." Evelyn giggles nervously and looks confused.

"Okay?"

Rayen jumps in, "He has been drinking since we got here."

"Oh. I see. Maybe I'll have what you've been having." Joshua bursts out a cough.

"No, you wouldn't like it." Rayen can't help but laugh.

"I should be going. It is 6 p.m., and I have some proposals to look over. Check, please!" The waiter comes over, and she stands to leave.

"I should be going also. Rayen is my ride. Evelyn." He nods. She fumbles trying to stand.

"I could take you home. I have a rental for the weekend. We could go for drinks. Anyway, I'm sure Rayen's in a rush to get to her work." Rayen turns to look at Joshua.

"No thanks. I really need to get home," he answers.

"Well, I could drop you home. It's really no problem," she insists. Rayen turns to Evelyn.

"Actually, I can have Sterling drive you too. We have all had a few drinks." Evelyn sighs in defeat.

Annetta Hobson

"No, I'm fine. Next time, Joshua?"

"Of course," he says unconvincingly. They all exit the restaurant. Sterling is holding the door open. Joshua gently holds Rayen's hand as she slides in the SUV. Evelyn watches as Joshua slides in behind her.

"How in the hell did this happen?" she asks herself.

"Spend the night with me, baby, please?" Joshua turns to her as the vehicle comes to rest in front of his apartment. She looks at Joshua. He is such a good-looking guy. A small piece of hair has escaped, and is dangling over his eye. She gently runs her fingers through it to smooth it out of his face. He always wears it brushed back but the curls seem to do what they like.

"Well?" He raises one brow. She matches his glare and hitches her brow. "I guess." She smiles.

"Sterling, that will be all this evening."

"Thank you, Ms. Vasu. Good evening, Mr. Manning." They enter the building, and his apartment is on the first floor. The apartment is dark, so he turns on the light when they enter. It is different than she remembers. There was no furniture. Now is it filled with furniture she helped him pick out. It has two bedrooms, and one he has made into the workroom. It is an organized mess. Drawing plans sprawl everywhere. Laptops and printers lay on his dual tables. A bookshelf with very little books also contributes to the clutter. They walk down the hall past his master bedroom and bath into his living room.

"Have a seat." She sits on his couch. She can see directly into his kitchen. "Would you like a drink, Rayen?" he asks as he enters the kitchen.

"Yes, water, please." He peeks around the wall.

"Nothing stronger?"

Light in the Shadow

"No. I want to be sober tonight, Mr."

"Are you implying something?"

"No. I'm just not interested in drinking tonight."

"Ouch!" he says as he reenters with bottled water and a glass of brandy for himself. He sits beside her, picks up the remote, and clicks it toward his 50 in" flat screen television mounted on the wall facing them. He clicks channels until he finds something he is interested in. They sit in silence for a while. He looks over and notices Rayen dozing off. "You want to lie down?"

"No, I'm fine," she yawns.

"Come, Rayen." He stands and pulls her up. They continue up the hall to his bedroom. He opens the door. His bed is huge; his room is adorned in green and beige décor. He has a sleigh bed with matching dressers. He pulls her over to the bed. "May I?" he motions his hands to lift her strapless yellow dress over her head. She yawns and nods. He slips her out of her dress. She is wearing no bra and white lacey boy shorts. He doesn't touch her body like she imagined he would. He walks over to his dresser grabs a white tank and slips it over her head. He bites his lip and groans. "Rayen you are such a wonderful sight. I never want this back. Just keep it and wear for me every now and then. " She gives him smirk but it is weak. She yawns. He pulls back his sheets, picks her up, lays her in the bed, and covers her up. He plants a kiss on her nose and leaves the room. She turns and falls asleep.

Rayen jumps up. She rubs her eyes. She is a little disoriented. "What time is it?" She reaches for her purse and searches for her phone, which is beside the bed in a chair with her clothes. "2:30 a.m.?" She clumsily stumbles to the bathroom. It is very dark, and she cannot see. She flips the light on and looks around. She flushes the toilet, washes her hands, and turns the light back off. She tips quietly back to the bed and sits on the edge. She takes in what is happening. "This thing with Josh is so foreign to me," she thinks. "How did I end up in this place? I feel so normal." She feels the bed move. Joshua sits up and turns the lamp on that placed on the nightstand next to his side of the bed.

"Is there something wrong?" She pauses.

"I haven't spent the night with anyone since I was a child."

"Do you want me to take you home?"

"No, no. It's just different," she says.

"Come over here." She turns to him and crawls to his side of the bed. "Lie down with me, Rayen." She snuggles in his arms. She feels so warm there. It is a feeling she never thought she would experience with anyone. He caresses her arm. His fingers tickle her skin. A chill runs through her and she shivers. Joshua feels her shake and responds, "Are you cold?" He lifts the cover and she slides under never leaving his arms. He runs his hands up and down her back. She looks up at him, and he glares back. He lifts her head to remove his arm. She lies back on the pillow. He sits up and sweeps her body with his eyes. He leans in and kisses her softly. She wraps her arms around his neck and returns with passion. He unclutches her hands and leans back to gaze at her. "Rayen, I swear I am mesmerized by you. When I was sleeping, I dreamed of you." She just watches him and says nothing. He trails kisses on her face to her neck and rests there a while. Gently he lifts her to ease her out of her underwear, then slides her legs open. He then takes his middle finger and inserts it inside of her. She lets out a small sensual wail.

"Do you like that?"

"Ooooooh, yes!"

Light in the Shadow

He laughs. He continues to slide his finger in and out of her. She is losing her mind. "Oh goodness! Please!" She pleads. He slowly slides it out. Her eyes fly open. She watches as he slides it into his mouth.

"There is nothing or no one as luscious as you are." He kisses her again. He then takes off the only thing he was wearing, his pajama pants. Rayen sits up and takes off the tank top he had put on her. He looks her over, he slides his hand up and he fondles her breasts. Then he leans in and slides the nipple between his lips. He takes turns sucking the left then the right. He then eases himself into her. She hums as if she were singing. He thrusts mildly in and out of her; he softly but repeatedly kisses her face, every inch of it. She returns the affection by kissing his neck. She grabs his behind, and he opens his mouth to let out a loud moan. "Oh, Rayen, you are too much for me." He starts to grind faster and faster. Finally, she let's go, and her moistness drenches him, sending him spiraling into his release.

When Rayen awakes, she is in the bed alone. She squints at her phone. It is 9:30 a.m. She notices she has a missed call and one message. She can't help but smell the wonderful aroma filling the apartment. Joshua is cooking breakfast. She sits up and begins to dial her voicemail. "Hey Rye. It's Evelyn. I was wondering, did you want to hang out today? It is Saturday. Don't be a bore! Call me." Rayen eyes widen.

"Rye? She hasn't called me that since we were fifteen. Even in college, we were distant from one another. So, why the best friend act?" she thinks, then deletes the message. She stands and puts on the tank top lying on the floor. Then, she finds her underwear and goes to the bathroom to bathe.

When she enters the kitchen, Joshua is standing at the stove, cooking. His back is so strong that his muscles flex as he stirs. All he is wearing is boxers. She clears her throat. He jumps. "You startled me!"

"Sorry," she smirks. She finds a rubber band sitting on the counter and pulls her hair up.

"You look amazing in my tank top," he mentions as he shuffles around.

"What are you cooking?"

"Well, I'm making French toast, scrambled eggs with sausage, and bacon," he gloats.

"Smells wonderful."

She takes a seat at the table. She folds one leg beneath her as she sits. He prepares her plate and sets it in front of her. "Eat up, sexy." She gives him a half smile and digs in. He makes himself a plate, sits across from her, and begins to eat. "How did you sleep?" he inquires.

"Very well," she says as she stands to get a bottle of water from the refrigerator. She sits back at the table. "By the way, have you noticed that Evelyn is completely taken with you?" she adds. He glances up at her from his plate.

"Umm, I guess?" he shrugs.

"I mean smitten."

"Rayen Vasu, I would never take you for the jealous type."

She sits up straight. "Jealous? Why would I be jealous? Enlighten me." She purses her lips.

"Well, darling, I have known them for a very long time. And every time I meet with her father and she is present, she flirts heavily."

"So, why have you two not dated?"

"She is the spoiled rich daddy's girl. Not my type."

Light in the Shadow

Rayen stares at him as he eats. She is feeling angry. "Could I be jealous?" she asks internally. "Anyway, she called me and wants to 'hang out'."

He chuckles, "Hang out, then." Rayen gets up again. She takes her plate and dumps it into the sink. She exits the kitchen. She dials Sterling and goes into the bathroom and dresses. When she returns to the kitchen, Joshua is cleaning.

"Thank you for breakfast," she says blandly. He turns to speak and notices she is dressed.

"You're leaving?"

"Yes, I really have work to do. I'm going home to get ready for Monday."

"Can I see you later, then?"

"I'll call you."

"Okay?" he says a little confused. She grabs her purse and proceeds to the door.

"Let me walk you out. I just have to put on a pair of pants."

She waits at the door for him. He walks her out to Sterling who is holding her door open.

"Good morning, Ms. Vasu."

"Sterling."

She nods as she almost mows him over to climb in the truck.

"Good morning, Sterling."

"Morning, Mr. Manning."

Before Sterling can close the door, Joshua grabs it. "I got it." Sterling nods and scurries around to get in.

"Rayen, have I missed something?"

77

"No, this was a big mistake." She closes the door. "Drive, Sterling."

"Yes, ma'am."

They leave and Joshua is standing at the curb. Rayen does not turn to see. Joshua throws his hands in the air in defeat. When she gets to her condo she is happy to be home. "Why did I let my guard down? He should have never been allowed in."

The day drags by, and Rayen buries herself in paperwork. She reads contracts, proposals, and employee files that she will handle on Monday. She sits on her bed in a sports bra and pajama pants with her laptop reading emails. She composes an e-mail, stating:

Mr. Drake,

All of the negotiations on the new project are finalized. They will begin construction at the end of the summer.

Rayen

She glances at her clock. It is 7:30 p.m. "I am starving." She gets out of her bed and enters her bathroom. She turns the water on in the bathtub. As the water runs, memories of Joshua and their intimate shower crosses her mind. She lifts her hand to lightly brush her lips. She shuts her eyes as the feeling of his touch invades her mind. She quickly tries to shake it off. She steps into the shower. Soon, her mind has traveled back to her starving belly. Rayen surveys the clothes in her closet and decides to wear her khaki pants that scrunch at the ankle with drawstrings. She compliments them with a brown satin camisole and beige blazer that gathers at the waist. Then she slides in her brown and beige wedge heels. She goes through the kitchen to her back door to enter the garage. She climbs in her car and heads out. "Where can I go?" she thinks for a while. "Oasis was nice, even with Evelyn pulling that Birthday stunt."

Light in the Shadow

She drives to Oasis. When she arrives she parks her car and enters. She is greeted at the door.

"Good evening. Do you have reservations?"

"No, I do not."

"Meeting someone?"

"No."

"Okay, right this way."

Rayen is seated, and a waitress approaches. "Good evening. May I start you with a drink?"

"Yes. White wine, please. And, for my meal, I'll have stuffed chicken breast over fettuccini. That's all."

"Great, I'll be right back with your wine."

Rayen examines the lounge. She watches as guests are dancing and enjoying the music. Suddenly, out of the corner of her eye, she notices a male approaching her.

"Ms. Vasu, we meet again."

"Oh goodness. It's the detective," she thinks. Calmly, she returns, "Mr. Pierce. Hello."

"How are you? And, call me Blake please."

"I'm fine, Blake. And, you?" she states too serious.

"I'm great. Why are you always dining alone? I could imagine there are many that would love to accompany you. Besides, being alone is not safe."

"I'm a big girl. I can take care of me better than anyone."

"Oh, I wasn't…"

"No, no. It's okay, Mr. Pierce. I know it is second nature for you to observe."

Annetta Hobson

He smiles sincerely. "Well, I am dining alone tonight also. My date canceled, and I was just leaving." He lingers a moment. Rayen sighs. "I am absolutely starving too," he mentions. She pauses.

"You wouldn't want to join me would you?" she asks sarcastically, praying the answer will be no.

"Thank you, Ms. Vasu. I am not as brave as you. Dining alone dampers my mood." He circles the table.

"Well, I've ordered. Maybe you should do the same. And, my name is Rayen. My colleagues and staff call me, Ms. Vasu." He straightens his tie, holds it to his chest, and sits. The waitress returns, and he orders lasagna and a beer. "Off duty?"

"Of course. No drinking on the job," he states, matter of factly. Rayen sips her wine. They sit in complete silence for a while. She glances at him.

"What does he want?" she says to herself. When Blake's food arrives, he is rubbing his hands together. She catches herself staring at his hands. She shakes her head and begins to eat.

"Oh my," he growls. Her eyes shoot to him.

"Why is his eating turning me on? I don't even know him. Damn Joshua for awaking these feelings!" she thinks.

"Are you alright?" Blake questions.

"Fine," she snaps. They continue to eat their meals. Blake takes a gulp of his beer.

"So, Rayen, you are here in town with Vista Corp?"

"Yes, I am. I've been here around a month."

"I know."

Light in the Shadow

She watches him as he gulps again. He places the mug on the table. He is a different type of good looking. He is the 'sexy TV detective'. And, Joshua is 'Smallville' cute. "I have witnessed you running about, around town," he says, invading her thoughts.

She returns with caution, "Oh, okay."

"So, how are you adjusting in our small town?"

"It's no New York."

"Are you from New York?"

"Yes."

Blake tilts his head. "You are a very austere woman. Do you ever smile?"

"Is this an interrogation, detective?"

"Oh, no! Sorry, I'm just curious. No matter how much I try to suppress it, the questioning cop in me comes out."

"You must never keep dates. Or maybe that's why you got stood up," she scolds. He smirks but it is not genuine.

"Touché." She softens a little. The waitress approaches.

"Would you like the check now?"

"Yes," he says before Rayen can respond. When the waitress returns, he hands her $150 and encourages her to keep the change. She thanks him and leaves.

"I can get cash and give my portion of the bill back to you," she states.

"No, consider it a thank you for allowing me to annoy you for the evening." He stands and nods. "Rayen, it was a pleasure dining with you. Thank you." He pulls out his card. "Here you are. Please call me sometime."

Rayen takes the card.

"I would ask you can I escort you to your car, but I'm hesitant," He jokes.

"And, why is that?"

"You appear to be a self-sufficient woman, and I don't want to do anything to offend you. I would like to stay in good graces. Have a good evening, Rayen." He grabs her hand to shake it. When his warm palm connects with hers, electricity surges through her.

"I am just all over the place!" she thinks. "Nice dining with you, detective."

"The pleasure was mine," he says with a captivating look. He holds her gaze until someone calls out his name.

"Blake!" A tall blonde comes dashing towards the table. She kisses him on the cheek. Rayen glances down at her hands. "I'm so sorry I stood you up. I have this case in Bingham Farms that is killing me. I could not get away."

"Blake buttons his blazer. I've eaten, Lauryn. Ms. Vasu was kind enough to take pity on me, so I wouldn't look like a dateless dope."

"Ms. Rayen Vasu, the young up and coming business tycoon."

"You know her?"

"No. I only know of her." She reaches out to shake Rayen's hand. Rayen stands and grabs her clutch.

"Hello. I'm sorry; you have me at an advantage." They shake.

Light in the Shadow

"I apologize. I am Lauryn Fleming. I read a lot, and I came across an article about you and your parents." Rayen places her clutch under her arm.

"Oh I see. Well, I need to get going."

"Thanks again for dinner," Blake says, lightly brushing her arm.

"No problem. Next time, no interrogation," she states as she walks away. He is entranced. He doesn't take his eyes from her until she disappears through the glass doors.

"Blake, I'm so sorry. But, you understand, right?" Lauryn pleads. He is not in the room anymore. His mind is still with Rayen. "Beautiful isn't she?" Lauryn interrupts his trance.

"Oh." He shakes off his thoughts. "What article were you speaking of?" he inquires. "Come, let's sit in the bar area. She tugs his arm. They sit at a small table.

"The article was about how her parents were murdered about ten or eleven years ago. Her father was the founder of Vista Corp, and she has recently stepped in to help rebuild the company in his image. They got some big contracts here in Michigan, and they are moving a part of the company here to Bay City." He scratches his chin. She continues. "Shortly after her parents were murdered, she went to live with her grandfather who was her only living relative. He then died from natural causes months later."

"My goodness! No wonder she is so edgy," he says concerned.

"Yes, but enough about her." Lauryn leans in to kiss Blake.

"Lauryn, stop."

"Why? You said we would try."

"I said we would go slow and see where things go!" Blake waves for the waiter.

"I love you so much, Blake. You have to give us another try."

"I care for you, Lauryn. That is the only reason I am even here tonight, but I am not where you are yet. It is going to take some time."

Lauryn hangs her head and tears began to fall.

"Please, don't cry."

"I have always been married to my job, and I have realized my mistake. You should understand that more than anyone, Blake."

"I love my job also, but I never put my work before you. My dad taught me to always remember what's more important."

"Will you ever forgive me?"

"I have forgiven you." The waiter intervenes. "Can I get you two anything?"

"Are you willing to throw away 5 years? You wanted to marry me for goodness sake!"

"Stop! Please?" He says as he dismisses the waiter. "I'll see you tomorrow at my father's retirement party. I can't do this right now." He stands to leave, and Lauryn is there alone.

Sunday morning, May 16th at 8 a.m., Rayen wakes, and the sun is shining in her window. She squints as usual. She stands and stretches. Her phone rings. "Hello?" She says with a yawn.

"Hello, sleepy head."

"Who is this?" She asks with a frown.

"Evelyn silly!"

Light in the Shadow

"Oh shit!" she thinks. "Evelyn."

"What happened to you yesterday?"

"I worked all day."

"Oh, well. You missed so much fun."

"Is that right?"

"Oh, yes. I went to an upscale club, and I met the District Attorney and his associates. They were having a few drinks, and noticed I was alone. All handsome fellows, I explained to them I was new in town. I told them about our company, which they knew of. Then they invited us to the Chief of Police retirement ball. So, do you want to go?"

"Why would I want to go a party on a Sunday?"

"Rayen, everyone who is anyone will be there: judges, business owners, the Mayor, and a host of other wealthy socialites. It could be a great breeding ground for future clients!"

"I guess you're right. Text me the details."

"Will do, and pullout the million dollar gown. I sure will."

"Okay," Rayen spits, totally annoyed.

She presses the end button and proceeds down stairs to eat breakfast.

While she is eating, her doorbell buzzes. She goes to the door and pushes the call button. "Yes?"

"Rayen, it's me, Joshua." She releases the button quickly.

"Come on! What is this?" she says silently.

"Come up," she says as she pushes the button. She opens the door, and Joshua is coming up the stairs.

"Hi," he waves.

"Hello," she returns. She motions her hand to wave him in. He walks pass her with his head hung. "What's wrong, Joshua?" she asks. She closes the door, and he turns to her.

"Rayen, what happened?"

"What do you mean, Josh?"

He smiles. "I like when you call me Josh." She purses her lips. "You just left abruptly. Neither warning nor explanation. I thought you enjoyed spending time with me."

"I did," she pauses. "I mean I do. It is so much. My head is spinning."

"Does this have anything to do with Evelyn?"

"I guess, a little."

"Why?"

"Joshua, please…"

He stops her with a kiss. He grabs her by her arms and kisses her deeply with every emotion he has ever felt when he was with her. She is breathless when he releases her. "Don't do that again," she demands darkly.

"I am sorry, but I crave you. If you end us now I won't be able to handle it."

"Evelyn may be better for you, Joshua; I am so new to this."

"I don't want her; I want you!"

"I don't know why. I am so lifeless." He hugs her ever so gently. She feels for him. "How could I do this to such a wonderful man?" She wonders. "The thought of you being with her made me so angry! I didn't want to deal with it, any of it. I can't get deep into this. If I get hurt, I will never recover. And, I

Light in the Shadow

will be emptier than I already am. I am merely a shadow of a girl who knew how to live."

"I won't hurt you, Rayen! I won't."

"You cannot guarantee that."

He drops his head as if he just got knocked out. She grabs his hand and leads him to the couch. "Sit down, Joshua. Don't hate me."

"Rayen, I could never hate you. I think I love you."

She gasps. "No, please, Joshua."

"I am a big boy, Rayen. I thought you were feeling what I was feeling."

"I don't know what I am feeling. I have never been with a man like this."

She sits on his lap and runs her fingers through his hair. "I'm sorry. I want you to find someone who deserves your love and can return it without thinking about it."

"I want you," he whispers.

Rayen sits at her dining table and watches Joshua while he sleeps on her couch. "What was I thinking? I can't get close to anyone. My secrets are too heavy. Too dangerous for me and him." Joshua turns and stretches.

"How long have I been sleeping?" She points to the clock on her wall. "3 o'clock!"

"Yes, I just couldn't disturb you." She says resting her chin on interlocked hands.

"Are you going to the big party tonight?" he inquires.

"Yes. Did Evelyn call you?"

"Yes, earlier this morning. I was hoping we could go together. Is that alright?"

"I was going to ask you anyway. Did Evelyn ask you to be her date?"

"She did, and I said no thank you. We would see each other there."

"Well, you better get going. The party starts at seven."

She stands to approach him. As soon as she reaches him, he stands to meet her. They embrace; he kisses her cheek. "Even if we never sleep together again, can we please still have this?"

"Josh, you have awakened something in me. I don't understand it, but I don't want it to go away. I need you. I will always need you. I'm sure of it."

She walks him to the door before he leaves he asks, "May I kiss you Rayen?" She looks up at him and leans in to kiss him. He engages her. The kiss is passionate. She breaks away, knowing where it will lead. "Please Rayen, once more. Can we just try it once more?"

"Joshua…I don't think that is wise. Give me a little time. I need to process this." He is in pieces over her.

"I need you, please?" She is torn. He makes her feel so good, but she doesn't want to get too deep. She is afraid. He slides his hand behind her head and stares in her eyes. "I have been with other women. It is something about you. You have captivated me." She really likes Josh, but she is not sure how she is supposed to feel. He breaks her from her reverie. He kisses her once more, reinvading her mouth. He slithers his tongue in searching desperately for her surrender. She doesn't give in. She gently pushes on his chest. He hesitates. "Rayen," he pleads through their kiss.

Light in the Shadow

"I can't, not today. Give me time. I beg you," she gently responds. He drops his head to her shoulder and inhales. She smells so nice, he thinks. He wants her so bad, but he cannot force her. He respects her.

"I'm so sorry. I will do as you wish." She grabs his head and plants one soft kiss on his lips. "I will see you at seven, okay?" He walks out of the door, sulking.

Rayen dashes out of the shower; she dries her body. She relives the torturing moment between her and Joshua hours earlier. She plops on her bed. "How did I get here?" She looks over at her gold evening gown lying across her bed. The satin dress has a strap that adorns one shoulder. The bodice is beaded with silver and gold beading. The dress is made to hug her every curve, and it is long, almost covering her feet. It has a long sexy split that touches above her knee and is decorated the same as the bodice with beading. The high-heeled shoes she chooses have Swarovski crystals across the strap that crosses her toes, and the other strap the wraps around her ankles. She dresses quickly, knowing that Sterling will be there shortly. She curls her hair in loose wavy locks and pins it to one side so that they cascade down the strapped side of the dress. Her bare shoulder is exposed. She thinks as she checks the mirror reflection. The bell buzzes, and she pushes the button. "I'll be right down." She explains as she grabs a silver clutch and bolts out of the door. Sterling is standing with the SUV door open to let her in. Joshua is already seated in the truck when she slides in. "Oh, goodness, Rayen. You look absolutely stunning." He kisses her cheek.

"You are a sight yourself, Josh." He looks so debonair in his black tuxedo.

Chapter 5

Sterling climbs in the driver seat and pulls off. When they stop, Rayen glances out the window. She spots a beautiful mansion. It resembles a small Whitehouse. "Where are we, Sterling?"

"Mayor Grant Winters' mansion. This is the destination of the Retirement party."

"Oh, Mayor Winters. Any relation?" she inquires.

"Yes, he is my father."

"Oh!" She says surprised. He steps out and rounds the vehicle to open her door. "Thank you, Sterling." They walk up to the door, and the place is glorious.

"Names, please?"

"Rayen Vasu and Joshua Manning." He looks at a clipboard and waves them in.

"Enjoy your evening." They step in and there are several people crowded in the foyer. It is beautifully crafted gray and white marble. A large chandelier hangs in the middle. Under it is a white marble table with roses and lilies in a grand vase atop it. They walk pass the foyer into the great room where the party is centrally located. Everyone is mingling. Then she spots Evelyn looking very elegant. She is wearing a black backless gown. It plunges just to the small of her back. It trails the floor like a small train but lifts to her knees in the front. The fabric is silk, and her legs are flawless. The dress twists at the bust line like a pretzel around her neck, with her cleavage peeking through. Tall black high heels finish the elegant look.

Annetta Hobson

"A million dollars indeed," Rayen thinks. She is giggling and talking to a very prestigious looking fellow.

"Rayen! Come." She scurries to her and leads her back to the gentleman. Joshua keeps up. "This is my boss and my oldest friend, Ms. Rayen Vasu of Vista Corp. Our General contractor/Architect here is Joshua Manning." They all shake hands and nod. Evelyn continues, "This is the district attorney, Trevor Huffman."

"Pleased to meet you, Ms. Vasu. It is great to finally meet you. I have heard so much about you."

"Really? Thank you. I am so sorry. I have not been introduced to anyone in town yet."

"Well, you should meet my wife. She will introduce you to everyone in town. Emily, honey, come here. The classical music is really low, so the woman he calls hears him and immediately hurries to his side. Trevor is maturely handsome. His wife is very slim, but not too tall with short bobbed brunette hair.

"Hello. I am Emily Pierce-Huffman. And, you are?"

"Rayen Vasu."

"Ahhh. So, you are Rayen Vasu," she says as if she recognizes a story in her head.

"You are very beautiful, my dear."

"Thank you. This is Joshua Manning."

"Come, Ms. Vasu. There are some people dying to meet you."

Joshua releases her arm, and she is whisked off by Mrs. Huffman.

"By any chance, are you related to Detective Pierce?"

Light in the Shadow

"Yes, he is my brother."

She brings her to a group of people conversing. They stop as they approach. One of the people is Blake. He is wearing a black tailored suit with a black tie and white dress shirt. He looks absolutely divine. "Everyone, this is Rayen Vasu of Vista Corp." Everyone smiles and nods. Emily continues her introduction. "This is my father, the greatest police chief to grace Bay City, Robert Pierce. My mother is Abagail Pierce. My baby sister, here, is Danielle, and her twin is Daniel. Then, of course, there is Blake."

"Hello," Rayen says with a quick wave. Blake steps forward and kisses her hand.

"Good to see you again, Rayen." She inhales when his lips brush her hand.

"Likewise," she states as she quickly pulls away. Daniel steps forward. He isn't as good-looking as Blake. He has copper blonde hair, untrimmed stubble, and he isn't wearing a suit. He has on a white dress shirt with some blue slacks. In an instant, she is yanked away. For a while, Rayen trails Emily as she introduces her to everyone at the party it seems.

Joshua finds Rayen talking to Judge Richard Caldwell. "May I have my date back, your honor?"

"Of course. She is quite amazing," the judge adds.

"Can I have one dance with the lovely Ms. Vasu?"

"Anytime, Joshua."

They dance to music being played by an orchestra. He leans his chin in and rests it on top of her head. Right then, she spots Blake starring at her. He is across the room dancing with Lauryn. "Your father and mother look wonderfully happy, Blake." He doesn't answer.

Annetta Hobson

"Blake!"

"Yes, Lauryn?"

She pulls back from the embrace.

"Do you hear me, babe?"

"Yes, Lauryn."

The music stops; applause erupts. Trevor grabs the microphone. "Thank you everyone for coming this evening. We are here to celebrate the retirement of Bay City's finest police chief. He has served our wonderful city for 35 years. Starting as a traffic cop, serving as a detective, then lead detective, and finally Chief of Police. Robert, I'm not just saying this because I'm married to your lovely daughter. You will never be able to be replaced. Bay City Police Department won't be the same without you. Hopefully, Blake, already a superb detective himself, will follow in your footsteps and make this City proud!" Everyone applauds, and he passes the microphone to Chief Pierce.

"Thank you D.A. Huffman. I just want to say thank you for your love and support through the years. I could not have done it without all of you." Everyone begins to embrace him one after the other. Lastly, he hugs his wife, who is crying.

Rayen is clapping, and Joshua has his arm firmly wrapped around her. She notices Blake's continuous glances in her direction. She taps Joshua, and he releases her. She exits the party to find the restroom. Blake notices her exit and proceeds to follow her. She enters the restroom and checks her make up. She touches up her lipstick and uses the restroom. When she is done, she washes then dries her hands and pats her hair. When she steps out Blake is planted against the wall. "Is that your boyfriend?" She looks up from her purse.

"Excuse me?"

Light in the Shadow

"The curly haired, Clark Kent, is he your boyfriend?"

"That is not your concern, detective."

"I just wanted to know if you have someone to keep you safe at night. There is a killer still on the loose, you know?"

She smiles to herself, "Oh, I know…"

"Why do you care about my well-being, Detective Blake?"

"I care about all my Bay City citizens." She begins to walk away.

"Wait, Ms. Vasu. I want to ask you on a date, but I can't if you have a boyfriend or fiancé, etc." She stops.

"Aren't you involved yourself, with Ms. Fleming?"

"I am not involved with anyone right now."

"I see." She pulls her card out of her purse and hands it to him. "Call me. We may be able to schedule something." He takes her card and smiles.

"Please don't toy with me, Ms. Vasu. I really want dinner or a drink with you."

"I never toy with anyone, detective. I am way too busy for that." She turns away so he won't see her smile.

"This week, Rayen?" Blake yells.

"I will check my calendar, detective," she yells back, exiting the hall and reentering the party. Lauryn spots Blake reentering the party, smiling with a card in his hand. He tucks it in his pocket and goes over to his mother. Rayen glides over to Joshua. He and Evelyn are chatting. Evelyn is obviously throwing herself at him.

"Joshua, you look so handsome this evening."

"Thanks, Evelyn."

"Joshua, I've wanted you for years. Tell me you haven't noticed. And, please don't tell me you are involved with Rayen." she spits in a drunken slur.

"Evelyn, did you drive?" Rayen interjects. Startled, she spins around.

"Umm, yes, I did."

"Well, you are intoxicated. I wouldn't feel comfortable allowing you to drive."

"Maybe Joshua can take me?" Evelyn adds. Rayen turns to Joshua. He shrugs.

"Sterling will drive you, and I will bring your car," she demands. She searches for Sterling and finds him conversing with his father.

"Ms. Vasu, thank you for hiring my son's driving service. It is a new business venture for him."

"The pleasure is mine, Mr. Mayor. He is very professional and reliable. And, I am impressed that he services me himself. He never sends anyone else." Sterling holds his head high as she speaks. She sees Sterling in a different light now. She knows he is working hard to prove himself to his father. "Sterling, can you take Ms. Drake home? I will drive her car when we retire, and you may pick me up from her house. They approach Evelyn, and she is staggering.

"Joshua, Joshua, how can you not want me? Look at me!" Joshua just stands there flushed with embarrassment. Before anyone notices, Sterling guides her out the door to take her home.

"Joshua, are you okay?" Rayen asks.

"I'm fine. I really feel bad for her. Excuse me. I'm going to check on her." As he leaves, a slow melody begins to play and

Light in the Shadow

most of the guests start to dance. Blake struts over to where she is standing.

"Everything alright?" She drops her hands to her side and turns to greet him. "Yes. My colleague has had one too many. Sterling is driving her home."

"And, your date?"

"He went to make sure she is alright."

"Well…can I dance with you until he returns?" She rolls her eyes.

"Why not?"

He grabs her waist with one hand and lifts the other. She places one hand in his and the other around his neck. He begins to twirl. "Not bad."

"I won't step on your feet, if that's what you mean." She drops her head to hide the hint of a smile.

"You smell delightful, Ms. Vasu. What are you wearing?"

"I don't remember. I spritzed something on me after I bathed."

He hums as if the thought of her bathing drove him wild. "I read your bio on Vista Corp's website, and you have quite an impressive story, Rayen."

"Thank you. But, from what I hear, you have an equally impressive one yourself."

"I suppose, but you have beauty and brains."

She doesn't respond. As he inhales her sweet aroma, Joshua approaches. "Rayen, I think we should go. She is refusing to get in Sterling's Escalade." He then walks away.

"I have to go."

"Okay, but I have intentions on calling you. I need to get to know you."

"Need is a very strong word."

"I know. That's why I said it."

He kisses her hand, and she leaves the party. Lauryn stops Blake in his tracks.

"What is going on, Blake? You are embarrassing me, falling all over her."

"Lauryn, we are not together. You didn't want anyone to know we split, so you are embarrassing yourself."

"But, you said we would try."

"And, I am trying. But, you neglected me. You dove into your work. I wanted to make you my wife, but you wanted your job. So, now you have it."

"I was new and the only woman. Marriage at that time would have destroyed all I worked for." He frowns.

"When we were together you didn't even make love to me. You abandoned me when I was your only support. No one believed in you but me, and you threw me aside. And, now that you have it all, you want your trophy husband." Lauryn eyes tear.

"That's not fair, Blake! The first new woman you see you want to throw all of this away?"

"You hurt me, Lauryn. I was humiliated in front of my family. My sister helped me pick out that ring. And, you turned me down," he whispers.

"No, I said not now. I could not start a family at that time."

Light in the Shadow

"I wasn't asking you to marry immediately or have my baby right then and there. But yes, I want children."

She smiles.

"I am done with this, Lauryn, done! Tell your parents. We are done."

The smile quickly leaves her face. "No, Blake! I am ready now."

"I asked you two years ago!" His voice crescendos.

"Lower your voice, Blake," Lauryn pleads.

"And, now you want to say yes? I'm going home," he lowers to a whisper.

"Can I come home with you?" she asks. "It's been months since we made love. Maybe that's what you need." He gives her a bland stare.

"I have been practically begging you for sex, and now all of a sudden, you're game."

"I have been very busy, but tonight we are celebrating, so making love seems evident."

"To whom, Lauryn? You baffle me with your logic. Good night."

He goes over to hug his father and kisses his mother on the cheek. Lauryn follows him as he exits the mansion. The valet brings his Camaro around, and he hops in. Lauryn jumps in the passenger seat.

"Lauryn, what are you doing?"

"I am going home with you. I refuse to lose you to some young tramp."

"Whatever," Blake says as he pulls out from the Mansion.

Annetta Hobson

Blake reaches his home. This place is not for a bachelor. He purchased it two years ago as a surprise for Lauryn. She never moved in. She wanted to stay in Mount Pleasant for her job. He moved in anyway. As he pulls into the garage, she gazes up at the house. "This is our home, Blake. You purchased it for us." Blake doesn't respond. He jumps out the car and proceeds to open the door. He loosens his tie and rips it off. He tosses it on the table and cuts on the light. He slides his jacket off and throws it onto the couch. He looks very agitated. Lauryn glances around and follows him into the living room. He has very little furniture, a couch and coffee table in the living room, a dinette set for two in the dining room. Two of the bedrooms are empty. He has an office that is directly next to his bedroom and bath. There is a bed, a recliner, and a 36" TV sitting on a stand in his bedroom. Blake strips down to his boxers then disappears into his room to find a robe. He moves about as if he is home alone. He finally drops onto the bed and clicks his television off. Lauryn peeks in the room, and his eyes are closed. She creeps in the room and sits carefully on the bed. He opens his eyes and glares at her. "What are you doing?" he snaps.

"I just want to start over. You were fine with that," she reminds him.

"I have been waiting on you for years, Lauryn. You are selfish. You only want to have sex with me because you think I'm interested in someone else."

"I want to make love to you because I love you, Blake."

She leans over to kiss him. She touches his lips to his. He doesn't move. He cares for Lauryn. They have a history. His intensions were to marry her. She stands and drops her beaded green gown on the floor. She is a very attractive woman. She is the model type, blonde hair, green eyes, perky breast, and legs to

Light in the Shadow

die for. She slides back onto the bed and reaches to rub his crotch. He grabs her hands. "Stop, Lauryn!"

"You have been begging for weeks to make love to me, and now you want me to stop?"

"Yes! Stop before I throw you out."

She leans back and looks at him. Tears dance at the crease of her eyes. She concedes, wraps herself in his comforter and goes to sleep.

Monday morning, Rayen gets up early and goes to the new office to greet her workers. Everyone is in the office, moving around as efficient like worker bees. She acquaints herself with the employees and goes to where they set up an office for her. She looks around her office. The office is much different than the office in New York; Rayen is very satisfied with it. She feels she is making all the right moves to satisfy her father's legacy. She exits her office and peeks in on Evelyn. Evelyn is embarrassed by her behavior last night, but she doesn't acknowledge it. "Hello, Rayen."

"Morning, Evelyn."

"My dad called and said he would send all the reports from the new contracts this afternoon."

"Good."

"Have you hired an assistant yet?"

"Yes, I have someone in mind, but she won't be here until next month."

"Who, Angela Taylor?"

"Yes."

"Oh. I know she is graduating next month."

"When Mr. Drake forwards the reports, please bring them to me. If I am not in my office, leave them on my desk," Rayen states as she leaves and makes her way back to her own office. When she gets there, Joshua is sitting back in the chair positioned in front of her desk.

"Morning, gorgeous," He beams.

"Morning, Josh."

"Do you like your office?" He sits up.

"Yes, it is quite nice." Rayen's cell phone rings. She snatches it from her desk. "Hello, Rayen Vasu speaking." A man clears his throat.

"Hi, Ms. Vasu. This is Detective Pierce." She pauses.

"I know this is sudden, but I would like to take you to lunch."

She can hear the commotion in his background and guesses that he is at work.

"I am at work right now. Can I call you back?" She snaps.

"I will be having lunch today at 12:30 at World Café. If you don't show up, I will know you are busy."

"Okay. Thank you." She presses end.

"I enjoyed myself last night, Rayen." Joshua says. "Well, until Evelyn's spectacle."

She returns sarcastically, "Well, she did eventually get in the car. Yes, when you agreed to accompany her."

"You followed, so it was all good," he jokes.

"This is so awkward, Josh. Evelyn continually throws herself at you. She has always been this way."

"Really?"

Light in the Shadow

"Yes, really, but I didn't mind because I was going through so much."

"So, what are you saying?"

"I am saying she was my friend, and she has always wanted things, no matter who has them. But, after I lost my family, I just did not care." She stares at her hands and picks her nails.

"Am I one of your things?"

"No, I…"

He smiles. "Rayen, why don't you ever speak about your parents or grandfather?"

Rayen sits in her chair behind the desk and slides her chair up.

"You always shut down when someone mentions them. One day you will have to let it out."

She clasps her hands together and plants them on the desks. "But, not today." She opens her laptop and begins to type.

"I'll let you get back to work." Joshua exits the office. Rayen doesn't look up.

She finally pulls eyes from her computer to look at the time. 11:30 a.m., the clock reads. She stops to think about what she should do for lunch. She gets up from her desk and struts down the hall to Joshua's office. When she turns to enter, she backs up. She spots Evelyn sitting at the corner of Joshua's desk. "So, Joshua, what are you having for lunch?"

"I don't know," he answers, staring at his computer.

"I could get lunch for you since you are so busy," she says as she rocks her leg back and forth. She is trying very hard to get his attention. She has never had him alone. "Joshua." She leans forward, exposing a full view of her cleavage. The more she leans, her breasts spill from her revealing pink satin blouse. She has way too many buttons undone. He finally looks up at her. He stares directly at her cleavage and swallows hard.

"Yes?"

"You want lunch?" she says in a seducing whisper.

"What did you have in mind?" he asks. She smiles like a child with a secret. "Well…" Rayen is disgusted by the sight. She scrambles to get as far away from Joshua's office as possible. She enters her office and closes the door.

"Why am I so annoyed by this? I am the one that wanted to slow things down. And, someone really wants him. I mean I want him, too, but, the hell with it." She walks to her desk to get her cell phone and purse. Quickly she dashes out of the office.

Rayen pulls up to World Café and checks her watch. "12 noon, I am on time, but if he is not here…oh well." She gets out and hands her keys to the valet. She enters the restaurant.

"Good afternoon. Welcome. May I get you a table?"

"Yes. I am looking for Detective Blake Pierce."

"Oh, yes, he is expecting you." She glances at a clipboard. "Ms. Vasu."

"Yes? He was expecting me? How did he know I would show?" She notes silently and follows the greeter. They stop at a quaint table in front of the window. Blake is glaring with a serious expression at the menu. "Detective."

"Ahh, Rayen, you made it," he says with a fabricated surprised tone. She sits in the chair next to him, the table seats three.

"Yes. I decided I was in the mood for food here," she states. The waiter interrupts, and they order.

Light in the Shadow

"You look lovely today, Rayen, but then again you always look very beautiful." The waiter sets glasses of water in front of them. She quickly grabs her water and drink.

"Thank you."

"I want to thank you for deciding to join me. I am flattered."

"Well I had to eat, and this has become one of my favorite places," she says. He smiles.

"Wow, he is so attractive. I mean gorgeous!" She thinks. He sips his water with his eyes glued on her. Their food arrives. They both eat their meal, and Blake asks for the check. "Oh, no. I got it this time," Rayen warns him.

"You know you are very demanding. I can tell you use your abrasiveness as a mechanism to keep people at a distance. I am not convinced. As a matter of fact, I want the challenge. I welcome it," he says, completely freezing her with his stare.

"I don't know what you mean," she says, playing coy. He reaches softly and seductively, grabbing her hand.

"Since the day I laid eyes on you in this restaurant, I haven't been able to think about anything else. I am dying to get to know you." She pulls her hand from his titillating grip.

"Well, Detective. I appreciate your kind words, but you are right. I don't like making friends." He smiles.

"Okay, but I am very persistent. I am a cop and a very good one. Persuasion is my specialty." She purses her lips.

"You are very arrogant, Blake Pierce."

"No, I am just good at my job."

"I've heard, but there's one thing."

"What's that?"

"I am not a suspect in one of your cases."

"No, but I always get my man, in this case woman."

She pays the check and stands to leave. "Thank you for lunch. It was…entertaining." She mocks.

"Will I be able to see you again? I was serious about wanting to get to know you," he says.

"I have your number and you have mine." She leaves to return to the office. He watches her exit the restaurant.

"I hope I didn't blow it. At least she didn't throw her food at me." He grabs his blazer and follows.

Rayen gets back to the office. She passes Evelyn's office and notices it is empty. "She is probably in Joshua's office bent over the desk. She has no shame," she mouths. She goes into her office and sits down at her desk. She searches for something to do. Her lunch with Blake crosses her mind. "Who does he think he is? So arrogant, and so fine. He really makes my senses react, not just when he touches me. When he looks at me, I can't think. I have never been so vulnerable to men. It's the sex. It has to be. But, I feel different around Blake than I do with Joshua. I had sex with Josh, and it was very nice, but I feel the urge to push him away. I haven't slept with Blake, and I want more of him. I am so confused. I need to talk to Angela. She is going to go crazy. But, she is the only person besides Margaret I trust.

"Rayen." He breaks her from her thoughts. She lifts her head, and Joshua is entering.

"Yes?"

"I thought you left for the day."

"Now, did you?" she says with extreme sarcasm.

"Yes. Where were you?"

Light in the Shadow

"I went to lunch."

"Why didn't you come get me? I would have joined you."

"I went to your office to get you, but you were busy with Evelyn."

He closes her office door. "Oh, I didn't see you."

"I know. I am going to call it a day." She stands to gather her things.

"Rayen, what is wrong with you? You wanted to slow things down and that's what we are doing, right?"

"That is exactly what we are doing." She brushes past him to leave, and he grabs her arm. "Rayen, tell me what you want me to do, and I will do it."

"I want us to go back. I don't want to feel jealous, and most importantly, I don't want to hold you back. I see how Evelyn desires you. She can give you all of her. I can't. Don't wait around for me. I really care for you, but I don't know what I want."

"You mean you are telling me you just want to be friends."

"Yes, Josh, I need your friendship. I need you as my friend. You have shown me that every man is not out to hurt me. And, I will forever be grateful for that. And, the sex was wonderful. It was the most intimacy I have ever had, but you are more than that to me."

He grabs her and hugs her. "No matter where I am, I will come. If you need me, call me, and I am there."

"We can still hang out right?"

"Of course." He kisses her forehead and releases her from their embrace. He opens her office door and leaves. She leaves behind him to go home.

***

"Pierce!" Blake's partner shouts through the station. "We got a lead on the Park murder."

"What is it, Wilcox?"

Samuel Wilcox has been Blake's partner in the Homicide division for 4 years. They have known each other forever. Samuel once worked with Robert, Blake's father. He is tall, African American, and his head is clean-shaven. He is 37 years old, married, and father of two teenage daughters. "This guy was busy. He had some assault charges in Ann Arbor at the college. His ex-girlfriend, Missy Alexander, got a restraining order against him a week before the murder. And, check this out…they both frequented the park to jog in the a.m. twice a week."

"So, she would have known he was there that morning. Let's go talk to Missy."

Blake gets up from his desk and grabs his blazer. They leave the station and jump into a gray Dodge Charger. "You will never guess what I did today for lunch."

"What?" Sam returns.

"I had lunch with that young lady I was telling you about."

"The Vista Corp girl? What's her name, Rayen?"

"Yes. Man, she is super-hot. I am really taken by her."

"Man, she is sexy as hell. You sure you aren't just horny? You have never even thought about a woman since you met Lauryn."

"I don't want to talk about Lauryn."

Samuel laughs. "Okay. What's special about Rayen? "

Light in the Shadow

"Man, I don't know. We bumped into each other literally about a month ago. And, touching her skin was magnetic. I been dying to see her ever since."

"I know you don't want to talk about her, but what about Lauryn, though? I know you are angry with her for not accepting your marriage proposal. But, you guys have been still seeing each other."

"Man, I don't want her. The day she said 'not now' I slowly fell out of love with her. Finally, we decided to go our separate ways. She was the one hiding our break up from everyone. I said I would try to work on us to please her. I didn't want to hurt and embarrass her. When I asked her to marry me, I really wanted to be with her for the rest of my life. But, when she turned me down that was the beginning of the end."

"You're not sleeping with her, are you?"

Blake laughs. "No, Sam! I wanted to, but she wouldn't even let me smell it. We haven't touched each other in about two months. Then, she sees me checking Rayen out last night. I basically had to throw her out to get her off of me."

"I would have given it to her."

They burst into laughter and continue to their destination.

Tuesday morning, June 1 at 10:30 a.m. Rayen jumps up and looks at her clock. *Oh, no. I am so late!* she runs to the bathroom and showers. She hurries to her closet and selects a navy blue pantsuit and a white blouse that ties in a bow at the neck. She dresses and slides on her black heels. She runs down the stairs and grabs two slices of toast. She takes a bite and runs outside. Sterling is patiently waiting, reading a newspaper.

"Sterling, I apologize."

"No problem, Rayen. I figured you needed the rest."

"I have had some late meetings. But, thanks for waiting."

"You are a loyal client. It is no trouble." He opens her door, and she hops in.

On the way to the office, she thinks about how quiet the office has been the last few weeks. When they arrive to the office, she dashes in. One of the secretaries brings her a cup of coffee. "Thanks, Karrie." She nods and sits at her desk. She tosses her purse and goes straight to work. "Joshua has been out of sight for weeks. Maybe he just doesn't want anything to do with me." She shrugs and returns to her work. She composes an email to Evan and schedules two meeting for the week. Her cell phone chimes. She pauses typing and looks at it. She sighs and answers. "Hello, Rayen speaking."

"Hi, Rayen. How are you?"

"Hello, Mr. Pierce. How can I help you?"

"Well, we had lunch a couple of weeks ago, and I haven't heard from you. I haven't seen you around town either."

She is silent for a moment.

"Rayen, are you there?"

"Yes. I have been very busy. My company's central office here has needed my undivided attention. I don't have an assistant yet, so I must do everything myself."

"I was beginning to think you were avoiding me." He chuckles nervously.

"I am not avoiding anyone. I have barely had time to eat."

"Today is my day off, and I was wondering. Would you be interested in dinner?"

She hesitates. "I…I guess I could do dinner. What time?"

Light in the Shadow

"How about eight?"

"I...umm, guess so."

"And, would you mind if I pick you up?"

"This guy has nerve..." she thinks. "Why not?" She gives him her address and ends the call.

"I have been avoiding him and Joshua. Joshua made it very easy. I don't need this. It is changing me. I don't like the way I am feeling. But, for some reason I can't tell this man 'no'. Mr. Blake Pierce. First of all, he is not just a cop; he is a homicide detective. I am playing with fire!" She pauses and slides her hand along her tightly twisted bun. "I have been thinking about him...and the things I would allow him to do to me. What am I saying?" She shakes her head. "Angela will be here Friday. I have to talk to her. I hope I don't shock her too much." She returns to her work.

About 2 p.m., Rayen looks at her watch. 'Knock, knock.' She looks up at the door.

"Come in."

"Hey. What's up?"

Her eyes widen. "Hello, Joshua. I haven't seen you in a while. Where have you been?"

He sighs. "I am so sorry I haven't called." She interrupts.

"No, Joshua. You don't owe me anything. I was just wondering. I thought maybe you needed to be away from me."

"No, It wasn't anything like that. My dad had been really sick. My mother called, and I was on the first flight out. I asked Evelyn to inform you." She gasps and cuts in.

"Of course I didn't get the message. But, how is he?" Concern washes her face. He looks at his feet. He expression turns grim. "Is your father okay, Josh?" She stands and places the tips of her fingers on the desk.

"Yes, he is better. He was really sick from the chemotherapy, and my mom panicked. I was so worried. Looking at my father like that was so hard. He has lost so much weight. I…I needed someone and you…just…" He can't get the words out.

"What are you trying to tell me?" She asks.

"You made it clear to me we were over, Rayen."

"Okay?" She slowly sits back into her plush chair.

"I thought Evelyn told you. I thought you didn't call me because you didn't want to lead me on. I was such a mess."

"Spit it out, Joshua!"

"I…I can't. I feel so stupid."

"What is it?"

"Evelyn and I…I mean she flew down a couple of days after I got there. I was a mess."

She hadn't even noticed Evelyn's absence; she was just happy she didn't have to deal with her. Mr. Drake had been sending everything directly to her. How could she have missed this?

"Are you telling me…" she turns her chair towards the window and stands. She stares out of it waiting to hear what she already knows.

"We have been sleeping together. I am so sorry." He rubs his hands through his hair. "I was sad and feeling rejected. My dad was very sick and she…she was there."

"No one told me, Joshua!" she shouts. She spins around to face him.

Light in the Shadow

"I am sorry, Rayen. You told me…"

"Don't! I know what I told you!" she waves her hand and places them on her hips. She paces back and forth behind her desk. She stops walking and looks at him. Afraid to see her expression, he glares at the floor. She walks toward him. He stands there looking apologetic. She stops when she reaches him. He still does not look at her. She takes another look at his face, walks around him, and leaves. As she is leaving the building, she spots Evelyn parking his car. She keeps going to where she sees Sterling standing. "Take me home, Sterling."

"Yes, Ms. Vasu."

"That bitch! What the hell? Ugh!" she screams in the privacy of her bedroom. "Was I that stupid to think I could do this shit? I should kill that fucking bitch. I should slit her fucking throat! She did this on purpose. I am a fucking mess!" Finally she plops down and falls across her bed. Tears pool under her eyes. "I don't cry. I don't cry!" She screams. She stands again and starts to pace. "I am coming apart. Wait, Rayen, wait!" she tells herself. "You told him to go to her. You knew she wanted him. You wanted it over." She calms down. "I need a drink." She goes down to her kitchen and grabs a wine glass from the cupboard. She uncorks the wine and sits on her couch. She drinks glass after glass, thinking. As she stares at the ceiling, her eyes start to tear. "He is such a great guy, and I ran him to that conniving bitch, Evelyn! What did I expect?" She lies down on the couch and unravels her hair. After a while she drifts off.

Chapter 6

"Excuse me?" Rayen turns around. There are so many people in the bookstore today. She tilts and turns, sliding through the thick cloud of people. "Excuse me?" She turns again to see who is talking. It is a guy with shoulder length brown hair, tall, and looks like he may play sports. "Who knew so many kids would be taking summer classes," he says. She shrugs. She turns and proceeds to make her way to the line with her books. He follows her, keeping up but bumping his way through. Finally, she gets in line. She makes her way to the cashier. The young woman scans her books.

"Your total is 654 dollars and 38 cents." She takes out her credit card, and the cashier swipes it. She signs and is on her way out.

"Wait up!" the brown haired guy yells. She doesn't stop. She picks up the pace. He speeds up and catches her. "Hey, are you trying to get away from me?" She turns toward him.

"Basically."

"Whoa baby! Don't be so mean." He smiles.

"Can I help you with something?" she says very unfriendly-like.

"I wanted to know your name. I have never seen you before. You are very cute," he says.

"I am not interested," she says as she turns to walk away.

"I haven't proposed anything yet!" he snaps. She walks out of the building and toward the parking lot. She gets to her car and he is right on her heels. "Look, I just want to get to know you." She reaches to open her car door. He stops it from opening and slams it back shut.

"I am not interested!" He leans on her car. She sighs very loudly.

"You. Don't. Have. To. Be," he spouts. He gets so close, she can feel his hot breath on her face.

"Rick!" a girl yells. He whirls around. "Babe, I was just telling this bitch to back off." He turns to Rayen. "I'm taken. Damn!" The girl speeds past him straight to Rayen.

"Bitch, you hit on the wrong man." Rayen attempts to get in her car once more. The girl slams the door. She rolls her eyes and turns toward the girl. "He is taken, you little shit-faced bitch!"

"Good!" Rayen spits.

"What did you say to me?" Smack! The girl slaps Rayen so hard she slams into her car door. Rayen reaches into her bag, but as she leans up to strike, she notices people in the distance. She doesn't want to make a scene, so she eases her hand out of her bag and gets in her car. The girl bangs on the door and Rayen pulls off. Rayen is pissed! She has a very dark look on her face. She whirls the car in a circle and goes back. "No one puts their hands on me and lives!" When she drives back, she sees them still in the lot arguing; she parks behind a bunch of trees. They finally get in their car and leave. She carefully follows their car. They are shouting so much, they do not notice Rayen trailing them. They drive for about twenty minutes and end up in town. They stop at an apartment complex. They park, get out, and walk into the apartment. She hurries in behind them. She reaches the foyer in enough time to see them get on the elevator. She watches the elevator come to a halt on the 3rd floor. She scans the lobby for surveillance cameras. There is one in the parking lot. She makes sure her car is at a safe distance. She finds the service stairs and scurries to the third floor. She peeks out of the stairwell door and catches Rick taking trash to the

Light in the Shadow

disposal room. She devilishly smiles and takes note of apartment 311. She then says to herself, "Can't take care of them here. It's too risky." She goes back to her car and waits.

Nightfall comes soon. She checks her bag and takes out a silver blade. Before she can get out of the car, she spots the couple walking. He wraps his jacket around the girl's arms. Rayen hops out and follows. It has gotten really late. They turn down a path through a wooded area. "Perfect! I am so lucky tonight," she thinks. They proceed down the path holding hands and talking. He stops and turns her around. They begin kissing. "Really?" she thinks. He stops.

"Hold on babe." She wipes her lips and snuggles into his jacket. He runs to a tree and unzips his pants. As he starts to stream, Rayen sneaks up behind him quiet as a mouse.

"Wrong night for a romantic walk," she whispers as she jumps up, grabs his mouth and slits his throat. He falls to the ground. The girl hears the thump.

"Rick? Babe?" She starts toward the sound. "Rick?" Right then, Rayen walks out. "What are you…"

"You slapped the wrong girl, you bitch!" Rayen scowls darkly. The girl glares at Rayen for a moment. She does not realize the danger until the glint of the blade catches her eyes. The girl turns to run. But before she can turn, Rayen catches her in mid stride and throws her to the ground. She is choked with fear.

"Please don't kill me," she says as her voice shakes. Rayen ignores her plea. She is blind with fury. She takes the blade and stabs the girl in the neck. She then slides it across, making sure she punctures her main artery. She watches as the girl's eyes go dark.

Annetta Hobson

"No one will ever hit me and live again." She stands up and scans her clothing. She is splattered with blood. She cases her surroundings to see if anyone is coming. She walks quickly back to her car and drives away.

***

"Buzz. Buzz." The doorbell startles Rayen. She stretches and yarns. She sits up and looks at her watch. "It's 7:45. How long have I been out?" She goes to the intercom. "Yes?" she speaks hoarsely into the intercom.

"Hello, Rayen. It's Blake."

"Oh, shit! I forgot all about him…" She buzzes him in. He makes his way up to the main door and she opens it. He scans her attire. She is wearing pajama pants and a tank top.

"Have you forgotten about me so quickly?"

"I apologize, Blake. I have had a terrible day. I fell asleep."

He steps in the condo. He looks especially delicious this evening! He is wearing a dark gray blazer with dark gray slacks and a black dress shirt. She turns to go to the kitchen. "Would you like a drink?" He follows her as his eyes travel up and down her body. She isn't wearing a bra and the tank is virtually shear. The pajama pants hug her in all the right areas. Her behind is like a ripe melon. He tries to shake it off, but he desires her so much right now. She turns. "Well?"

"Oh, umm. Do you have beer?"

"No, I do not. But, would you like wine, brandy, or bottled water?"

"Water is fine."

"Okay, have a seat."

Light in the Shadow

She points to the couch. When she enters the kitchen, she places her hands on the counter.

"I do not feel like this right now." She hangs her head and relives her conversation with Joshua. When she does not return, Blake stands and steps in the kitchen.

"Is everything okay?" He shocks her from her reverie. She whips around.

"I'm fine." She rubs her forehead. "Maybe I should take a rain check. I am not my usual self today." He creases his brow.

"Is there anything I can do?"

"No. I just need to be alone," she sighs. He drops his head and looks around.

"Okay, maybe some other time. I hope all is well." He turns to head for the door. He is very disappointed. She trails him.

"Blake, I really don't think this is the right time to start dating." He stops walking and turns to look at her.

"Rayen, I know I come on strong, but I am great company," he says, trying to convince her. She rolls her eyes.

"Look, I think you are a nice guy, but I am not the dating type." He raises his hands.

"Okay, I hear you." She turns her head away from him.

"I tell you what, talk to me. I am a good listener. We don't have to go on a date. We could just talk." She folds her arms and eyes him. He is standing there with a genuine look of concern on his handsome face. "Oh, no! Been there, done that," she says underneath her breath.

"What happened? Everyone needs someone they can vent to. I am a police officer. I listen to people every day."

"Again as I have told you before, I am not one of your suspects. Women don't respond to police harassment."

He chuckles. "Oh, I see. Now I'm harassing you." He makes a face that implies he was stung. She softens a little.

"I apologize. I am just a mess this evening. She runs her fingers through her beautiful black hair. He steps toward her. She bulges her eyes.

"What happened?" He gently grabs her arms. She drops her arms to her side.

"Okay." She gives in.

She walks back to the living room and plops on the couch. She lifts her glass and looks at it. Hold on. I need a refill." She goes to the fridge to grab a chilled bottle of wine. She pops the cork and returns to the couch. "Have a seat, Blake." She waves her hand toward the spot next to her. He takes off his blazer and sits. She leans her head on the back of the couch. Her hair falls behind it. She stares at the ceiling for a long time. He turns to her and just watches. She breaks the silence. "I was so sure of myself when I stepped off the plane from New York. I just thought 'this town is going to be my temporary residence.' That's it and nothing more. I am a very private person, Blake." She lifts her head to look at him. He is looking back, giving her his undivided attention.

"Has that changed?" he questions in almost a whisper.

"Kind of. My hatred and loathing of those who hurt me has been my armor."

He places his arm on the back of the couch and leans to get comfortable.

"I met Joshua about a week after I got here. I was so impressed with his work ethic."

Light in the Shadow

He sits back up straight. She catches a glimpse of him out of the corner of her eye. She doesn't stop. She really needs this off her mind. "I am new at this, so bear with me," she says.

"New at letting people see you human."

"No, vulnerable. I never let anyone see me sweat," she snaps.

"Okay."

She begins again. "He crept in, and I don't know how. It was like one day we were friends, then it turned into something else." He raises his eyebrows. She pretends not to notice. "I just wanted it to stop. The emotion was too much. I was jealous, and that is not me. I was emotional and I hated that feeling, so I wanted it to end."

"So, you ended it?" he asks.

"Yes, I did, and I told him to date my colleague's daughter." He interjects.

"The drunk girl." She smirks.

"Yes. My life was so uncomplicated before I came here." She pauses and looks as if she recalled a painful memory. "He went to go visit his sick father. I didn't even notice he was gone for weeks…she flew down there to be with him and his family. She got him. She has wanted him for years, and she got him."

"And, that upsets you?"

"Yes, I care for him. He is the first friend I have had in eleven years."

"He is the reason I can sit here and talk to you."

She looks at him once more. He straightens himself and sits forward. "Rayen, may I say something to you?"

"Yes."

"First, do you love him?"

"Not in a romantic way. I care for him dearly. But, I don't want to be intimate…" She stops. He glances at her.

"Did he do something wrong?" She knows the conversation has taken a turn.

"I don't know." She lays her head back to rest it on the couch once more.

"I see. You want him to stay in the friend zone."

"I guess. Yes."

"What about me? Do I get to be in the friend zone?"

"I haven't decided yet. I like you, Blake. It is different than Josh. But, I don't know what to do with all this."

"Rayen, after you lost your parents and grandfather, did you see a therapist or someone?"

"No. I didn't need anyone. I took care of myself and kept everyone at a distance so I would never feel that loss again."

"Rayen, you need someone. For eleven years, you have been a loner, and it is just not healthy. You need someone to nurture you and to care for you. You can't have a healthy relationship until you get that. I see you, the real you. I see that hurt little girl who lost everyone. You're a girl who became a shell to protect herself. Your father or grandfather was supposed to be here to give you all of the love and affection in the world."

Rayen shoots up. This conversation has gone too far. "That's enough! You can go now!" Blake sits up.

Light in the Shadow

"Rayen, you have to face this. You need someone or you will go insane inside yourself. Please don't keep pushing people away."

"It's...it's all I have known. Being inside myself is what I know."

"It's okay to let people in. Let someone in, or you will be alone forever."

"I don't care! I have survived fine without anyone!" she walks into the kitchen.

"Until now," he says softly. He follows her in the kitchen and stands behind her. Her arms are folded. He reaches out to touch her, but she walks away. Tears are forming.

"No, not now!" she thinks. Suddenly, she bursts into tears and begins to cry. Tears are streaming. She cannot stop them as she covers her face. "Leave now, Blake." She states through her wailing.

"I won't leave you like this."

"Please go," she says a little softer. He steps over to her and embraces her from behind.

"Let someone take care of you. You need it to survive."

"I need nothing and no one." She wiggles out of his arms. The tears won't stop. She walks over to the counter. She places her hands on it to steady her stance.

"How long has it been since you have let go?"

"Eleven years," she cries. She is sniffling, and the tears just will not stop falling. She runs up the stairs to get away from him. She runs in her room and slams the door.

Knock! Knock! He bangs on the door. "Rayen, are you okay?" she doesn't answer. He turns the knob, and she is sitting in the corner of the bedroom with her hands around her knees. She has finally stopped crying. Her head is buried in her knees. He takes off his shoes and tips lightly to where she is sitting. He slowly plants himself beside her. He doesn't speak.

"I haven't cried in eleven years," she says softly with a hoarseness to her voice.

"How did it feel?"

"Why? Why did you pull that out of me?"

"Rayen, you have to give yourself the chance to feel every emotion. It is something we all need." She lifts her head.

"It felt terrific." Her hair falls into her eyes. He gently slides it back in place and puts his arm around her.

"See, I am not all bad." She smiles lightly.

"I guess not."

"Wow! I get a smile too?"

She continues smiling and leans her head on his shoulder. They sit there silently, his arm firmly wrapped around her shoulder. They are in that position so long, they fall asleep right there on the floor in the corner. Rayen hasn't felt like this since before her parents died.

Rayen opens her eyes. The sun is shining down on them. They have stretched out on the floor. He is lying on his back flat, and she is beside him with her head on his chest. She has her arm wrapped around his waist. His arm is around her neck with his hand resting in her hair. She lifts her head and glances at his face. He is so very handsome. She stares at his face for a while. She is embarrassed. "I must have been tired. I can't believe I let him in." She plants her hand on his chest for support to sit up. She stands and takes a quick peek at the clock. "Oh, no. It's 9 a.m.! Blake, wake up!" She bends to nudge him.

Light in the Shadow

"Blake!" He turns on his side and wraps his arms around himself and snuggles into her carpet. "How can he sleep so hard?" She stares at him. "Oh God! How cute is he, lying there tucked in himself? Wow, I cried in front of this man. I cried, period. What has happened to me? Whatever it is, I don't hate it that much." She grabs a sheet and pillow from her linen closet. She places the pillow under his head and covers him with the sheet. She runs to shower and dresses for work. She throws on a cream linen dress with a thin black belt. To complete it, she slides into a black short jacket. She slips on her cream heels. When she returns to the room, he is still sound asleep. He must have been tired. So, she allows him to rest. She writes a note.

> Blake,
>
> Thank you for the most interesting evening ever. You helped me so much more than you could imagine. You are definitely good at getting things out of people. I guess your interrogation worked for the best. See you later. Lock the door when you leave.
>
> Rayen.

She walks out of the door, and Sterling is waiting at the SUV. "Good morning, Sterling."

"Morning, Ms. Vasu." She steps inside of the vehicle. He closes the door and scurries around the truck to drive her to work. Before they get to her office, she speaks to Sterling.

"Friday morning, I need you to pick up someone from the airport."

"Yes, ma'am."

"Sterling, please don't call me ma'am."

"Yes, Rayen."

Annetta Hobson

She smiles and turns to look out the window. She is feeling better than she has in a very long time. Sterling looks at her in the rear view mirror and is pleased to see a smile on her face.

She arrives to the office. She swings open the glass doors and prances in. She approaches her office, offering good mornings to everyone she passes. She enters her office and sits at her desk. She has several messages from Mr. Drake. She reads the messages, and she dials his number. "Hello, Mr. Drake. You need to speak with me?"

"Yes. Good morning, Rayen. I need you to put together a meeting for the owners of a casino in Mount Pleasant. They would like us to consider a contract for building a luxury hotel. I need you to go to Mount Pleasant tomorrow, stay in the current hotel, and meet with them Thursday. I apologize for the short notice since you must leave tomorrow. If they are interested in a contract with us, see Joshua when you get back to start on some plans."

"I will book my room today."

"Thank you. I will forward all the details to you right away."

They end their call. As soon as she receives the details, she immediately calls the hotel to book her suite. She pushes her seat away from the desk and rises to leave her office when Joshua knocks on the wall. "Am I disturbing you?"

"No, Josh, of course not. Come in."

He walks in carefully.

"I am glad you are here. I was on my way to see you."

"Oh, okay. What's up?" he says with some alarm.

"Mr. Drake contacted me this morning about a potential client in Mount Pleasant. Should they decide to give us the contract, you will have to start work with them immediately."

Light in the Shadow

He sighs in relief. "No problem. When is the meeting?"

"I am going up there tomorrow to stay at the current hotel. The meeting will be Thursday."

"Do you need me to accompany you?" he asks.

"Oh, no. If they select us for the contract, you can meet with them next week. Just have something in mind."

"You sure you want to go alone?"

"I am positive. I travel alone all the time." She sits back down and begins her daily work.

"Rayen, are you okay? You seemed pretty upset yesterday."

"Joshua, I am great. I just want us to remain friends, okay?"

He tilts his head to the side and glares at her. "Why is she so happy?" he thinks.

"I haven't witnessed this side of you before. Has something changed?"

"A lot has changed, Josh. I have discovered a new me. And, it feels great. I have you to thank you for that."

He scrunches his brows. "What does that mean? I slept with Evelyn, and now you are happy to be rid of me like a lost dog or sick puppy?"

"Of course not. I was very hurt by it, but I wanted that for you."

She stands and motions toward him. She hugs him tight. "Be happy, Josh. Whatever you do, I will support you. You are my first real friend in a long time. I never want to lose you."

She grabs his face between her hands and kisses his cheek. He smiles and returns, "Rayen, I don't think I have ever seen you fully smile. You have such a beautiful smile. Do it more often."

"I will. I promise. Now get to work." She sits and gets back to work herself. She works all day. After some time passes, she notices Blake hasn't called. "Maybe he is busy," she thinks.

The day goes by slowly, but finally it is time to go. She gathers her files and heads to the closest desk that sits outside her office. "Julie, could you file these for me?" She hands the young lady the files and heads back into her office to prepare to go home. Her phone rings. "Ms. Vasu speaking," she says as she grabs her things.

"Hi, Rayen. It's Blake."

"Hi."

"Why didn't you wake me?"

"I tried, but you were sleeping so peacefully. I decided not to disturb you."

"I got your note. You approve of me interrogating women now?" he chuckles.

"It was so therapeutic. I never knew crying your eyes out could be the best release. I have a whole new feeling inside. I am smiling. I don't smile, Blake. You were the perfect solution for my issue."

"Wow, you are too kind, but I won't say I told you so."

"Okay, okay. So, I was wondering…"

"Well, I was wondering, since we didn't go out last night, how about today?"

"I would love to go out, but I have to go to Mount Pleasant for two days. I'll be locked up in a hotel and meetings. I figured I would get a day of fun first before I go."

Light in the Shadow

"Mount Pleasant, when?"

"Tomorrow."

"Have you ever been?"

"No."

"I can show you around, and we could hang out. I could take the next couple of days off. That way you won't be there all alone."

She pauses. "I guess that would be good."

"Cool! Let's go today! I'll go home and pack. I'll be there in an hour."

"Ummm, okay?"

"See you then." He hangs up.

Rayen is just sitting there trying to figure out what just happened. She dials Sterling.

"Sterling, I am ready. I am going on a business trip, so I won't need you again until Friday."

"Yes, Rayen."

She ends her call and turns to the window. "Bay City is really breathtaking," she thinks as she watches the boats glide pass back and forth under the bridge. That is why she loves her office. She gets up to leave, and Joshua is at her office door again.

"Since you are leaving for two days, can we hang out tonight?"

"Oh, I decided to just go today."

"Are you leaving now? It's only 2 p.m."

"Yes. I'm going to get an early start."

"Okay then. I'll see you Friday." He waves.

"Bye."

When he leaves out of her office, she notices Evelyn waiting for him. He grabs her around the neck when he gets to her, and they leave out the building. She is as happy as a schoolgirl.

When Rayen gets home, she dashes up the stairs. She pulls out her suitcase and begins to pack. She is so excited. She cannot contain it. She packs anything that is sexy so she can look her best. She packs a couple of bikinis to sit by the hotel pool. Soon, she hears her doorbell. She hurries down the stairs to open the door. Once she opens it, she runs back up to get her luggage. "Are you ready?" he yells up.

"Yes," she says. She drags her suitcase down the stairs, and he rushes to grab it from her. She locks her condo up, and they go down to his car. She spots his red convertible Camaro.

"Very Nice."

"It gets the job done."

He opens the door for her to climb in, and then, he loads her luggage in the trunk. He pulls off, and they hit the road.

They drive on Us-10 W for about an hour. "Are you hungry, Rayen?" Blake asks. She is half sleep as she rocks her head from side to side with her eyes closed.

"Is that a yes or no?"

"What did you have in mind?"

"I'll just stop at a diner, or would you rather wait to eat at the hotel?"

"Let's just go to the hotel."

"Okay."

Light in the Shadow

Blake continues on the highway until they get to the hotel. When they get to the hotel, it is much nicer than she imagined. It is a casino resort hotel. They get out of the car and unpack their luggage. The valet takes the car, and they check in.

"Good afternoon, Sir."

"I called and reserved a room for two nights under Blake Pierce."

"Oh, yes, Mr. Pierce. There is one premium suite with a bedroom, two beds, and a living room."

"Rayen, are you fine with that?"

"Yes."

"Here are your room keys."

Rayen opens the door to the room. Blake takes in their luggage. The living room looks like it belongs in a really nice posh apartment. It has a brick fireplace, lacquered wooden tables, a tan couch, and a matching tan love seat. The room has two queen-sized beds and a tan chaise in the corner. The flat screen TV is mounted to the wall over the dresser.

"Thank you for allowing me to tag along, Rayen."

"I am glad you wanted to come because it would have been just another boring business trip."

"Well, what would you like to do first?"

"I don't know. You've been here before. What do you suggest?"

"Let's just change and eat. Then, we can hit the casino."

"Okay."

Rayen goes into the bathroom and turns on the shower. She undresses and gets in. The water is so relaxing. She almost gets lost in the stream. She washes and turns off the water. She peeks out of the bathroom and quickly jolts into the room. "Left your clothes?" Blake startles her.

"I forgot them. Not used to sharing a room with a man," she answers honestly. He laughs.

"I've seen it all, Rayen. I assure you."

"Well I doubt if you have seen anything like this."

The smile leaves his face. "You're right. I have never seen anyone as spellbinding as you."

She sits on the bed. "What is so special about me? Men always say that, but really, what is it? Beauty is nothing."

"Rayen, you are right. Beauty is nothing without brains and sensuality. It is nothing without mystery. You are all of that, and it makes you a hell of a beauty."

She looks down at the hand clutching the towel.

"Thank you, Blake. You make me see things, everything, so differently."

"Bumping into you that day was like destiny. I was so stuck, stuck in a situation that I was miserable in."

"Lauryn?"

"Yes, Lauryn."

He explains the whole proposal issue, the house, and her not wanting to settle down until her job was stable. He told her how Lauryn was still pretending that they were still together.

"Were you upset with her for being driven?"

"No, not at all. That is what originally attracted me to her and her love for the law, like me. Our parents loved us together

Light in the Shadow

but she wanted to wait. I had no problem with waiting, but she didn't take my ring. She wanted her career."

"Okay."

She steps toward him. "You are actually a great guy, so..."

He interrupts her, "Enough of that sad story. Let's go have some fun."

Rayen and Blake get back to the room from the casino very late.

"I am exhausted and very drunk," she says.

"I second that!" he says as he bursts through the door of the room. He falls on the floor.

"Are you okay, Blake?" she questions and helps him up. He laughs.

"I am fine." He is smiling a brilliant smile. It is so enthralling. As he rises, they end up face to face.

"You do something to me, Blake. I don't know what it is, but I like the way you make me feel." He reaches for her face, cupping it between his hands.

"I feel the exact same way. I cannot believe I am here with you." She takes a deep breath. He leans close and touches her lips with his ever so gently. The kiss sends magnetic jolts through her entire body. She wraps her arms around his neck. She kisses him back but more passionately. They swivel, and the kiss becomes heated. Their breathing is heavy, and his hands slowly trail down her arms to her hands. He rubs her hands and intertwines them. He lifts them up and places them behind her back. She is aching with want. He gently backs her into the bedroom. He releases her hands and lifts her off her feet. She wraps her legs around his waist and the kiss gets deeper. He lays her on the bed and breaks his lips from hers. "I want to look at you." He slides her shirt over her head. She lifts the top of her body from the bed to help him along. "Rayen, I don't understand why no man has ever been able to keep you. But, if you allow me, I will never let you go." He leans down and trails kisses down to her breast. He sits her up straight and unfastens her bra. He slides it off. He lays her back down on the bed. He grabs her breasts gently and fondles them. "Your delicate skin drives me wild. I love it," he moans against her breast. "Umm. It's so soft." He drags his lips back and forth. He rubs them across the hardening nipple. He plays with it between his teeth. She is squirming like a fish. He then sucks the nipple into his mouth. He slurps and sucks strategically. He is very skilled. "Turn over on your stomach," he commands. She lifts up out of breath and obliges. When she flips over, he drags his eyes over her back. He places his hands on her shoulders and very gently rubs down to the dip above her behind. He leans in and rubs his nose across her butt cheeks. Cupping them, he squeezes them together. His touch makes her shiver. She lifts her head to look back at him.

"I want you, Blake. I want you to do whatever you want to me." He sits up and turns her over.

"I wanted you ever since the day I met you." He gets up and climbs beside her. She lies back and he rubs her breasts once again. He reaches up, takes her hand and places it on his erection. She gasps. "It is very, very nice," she thinks. She strokes it up and down. She places her hand on the button and tries to unfasten his slacks. He stops her. He grabs her arms and wraps them around her. Then he snuggles in beside her.

"Rayen, I want you so bad, my mouth is watering."

"Then take me. I want you. I want you more than I ever wanted anything."

"Well then, you will feel the same when you are sober. I have longed to find someone like you. So, I will wait until we are not incapacitated. I want to savor the moment. We must be sober for that. I want to remember my first time with you," he whispers. His mouth is so close to her ear the heat from his breath is sending her into a frenzy.

"I want to remember it also," she breathes. He places his arm underneath her and wraps the other around her. He plants one last sweltering peck on her ear. They lie there for a while. Soon they both fall asleep in an impassioned embrace.

Chapter 7

Meeting a man like Blake is a once in a lifetime opportunity. He could have made love to her last night, but he didn't. He is like no other. Not even Josh would have turned down a chance to ravish her. "Good morning, Rayen," he whispers in her ear accompanied by a kiss on her lobe. "What's wrong? Why are you staring into space?" She smiles.

"Thinking about last night and how wonderful it was. We were intimate without being intimate. I will never forget it."

"Me neither. But, we were pretty toasted, and I want to be fully in control when I indulge that glorious body of yours."

"Likewise."

He slides his hand from underneath her and sits up. "You want to shower first?"

"Doesn't matter." She sits up and looks for her shirt.

"Let's go outside of the resort for breakfast. I know of this place. It serves whatever you want for breakfast."

"Sounds great." She grabs her shirt and slides it on. She then goes and turn on the shower. She takes her clothes off and steps in. She tilts her head under the stream. She has her eyes closed. The warm water feels so good to her. Suddenly, she feels hands around her waist.

"Mind if I join you?"

She takes her hands and wipes the water from her eyes. "No, not at all."

"I'm sorry I got you worked up last night and didn't allow you to release."

"I was on fire, but it's okay. I was so drunk I felt right to sleep."

She reaches for the soap. He stops her hand and spins her around so that her behind is touching his shaft.

"I want to make you release, Rayen. Can I do that for you?" he speaks as his erection rises against her.

"Yes…" she purrs. He rubs his hands across her pointing nipples. He kisses her neck, tasting her wet skin. He takes his tongue and glides it along her back with his hands never leaving her breast. He then slides one hand from her breast to her navel. He takes the soap and makes circular motions into her skin on her stomach. The other hand remains on her breast fondling her nipple in between his fingers. Finally, he reaches her thigh and gently tugs for her to open her legs. She lifts her leg and places it on the tub. He then reaches in and rubs her center. His skilled fingers whirl around and around rubbing slower and faster. He takes turns rubbing and inserting his fingers inside. He is driving her wild. He kisses her ear. His tongue toys with the lobe.

"You feel so warm inside," he moans. He slides his finger out and rubs the bulb. She moans.

"Oh, yesss. Oh, yesss." He slides his finger back in. he adds another. In and out, the rhythm is sending her to the edge. Her eyes roll. He switches back and forth until she screams. "Uh!" she lets out a loud cry of ecstasy. She flinches and jerks forward. Her body goes limp and she collapses back onto him as he holds her up.

"Oh my." She turns around to face him and kisses him deeply.

"What about you?" she asks virtually out of breath. He looks at her.

Light in the Shadow

"I simply wanted to see you explode in my hands. It was so intoxicating to watch." She blushes.

"Okay, but now I want you to get yours."

"It's okay. I will just fantasize about you singing that orgasmic song, and it will be gratifying." He rolls his eyes closed and inhales.

"No. I want you to be physically gratified as well." He takes a towel from the towel bar and washes his bulging erection. He cleans the rest of his body and gets out of the shower. She stands in the stream of the water thinking. "How in the world could any woman turn him down for anything? He is so tantalizing. I want him, all of him."

Rayen turns the shower off, dries herself, and proceeds to the bedroom. Blake is looking for something to wear. He searches through his suitcase. She walks up behind him and wraps her arms around his waist. He turns around to face her still naked from their shower.

"Blake, I want you to make love to me. I have shown you so much of me, and I want you to have me in every way."

"What about breakfast?"

"Fuck breakfast!" she yells. He laughs. She grabs him, her hand can barely wrap around it. "It is very impressive, you know."

"Thank you," he says with a consuming glare. She fondles it for a while but she wants to do more. She pushes him back onto the bed.

"I don't just want you like this, Blake. I have never met anyone like you. Say you will be with me. You wanted me; now I want to give you me. You opened me up. You made me laugh again. Can I be with you and no one else?" Before she can stop the words, they flow out of her mouth like a river. His eyes grow wide.

"Absolutely, Rayen," he returns. Her gaze is penetrating him. The moment is so passionate; they don't say another word. She climbs him like a cat. She opens her legs and straddles him. She leans in and kisses his lips. Then, she licks her own lips. He just watches. He is mesmerized by her every movement. He is as hard as a rock. She slides off of him and stands back to look at him. She then leans over and grabs his erection. Then she slowly drags her lips along the sides and slides it into her mouth. He relinquishes a drawn out moan. She slides her mouth down and presses her lips against the sides. She licks the tip as she brings her mouth back to the top. She slurps in and out, up and down. She twists her mouth as she strokes the exposed skin. He is reveling in each motion. He lifts his head from the bed to watch her work. Secretly she is hoping she is doing it correctly. He pulls himself from her mouth and stands.

"Was I doing it wrong?" she asked.

"Hell no! You were perfect." He scoops her up and lays her on the bed. He pushes her legs open as wide as he can. "Now I will return the favor." He dips his head between her thighs. He takes his tongue and pushes it into her. He uses his tongue like a dip stick, bobbing and dipping. Her body is lifting off the bed. He takes that as an invitation to go in further, so he grabs her legs and put them on his shoulders. He goes to work. She watches as his gorgeous ruffled hair brushes her thigh. The bottom half of her is hitched in the air. He grabs her bottom and digs in even deeper; now her legs are wrapped around his neck.

"Ohhh, Blake." She leans back and clenches the covers. She turns her head and buries her face into her hair. He sets her body down on the bed and climbs up to meet her eyes.

Light in the Shadow

"Don't let go yet, baby. We are just getting started." She grabs his face and attacks his lips. He welcomes the siege. They kiss for a while and he turns her over again. "Rayen. your body is like a perfect painting. I just want to take my time and explore every part of it." She cannot respond. He kneels on the bed. He lifts her foot and begins to slide every toe in his mouth one by one. She is rocking and wiggling. She can't take it. He inserts a finger inside her. "Your walls feel like soft wet padding. I can't wait to feel them around me." He lays her foot back on the bed. As he moves up to her face he slowly plants wet kisses up her thigh. He kisses her lips again. She wants him inside her.

"Please. Take me. Now!" He smirks and brushes his mouth across her cheek.

"Oh, I'm going to give it to you." He grabs his throbbing erection and finally inserts it inside her. She sighs in erotic relief. He thrusts gently in an out. He throws his head back and shouts.

"Oh, shit! You feel so good. Ohhh." He moans as if he is in pain. She begins to rock her hips. She swirls and bucks, answering his every stroke. He kisses her neck. The passion between them is high. Her eyes roll into her head. She grabs the sheet and twists it into her fists. He places his hands on top of hers and squeezes them. She releases the covers and intertwines their fingers. His strokes become quicker and shorter. She grabs his firm cheeks and wraps her legs around him. She strikes back, stroke for stroke. They spiral together, falling apart and screaming out in a roar of passion.

Rayen's head rests on Blake's bare chest. They are both laying there, reveling in their intense performance. "You think someone heard us," she says.

"I don't care. That was amazing," he remarks as he strokes her hair. "I never could have imagined it being that wonderful."

"Are you good at everything you do Blake?" she wonders out loud. He smiles.

"I most definitely try." She smiles in turn.

"I feel you smiling."

He says, "You make me smile."

"You made me cry first. But, I guess I had to cry to smile," she states.

"Can I ask you something, Rayen?"

"Shoot, Detective."

He smiles. "Did you mean it when you said you wanted to be with me?" he asks slowly. She pauses. Her heart starts to pound.

"Well…the way you make me feel is indescribable. After spending these last couple of days with you, I really don't want it to end. So, yes, Blake. I meant everything I said." She rubs his chest.

"Good. That means I won't be in the friend zone where sex isn't allowed." She sits up and looks up at him. Her eyes fix on his beautiful ocean blue glare.

"The way you make me feel is not within an inch of what Josh and I had. You have taken me to another world. And, I want to live there. I never want to leave. He opened the door, but you made yourself at home." He kisses her temple. She closes her eyes and enjoys all of the feelings he has pulled out of her. They fall asleep again wrapped in an embrace. Suddenly her phone chimes.

"Hello, Rayen speaking," she says sleepily.

"Hey, I was calling to check on you."

"Josh?"

Light in the Shadow

"Yeah, you are asleep at 5 p.m."

"5 p.m.!" She sits up. "My goodness, the whole day has gone."

Blake's eyes open. He lifts his arm from behind her head and rubs it.

"Is everything alright, Rayen?"

She slides out of bed and heads for the living room.

"It's fine. Go back to sleep," she whispers to Blake while covering the phone. He turns over and she scurries to the couch. "What's up, Josh?"

"I just was worried since you are there alone and I hadn't heard from you. I almost came down there"

"I am doing great, and I am not alone." She is still speaking in a hushed tone.

"Oh!" he says, surprised. "Who went with you?"

"I am having fun. I have a meeting tomorrow, and I will see you when I get back with the details, okay?"

"But, Rayen?"

She ends the call. She goes back to bed and cuddles with Blake. He turns to receive her back into his arms. "We should have gotten a single bedroom," she says as she nestles back into his chest. He kisses her hair.

"I wouldn't have dared. You would have thought I was a dog."

"Never." She smiles, and he goes back to sleep.

Annetta Hobson

Rayen runs to the shower, "I cannot be late for this meeting, so you have to pack our things and check out." He runs behind her and grabs her.

"I am not ready to go. I don't want to leave from this place... ever."

"Me either. This is by far the best time I have had in so long," she says beaming. "I can't believe I am doing this! It feels so impulsive. I have always done things with structure and planning. When I think about not having this, I feel panicked. I am kind of nervous," she says looking into his eyes.

"Actually, I have a question for you." His mood lightens.

"You with all of the questions, Detective," she says and rolls her eyes.

"Will you...should come home with me so I can reintroduce you to my family. I want them to get to know you." He laughs almost uncomfortably. "They have to meet you as my new...girlfriend."

"Girlfriend?" she thinks as she states. "That sounds so juvenile."

"What should I call you, then?"

"Umm, let's see. How about the new woman in your life?"

He slides his hands through his hair. "You can call me whatever you like, but I will call you my girlfriend. It just sounds exclusive."

"That's fine, Blake. But, I have to go my meeting. It is in one hour. He kisses her and slides his hand across her behind.

"Oh, no! You are an animal. We did this all day and night. I'm sore."

Light in the Shadow

"You want me to kiss it and make it better?" he moves his hands around between her thighs. He bends to his knee and puckers. He motions his lips to her center.

"No, Blake!" she runs and jumps in the shower. She gets ready for her meeting. When she comes from the bathroom, she is dressed in a pencil black skirt and silver blouse. The heels she is wearing are silver as well. Before she leaves, she gives him a soft seductive, lingering kiss. "I'll see you in the lobby after my meeting." She waves.

"Okay. I'll anticipate your return," he laughs.

The meeting goes smoothly. She is offered the contract and is very happy. She enters the lobby and finds Blake impassively waiting. "Got the contract!" she tells him. He returns the excitement.

"That is terrific! Let's celebrate tonight when we get home. We could go for drink after we come from my parents place?"

She adds, "Whatever you want, Blake. I am just so excited about us. I am looking forward to exploring this."

"Me, too. But, I have to eventually go back to work, as do you," he reminds.

"I know. Let's go," she says disappointed.

They arrive in Bay City at 3:30 p.m. on Thursday afternoon. He takes her home first. He unloads her luggage and takes it in her condo. He sets it down at the door and grabs her around her waist. "I will always treasure Mt. Pleasant," she smiles with a little laugh.

"I want to always be able to make you smile, Rayen," he exclaims seriously.

Annetta Hobson

"I strongly believe you will. Keep your interrogating ways, Detective," she returns, giving him a sweet kiss. He kisses her back once more. He dashes out to go home and unpack.

She goes in the kitchen to find a snack. She grabs some grapes and has a seat at the dining table. "I am so glad I let him stay Monday night. I am so happy right now. Wait till Angela gets here. I should have moved to a small city years ago." She pops some grapes in her mouth and grabs her phone. She dials Joshua.

"Hello?"

"Hi, Josh."

"Hi, Rayen."

"I was calling to inform you that we got the new contract."

"That's great! When do you want to go over the designs?"

"We can do it Monday."

He pauses. "What are you doing tonight? You want to have dinner or a drink?"

"I have a date."

"Oh…do I know him?"

She tries to be gentle. "Why, Josh? We don't have to do this. You have Evelyn now. And, I have decided that I am moving on, too. You will see him eventually. And, yes, you know of him."

"I don't understand. You said you didn't want to be with anyone and that you were confused!" he exclaims.

"Okay. Josh, please. Let's not do this. Your friendship means so much to me. Let's not ruin it."

Light in the Shadow

"You know what, Rayen? We will always be friends, but I gave you something I haven't given to anyone in a very long time. I gave it to you, and you threw it back at me."

"I didn't mean to, Josh. I just can't make myself feel something I do not feel. I will always cherish what you have given to me. I will never forget what you did for me. But, I truly love and honor the friendship you have bestowed upon me. Please don't be angry or hate me. I couldn't handle that," she says sorrowfully.

"Alright, Rayen. I will take whatever you have to offer me because I care about you. But, this guy better not hurt you. If it lasts," he says sarcastically.

"No one is going to hurt me. And, I don't even know where this will lead. So, I'll see you Monday." She cuts the conversation off.

"Okay, Rayen. Okay."

She ends the phone call and continues to snack on her grapes.

Rayen turns off the shower and strolls to her closet. "I really want to look good tonight. I have never had an adult relationship with anyone, really. Blake makes me feel so out of whack. My stability is crumbling emotionally. The shell I have used for protection is slowly being chipped away." She steps back and closes her eyes. She remembers his touch. "Am I moving too fast? Was I hasty in jumping into being his 'girlfriend'? I have so many secrets, secrets that could hurt us both. But, I know I want him all to myself. I have to keep my secrets safe now to have him in my life. It's the only way to accomplish that." She touches her lips. She can feel the tingle from his tender but sensual kiss. She opens her eyes and shakes it off. "I must get ready."

Annetta Hobson

She decides to wear a black dress. It has thin straps, a sweetheart plunging neckline, and it gathers from under her breasts to the bottom of the dress, which ends above her knee. She chooses silver sling back stilettos. She grabs her silver handbag and starts down the stairs. When she enters her dining room, the bell buzzes. She dashes out the door to meet her date. "Wow! You look marvelous, Rayen."

She drags her eyes over Blake. He is wearing a blue dress shirt no tie and black slacks. He has such a grand body! He looks good in anything and especially nothing.

"You don't look bad yourself, Detective."

He smiles a shy schoolboy smile. He opens the car door and takes her hand. She slides in his car and he closes the door. He jogs around to the driver door. He gets in and they are on their way.

Rayen stares at her hand. She is silent during the drive. Blake asks with concern, "What's wrong, Rayen? You are so quiet."

"I have never done any of this before. I am very uncomfortable."

"Is it too much for you? Tell me and we can turn around. I am just a family man. I like for my family to meet whomever I date."

"I'll be fine. I just need to adjust my brain to all of this."

He reaches across to Rayen's hands and clenches them. She lifts her eyes to meet his and smiles. "Your beauty enslaves me, Rayen. It is like looking at a diamond that glistens, and I can't look away from it."

Light in the Shadow

She looks down again. "There have been many men to compliment me. But when you say those things to me, I feel giddy like a child." He smirks and releases her hand.

The car drives into a driveway that circles around a tree placed directly in front of the main door of the lovely colonial style home. He puts the car in park.

"Are you sure you don't mind?"

"I'm fine, Blake. Let's go."

He steps out and walks around to her door. When she opens the door, he takes her hand to help her out. She steps out and they walk to his parent's door and knock. A young lady a,nswers. "Hi Blake!" she shouts.

"Hey, Danny." He hugs her then turns.

"Rayen, you remember Danielle, my sister?"

"Hello, Danielle."

Danielle looks Rayen up then down and replies, "Hi. Please come in."

"Where are Mom and Dad?"

"They are in the family room."

They follow Danielle to the family room. Blake looks at Rayen. He whispers to her. "You okay?" She nods. When they enter the family room, everyone is laughing and talking. The room becomes silent as Rayen, Blake, and Danny enters. Blake's dad, Robert, stands.

"Hello again, young lady." He walks over to Rayen and embraces her. She is surprised by his gesture, but she hugs him back. After Robert releases her, Blake introduces her to his family once more. Everyone exchanges friendly hellos.

"Mom, you remember Rayen?"

"Yes, sweetie. How could I forget such a delightful face?" Abagail says. "My son has been speaking about you since you came to town." Rayen smiles and glances at Blake. Emily stands and invites everyone to the dining room for dinner.

They all sit at the table and begin to eat. "So Blake, what's up?" Daniel says.

"Nothing much, brother."

"What I mean is…what's up with you and this 'Angel' you brought with you this evening?"

"Well this is the new 'lady' in my life." He glances at her then winks. "I am excited about us, so I wanted you guys to know that." Daniel laughs.

"So, you are telling me that you are totally over Lauryn?" Abagail interrupts.

"Daniel, that is enough!"

Blake coolly remarks, "It's okay, Mom. Daniel, I am totally and completely over Lauryn."

"Does she know this?" Daniel smirks. Just as he prepares to answer, Lauryn prances into the dining room.

"Hello everyone," she announces. "I am so glad I did not miss dinner. I am famished. I stopped at my Mom's, but she had already eaten." She goes on. "Is it okay that I just came in? The door was open…" She stops and scans the room. Everyone stops eating. Rayen tenses. She wipes her mouth with her napkin and slides slightly away from the table. "What the hell is this, Blake?" Lauryn yells. Blake stands and motions toward her.

"Why didn't you call first?"

Light in the Shadow

"I have been calling you for days. I've messaged and emailed you with no response. That's why I just drove up." Blake grabs her arm and takes her into the kitchen. She begins to cry hysterically. "I knew it! I knew it! You are with that now? Are you kidding me, Blake? Really?"

"Lauryn, I haven't talked to you in a while. Why are you here?"

"We never talked all the time. I didn't think you had…What is this?" she cries.

"I am with Rayen now, Lauryn. I thought I made it clear the last time we talked. We are done."

"Are you fucking kidding me?"

He grabs her arm. "Do not disrespect my parents' home." She drops her head into her hands.

"I know I hurt you, Blake. Please don't do this. Please? I love you so much, baby. I can't live without you." She drops to her knees.

"Get up, Lauryn. Don't do this." He grabs her shoulder. Rayen enters the kitchen.

"Blake, I have called Sterling. I think I should go."

"Rayen, no. Don't leave. I really want you here. Call him back." Blake insists. Lauryn marches up to her and points her finger at her.

"Bitch, let me tell you one thing! He is mine. I have invested five years into this man, and I am not letting him go!" Rayen raises her brow. Before she can react, Blake steps in front of her.

"Lauryn, that's enough! Get out of my parents' house. Now!" Emily enters the room.

"Lauryn, let's go, honey." She wraps her arm around Lauryn's shoulder and guides her toward the door. Her luxurious blonde hair swings as she is whisked out of the kitchen.

"Blake! I love you..." she wails. He looks at Rayen and steps toward her. He grabs her face between his hands.

"I am so sorry. I had no idea she would be here. Please tell me that this doesn't change anything." She looks away. He brings her face back to look at his gorgeous blue eyes. "I don't want her anymore." He kisses her deeply. When he releases her, she puts her arms around him.

"It doesn't change anything." She smiles. He breathes deep.

"Thank goodness. All I want is you, and no one will change that." They smile at one another.

Emily walks Lauryn to her BMW. "Lauryn, why are you here, hun? Blake did make it clear that you two were no more." She sniffles.

"I thought we were still working on it."

"He was being polite so you wouldn't be embarrassed. I know you haven't told your parents."

"They love him so much, and I didn't want them to know I ran him away. I still love him, Em. I didn't know my job would make me leave him waiting two years for my answer. I understand I messed up, but I thought I had time."

Emily says sincerely, "Blake is a family man. He has always wanted a family. You crushed him, Lauryn. I am so sorry, but he has moved on."

"How does he know she will give him what he wants? I am here! I am ready. Why would he take a chance on someone new?" she continues on. Emily shakes her head and crosses her arms. Lauryn leans on her car, still sobbing. "I'm sorry. I am not

Light in the Shadow

giving him up that easily. If I have to get an apartment here I will. I can't let him go. I see my future with this man."

Emily pleads, "Lauryn, don't." Lauryn slowly raises her head to see Blake and Rayen exiting the main door. He puts his arm around Rayen as they walk to his car. He kisses her cheek and she leans in to fully receive it. Lauryn wipes her eyes and hugs Emily. Blake spots them, and the smile leaves his face. He releases Rayen. Emily urges Lauryn to get into her car. She starts the engine. She takes another look at them and drives away.

"So, where to?" Blake says.

"I don't know," Rayen responds. She stares out of the window, thinking.

He states apologetically, "Rayen, I didn't know that would happen."

"It's fine," she returns quietly. He glances at her out of his eye.

"What are you thinking about?"

"Just that I will not give in like I did with Josh. I really want to explore this with you, Blake."

He smiles. "Let's go to my place, okay?"

She says with a small smile, "Okay."

He drives to his house. He turns into his driveway and pushes a button. The garage door lifts, and he pulls in. He turns the engine off and looks over at Rayen. "My life has been a ball of confusion for two years. Should I wait? Should I move on? But when I met you, it all became clear. I hope I don't run you away by laying all this on you so soon."

"I am enjoying this. It's something I never dreamed I could have," she responds honestly. They get out of the car and go into the house.

"Let's have a celebratory drink." He grabs her hand and whisks her into the kitchen. He retrieves a bottle of wine, grabs two glasses, and then goes up to his room. "Welcome to my humble abode." He sets the glasses and the wine down. He turns to Rayen and grabs her in an embrace. He kisses her on her lips and smiles. She looks into his eyes. "You are so damn fine, Rayen." He shakes his head. He doesn't believe after all the admiring from afar that he has her there with him. She looks down, and her lashes sweep his cheek. He kisses her eyelids. He lifts her up, she wraps her legs around his waist, and they kiss passionately. He blurts out through the kiss, "I feel so lucky because you and Josh didn't work out." She leans away from his lips.

"I don't want to talk about Josh." She cradles his head and kisses him deeper than she has ever thought possible. He moans in pleasure. He places her on the bed, takes off her shoes, and lifts her dress over her head. She is only wearing a lacey thong with rhinestones trailing the strings on the sides. He quickly slides them off.

"Lay back, baby. I want to taste your delicious treat." She leans back and spreads her legs apart. He leans in between her thighs and begins tasting her. "You taste exquisite," he resounds as she hums in delight. He licks her bulb and then her center. He laps her up like he is licking milk from a bowl. He is driving her wild. He pauses, reaches down to the floor, and grabs the wine. "I want to drink from you. The mixture will be like no other." He pours the wine in her belly button and slurps it up in one motion. Then he goes straight back to her center and slurps the lips of her womanhood.

Light in the Shadow

She breathlessly whispers with pleasure, "I'm going to….oh, Blake." He stops.

"Oh, no. Not yet baby." She twists and moans. He stands and takes the tip of his member and rubs it up and down her center.

"Oh, yesss! Blake, yesss!" Finally, he thrusts his erection inside her. He rocks his hips in and out. She immediately wraps her legs around him and matches his rhythm. She kisses his lips. "Oh Blake! What are you doing to me?" He leans into her hair and growls. His movement quickens. She matches his stroke. Their breathing becomes rapid. And, tears began to stream down her face. Finally, they both cry out in dramatic release. He lifts his head from her hair and run his fingers through it to remove it from her face.

"Rayen, what is it? Why are you crying?" he says with concern. She lifts her arm and hides her eyes. He continues to gaze at her, never removing himself from her.

"You are absolutely amazing, Blake."

"Oh, no. You, my dear, are what I call amazing." He leans in to kiss her lips, and she meets him. He falls asleep inside her. She is so tired that she cannot help but to follow him into slumber land.

Blake awakes in a jolt. His manhood is so stiff from being incased in her moistness all night. He slowly begins to move. "Ohhh," he moans. She opens her eyes and looks at his eyes tightly shut in pleasure. She lifts her knees and grabs her ankles. His eyes shoot open and he cannot contain the delight in his face. "Whoa, Rayen! I am not going to last…" Before he can stop it, he bursts with excitement inside her once more. He collapses on cue as he lets out a loud cry. "You were so deliciously wet, I could not help myself. Do you want me to help you release? Name it and I will oblige." She stretches as he lifts out of her.

"I am good, Blake," she replies.

"Oh, no, baby, I am giving you this gift." He hurries to the restroom, gets a washcloth, and washes her. He then inserts his pointer and middle finger inside her and works his magic. Before she can protest, she is screaming out an orgasm.

"What time is it?" she inquires. He sits up and walks over to his dresser and looks at his watch.

"3:30 a.m. And, I need sleep. I have to go to the station in the morning. My hiatus is over." He kisses her on her lips gently and places the covers over their naked bodies. He wraps her in his arms and goes back to sleep.

Rayen stretches and rolls over. "Good morning."

Blake says smiling, "Morning."

"Did you sleep well?" He leans over to kiss her. She closes her eyes and enjoys the soft tenderness of his lips. She inhales.

"I have to go. I must get my house ready for my sister's arrival."

"Your sister?"

"Angela is Margaret's daughter. She is the woman who helped raise me. Angela and I have always been like sisters. I didn't get to attend her graduation, so I would like to go and get her a present."

"Well, do you want me to take you home or would you like to call Sterling?"

"I need my car. Do you have time to take me home?"

"Of course. I can go in early to catch up on some paperwork."

Light in the Shadow

He leaves the room to go turn on the shower. Rayen watches him. His body is so chiseled. She has never desired anyone the way she desires him. "Come on, get in with me!" He shouts from the bathroom. She sits up and throws the covers off of her. She dashes into the bathroom to find him already in the shower. The water is flowing into his face he has his eyes shut. He wipes the water from his eyes. He waves his hand inviting her in. She steps in and wraps her arms around him from behind. She kisses his back and then runs her tongue down the line that leads to the small of his back. "Rayen, if you keep that up, I won't make it to work." He looks back and smiles. She releases him. They wash and step out. They get dressed and head out of the door.

"When can I see you again, Rayen?" he questions.

She remarks, "I don't know. I want to spend some time with Angela, and you have to catch up on your work. We will just have to be spontaneous."

"I will count the hours and minutes until I see your face again," He laughs. "We will talk though."

"I really enjoyed this whole week with you, Blake. It was incredible."

"Even with the drama at my parents' house?"

"Yes, especially with the drama at your parents' house."

"Seriously, I would like to go back so you can get to know my family. I am very close to them, and I want them to know you."

"That will be fine. They seemed to be lovely people with the exception of…"

He interrupts her. "Daniel, I know. He can be a total ass." She smiles shyly. "Well, here you are, home sweet home," he says trying not to seem disappointed that their time together has ended.

"Thank you again for a wonderful week. I will never forget it, Blake."

"You won't have to, Rayen. There is plenty more where that came from."

He smiles and reaches over to hold her face. He then places a soft and tender kiss on her lips, leaving the feelings of his gentle touch lingering. "See you later."

"Until next time, Detective," she says with a small smile. He watches as she walks to her door, waves, and then goes in.

Chapter 8

"Excuse me. Pardon me." Angela whispers as she makes her way through the sea of people entering the airport from the terminal. She spots a handsome gentle holding a sign with her name on it. "Angela Taylor," she answers the poster. "And, you are?" She glances at the young man's face. "Wow he is cute," she thinks.

"I am Sterling Winters from the car service, Ms. Taylor." He takes her bags, and they head toward the Cadillac Escalade. He slides her bags into the trunk and proceeds around the truck to open her door. She says with a coy flirting smile, "Thank you, Mr. Winters."

During the drive, she questions Sterling. "So…Sterling, how does my sister like Michigan?" He glances up at the rear view mirror.

"I don't know, Ms. Taylor. But, this is a lovely part of Michigan. Bay City has beautiful scenery. There are lots of sites to enjoy. Are you here to stay?"

She returns, "Well, Sterling, that is up to my uptight sister." He smiles as if he has a secret and continues to drive. Angela revels in the cozy atmosphere of the city. "It's so different from New York."

Finally, they arrive at Rayen's condo. "Wow this is nice! It is like a house, but it's a condominium?" Angela wonders aloud. Sterling steps out and walks around to open her door without response to her outburst. "Thank you," she states as she touches his hand. She walks up to the door. Before she can buzz the bell, Rayen swings the door open.

Annetta Hobson

"Hello, Angie." She embraces her. Angela is stunned! Rayen hasn't called her Angie since she left for Las Vegas, and she notices she is smiling.

"Okay, who are you, and what did you do with Rayen?" She smirks.

Rayen speaks nonchalantly, "What do you mean? I am just glad I've got someone I love here. You have no idea what I've been through. Come in, so I can tell you everything." She trails behind her with a bewildered look on her face.

"Sterling, please take her bags to that room at the top of the stairs."

"Yes, Rayen."

Angela watches him as he climbs the stairs. "How can you have him work for you?"

"What?" she asks.

Angela goes on, "He is so fine, Rayen! I want to eat him alive." She laughs at her.

"I have really missed you Angie." She stares for a moment with shock as Rayen exclaims, "What!"

"You are laughing, Rayen. You are laughing, and it is a glorious sight."

She blushes.

"What has happened to change you so drastically? A man? This city? What is it?"

Sterling jogs down the stairs. "Anything else ladies?"

Rayen responds, "No, Sterling. Thank you."

"Maybe some other time. I have something you can to do to me," Angela whispers as both of them laugh. Sterling smirks then leaves.

Light in the Shadow

Rayen grabs her hand and yanks Angela along. "Let's sit. I have cooked and bought lots of wine. We need to talk and have a girl's night in." She leads her into the dining room.

"You cooked? Girl's night in? What in the hell is going on?" Angela says with unbelief. They sit at the table. Rayen serves the food, and they indulge in a few glasses of wine.

"After we eat, I have a surprise for you. Since I missed your graduation, I wanted to give you something special."

"You are like this breath of fresh air."

They finish their meal. "Very delicious, Rayen," Angela resounds.

"Thank you. I have so much to tell you. Let me start with this. Growing up with you and Margaret has helped me so much. More recently, have I noticed the influence you have bestowed on me," she states.

"Thanks! Lord knows I have tried," she jokes.

"I love you guys so much, and I will start to tell you more often."

Angela eyes began to tear.

"Don't cry. I have so much to share."

"Go on before the waterfall opens."

Rayen begins with explaining her relationship with Josh then how he and Evelyn began. She explains their friendship, longing for more, the sex they experienced, and the rejection. Then she explains about Blake and how he makes her see things, how she cried, and laughed. She talks about Mt. Pleasant. She tells her about Lauryn and the scene at his parents' home. She talks about every detail that leads to this morning.

"Wow, Rye! You have been busy. Two delicious men? I am jealous. I didn't think you had it in you. Joshua and Blake. I can't wait to meet them. And, I can't wait to see that bitch, Evelyn!"

"Oh, Angela, the hell with her. I am so happy she stepped in. Blake is wonderful."

"He has to be. You are laughing and crying. How was the sex?"

"With?"

"Both."

"Well with Josh, it was like first-time young girl sex."

"I had sex with my boyfriend in Mom's basement"

"But, Blake makes me feel like a woman. I feel sexy, seductive. I feel like we are having sex with each other, not 'he is the teacher, and I am the student'. I mean it was great with Josh, but with Blake it is so much better."

She rubs her lips and her eyes become distant. It is as if she is recollecting her moments with him. Angela giggles, "You are in love, Rayen. I never thought I would see it, but finally someone has unlocked the dusty box your heart was in."

They move into the living room and turn on some music. Angela sits on the couch, and Rayen is on the floor beside her. They laugh and talk for hours. The hours fly pass. Soon, they both fall asleep.

Rayen jumps up; she realizes she is still on the floor. She sits straight and grabs her head. She hears her phone vibrating. She searches for it and locates it on the end table. "Hello?" she whispers with her voice scratchy. She squints to look at the time. The clock reads '4 a.m. "Hello?" She repeats.

Light in the Shadow

"Did I wake you, Rayen?' She immediately recognizes the voice.

"Hi, Blake."

"I just left the station. Before I go to sleep, I had to hear your voice."

She smiles. Angela lifts from her slumber. "Is that him?" Rayen nods.

"I won't keep you. I just haven't been able to focus. I close my eyes, and I smell your sweet scent."

Rayen blushes. Angela cannot believe what she is seeing.

"I don't know how long I will be able to stay away. Your sister may have to meet me soon."

"I am very happy you called. Your voice is a refreshing sound to wake to."

"Be careful for what you ask for, Rayen. I will be tempted to drive over there right now."

"No, don't. I am spending time with Angie. Maybe we can steal a moment or two tomorrow?"

"Maybe? I am trying to just not go to work and spend all of my nights and days in your arms." Her smile is so large, Angela starts to smile also.

"I am tempted to keep you on the phone, but I'll let those beautiful eyes go back to resting."

"Okay, we will talk later."

"Alright, Rayen, until then."

She presses the end button and sets the phone back on the table.

"Okay, Rayen. You two are in love!"

"I don't know. It is too soon for that. I don't even know what it feels like to be in love."

"Well, first, does your heart flutter when you see him or talk to him?"

"Umm, I guess."

"Okay, do you miss him as soon as he leaves you? And, do you become impatient when you have to wait to see him?

"Yes?"

"Finally, do you find yourself wondering why he hasn't called?"

"Yes."

"You love him! Oh my goodness! You love him, Rayen!" Angela screeches. Rayen jumps to her feet.

"I do? Oh my. What if I do? What if he finds out? No! What if he doesn't feel the same way?"

"Calm down, calm down. If he didn't feel the same way, I think he wouldn't have thrown what's her face out of his parents' house on her head."

"You're right."

Angela jumps up. "You should tell him!"

"Oh no, no, no!" Rayen exclaims. Angela laughs. "What if I tell him and he doesn't feel the same? I would be ruined, and I would be worse than I was before."

"Can I ask you something personal, Rayen?"

"It depends?" She hitches her brow.

"Were you a virgin when you came to Bay City?"

Rayen looks down at her hands. She is very quiet for a while. "Basically I was. I have never been with a man in a

Light in the Shadow

pleasurable way," she whispers. Angela recognizes the pain in her face and quickly backs off.

"Well now you have, and from what you tell me, it was good!" She jokes. Rayen's eyes lighten.

"It was beyond good." They both begin to laugh.

"Before I forget..." She stands and jogs to the closet by the door. When she quickly returns, she is holding a medium sized velvet box.

"Oh, Rayen, what's this?"

Rayen hands her the gift box and Angela opens it. "Oh, thank you!" She gently removes a diamond icicle shaped pendant on a gold necklace, an exact replica of Rayen's. She grabs it from her. Angela turns so she can put it on. The dagger shaped pendant extends down to the tip of her cleavage. "Very nice, sis, thanks."

"It can also be used as a weapon...if you are in trouble."

Angela forces out a smile. "A weapon?"

"Never mind. It costs a pretty penny," Rayen jokes.

"I am sure it did. Thank you again." She hugs her. They sit there for a moment locked together.

"Okay, let's go to bed. It is so late."

"Rayen, I don't mean to sound sentimental, but I am so happy right now. I will never forget today. For as long as I live."

She smiles, and they go up the stairs to sleep.

Rayen opens the refrigerator. "What should I have for breakfast?" When she shuts the door, Angela is coming down the stairs.

"That bed is so freaking awesome! Best sleep I ever had."

"I spent a pretty penny for that too, so it should be," she remarks.

"What are we going to do today?"

"I don't know. What do you want to do?"

"One thing I would love to do is get some of what this city gave you, starting with that scrumptious looking specimen, Sterling."

"No, Angela, not Sterling."

"Awww, why not?"

"The company has a great professional relationship with him that makes his father very proud right now."

"So, he is trying to impress daddy? Oh no! He is not one of them."

"His dad is the Mayor, Angie."

"Really?" A glint of interest flickers across her face.

"Angela!"

"What?"

"No."

"Okay! Be selfish with your Bay City men!"

"You can talk to anyone except for him…oh or Blake's brother, Daniel. He is an ass."

"Oh, Mr. Charming has a brother?"

"Yes. Mr. Not-so-charming."

"Okay, let's just eat."

They have breakfast, joke, and talk for a while. Then, they go back to their rooms to get some Saturday rest.

Light in the Shadow

Angela peeks in Rayen's room. "Can I come in, Rye?" She sits up. "Come on." She runs and jumps in her bed. "Are you going to stay in bed all day today?"

"I just wanted to relax and spend some alone time with you. Why? Do you want to go out?"

"Hell yes."

"Okay, its 7 p.m. now. Let's go for drinks."

They get dressed and head out.

"Where are we going?" Angela asks.

"Latitude, I guess." Rayen shrugs. Sterling nods and drives to their destination. "Wow! This place is really crowded tonight," she blurts out. Sterling helps each of the ladies out of the SUV.

"I'll call before it gets late. If not, come back at 1 a.m."

"Yes, Ms. Rayen."

Angela bats her eyelashes at him before he gets back in the truck to leave. He smiles.

They enter the lounge and head towards the back. "I hope we can get a table!" Angela shouts. "There is one." They find a table adjacent to the bar. The waitress approaches.

"What can I get for you ladies this evening?"

"I would like a blended Mojito," Angela says.

Rayen enters, "I'll just have a Cosmo." The waitress smiles at them and leaves. She returns with their drinks. They drink, laugh and enjoy the music.

"Angela, you're here?" They turn to find Evelyn and Josh standing behind them. "I am," she states sarcastically.

Joshua interrupts the ladies before going any further, "Hi Rayen. How are you?"

"Fine, Josh. You?"

"Good."

"There are no tables, babe," Evelyn says disappointedly. She let's go of Josh's arm and leaves to search for a table.

"You must be Joshua." Angela stands.

"Yes, and you are Angela." They shake hands, and she sits. She winks at Rayen and looks at Josh's butt.

"He is so fine!" she whispers through her cupped hands to Rayen. Rayen smiles.

"What's up, Josh? Are you guys celebrating?"

"Yes. Mr. Drake called and gave us the details from your meeting in Mt. Pleasant."

Rayen beams at the thought of Mt Pleasant. "Oh, good." Evelyn returns, rolling her eyes.

"No table, Joshie."

"Well, we should go. Good seeing you, Rayen." He turns to leave.

"Why can't we just join you guys?" Evelyn blurts.

"No! We are expecting dates," Angela interrupts. Joshua raises a brow. "Sorry," Angela snorts. Without one word, Evelyn grabs Joshua's hand and pulls him towards the door.

"That bitch has a lot of nerve!"

"Angie, don't waste your time or anger on her. Let's enjoy the rest of the night."

They drink their drinks and relish in the atmosphere.

Light in the Shadow

"It's getting late, Angela. We should go," Rayen announces. "No. I don't want to go. We are having so much fun. I haven't danced and drank like this in so long. I recently graduated from college. I should be able to enjoy myself," Angela returns, pouting.

"Very true, but I'm tipsy, and you are drunk. It's not good to be out like this."

"Oh, there you are! The old Rayen resurfacing."

"I just have to be safe. You never know what danger is waiting for two young drunk women."

"Oh come on! Nothing is happening in Pleasantville. Maybe New York, but not here."

A dark glare crosses Rayen's face. "It could happen anywhere."

"Whatever, party pooper!"

Rayen turns and takes a gulp of her drink. "Whoa, this is my song!" Angela jumps up and starts to dance. She motions toward the dance floor. Rayen watches carefully. She begins to dance very seductively. As she is grinding, a guy slides up behind her. He begins to grind on her. She is so drunk, she just leans into him. He begins to lick and suck on her neck. Angela just lies into him. Rayen shoots out of her seat and motions to the dance floor. She bursts through the dancers on the floor. She grabs Angela's arm. "Let's go! We are leaving now!" Angela leans her head forward and rolls her eyes.

"Angie, what would your mom say?"

"My Mom is in New York, Rayen."

The man purses his lips. "Look, baby, join in or get the fuck out! Cock blocking bitch." Angela tries to pull away, but he brings her close to him.

"Let her go! Now!"

"Or what? You going to suck my cock?" He laughs. Rayen pulls Angela's arm. She staggers forward. He grabs Angela again, but this time, he pushes Rayen. She looks around, and her eyes rest on him. They are cold and dangerous. Rayen lets Angela go and steps to him.

She leans close to him and whispers, "You pushed the wrong woman." He steps back.

"What, bitch?"

He staggers back and tries to grab her. Before he can, she bends her arm, clutches her wrist, and hits him in the throat with a clean and swift movement. Angela gasps. He hits the floor holding his neck.

"Somebody help him! He can't breathe!" a woman yells. Rayen snaps out of her darkness and pulls Angela off the dance floor. Before she can get to her table, security stops her.

"Ma'am, what exactly just happened?" People are panicking. Someone calls the ambulance and police.

When the police and paramedic arrive, Rayen and Angela are sitting at the bar with a security guard standing beside them. The man Rayen hit is strapped to a stretcher and has on oxygen. Two cops approach them. "We need to ask you some questions." Angela is drinking water.

Rayen lifts her eyes slowly to look at the officers. Angela starts to speak, "Officer, my sister was just protecting me."

"And, how is that, Ms.?"

"Taylor. Angela Taylor."

The one officer starts to write on his pad. "And, you are?" He says to Rayen.

"Ms. Rayen Vasu."

Light in the Shadow

"Okay. Now, what happened here?"

Angela begins to explain the events, and the officer is writing as she speaks. The other officer stands beside him with his hands on his hip. "Now, you give me your version, Ms. Vasu." "That asshole was disrespecting my sister. Then, he struck me. He is very lucky that he was only hit in the throat," she says way too calmly.

"What does that mean, Ms.?" he returns. She looks down to the floor to control her rage.

"Nothing, officer. He was trying to take advantage of a drunk young woman. When I tried to take her home, he became aggressive." The officer closes his book. Rayen looks around the lounge. It is practically clear and very late. "Well, ladies, I am going to take you in. We will talk until I am sure he is okay. I will also check your stories with the statements from others," the officer informs. Angela bursts into tears.

"What! Are you kidding me? He assaulted us! Rayen, I am so sorry. I should have left when you told me."

Rayen turns to her in a low tone, "Calm down, Angie."

"My Mom is going to freak! Oh, no. She is going to shit bricks!"

"Calm down, Angie."

The officer motions for them to stand and leads them to the police cruiser. "I am so sorry, Rayen. My second day here, and I have you being escorted to the police station. I'm so, so sorry!" She rolls her eyes and get in the police car.

The ride to the police station is a quiet one. The only sounds are of Angela sobbing. When they arrive, they are led inside. The station is basically deserted. The only occupants are the detectives in the back. All of the officers hurry to get a glimpse of the woman who took out a guy with one blow.

"Rayen?" Blake yells. Angela wipes her tears.

"Is that umm…Blake? Wow, he is absolutely decadent!" she says through sniffles.

"Are you the woman who hit the guy with a death blow?" He jokes. She jerks her head up and looks at him in horror.

"Death blow?"

He remarks, "Just kidding. The guys around here are having a ball with this one. What happened?" She doesn't respond.

"You know them, Pierce?" The officer inquires.

"Yes, this is the new lady I am dating." He smirks. Whistles echoes through the station. He tugs at his blazer and clears his throat.

"Wow, Blake. She's a knock out!" his partner interrupts. "I just want to make sure the dirt bag she cocked is okay. You need to watch this one, Pierce. One false move, and she could take you down." He laughs and invites the women to sit.

"I heard there was some sort of ninja move performed. Is that an exaggeration, Rayen?"

"Ninja…no. Karate or Judo, yes. It was a move I learned for self-defense. I am a black belt."

"Oh? You didn't mention that," he says, looking surprised.

"I didn't feel it was important. Does it change things?"

"No, it's just…never mind."

He stands to walk away. She looks at her hands. "Oh, no. Rayen, please forgive me. I hope I didn't ruin things for you," Angela resounds sadly.

"Shhh, Angie. Don't worry. Just calm down," she replies.

Light in the Shadow

They sit in the station for hours. No one else speaks to them. Angela is nodding at the table. She finally rests her head on it and falls to sleep. Rayen is calmly sitting with her hands in a ball atop one another. She isn't nervous at all.

"At least I didn't kill him like I wanted. I wanted to kill him so badly. He is lucky we were surrounded by all those witnesses," she thinks.

"You ladies are free to go," one of the officers says, interrupting her thoughts.

"Oh, okay. Thanks." She nudges Angela. "Time to go." She jumps up.

"Oh…Okay. Umm…is that douche alright?"

"He's fine, just very embarrassed," the officer replies. Angela giggles. "Here are your purses. The security guys dropped them off." They grab them from the officer. They proceed to the door of the station to leave.

"Rayen, wait!" Blake calls. "Let me take you home."

"Oh, no, thank you, Detective. I am calling Sterling. He dropped us off," she retorts. Angela steps outside so they can talk alone.

"Rayen, I apologize. I just was thrown that it was something about you I didn't know."

"No, no. It's fine. I am just tired, and I don't want you to have to leave work."

"My shift just ended. Its 4 a.m., remember?" He smiles. She glances at the floor.

"Blake, I saw the look in your eyes. I don't know why, but you were embarrassed."

He begins, "I…" She stops him by placing a finger on his lips.

"I understand you are a lawman and I chopped some guy at a bar. It is just uncomfortable, but I will not apologize for learning to protect myself."

"You are interpreting this in the wrong manner. I really care for you. I actually adore you. You could have plucked his eyes out, and it would have not changed the way I feel about you. The jerk deserved it. I was just surprised and didn't know how to react. I promise, Rayen, it's nothing. Whatever there is about you, I will accept it. I haven't met anyone in a while that I just wanted to drop everything for. I am here, and I don't plan on going anywhere. What about you?"

"What do you mean?"

"Are you going anywhere? Are you serious about this?"

"Of course I am. Blake, you know what I told you."

He smiles so big. "Are you begging yet, Pierce?" Sam screams. And, the guys start to laugh.

"Fuck you, Wilcox!" He turns back to her. "May I take you home?"

"Yes. Please take me home."

Blake brings his Camaro around to meet the ladies in front of the station. He gets out and opens the passenger door for them. Angela climbs in back. He looks around and whispers to Rayen, "I missed you. I wanted to rip you out of that dress when I spotted you standing in the station." She smiles. "Can I come home with you? I would love to sleep on your floor again," he asks, seductively kissing her ear. A shiver runs chillingly down her spine.

Light in the Shadow

She stokes his cheek gently as she whispers, "I am dying being away from you. I lie in the bed thinking about you." He kisses her again, and puts his arms around her. He slides his hands down her back to her behind. She inhales. "Blake, not here. You are starting something we cannot finish."

"I am mad about you," he breathes into her ear. She leans in and revels in the moment. "Let's go before I start ripping your clothes off right here." He grabs her hand to help her in the car. She gets in and they head towards her condo.

"Blake, I love you for finding Rayen," Angela says. He turns his head slightly to look at her and smiles.

"It was my pleasure." He reaches over and caress Rayen's upper thigh.

"I have never seen her with any guy, let alone smiling and blushing. You are unimaginable," she continues.

"Thank you," he exclaims as they arrive at the condo.

They get out the car and walk to the door. Rayen lets Angela in, and she hurries up the stairs. Blake steps in the doorway.

"I was about to keel over," he says.

"Why?" she asks.

"I thought you were going to be done with me after the talk at the station," he states with relief.

"Never. I think…I'm in...love." She slaps her hand over her mouth. "Shit!" He smirks. "That just slipped out! I'm tired and still a little intoxicated," she rambles. He hushes her with a kiss. She stares at him and blinks.

"Good because I am definitely in love with you," he speaks softly. She places both hands on his face and gently caresses it. Tears start to stream down her cheeks.

Annetta Hobson

"I haven't known love. Ever since I lost my parents, love has been unattainable. I believe what I feel is love. It is just…I feel so safe with you. I feel…like someone else…please don't hurt me. Please. I know it's redundant. But, I couldn't handle it."

"I know for a fact I would never do anything to intentionally hurt you. You saved me from a lie, a lie that was stripping away my being. I was a zombie until I bumped into you at World Café," he states honestly.

"It is really late."

"Okay, I'll go."

"No, no. It's too late for you to drive home. Stay here with me, Blake. I don't want you to go." He grins very wide, grabs her hand, and leads her up the stairs.

They step inside her door and survey the room for Angela. "She's in bed," Rayen states.

"Come, let's get you in your PJ's 'cause I am dying to get you out of that dress," he says. They start to kiss. The kiss deepens. He scoops her into his arms and carries her up the stairs to her bedroom.

"Knock, Knock." Rayen jumps up. She glances over at Blake still sleeping like a baby.

"Yes?" She says her voice a little groggy.

"It's me, Rye. Can I come in?"

"Uh, Angie, I'll be right out!" She jumps out of bed and runs to grab her robe hanging on the back of the bathroom door. She slides out of her door and closes it.

"I am guessing Blake stayed?" she teases.

"What is it, Angela?" she whispers.

"I just wanted to apologize again for last night."

Light in the Shadow

"It's no big deal."

"No. You opened your home and your life to me. I don't ever want to destroy that. You are the only family I know besides Mom. You have a great thing going here, and I do not want to ruin it." Angela opens her arms and wraps them around her. She slowly hugs her back.

"Oh, and, Rye?"

"Yes?"

"Please, don't tell Mom."

They burst into laughter. "I am going to let you get back to that fine man in there." Angela nudges her. Rayen smiles.

"He loves me, Angie. He says he loves me." They embrace once more. Rayen enters her room and climbs back in bed in front of Blake. She snuggles close to him. He breathes out and wraps his arms around her and they sleep.

The bell buzzes. Angela runs to the speaker. "Yes?"

"It's Sterling," the voice answers.

"Come on up," she replies. He enters the condo. Angela holds the door open while clutching her robe.

"I heard about what happened last night. How are you and Ms. Vasu doing this morning?" he says, making small talk.

"Thank you, but we are great. How did you find out?"

"There is nothing in this city I don't know about."

"Oh, I see. I will tell her you came by. Thanks again."

"Anytime, Angela." He displays his big band boy smile and turns to exit out of the door. She leans on the door, thinking.

"The hell with what Rayen is talking about!" She closes the door and goes back in the kitchen to make her meal.

Angela begins watching television. She eats her ham and cheese sandwich she prepared. When she lifts her cup to drink, Blake comes stumbling down the stairs.

"Whoa! What's the hurry?"

"Good morn…I mean afternoon, Angela. I am so late for work. Rayen has me totally gone, and soon my job may be."

"I doubt it. From what I hear, you are top dog around here."

"Yes, but even the top dog has to show up. Anyway, it was a pleasure finally meeting you."

He hurries out of the door and slams it behind him. Angela smiles and continues to eat.

Rayen opens her eyes. She stretches and turns to touch Blake, but she finds an empty space. She sits up, and there is a note on the pillow.

Rayen,

You were sleeping so peacefully. I didn't want to wake you. It is so nice waking to such a stunning beauty. This has been a whirlwind for me, but I welcome it with open arms. I have to see you later. I must taste those lips every single day. I am addicted to you. And, making love to you is a bonus. I want to smother you with my affection. Don't get tired or annoyed with me; I am not fond of withdrawals. I get off at 4 a.m. Say I may be with you again tonight, or I will die. Well, maybe not die but be very sick.

Reluctantly leaving your bed,

Blake

She beams as she reads the note. Blake cannot be real. He is everything she ever could have imagined a man could be. "What if he finds out about my past? He would lock me away, and I would die lonely and in love. Why am I letting this go so far?

Light in the Shadow

It's because I am in love, and I can't stop it. It's like a run-away locomotive with no brakes," she thinks. Angela breaks her from her thoughts.

"Can I come in?"

She answers, "Yes."

"Oh my goodness, Rayen! He is so beyond hot. You have hit the man lottery here. First Josh then Blake," Angela yells as she jumps on the bed and lies back. She lifts two fingers. "Two, two. I am so darn jealous!" Rayen runs her hands from the front to the back of her head to smooth her hair.

"Why?"

"Because I have always wanted to find a man like Blake or Joshua; you didn't. But of course, the one who is not looking gets the ultimate prize. It's not fair."

"Angela, it hasn't been easy. No, I wasn't looking, but I realize now what I was missing. I was even lonely."

"I know, Rye. But, I have met so many jerks! I hope I find someone here also. It took you a month or two. Maybe I'll have it soon also."

"I sure hope so. Because Blake makes me feel so...oooo."

Angela screams and kicks her legs. Rayen rolls her eyes. "I am sleeping all day. So, if anyone comes by or calls, please take a message. Your job starts today instead of tomorrow," she commands.

"That reminds me. Earlier, Sterling stopped by to see if we were okay. He heard about what happened and was very concerned," Angela returns.

"Really? What did you say to him?" she hitches her brow.

"Nothing but thank you. That's it."

"I will see everyone tomorrow."

She plops back on her pillow and throws the cover over her head.

The phone startles Angela. "Hello!"

"Hi, may I speak with Rayen?" the male voice asks.

"She is sleeping, Blake. I have her phone because she wanted to rest. What time is it?"

"It's 4:15 a.m."

"Hold please."

She dashes to Rayen's room and peeks in. "Are you up, Rye?"

"Yes," she replies as she switches the light on.

"Blake is on the phone." Angela steps in and passes it to her.

"Yes?"

"Hello, sexy."

"Hi, Blake."

"You got my note?"

"Yes I did. Very romantic."

She smiles.

"Good. May I have my daily dose of you?"

"Come on over."

"I am already outside."

"That is very presumptuous of you, Detective."

"Well, I was just hoping you wanted to see me just as bad."

"Of course. I'm coming to buzz you in."

Light in the Shadow

She ends her call, jumps up, and scurries to the door.

When he gets to her, she pushes the door open. "You look edible in those boy shorts and tank. I am trying not to want you so much, but you ooze sexy." He smirks seductively.

"You look just as appetizing in your work suit with your shirt slightly open. What you do to a suit should be a crime." She reaches up around his neck and locks her hands. She then pulls herself up onto him and wraps her legs around him.

He resounds, "Oooooooo! I am such a fortunate man." They kiss passionately. He then turns to carry her up the stairs with her still clinging round him like a book bag wrapped snug around his front.

Angela peeks from her room and smiles. She closes her door and dials her Mom. "Hello? Angie, is everything alright, baby?"

"Yes, Mom. I thought I'd call and tell you Rayen is in love. She has found Mr. Perfect."

"Oh my! Is that right?"

"I know its early, but I couldn't hold it much longer. Mom, she is really happy here."

"I have wanted that for her ever since her family was taken. She deserves it."

"I know. I'll call you later. I need to get to sleep. Work is in a couple of hours. I love you."

"I love you, too. And, give my love to Rayen." "I will."

Chapter 9

Thursday, December 16th at 2 p.m., Angela types away on her computer. She glances up at the clock. "One more hour."

"Angela can you step in here please?" Rayen calls. She rises from her desk directly in front of Rayen's office and goes in.

"Yes, Ms. Vasu."

"Angela, I need you to take notes from this call I am about to make."

"Okay."

She runs out to her desk to grab her pad. Rayen picks up the office phone and dials the casino resort client. "Hello, this is Ms. Vasu. I am calling to get the final plans you and Mr. Manning went over." She waves for Angela to start writing. She talks more about the details. "Okay, fax them over. I'll be waiting," she says as the call ends. Angela pauses to looks at Rayen. "Can you call Joshua in here please?" she directs, beginning to type on her computer. Angela goes to her desk and calls Joshua's office.

"Hello, Joshua. Its Angela. Rayen needs you in her office please."

"No problem, I'll be right there," he returns.

Joshua enters Rayen's office. "You wanted to see me, Rayen?" She looks up at him from her computer.

"I need your version of the plans for the new casino resort hotel."

Annetta Hobson

"I have it. I just received it back Tuesday," he responds. "They are faxing me their copy but I would like to view them both," she states with authority.

"Okay…" He lingers. Then he walks over and closes Rayen's door. Her eyes shoot up to him when she hears the door close.

"Was there something else?" she asks dryly

"As a matter of fact, yes." He walks around the chair directly in front of her desk and sits. "I don't know if you knew, but last month, Evelyn and I decided to call it quits. It has been very uncomfortable working with her since then. Her Dad has contacted me about it. I don't want to jeopardize my job by telling them both to go to hell. So, can you please help me?" Rayen pushes her chair back and stands. She walks over to the window and peers out of it.

"I really don't want to get involved. However, you are the best at what you do. I will find a way to talk to them both. This is a major deal we are working on, and the strip mall is almost complete. Soon, we are about to begin the condominiums. I really need you at 100%. I will speak to Evan right away."

"I know this is not professional, but it has gotten a little difficult."

"I understand."

He walks over to the window to get close. "Are you still dating that cop?" She backs away.

"Yes I am."

"I still love you, I will always love you, Rayen." He gets so close; she has to circle the desk to escape.

Light in the Shadow

"Joshua, Blake and I are very serious. We have been together for six months. I love him. I still love you as a friend, but he is who I want to be with," she explains.

"I wish it had been you and I. I could have loved you like he does."

"But, I couldn't have loved you like I love him."

Right then, Angela steps in. "Oh, I'm sorry. Am I interrupting?"

"No, Angela. Come in," Rayen says, welcoming the interruption.

"You have a delivery," Angela announces. She smiles.

"Send it in." She walks out and asks the person to bring it in. A gentleman steps in with a bouquet of flowers so big, they cover the top half of him.

He then speaks, "Hey, baby!" She sashays over to him to plant a great big kiss on his lips.

"Blake! These are beautiful."

"But, they don't hold a candle to you." He hugs her and closes his eyes to enjoy her touch. "I came to whisk you away for a day of relaxation and fun. Can you go?"

"Yes, it is almost time to go anyway. Where are we going?"

"You'll see."

"I'm sorry, Joshua. Are we done?"

He glares at Blake and then at Rayen. "Yes. Just let me know the outcome of that favor." He nods at Blake and struts out of the office.

"And, his problem is?" Blake questions as he sets the flowers on her desk.

"He broke up with Evelyn and her Dad is giving him a hard time. She must still want him," she speaks nonchalantly.

"But, does he still want you?" he asks. She turns to walk to her desk. She bends and retrieves her purse from the draw. He grabs her brown cotton pea coat from the coat rack and opens it to receive her.

"Does he?"

"Yes, but he knows I love you and only you."

He slides her coat over her shoulders. He kisses her in her hair. "Lauryn's Dad tried to bully me at first. When he found out we were done and that I had moved on, he tried to convince me that I was just trying to get back at her for making me wait to get married."

"What did you tell him?" she inquires.

"I told him I found someone that I wanted to be with more than anything else. Lauryn and I are done. He argued with me and even threatened me. But, I didn't care. I found you, and no one can change that," he states. She smiles as they leave her office holding hands.

"I'll be home late, Angela," she announces.

"No, she won't be home tonight, Angela." He corrects her. Angela smiles.

"Okay, have fun!"

As they leave, Evelyn exits her office. She stares at Rayen and Blake. She drags her eyes up and down to examine their body language. "Hello, Rayen…Hello, Detective Pierce." She slithers his name out of her mouth. Rayen's eyes widen. He waves at her with the hand that is not interlocked with Rayen's. "I need some advice," she says as she approaches them. They stop.

Light in the Shadow

"What would that be?" Rayen spouts.

"For the detective," she spits.

"I am off duty, Ms. Drake," he says sternly.

"Oh, it's general." She gets close. Rayen pulls him towards her.

"Call the station, Evelyn!" she smiles.

"I promise it is quick." Rayen's eyes begin to darken. Her rage is brewing. Blake breaks down slightly.

"Go ahead, Ms. Drake. I want to leave so I can enjoy my beautiful lady." Rayen snaps out of her darkness. She looks at Blake. He is waiting for Evelyn's response. He appears very annoyed. He then leans over and kisses her on her ear. Evelyn scans the room.

"Nevermind, Detective Pierce. I can get the info from the station." She flips her hair and storms back to her office to retrieve her coat.

"Thank you, Blake," Rayen purrs.

"For what?" he says.

"For being you," she returns. They leave out of the office.

"I am going to die if you don't tell me where we are going." Rayen screams.

"We're almost there," he adds. They drive for a while. They arrive at a beautiful stretch of condominiums directly on the river.

"Oh my! These condos are absolutely stunning, Blake!" He does not reply as he just smiles. He walks around and opens her door. She steps out of the car and he grabs her hand. "Who lives here?" she asks. He puts his arm around her shoulder and leads her up to the home. They walk up to the door. The beige stone appears to be newly built. The windows are trimmed in brown. The door is the exact color of the window trim. They are connected but each has its own driveway. The neighborhood is serene. There is snow covering the trimmed grass and skeletons of beautiful flowers. From the front, you can see the river stretching across the back. Each condo has its own dock. In the distance, the bridge is visible. You can see the ships passing as the bridge lifts and lowers. "Blake are you going to tell me anything?" He walks to the door and pulls out keys. He puts one in the lock and turns.

"I bought a new house." She laughs.

"Are you serious?"

"Yes, the old one was for Lauryn. We are history, so I decided that house should be as well." She smiles. Tears threaten the base of her eyelids. He grabs her around her waist. "What's wrong, Rayen?" She shakes off the annoying linger of her teary response. "I wanted all memories of Lauryn gone. I waited for years to start with Lauryn, and she didn't want this. I want to start early with you."

"I don't know what to say. This is like a dream or a scene from a romantic movie," she huffs. He laughs.

"Tell me I am the guy who gets the girl this time."

She returns, "Oh sir, you definitely get the girl." They walk in. There is a huge foyer, and the ceilings are tall. Then they enter the living room. It is gorgeous! There are hard wood floors throughout. The dining room is connected to the living room with no separating walls. The kitchen is open with an island in the middle. It has granite counter tops and cherry oak cabinets that align the wall. He then leads her up the stairs to the master bedroom that has a bathroom next to it. Down the hall there are

Light in the Shadow

three more rooms. They have a half bath that separates two of them.

"One day I want you to share this with me." Her skin turns a faint shade of crimson. "Oh! I have something I want to show you," he resounds as they walk to the last room at the end of the hall. When he opens the door, there is a picnic set up in the room. He has a fluffy throw in the center of the floor. There are champagne and crystal wine glasses. He has lobster tails, fresh tossed salad, and French bread sticks. Then for desert, there is a delicious looking strawberry cream cake covered in fresh strawberries.

"Oh Blake, this is the sweetest thing anyone has ever done for me!" she squeals.

"This is just the beginning. I want to do everything I can to make you feel like you are the one. I have a gift for you. I know you have your own money, but I want to be able to give you things."

"Blake!" she exclaims. He shakes his head from side to side and hushes her with his hand.

"Here, it's not what you think." He hands her a glorious blue velveteen box with bright blue bows on it. She slowly grabs it. She opens it. It is a dazzling diamond ring. It is princess cut set in a white gold setting. There are little diamonds that circle the band and stop just before the inside of it. It is about 5 karats.

"Why did you buy this?"

"It's not an engagement ring. It is just to show you I am here to stay. It is my promise that one day I want you to marry me. You don't have to accept it now. I want you to take it and wear it proudly, saying you are mine, no matter what."

"I don't know what to say."

Annetta Hobson

She stares at the box. He starts to fidget. He is so nervous. She takes the ring out of the box and hands it to him. "Can you put it on my finger?" His eyes widen and he smiles ever so bright.

"Rayen, it is crazy how much I love you right now." He slides the ring on her ring finger. He kisses it soft and seductively. "I am moving as slowly as possible because I know this is new to you, but I really want to spend the rest of my life with you," he states. She smiles and spreads her fingers in the air to look at the beautiful ring.

"I love the look of this on my finger." He kisses it once more.

"Let's sit and eat." They sit on the floor and Blake's pours some champagne. They drink and begin to eat. Blake watches her. "I love the way it looks on your finger too." They finish their meal. He grabs some pillows and a comforter out of the closet. He spreads them out and pats the floor for her to join. She crawls over to where he has laid a make shift bed.

"You didn't have to sell your house and buy a new one," she softly speaks. He reaches for her to get closer to him and wraps his arms around her. She snuggles into his chest. He inhales the scent of her hair.

"That was the past, and I want it out of my life," he responds.

"I know. I just don't want you to think I need you to do all of this. I don't plan on going anywhere, and I hope you don't feel you have to do this to keep me."

"I know, Rayen, but I am a man that knows what he wants. And, when I find it, I go for it full throttle."

"Okay."

Light in the Shadow

They lie there for a moment, still locked in an embrace after their talk. "Let's go down to the back patio," he suggests. They go downstairs through the kitchen. They step through the French doors.

"This is absolutely breathtaking. I love the view." She sips from her wine glass as she continues. "You know everyone is going to think this is an engagement ring,"

"I don't care. Do you?"

"No, but what will I say?"

"Say whatever you want."

"Do you want it to be an engagement ring?" He leans back to look at her face.

"I don't know? I know I want to be with you and no one else. The thought of marrying you makes me happy. My Parents strongly believed in being married and they were so happy."

"So do my parents. That's why I am so adamant about having a family. It is more important than anything else."

As they talk, a large ship's horn interrupts them. They stop talking and watch as the ship passes. "It is so peaceful on the water. Living here will be the best thing for you. When are you moving in?"

"This weekend. I have been staying at my parents after I sold the house. No one knows yet. I am having a small get together on Saturday."

"You hid it well. Is that why you have been coming to my condo, so I wouldn't know?"

"Yes, you are correct." He laughs. They glare at the water for a while. "It gets really cold in the winter on the water. It will be more romantic in the summer." They head back in and back to their indoor picnic. They sit on the throw he laid out.

"Can I ask you a serious question?"

"Of course, Rayen."

"Well…are you sure you are not just moving fast because you just want to be a married man, or are you that much in love with me?"

"Rayen, I would never marry just to get married. I love you. And, I know you are the one. I am actually going slowly. I am trying not to run you off."

"Well, why did you wait so long to ask Lauryn?"

"I wasn't sure she was the one. I waited because I didn't feel strong about it. After being together for so long, it just seemed like the right thing to do. So when she basically said no, I was pissed because I felt like I wasted my time and love on her. We were just not meant to be, but you and I are!"

She smiles then turns away. When she returns her eyes to his, her expression becomes intense. "What about children? I don't know if I want children."

"Why, Rayen? Children are the ultimate gift."

"I can't imagine it. My parents were taken from me. I don't think that I could put a child through that."

"Just because it happened to you doesn't mean it will happen to our child."

She smiles again. "Our child."

"Let's cut this conversation and start practicing."

"Practicing?"

"For our future child."

Light in the Shadow

He lays her back and began to unbutton her blouse. She places her hand at her side. He opens the blouse and hungrily stares at her. She slides her arms out of the blouse. "I just want to make love to you, Rayen, endlessly." He then slides her out of her skirt. He scans her body. She is lying there like food on a platter. He wants a taste. He begins kissing her stomach. He plants soft wet kisses along the line beneath her belly button.

"Do you mind if I get right to it? I really want to feel you. I want your moistness to drench me."

"Yes, I want you inside me. I need it now."

He looks into her eyes and kisses her, invading her mouth. He slides his slacks and his boxers off. He pops the buttons pulling off his shirt. He slides his hands through her luxurious hair. He stares deep into her eyes and enters her. He slides in and out of her, enjoying every stroke. "It feels so good," he whispers. He begins to grind, plunging deeper. He circles his hips around and around. She answers him as she matches his desire. She grinds back, lifting her body from the floor, circling her own hips. She has become so skilled with her body movements, resembling that of professional dancer. He moans each time she pleasures him with movement. "Oh, woman, you have put a spell on me with your delicious center." They buck back and forth breathing heavily. The movements become rapid. She wraps her legs around him. He caresses her legs as she lifts them. He kisses her passionately. Her head is spinning. The movements become even faster. Soon, he groans loudly, releasing inside her, and she immediately follows. He collapses on top of her. She drops her legs, wraps her arms around him, and strokes his back slowly.

"I love you so much, Blake. And for the record, if this was an engagement ring, I would have said yes." He jerks his head to look at her. The sweat from their heated moment slings in her face. She turns her head and wipes the sweat.

"Really, Rayen? You would have said yes?"

"With my entire heart, definitely yes. I love you like I have never known I could love."

Blake slides beside her and wraps his arms around her in a soulful embrace. Rayen closes her eyes and nestles deep into his hold. He cradles her and kisses her hair.

Blake watches her serene somber. He is entranced by her beauty. "She wants to be my wife. Where have you been all my life? I've wasted my affection on Lauryn, and now she wants to destroy the love we share. I should whisk your beautiful ass away tonight, but then my parents would be angry they didn't get to share that with me. They know I am gone. You got me acting like a love sick teenager," he whispers to her while she sleeps. He scoops her head up in his arm so she can rest on his muscular chest. She wiggles and snuggles in. He lies back with one arm around her and the other resting beneath his mussed golden hair. He stares at the ceiling wondering about marriage and family with her. He stares so long; he begins to drift off.

Rayen jumps up and looks at her watch. It is 6 a.m.! She needs to be in the office today at eight. She balances herself on her palm to stand. Blake doesn't flinch. "He sleeps so hard." She laughs. She begins to dress. She nudges him. "Blake, I have to go home and change for work." He turns over and lies on his stomach. He moans as he flips.

"Come on sleepy head. I have to go."

"Baby, take the car and come get me later for work. I am exhausted. You wore me out yesterday with that good moist toy between your thighs."

Light in the Shadow

She smiles. He points towards the keys in his pants pocket. She grabs his pants and his keys falls out. His phone chirps very low from his pocket. She grabs it and pushes the button so it doesn't disturb him. She tries to silence it when she spots a text.

Text Messages (2)   Picture message(1)   Missed calls(4)

December 17th, Friday 2:25 a.m.

From: Lauryn

> *Hi baby! Just because you ignore me does not mean I am going away. I will never stop loving you. I want to be your wife, and I will. So, play with your little bitch. Get it out of your system and come back to me. That home you bought two years ago is ours. That bed is the one we made love in. I will do whatever it takes to get you back. I wish I would have kept the baby you planted inside me. I still cry about it. I was an idiot. Give me one more chance, and I will never fuck up again. I love you!!!*

December 17th, Friday 3:05am

From: Lauryn

> *Baby, please answer me. I know you have not gotten over me that quick. Five years does not just go away!!! We shared more than that little tramp could ever imagine. You complete me, and there is no one else for me. Please, do not do this to me. I will never give you up. You are MY soul mate. MINE!!!*
>
> *I will be up there tonight. When I get there, I am coming to see you. I do not care if she is with you or not. I will come to the station if I have to. That bitch better let you go, or I will make her wish she never step foot in Michigan!!*

I love you, Blake!!!

(Picture retrieved)

From: Lauryn

December 17th, Friday 4:21am

> *Rayen gasps when the picture loads. "This woman is desperate. A nude picture, really?" She rolls her eyes. The picture is of Lauryn on Blake's bed with her blonde hair draped over her breasts. She is lying back on her arms. Her long legs are arched to one side. She has on a pair of red heels. Someone took the picture. "I am assuming Blake snapped this." She places the phone back in his pocket and turns to check if he is still sleeping peacefully. He snuggles his head deep into the pillow. She smiles and leaves. She unlocks his door and gets in. She drives to her house to change. When she arrives, she goes in and showers. She hurries about and runs to her closet. Angela is dressed and drinking coffee in her room. She spots Rayen hurrying past.*

"Hey lady," she yells as she peeks out.

"Hey," Rayen returns. She follows Rayen into her room. Rayen is running around from the bathroom to the room, getting ready.

"Well, did you enjoy yourself?" Angela asks playfully.

"Yes," she states.

"You did? You aren't acting like it."

"I don't want to be late, Angie."

Light in the Shadow

As she slides on her cream blouse and buttons it, Angela spots the diamond. "Eek!" she screams. "Did Black give you that?!"

"Yes, Angela," Rayen responds.

"Oh my goodness," she says, admiring it. Rayen slides on her beige pencil skirt and blazer to match. She finishes the look with knee high brown butter leather boots.

"Did he…oh my…did he?"

"It is a promise ring. He was afraid to ask so soon. He thought it would scare me off."

"Whatever! That is an engagement ring. You wearing it definitely screams a yes! I want to be your maid of honor. I want to help plan. I cannot wait to tell Mom. She is going to freak. When is the wedding? Are you having kids? I want to be an aunt. Yay!" Angela goes on and on.

"Calm down. We haven't gotten that far."

"I'm sorry. I knew he was the one. But, since Joshua has broken it off with Evelyn, he wants you again. What are you going to say to him?"

Rayen stops walking and turns to her.

"Nothing. It is none of his business. I have to go, and so do you."

They walk out the door, and Sterling is awaiting them as usual. "I am driving today Sterling." Rayen informs. "Yes ma'am," he returns as he opens the door for Angela. She then hops in Blake's Camaro and drives off.

All day at the office, people eyeball her new ring. They all just watch her. She gets the plans from the resort and scans them. She grabs Joshua's version to compare the two. "Angela, call Josh." Rayen directs from her office.

Angela replies immediately, "Right away." Minutes later, Joshua appears at her door.

"Knock, knock." She motions her hand towards him to enter. He steps in and sits.

"What's up?" he questions.

"Well, I was going over the plans. It appears that you have an extra space on your copy," she answers sternly. He stands and walks around her desk to investigate. He leans over her and inhales her intoxicating scent.

"Umm…yes. Victor called me and asked me to add another banquet hall."

"Victor?"

"Victor is their head of design."

"Next time, just inform me first."

"Okay, I will."

She turns to look at him. He backs up and moves back to his seat.

"While I am here, can you speak with Evan?"

"Oh, of course."

She grabs her phone and dials Mr. Drake.

"Hello. Hi, Mr. Drake."

"Hello, Rayen. How is everything?"

"Everything is on schedule so far."

"So, what can I do for you?"

Light in the Shadow

I don't know how to put this, so I will just spit it out. I know Joshua and Evelyn broke up."

"Don't worry. Those love birds will work it out." He cuts her off.

"No, Evan. That is what I am calling about. Joshua is feeling very uncomfortable. He says he doesn't want to jeopardize his job, but he feels as if this is becoming a problem since you became involved and all."

"Evelyn told me they were serious, and she wanted to spend her life with him. I had no idea it was not mutual."

"I do not know nor do I want to know the details, but I treasure his presence, and I want everyone to be able to maintain professionalism."

"Of course, Rayen, I agree."

"Could you possibly pass that along to Evelyn so we can work in a peaceful environment?"

"Yes, right away. I can contact her now. Give my apologies to Mr. Manning."

"I will. Thank you so much."

They end their call. Joshua is very pleased. "This has been bothering you?" Rayen questions.

He answers, "Yes. I don't want to harm my dad and Evan's friendship. I definitely don't want my business arrangements affected, so thanks a lot."

"No problem," she says as she tucks her hair behind her ears. As soon as she does that, Joshua spots her ring. "What's that, Rayen?"

She quickly scans her clothing. "What?"

"Your ring finger. Is that what I think it is?"

"My personal affairs shouldn't concern you, Josh."

He abruptly stands and storms toward her desk. He slams his fist on it. "But, damn it, it does. Why the fuck can't I get over your ass?" He storms out of her office and slams the door.

Angela runs in. "You alright, Rye? I mean, Ms. Vasu?" she waves her hand.

"I'm fine."

"He spotted the ring, huh?"

"Yes, he did."

Moments later he storms out of his office with his brief case and bomber jacket on. Rayen just watches him leave. Evelyn runs out of her office just in time to catch his dramatic exit. She looks around and spots Rayen watching. She storms toward her office. Rayen sees her coming. "Shit." She enters and closes the door. "What is it Evelyn?" she asks.

"You fucking called my Dad. How fucking dare you?" She paces back and forth staring at Rayen. "It is bad enough the man I love wants you. He broke it off with me because he couldn't think about anything else. Then on top of it all, you call my Dad? You have hell of a nerve to do that! Yes, I tried to convince Dad to get him to come back to me! I was desperate, but you are always in the way. Connor wanted you and now my Joshua. He is mine!" She screams.

"I don't want him Evelyn. I didn't want Connor either. We were kids."

"You think you are so special because men think you are beautiful. But, women hate you. I hate you!" She stands.

Light in the Shadow

"I could care less what you bitches think of me. I hate them and you, too. Get the fuck out of my office before I drag your ass out bleeding."

She whispers so low it is barely audible. "What did you say?' she asks, eyes wide.

When Rayen steps close, Angela quickly bursts in and says, "Why are you yelling? Get out of here." Evelyn whisks around towards Angela.

"I was leaving anyway. I was just informing my boss of my transfer. My Dad is sending me to the office in New York." She flings her hair and storms from her office.

Angela closes the door. "What just happened?" Rayen sits in her chair and slides it under the desk. She unbuttons her blazer and slides it off.

"She still loves Josh, and apparently women hate me." She begins to type on her computer.

"I don't, Rayen. I love you and your beauty," Angela says with encouragement.

"My beauty is my curse. That is why there is merely a twinkle of light in my enormous shadow," she speaks softly.

"What, Rayen?" Angela states, puzzled.

"Nothing, pay no attention to my rambling," she returns in her stern voice. Angela shakes her head and exits. Rayen continues to work on her computer. Her day started in a tornado. And, it is going to get worse…because Lauryn is going to Blake's job, and she plans to be there.

Chapter 10

Blake reaches over and grabs the pillow. "Ummm." He inhales the scent. He lies back and slides his hands behind his head. He clasps his hands together to rest on them. He stares at the beautifully painted taupe ceiling. He reminisces on the night before. "I can't believe she accepted my ring. I was so afraid she would run. I thought that she would say I was moving too fast. She actually said she would marry me if I had asked. After Lauryn, I never thought I would want to ask anyone to marry me ever again." He wipes his face and stretches. He crawls over to his pants and peeks at his cell phone.

It's 2:30 p.m. He notices he has missed a call. "Four missed calls?" He scrolls down to see who called. "What the fuck? Lauryn?"

He slams the phone on the floor.

I could barely get a call from her when I wanted one, and now she won't stop. What is wrong with her? It's over!

He stands and walks to the bathroom. He turns the shower on and takes off his boxers. He steps in the shower. He places his hands on the wall and bows his head so the water runs down his face. He grabs his body wash and washes his hair. As he rinses, he reminisces on the rare times he spent with Lauryn. The times she washed his hair in the shower and the way they would make love after.

She loved to wash his hair. She said his hair was gorgeous and she loved how it looked after it was clean. It is curly like an eighties hunk, the wild look.

He recalls why he fell in love with her. They had fun in the beginning. Their relationship was not perfect, but when they were together they were happy. He remembers how perky her breasts were and how she loved for him to gently bite her nipples.

He thinks about how she enjoyed putting him in her mouth. She was quite the lover when she allowed time for it. That was the only reason it dragged on for five years. He shakes his head really hard to release the thoughts of her.

What am I doing? She is really trying to get in my head. He lathers up his body and rinses off. *I can't believe I am actually thinking about her. She hurt my heart, my pride, and made me look like a fool. I don't love her nor do I desire her anymore.*

He steps out of the shower and dries off and goes to his new closet. There is only a black blazer, white shirt and black slacks. He gets dressed and heads down stairs to find a bite. "I must go shopping. I have no furniture, clothes, or food here."

He looks around in the doubled door titanium refrigerator. All he finds is some strawberries he had left from his indoor picnic with Rayen. His picnic with Rayen went just as he hoped it would. He relives how her hair blew in the chilled air as they watched the ships ride pass in the icy water. *I could watch her for hours without doing anything. I am beguiled by this woman with no imagination of anything else. She is just an extraordinary woman, and she returns my affection. As tough as she seems to be, she is just as smitten as I am. I think.*

He eats the strawberries and sits on the counter, waiting for Rayen to arrive.

Blake walks over to the window and catches a glimpse of Rayen approaching. He runs and slides on his shoes. He grabs his keys and hurry out of the door. She spots him coming out. "Am I late?" She looks at her watch as she slides out of the car.

Light in the Shadow

"No, I don't have a TV yet, so I was just twiddling my thumbs." He jogs over to her and scoops her into his arms to plant a luscious kiss on her shiny glossed lips. "Ooooo. I missed you," he whispers.

She leans back to look into his eyes as she says, "I really missed you too, Blake. I had such a terrible day. I couldn't wait to get back to you."

"What happened?" he says, concerned. She explains her incident with Josh and her blow up with Evelyn.

"He was upset about the ring?"

"Yes. Very…"

"He still has feelings for you, but Evelyn is in love with him?"

"I guess, but she is just obsessed. She is smothering him. Anyway, her father is sending her off to New York."

"Why doesn't Joshua want her? She is very sexy, smart, and successful."

She hitches her brow. "Very sexy, huh?"

"Oh no, not nearly as sexy as you."

"Great save, Detective."

He laughs. They stand with the driver door open, kissing and rubbing each other for a moment. He breaks their kiss. "I need to go before I carry you in the house and rip those clothes off you." She smiles, and they unleash their grasp of one another. He gets in the driver seat and they leave.

When they get to Rayen's condo, he sits there for a moment. Rayen opens her door to step out. "Wait." He grabs her hand. She turns to look at his face. "Rayen…" she lifts her eyebrows in worry.

"Yes, Blake?"

"How did this happen? You really do something to me, and it's not just about your beauty. It is the way you sashay into a room, the way you swing your hair when you release it from being up, the smell of your skin, the evil look you give people when you feel threatened, and even the way you dress. It's like you have a spell on me." He shakes his head.

"I love you, Blake." She kisses him to stop him from going on and slides out of the car. She waves before she disappears into her house.

When Blake gets to work, he has a lot of paperwork. He is helping the traffic officers with their daily reports. Samuel walks over to Blake's desk. "What are you doing?"

Blake remarks with sarcasm, "I am helping out, something you should do."

"No thanks man. I am a detective, not a traffic or patrol cop," Sam returns with more sarcasm.

"Okay, Wilcox. You know my dad wants me to take over one day, so I have to be willing to do everything," he reveals sincerely.

"Well, not me. I do what I am paid to do," he laughs. Blake continues to read and type on his computer. He separates papers and enters information in the system.

"Well, I think we found Missy Alexander."

"Really? When can we question her?"

"Chicago police already questioned her about a robbery her new boyfriend was involved in."

"She is in Chicago?"

Light in the Shadow

"Yes, and I informed them that she was wanted for questioning in a murder investigation involving her fiancé."

"Well?"

"They allowed Detective Kate Bergman and Detective Adam King, the new chief's son, to go down and question her last night. We will know something in a couple of hours."

"Alright then. Just keep me posted."

He peers back at his computer screen and gets back to work.

"Hello, officer. I am here…"

"To see Detective Pierce? I remember you, Ms. Fleming."

Lauryn smiles. "You should remember your colleague's fiancé." She lifts her hand and displays the ring Blake gave her two years ago. She looks at the door and reminisces on the day he gave it to her…

***

Two years ago, Thursday June 25th, 9:39 p.m. at Charlevoix's Lounge in Mt. Pleasant. He surprised her by driving up from Bay City. He was waiting outside the federal building with a bouquet of the most exquisite flowers. She smiled because he looked so gorgeous. His golden blond hair curly and wild like she loved. He was wearing a black suit with a black and gray swirled tie and black shirt. He makes a suit look like a sin. She ran to him.

"What are you doing here, babe?"

"I just wanted to see you. I couldn't wait till our weekend."

"Well, these are some beautiful flowers."

He smiled. They got into his white Cadillac CTS and headed out. They pulled up in front of the lounge, and the valet guy takes the car. They walked in, and their families were there to surprise them. Lauryn's parents with Blake's entire family stood when the couple entered the private room. The room was beautifully decorated. It had balloons, flowers, and candles. Emily stepped up. "Hi, Lauryn. How are you?" She hugged her. She was so confused. Blake grabbed her hand and pulled her to the center of the room. "Lauryn, we have been together for three years." She scanned the room nervously as he spoke. "You are driven. I know you love your job, and I love you for that because we are so alike. I have asked your father, and he has given me his blessing. Her mouth dropped.

"Blake, I..." he continued.

"I want to share my life with you." He dropped to one knee in the middle of the room. He pulled out a square box and popped it open. It had a lovely pear-shaped 4-karat diamond solitaire with a gold band in it. "Lauryn Fleming, will you do me the honor of being my wife?" Her face flushed red. She pulled him off of his knees. She was no longer smiling.

"I'm sorry, excuse me, everyone." They all looked at one another. She pulled Blake out of the private room. Blake's face was flushed with embarrassment. "What's wrong, Lauryn? You don't want to marry me? I bought us a beautiful home. The one we used to drive past all the time. The one you said you wanted. I got rid of the apartment. I want to have a family with you...say something to me, Lauryn."

"Blake...I, I just got the respect I deserve, and my position is solid. I can't leave Mt. Pleasant. I love you so much, but...I can't marry you right now. I can't have a family now. I need you to understand, I am not saying no, just not now," she stated apologetically as she grabbed his face. His eyes were very sad. He gently pulled her hands down. "Just keep the ring. When you put it on, I will know that you are saying yes."

Light in the Shadow

***

She smiles at his last words. She looks down at the pear-shaped diamond on her finger. She was so deep in her thoughts, she did not notice the officer leaving the desk. He returns. "I think Pierce stepped out for lunch, so you can wait in the interview room. That's where they eat lunch."

"Okay, don't tell him I'm here. Just let him come back," she directs.

"Okay, will do," he says. She goes into the interview room and lets down the blinds. She has on a long black coat with a white corset and white thongs underneath. She has on black thigh high boots to match her coat. She walks around the table tracing the edges with her finger. Finally she sits.

Blake enters to the station with Sam. They are discussing the details they received from Bergman and King. "She eluded us for so long man. She disappeared the day we went to question her. She emptied his accounts and fled," Sam states.

"And, she has no alibi," Blake resounds with excitement.

"Slam dunk!" Sam screams. They walk pass the front desk. They laugh as they enter the interview room. Sam stops in his tracks. "Whoa!" Blake turns to see what Sam is gawking at. His eyes scan the room and he spots Lauryn sitting with her legs stretched to reach the table. The heel of her black boots rests on the edge.

"Lauryn, what the hell are you doing here?" She stands and slithers toward him. She releases her coat and let it fall open.

"Damn!" Sam screams. "Looks like you've been keeping in shape, Fleming." She throws her head back and swings her hair. Sam slaps Blake on the back. "I think I'll eat at my desk and leave you two alone." He leaves the interview room before Blake can protest.

"Lauryn, get the hell out of here! You are out of line!" he yells. She lifts her hand to show him the ring.

"I told you I am ready, baby. See, I love you. I am ready to have your child. Can she promise you that now? I am at a place where I can give it all to you now! You have to wait for her. She is young and ambitious like I was. She has to build her company in the name of her Dad. Marriage and children are not in your near future with her." She walks over and stops when they are face to face. "I love you, Blake," she whispers through her teeth. She caresses his face. He grabs her hands to break her grasp. She leans forward and presses her lips to his. She desperately kisses his lips. He grabs her shoulders and pushes her back.

"Are you insane?"

Rayen pulls up to the station. She checks her watch. "1:30 a.m." She leans back and turns off the engine. She saw Blake and Sam leave when Lauryn arrived 30 minutes ago. "Maybe I should just call him and tell him about the text. I don't like being deceitful. He doesn't deserve this." Just as she picks up the phone to dial, Blake and Sam return. She watches as they enter the station. She debates if she should go in. After about 15 minutes, she gets out of her car. She enters, but no officers are at the desk. She searches the rooms. Midway down the hall, she runs into an older officer.

"Hello, young lady. Can I help you?"

"Yes, I am looking for Detective Pierce," she answers. "And, you are?" he interrogates.

She coolly responds, "I'm Rayen, his girlfriend."

"Go to the interview room, I think. They always have lunch in there at night."

Light in the Shadow

The officer shrugs as she says, "Thanks." He points her to the room and goes his way. She gets to the interview room, and the blinds are drawn. Her heart drops in her stomach. She feels her breathing speed up. She clasps her chest. "What's wrong with me?" She listens to the door first. She really can't hear anything but muffled sounds. Her heart beats becomes more rapid. So she turns the knob very carefully and opens it slowly.

"I love you! Blake, please don't do this! I've been calling and texting you. Why haven't you answered? When will you realize she is not the one, but I am? Does that mean anything?" she pleads.

"No, it doesn't, Lauryn! Something is wrong with you. You can't be functioning at work like this," he exclaims.

"I don't care about anything but you." She tosses the coat on the floor and leaps in his arms. "I need you, baby, please. I can't spend another day without you. He looks at her with pity. He shakes his head. As he is attempting to put her on the floor, the door slings open. They catch eyes. Rayen's eyes are wider than he has ever seen.

"Blake, I…" She turns to leave. "I am the biggest idiot ever. Why did I come?" Blake drops Lauryn on the floor and chases her.

"Rayen! Rayen!" She looks back at him as tears stream down her face. She stops and allows him to catch up. "Rayen, it is not what you think."

"It doesn't matter. I got what I deserved," she softly speaks.

"What are you talking about?" he asks, puzzled.

"Never mind. I've got to go." She walks out of the door, jumps in her car, and drives off. Blake just stands there and watches her car drive away.

Annetta Hobson

After a few minutes, he reenters the station and walks over to the lobby to sit. He looks up at Lauryn. "You didn't want me. And, you don't want me to be with anyone else. You just showed up here and ruined my relationship with someone I am very much in love with. Why?" He speaks almost inaudibly.

"I didn't just show up. I called, and I texted you. I said I was coming. When you didn't reply, I just came. But, I always wanted you, and I always will," she says painfully.

"A text that said what? I didn't receive any text. When?"

"This morning, and I sent that sexy picture you took of me in our room."

He sits there with his head down. The other officers come to poke fun at him. "Awww, Pierce. Two women, one night. Drama." One of them says. Sam doesn't laugh.

"Lauryn, you should go." She looks at Sam and rolls her eyes.

"I am not leaving until Blake tells me to." She looks at Blake. He doesn't respond. Sam walks up to Blake and nudges him.

"Come on man, go call Rayen." But, he just sits there and says nothing. Lauryn sits next to him. She puts her arm around him. He is staring at the floor, and his hands are clutched together in his lap. Lauryn kisses his hair. She rubs his back, but he doesn't move. Finally, he stands.

"I'm going home, Sam."

"Okay. Are you gonna be alright?" Sam asks with concern. He tries to smile. He goes to the back and grabs his jacket. No one says anything else.

"What about me? Please…" Lauryn trots behind him like a puppy. He gets in his car and Lauryn hops in. He looks at her.

Light in the Shadow

"Please go."

She sternly states, "No."

He reasserts, "Lauryn please get the fuck out of my car!" She hops out, and he speeds off. She runs to her car and follows him.

Blake drives with one hand on his head with his elbow resting on the door and the other on the wheel. Before he realizes it, he is in front of Rayen's condo. He steps out of his car, walks up to the door, and pushes the buzzer. He waits for what seems like forever and then Angela finally answers. "Yes."

"Angela, let me in. I need to see her," he asks.

"I'm sorry, Blake. She doesn't want to talk," she returns.

He pleads, "I didn't do anything. I need to see her, please?" Angela sighs. She feels terrible for doing this to him. Rayen was explaining everything to her when he buzzed. She doesn't understand why she is reacting this way.

"I can't. Maybe you should call her tomorrow." He drops his hands to his side and slowly walks to his car. Rayen goes to the window just in time to see his handsome face. He looks so sad. She wants to call to him, but she doesn't. She closes the window and goes to her room. She lies across the bed and cries herself to sleep.

Blake drives to his parents' home. He just does not want to sleep on the floor tonight. He pulls in their circle drive way and parks his car. He lays his head back for a moment to think. "I am being punished for thinking about her. I let myself think about the past when she is my future." He lifts his head snatches his keys out of the ignition. He walks up to the door. He takes out his key to their house and enters. As he closes the door, his Dad greets him.

"Hello, Blake. I thought you were staying in the new house. Is something wrong?" Before he can close the door, Lauryn steps in. "Lauryn, what are you…" he stops and looks at Blake. Blake looks at her.

"What are you doing, Lauryn?" he says exhausted.

"I want to be here with you. Please?" she begs. He looks at his dad.

"Son, we will talk later this morning."

"Alright, Dad," he whispers. His father heads down the hall and up the stairwell to his bedroom. Blake looks at her and rolls his eyes. "Why are you here? Just go home, Lauryn. I am done with this." She steps toward him.

"I am not going home. I came to get you back, and I am not leaving." He turns away and mopes down the hall to the guest room. Lauryn carefully follows. He enters the room. When he tries to close the door, she slides her high heel boot in the door.

"Lauryn, I don't have the strength to fight you tonight…this morning…whatever." He slides off his jacket and lays it on the rocking chair. He plops on the bed and lies back. "Get out, Lauryn!"

"No!"

"Fuck it! You are a crazy ass woman. Why weren't you so adamant six months ago, shit, a year ago? Why now? I love her, not you. I don't want you, I want her! And, you fucked it all up!"

"I will take you. She doesn't know you like I do. If she doesn't believe you, she doesn't deserve you. I would never doubt you. I made mistakes and embarrassed you. I made you wait on my answer, aborted your child, and…" He jumps up.

Light in the Shadow

"What? You did what Lauryn? Please don't tell me that. You are making that shit up! Are you?" He stands, tears weld in his eyes. He walks over to her and grabs her arms. "You killed a child of mine? You know I want children. How could you do that shit! I don't believe you. You are fucking lying!" He releases her and walks to the window. As much as he wants to cry, he doesn't. The tears just set there. She continues on.

"I promise it is true. I have proof. I kept the ultrasound picture. It was right before you met her. I kept begging you to just try to make it work. I wanted that baby so bad. I really desired for us to be a family, but you met her and dropped me. I was so lonely and hurt. I wanted to tell you the night I came here. But, you were with her. And, I was going to tell Em, but I decided to just end it." He turns to her.

"That's why you've been acting like this?"

"Yes. Being pregnant with your child for those months made me see things differently. Nothing and no one is more important to me right now. I wanted your child to grow inside me, but I had to have you along with it. I couldn't do it alone. I just couldn't." She begins to cry. "It was the hardest thing I ever had to do, and I did it alone." He walks over to her and sits. He pulls her down on the bed.

"I am so, so sorry you experienced that. You should have told me." She wipes her eyes and look up at him.

"Would it have made any difference?" she asks.

"I don't know. I would have been there for you though," he answers honestly.

"I want your child inside me again. I really do. Please give me another chance," she speaks through the continue flow of tears. He places his arms around her and holds her. They sit in silence for a few minutes. She dries her eyes on his t-shirt. He laughs. She slips out of her coat. He drags his eyes over her model type body. She is in perfect physical shape. When he looks up, her breathing is rapid. Her chest rises and falls. She gazes into his eyes. "I have always been mesmerized by your beautiful blue eyes." He turns away. She grabs his chin and pulls his eyes back to hers. "I want to have your baby. Please let me be with you forever." She kisses him. He pulls he face away from her grasp.

"No," he whispers. She smiles. He isn't yelling. She feels as if she is wearing him down. She reaches for his pants to unbutton them. He grabs her hands. "No." she slides his hands off of hers. She unzips them and gets on her knees.

"I want you in my mouth, Blake. I know her lips don't feel like mine. I know her tongue doesn't circle it like mine." She licks her lips. "I know her mouth doesn't slide up and down around and around it like mine." He doesn't speak. He just watches her as she licks her lips and rubs his erection through his pants. She glides up his legs, plants a seductive kiss on it, slips her hand into the slit in his boxers, and then pulls it out. She shakes it in her hand. It is very stiff. "Oh, yes, just as I remember. I have dreamed of you, all of you in my mouth. Ooooo, look at it. I know this is too much for her. I was built to handle this." Just before she slides her mouth over it he grabs her head.

"Stop! Lauryn, I can't. I really love her." He stands and tucks himself back in, then zips his pants. He grabs her shoulders and urges her to stand. "I am so sorry you felt you had to abort our baby. I wish you hadn't, but we are never going to be together. I love Rayen, and that is not going to change." She stands and reaches for her coat.

"I am not done. I will never stop. I have felt you inside me. I have felt our baby grow inside me. I long to feel it again, even

Light in the Shadow

though it was for a few months. No matter what I have to do, I will get you back." She eases her coat on and ties the belt. She then walks over and kisses him on the lips. She smiles and walks out down the hall and out of the door. He follows and locks the door. After he locks it, he leans against the door and breathes. He shakes his head and walks back to the room. He undresses, but leaves on a white Hanes t-shirt and boxers. He climbs in bed and falls asleep.

"Rayen, would you like breakfast?" Angela says as she knocks on her door. She doesn't answer. Angela nudges at the door. When she peeks in, she sighs. "Rayen, this is so dumb. Tell him you looked at his phone. I'm sure you guys will get past this. Just tell him." She peeks out from under her comforter.

"I can't. He'll think I don't trust him. Why did I erase the messages? It was so juvenile of me." Angela sits on her bed.

"Talk to him," she whispers.

"I showed up to his job like a stalker. He is going to think I am nuts!" She throws the comforter over her head. "I am never leaving this spot, at least not for the rest of the weekend." Angela throws her hands in the air and leaves. Rayen closes her eyes. "Why can't I act normal? I may have destroyed the only normal relationship I've had since my…" She starts to cry. She holds her hand in the air against the comforter. She stares at the ring on her finger. She hasn't removed the ring since he placed it on her finger, not even to wash her hands. She pushes the cover down to her waist. She looks up at the ceiling, and slaps both her hands over her eyes.

Chapter 11

Sunday morning, December 19th. at 9:30 a.m., Rayen sits up. The sun is extremely bright. Snow has fallen the night before. It is not very much, but it is covering everything. Rayen slides out of bed and walks over to enter the bathroom. When she steps in, she glances at the mirror. Her eyes are puffy from crying. She wants to call Blake, but she is afraid of telling him about the picture and the texts. "I could have prevented the whole ordeal." She shakes her head, grasps the sink, and steadies herself. Knock, knock! "Come in, Angie!" she yells from the bathroom.

"Are you okay?"

"Yes, I am fine."

"Why won't you talk to him?"

"I can't. I am so foolish."

"Okay. Well, we need groceries today. There is nothing to cook."

"I guess I can go to the store. I will get dressed."

Angela goes to her room. Rayen gets dressed. She slips on a pair of dark blue jeans and a black cardigan sweater. She slides on a pair of black riding boots. She pulls her hair into a ponytail. She grabs her black pea coat and keys. When she gets to the garage, she climbs into her car. She leans back, starts the engine, and the garage door lifts. She heads to the store.

When she gets to the market, she retrieves a basket and goes in. She scans the shelves for things she and Angela enjoy eating. "Oh, Angela wanted Oreos." She searches for the cookie aisle. When she finds it, she turns her basket and Lauryn is standing there glaring at the different types of crackers. Rayen tries to turn back, but she spots her.

"Ahhhh, the young and very beautiful Rayen Vasu. The little CEO that stole my man," she laughs sarcastically. Rayen stands straight.

"Excuse me." she tries to pass. Lauryn positions her basket so she can't. Rayen stiffens and looks to the ceiling. "What would you like to say to me so I can continue shopping?" Rayen spits with venom in her words.

"Well…" she smiles. "I want him back. I will have him back, especially after yesterday."

"What do you mean?" She hitches her brow. Lauryn laughs and tosses her gorgeous blond hair.

"We went back to his parents' home after you rejected him. I shared details about our child I was pregnant with earlier this year." She stares Rayen right in her eyes. Rayen gasps as she Lauryn licks her lips. "He was very torn about it. We shared a luscious treat after our talk. Sorry, I was always the one, honey." Rayen looks at the ring. Lauryn follows her eyes. "Oh! He proposed?" her eyes grow wide. Rayen doesn't speak. She slaps the basket out of the way and grabs her hand to get a better look.

"Let me go, bitch!" Rayen snaps. She snatches her hand back. Lauryn runs her hands through her hair and looks around nervously.

"I have one too!" She displays her hand with an engagement ring on it. Rayen shakes her head.

"How pathetic are you? You kept a ring for two and a half years and then decide to put it on after he has moved on. Oh, yes! You are on your way down the aisle." Rayen states sarcastically as she rolls her eyes. Lauryn purses her lips. She

Light in the Shadow

steps closer. Rayen does not move. She just drags her eyes down to her feet and back up to her eyes.

"Pathetic? Is it pathetic that we went to the guest room at mom and dad's? Was it pathetic that I got on my knees and put him in my throat? And, I enjoyed every fucking minute of it." Rayen steps back and turns away so she does not see her tears welding. Lauryn smiles. "Yes, Rayen. Be hurt. He loved it. I gave him something you will never be able to provide as I do. All I have to do is get him alone, and he forgets his distractions. He always said I was the 'BEST' he ever had." Lauryn stares at her to see if she will react, but Rayen does not give her the satisfaction.

"I have to go. I am buying groceries for my new apartment!" she says with a huge smile and sashays to the next aisle. Rayen is horrified. She turns her cart to continue shopping, but the confrontation with her was just too much. She leaves her cart and dashes from the store. She gets into her car and slams the back of her head against the seat. Tears are streaming down her cheeks. She strikes the steering wheel again and again until she screams. "What the fuck is wrong with me?! First, I don't attract anyone but rapists and losers. Then, I push the men I do love to other women." She leans on the wheel and cries for what seems like hours. She looks at her watch. It reads, "12:15 p.m." She wipes her eyes, starts the car, and heads home.

Half way to her condo she thinks, "Fuck this!" She twirls the car around and heads to the Pierce home. She pulls into the driveway and parks behind Blake's Camaro. She sits in her car for a moment. She finally gets out of her car and approaches the door. She pauses for a minute to build up the courage.

Emily answers the door. "Rayen? Hi."

"Hello, Emily. Is Blake here?"

"Yes, yes, come in. I just made a great lunch. Are you hungry?"

"No, thank you," Rayen says as she follows her. She rubs her hands together to contain her nervousness. They walk down the main hall as they pass the guest room. Rayen looks in. She spots the bed he slept in. Her tears form in the crease of her eyes. She looks to the floor. Emily asks with concern, "Are you ok?" Rayen sniffs.

"No." Emily stops walking and hugs her.

"What's wrong?" Danielle steps out of the family room.

"Who was at the…Oh." She returns to the family room. Emily grabs her hand and leads her there. Blake is sitting next to his father watching television. Everyone's eyes rest on Rayen. Blake shoots out of his seat.

"Rayen! What…" He hurries to her and places his hands on her shoulders. "Why are you crying?" She wipes her eyes with her hand. Emily sits down in his spot.

"I am so sorry for interrupting your Sunday," Rayen says, sniffling to his family. She is a mess, and Blake has not witnessed this side of her, even after the night she first shared her feelings. He softly touches her back to lead her out of the family room and into the guest room. When she enters the guest room she looks at the bed. She scans the room. Finally, her eyes rest on him. He stares at her with worry.

"Is this about what happened at the station? Because it is not what it looked like." She shakes her head.

"No, I know that. I ran into Lauryn at the market… " He stops her.

"What did she say?" he says as he turns away.

Light in the Shadow

"First I want to tell you I believed you." She speaks slowly. "I knew she would be there." He turns toward her again.

"How?"

"When I got your keys, your phone fell out. I read the texts she sent and erased them. That is why I didn't want to face you last night. I was ashamed of my childish actions. I thought you wouldn't want a woman that sunk to such childish lows." He walks over to her. Before he can embrace her, she places her hands on his chest. "No!"

"I thought you said you believed me?"

"Lauryn was at the market."

"Oh. What did she say to you?" he says in a hushed tone. She turns her back and begins to cry. "She said she made love to you with her mouth! In this room on this bed!" He widens his eyes.

"What!"

"So, are you telling me she wasn't here?" she questions through her tears. He turns and walks to the window.

"No, she was here, but I didn't let it get that far."

"And, what does that mean, Blake?" she resounds with a glare. He slides the curtains open and places his hands on the window seal.

"We were talking about the baby... and she kissed me a couple of times. And, she did try to... but I stopped her."

"How far did she get?"

"She tried...she got me at a vulnerable time, but I stopped her."

"How fucking far did she get, Blake!"

"She stroked it and pulled it out. But, she didn't get any further. I swear."

Her mouth drops open. "That was far enough. Why did you bother? She basically had you in the palm of her hands. I'm done with this shit! I am sick of all the drama that comes with relationships and sex!" She turns to walk away. He reaches for her shoulder.

"I promise I don't want anyone else but you. Please Rayen!" She starts to cry again.

"Why? I ruin every human relationship I ever encounter." Danielle knocks on the door.

"Blake, is everything ok?"

"Yes, Danny, go away!" he quickly returns as she continues.

"I am so tired, Blake. I just can't do this. I am new to this and it is really too much."

He iterates, "So, now you are going to tell me to go be happy with Lauryn? Fuck that! She dismissed my proposal, killed a child I never knew about, and now she thinks things is back the way it was?" Rayen turns to him with a sigh.

"No. I don't want you to be happy with her. I want you to be happy with me. How can I do this?" He places his finger under her chin and tilts her face to his. "Whether you know about relationships or not, hardships are a part of making it work. Exes and other obstacles will come. But, what determines the strength of it, is if you grow closer or further apart. When love is involved, it is difficult to break that bond." He takes both hands and caresses her face. "She tried to seduce me because she knows I don't love her anymore. And she used the abortion to try and break me. It didn't work. Now that I found you, no blowjob in the world could pull me away." He smirks.

Light in the Shadow

"Oh my! I understand now since you put it that way." she says sarcastically. He pulls her to the bed and sits down. He yanks her onto his lap. He tries to kiss her. She pushes his face. "I am still pissed at you."

"Why, baby? I didn't do it."

"She should not have been in here."

"I was so down about me and you; she just forced her way in. I didn't have the strength to fight with her."

"Well, get used to it. She has an apartment here."

He slaps his forehead and his hand rests there. "Damn her! She says since she experienced pregnancy she wants it again with me."

"She can want all day, but it doesn't mean she'll get!"

"Oh, so you aren't giving me away?"

"I guess not. I do love you a fucking lot!"

He laughs. "How does such a beautiful mouth spit out such filthy words?"

"I am only filthy when I have to be." Her mouth forms a dark smirk.

"Oh really? How filthy can you be?" he asks curiously.

"One day I'll show you but I may have to kill you," she answers.

When Rayen and Blake emerge from the guest room, the Pierce's are gathered at the dinner table. "All is well brother?" Daniel blurts out. He kisses Rayen on her cheek. She smiles.

"Have a seat and eat with us Rayen." Robert says pulling out the chair next to him.

"No, I don't want to impose," Rayen replies politely.

"Oh, please child. Sit and eat with us!" Abagail scolds. "Okay?" Blake caresses her hand and pulls her to the table.

"Where is Emily?"

"Oh she went home to the kids," his mom answers. "By the way son, I can't help but notice that beautiful ring on Rayen's finger. Is there something you want to tell us?" Rayen grabs her hand and places it behind her back.

"No, Mom. We are just very serious about one another," he speaks feeling like a child again.

"Good. I am so glad you are happy." She smiles.

"Two years of agitated Blake is no joke!" Daniel spouts. Blake cuts his eyes at him. Blake grabs the chair his Dad offered Rayen and she sits. He slides her to the table. He then sits beside her.

Dinner is delicious. Abagail prepared stuffed chicken breasts and green beans. She offers lemonade, but Blake gets the red wine and pours Rayen a glass. They chat after dinner. Daniel questions Rayen. "So, are you ok dealing with a stalker? Who would have thought Lauryn's gorgeous ass would be a stalker?" Rayen smiles.

"Let's just say I love Blake very much and I am willing to do things I never considered before." Blake smirks and gently lifts her hand and softly kisses it.

"I love you, too." She smiles.

"Would anyone like desert?" Abagail offers. She places a pie on the table. It appears to be apple. She then brings out ice cream. She slices the pie and scoops ice cream on each desert plate. When she slides Rayen a plate she glares at it. Her Mom used to love hot apple pie and ice cream. She eats it, and the memories flood her.

Light in the Shadow

Everyone begins to leave the table after finishing dessert. "Thank you for staying with me Rayen." Blake stands and pulls her to her feet. "If you would not have forgiven me, I don't know what I would have done." He buries his face into her ponytail.

"Your family is so great. I love the closeness between you all. When I am around them, I remember how much I miss my mom and dad. Over the years, I have not had the opportunity to mourn them. Since I have met you, I feel everything, and it is almost overwhelming." She drops her head towards the floor.

"I am trying to handle all of these emotions." He lifts her head.

"It is good to feel emotions. You can't love truly until you know desire and mourning."

"I know," she whispers. He kisses her softly on her lips. She closes her eyes to enjoy his moist delicious kiss. He releases her lips with one more lingering touch.

"I should go. I need to get ready for work in the morning."

"I wanted you to stay with me tonight."

"Oh, no, not here!"

"Of course not. I was hoping you would come to my house or I could go to yours?"

She smiles at him. "Come home with me."

"Oh, I would love to. My furniture will be there this week, so you can come home with me more often."

"Let's go."

"Let's say goodbye to everyone first."

Together they walk down the hall to the family room.

Annetta Hobson

"We are leaving." Blake step towards his mother.

"Okay, son. I will see you later," she says kissing his cheek. He hugs his Dad. "Come here, Rayen." Abagail motions to hug her. She hesitates. "Come on, honey." Rayen obliges. She feels so comfortable in her arms. She hasn't had a motherly hug in a while.

"I should call Margaret. I miss her. And I am sure Angela does also." She thinks.

"What are your plans next week for Christmas, Rayen?" Abagail asks.

"I haven't really thought about it. I rarely celebrate holidays," she states honestly.

Abagail continues, "Please come and join us. The whole family will be here. You can meet Emily's children." She looks at Blake.

"I don't know. I wouldn't want to intrude on such a special time for you guys."

His mom speaks with persistence, "I will not take no for an answer." She gives in.

"I didn't have plans anyway, so why not." Abagail smiles.

"Great, I will see you then." They finish with their goodbyes and leave.

"I am so grateful we patched things up. I was so afraid that you would leave me. I was going mad with anticipation," Blake says dramatically.

"One day of madness. However did you survive?" Rayen states playfully.

"Can we please get back to our card game?" Angie replies with irritation. Blake pretends to be tired as he yawns.

Light in the Shadow

Rayen yawns as well as she says, "It is very late, and we need to get to bed Angie."

"Sure you do, Rayen," she remarks sarcastically. Rayen smiles as she tries to convince her.

"I really am tired." Blake slams his cards on the table, staggers around to Rayen, and scoops her into his arms. Angie smiles as she watches them leave. She rolls her eyes and shakes her head.

"Steady now, Detective. You have had one too many drinks," Rayen says playfully.

Blake whispers sensually, "I need you now." He carries her up the stairs and to her bedroom. He throws her on the bed. She bounces then lies back.

"I have never had the pleasure of seeing you in jeans."

"I don't wear jeans. I just have them for days that I have my other clothes cleaned."

"You look so damn good in them."

"Why, thanks."

He motions toward the bed. "I am going to slide you out of those jeans right now."

"Wait." She holds up one hand. "I need to ask you something."

"Okay?" he sits on the edge of the bed with his back to her. She slides to the edge so that she is sitting next to him. "She claims she is the best you ever had," she rubs her legs. "She said she gave you something I will never be able to give you. She said all she has to do is get you alone." He turns to look at her.

"She is a delusional fucking mess. She got me alone, and all she got was disappointment. How can she be the best I ever had when you are everything I need and want? The only thing you haven't given me is a child and neither has she."

"You really want a child?"

"Of course, we talked about this. I want children, don't you?"

She stands and moves over to her dresser to remove her jeans.

"Rayen, don't you want children one day?"

"I don't know. I explained my concerns before. Children are easily damaged, especially when the parents are not there to raise them."

He stands and walks over to her. He turns her around to face him. "I am a family oriented man. I would never leave my children no matter the circumstances. I told you that I need to have children one day. Have you even considered that, for the future I mean." She pulls away and slides her sweater over her head. She yanks her rubber band out of her hair and it spills down her back. The only things she is wearing now are red satin underwear, and a red satin camisole. She trots back to the bed and slides under the covers. "Rayen, answer me," Blake demands. She turns away and buries her head in the comforter. He reaches over her and pulls the covers off her face.

"Okay! I have never ever considered having children. This world is too wicked. I am…there are just things you don't know about me. You may not want me to be a mother to your children." He slides in bed next to her and she moves away.

"What else is there to know, Rayen? You are smart, beautiful, and you care about people. You love me, right? One day you want to be my wife, right? What else is there to know?" She glances at him.

Light in the Shadow

"There are things that you may never know about me."

"You want to be with me don't you?"

"Of course, Blake. Forever."

"Well, we will work everything else out later."

He snuggles in and wraps his arms around her. She breathes in and thinks about how she will ever explain her methods of defense. Soon, his body relaxes, and she knows he has fallen asleep. She turns and glances at him. His expression is serene. "I wonder if he will feel the same when he discovers the truth?" she thinks. She turns and stares at the wall as she drifts off.

The week has flown by. The disaster of the past weekend haunts Rayen while she works. For a moment, she cringes at the thought of Lauryn. She despises her. She almost let her win. "I would die if she has Blake," Rayen thinks. She daydreams about her mornings with Blake. He has been at her house all week. He goes to work and returns in the morning at four. "His furniture will be delivered today, so he went to his home from work. I really didn't want him to go." While she is caught in her thoughts, Joshua walks in. "Hello, Rayen."

"Hi, Josh. What can I do for you?"

"I just wanted to apologize for my outburst last week. I was out of line and for trying to dodge you, which you didn't even notice by the way."

"I am sorry as well. I have had a world of drama lately."

"Oh, trouble in paradise? Can't be," he states sarcastically.

"Oh, shut up, Josh. Apology accepted. Would you like to go out for drinks tonight? It's Christmas Eve, and Blake has to work. Angela and I are dying for a chance to unwind. Not to mention it's Friday. So, what do you think?"

"That will be great, Rayen. I need to get out. I have been very busy for the last couple of weeks just working. What time?"

"Um, what about 7:30 or 8? We can meet at Latitude."

He laughs. "Are you even still allowed in Latitude?"

"Yes, that incident is almost forgotten."

"Almost?"

Her office phone rings. She smiles and answers her phone. "Ms. Vasu."

"Hi, Rayen! It's Margaret."

"Hi! How are you? I was just thinking about you, Margaret."

Joshua raises his hand to let her know he will wait outside her office. She nods at him as he steps out.

"I got a phone call from Joanna Shaw, and she needs to speak to you, honey."

"Joanna Shaw, the detective that was assigned to my parents' murder?"

"Yes. They have some new evidence, and she wants to talk to you about it."

"Okay, when?"

"First thing Monday morning. We are going to fly down there to meet with you. I don't know what it is, but I would like to be there for you."

"Really? Must be some very important details if she is flying down."

"I think so."

Light in the Shadow

"I wish you could be here for Christmas. You should not have to spend it all alone."

"I am fine. I am coming Monday, okay?"

"Okay. Send me your flight information, and I will have a car to pick you two up."

"I will. How are things with you and Blake?"

"We are fine. Some things about relationships are beyond me, but he is someone I want to learn them with. I am spending tomorrow with him and his family."

"The family, huh? My next question is do you love him?"

She pauses. Margaret has surprised her. "Yes, I do. I have never felt this way about anyone. So, I suppose I love him a lot. And, Aunt Margie?" Margaret is surprised. She can barely answer,

"Uhh, yes, sweetheart?" Rayen hesitates then speaks.

"I love you and miss you so much. Merry Christmas!" Margaret gasps.

"Oh my goodness, Rayen! I miss you too and Merry Christmas!" she says choking back tears. "I am overjoyed with happiness, Rayen. You have finally let someone in that has opened a door that we can enjoy also. Thank you, honey, so much!"

"Thank you for being there for me and accepting the responsibility of taking care of me. I am eternally grateful to you. I have to go, but I will let Angie know you will be here. We will make sure you get a little vacation out of this."

"Thank you, Rayen," she says, hoarse from crying,

"I will see you two Monday, okay?"

"Okay. Goodbye."

She hangs up the phone. She keeps her hand on the receiver. Joshua peeks in the door when he hears her end the call. "Should I leave you alone?" Joshua breaks her reverie.

She returns, "Oh no, I'm fine."

"Okay." He steps in and sits in the chair facing her.

"How is everything with Evelyn and her dad?"

"Fine. I wanted to thank you for that. She left Sunday. We had lunch to show that there were no hard feelings."

"How was that?"

"Great until she asked for goodbye sex!"

Rayen chuckles. "Well, can you blame her? You are very good at it." She grabs her mouth. "I am so sorry. That was so inappropriate. I apologize." She looks at her hands. Her face flushes.

"It's good for the ego. And, I am so glad you remember I gave you your very first orgasm," Joshua states with a smirk.

"I never told you that!" She spins her chair to turn away.

"You didn't have to." His eyes close.

"I felt the way your body shivered. I miss that feeling…your body exploding around my…" he clears his throat and his eyes reopen. "It's the very reason I broke it off with Evelyn. She just wasn't you."

"Joshua," she warns.

"I know. I'll shut up," he sighs as he gives in. She spins her chair to face him, but they avoid eye contact. "I guess I will see you at about 8, okay?"

Light in the Shadow

"Okay." He walks out of the office and shuts the door. "Does the drama ever end?" She thinks as she returns to her work.

"Angela, are you ready to leave?"

"Yes. Just let me finish going over the New York lists. Mr. Drake is having me pick up all of Evelyn's work."

"Why? He hasn't contacted me."

"Oh, she quit. She didn't want to work in New York, so she informed him of this yesterday."

"Really? Does Joshua know?"

"I didn't think to ask. It's a little unusual. Didn't you think?"

"Yes. Maybe he didn't want to bother me after our discussion. I will need to speak with Evan." She walks down the hall to Joshua's office. "Josh are you busy?" She catches him off guard. His eyes widen as she enters his office.

"No, come on in. What can I do for you?" He is still embarrassed about his comment earlier as she continues.

"I wanted to know if you were aware of the Evelyn situation."

"What situation?" He asks. She explains what Angela told her about Evelyn and her father.

"I wonder what she is up to. I will find out, but not right now."

"I understand. Just enjoy your weekend."

"Are we still on for tonight?"

She scans his face. She does not want to disappoint him by canceling. "Yes of course. I agree to deal with this issue on Monday." She turns to exit his office.

"Rayen?" he calls as she lets out a long sigh.

"Josh, let's just leave it be."

"Okay. See you tonight," he surrenders. She leaves and returns to her office.

Rayen's phone rings and catches her off guard. "Hello," she snaps.

"Hi, baby," the voice resounds sensually making her smile.

"Hi, Blake."

"I am missing you so much right now. I wanted to come home to you after work this morning," he remarks softly.

"Why didn't you?" she says playfully.

"Well, I would have missed the arrival of my furniture. I would like to have a bed for you to sleep on when you visit me. Wouldn't you agree?" he questions. She smirks.

"I would."

"I'm just sitting here at work thinking about how scrumptious you were yesterday. I should have come by before my shift and got a little something to tide me over," he states. She blushes.

"I would have loved that."

"The furniture guys left; I laid down to see how comfortable the bed was. And, the next thing I knew, I fell asleep. Then it was time to get to the station. But, don't worry. I want to pick you up after my shift so we can break that new bed in. Attack dogs couldn't keep me from between those thighs," he spoke without holding back.

"I will be counting the hours." She returns.

"What are you doing now?"

"Well, Angela and I are getting dressed to go out for drinks."

Light in the Shadow

"Where are you going?"

"The Latitude. Where else?"

"Be careful. No karate moves tonight, okay?"

"Yes sir, Detective."

"Seriously, I love you so much, Rayen. I need to come home to the perfect unscathed ass I left."

"Oh, Detective, you say the dearest things."

"Oh, I know. I will be anxiously waiting with my mouth watering to slurp you up."

She shivers. "Keep it up. I may be at the station for a midnight questioning session in your car."

"Oh, please do, Rayen! Please do!"

"I have to go. Angie is ready, and I'm standing here with a towel as water trickles down my leg!"

"Oh no! Don't tell me that."

"Goodbye, Blake!"

"Rayen, what are you doing to me?"

"Goodbye."

She smiles as she presses end. She runs to her dresser and takes out a sexy blue lacey bra and thong combo. She then prances to her closet to find something to wear. She selects a long sleeve cream wrap dress. She slides her arms into it, wraps it around her body, and ties it at her hip. She slides on some black ankle boots. She grabs her black mink jacket and heads down stairs. Angela is waiting at the door. "Oh wow! You look so hot, Rye." Rayen looks at Angie.

"You look great yourself," she responds. Angela is wearing dark blue mini pencil skirt with a sky blue cashmere sweater.

She displays her long black leather high-heeled boots. Sterling steps in the door as they are talking and slides her long black trench coat on.

"Hello, Sterling."

"Hello, Rayen. How are you?"

"Fine. Are you spending Christmas with your father?"

"No. As a matter of fact, I have a young woman I am seeing now, and I will be spending it with her."

"Oh, that's great Sterling!"

"We don't want to keep you out too late and have her upset with us."

He smirks and cuts his eyes at Angela. Her eyes shoot nervously to the floor. "Okay, let's go. No need to stand at the door talking all evening," Angela snaps.

"Okay, Angela," Rayen suspiciously eyes her. Sterling holds the door as they exit.

When they arrive at the Latitude, there is a nice crowd gathering. The snow is slushy on the ground. Sterling pulls in front and scurries to open the door. Angela steps out first. He grabs her hand ever so gently to escort her out of the truck. Rayen notices their exchange. He then grabs her hand to help her out. "Thank you, Sterling. Why don't you join us this evening?" He is startled by her invitation.

"Well…" he looks down at what he is wearing. "I suppose I can."

"It's Christmas Eve. No use to just work without play," she adds. He takes off his coat and removes his blazer. He tosses the items into the car. He is looking very handsome in all black as usual. Angela gawks at Rayen. "What is wrong with you,

Light in the Shadow

Angela? You are behaving very strangely," Rayen exclaims quizzically.

"Am I? Sorry, nothing's wrong with me." She smiles and Sterling hands the valet his keys, grabs them both by the arms, and they enter the lounge together.

When they are inside, they search for a table. Rayen spots Joshua. He waves them over. When they arrive at the table, Sterling pulls out the chair for Angela. Joshua stands and does the same for Rayen.

"Sterling, what a surprise. Are you working tonight?"

"Yes, but Rayen invited me to join you guys. How are you?"

"Fine."

Rayen scans the lounge. There is holiday décor everywhere. The place is adorned with green and red. It is really lovely. A waitress approaches the table. "Merry Christmas. Welcome to the Latitude. May I offer you our signature drink for the evening?" The all agree to try it. She walks away to retrieve their order.

"So, Angela, when were you going to tell me you and Sterling are an item?" Rayen blurts. Angela is caught by surprise.

"Oh, I…"

"How long have you two been dating, Sterling?" she asks him. He smiles.

"About four months?" She turns to Angela, but she looks away.

"Really, Angie? When were you going to tell me?"

She carefully answers, "I'm sorry, Rye. You said don't, but I liked him so much. One day we were talking; he stayed over. We have been seeing one another ever since."

"I'm sorry, Rayen. Please, don't be upset. I truly value your business," Sterling states. She drags her eyes from her to him without speaking. Joshua interrupts.

"I am sure you two will be fine. Rayen is just worried because you are like her little sister. She doesn't want you to get hurt."

"I understand that, but I am grown," Angela offers defensively.

"You are, but your mother instructed me to watch over you."

"Mom knows, Rayen. He has spoken with her and everything. She is excited about meeting him Monday."

"Really? She told me nothing."

"I asked her not to. Don't be angry. You just overreact to everything. You have been caught up with Blake…"

"And, you used that to go behind my back?"

"Let's not do this here, please."

"I am done with it. Sterling, I just hope you are what you appear to be. I don't want this to harm our professional relationship."

"It will not. I assure you."

The waitress returns with their drinks. They sit awkwardly in silence sipping their drinks for a while. Sterling stands and holds out his hand for Angela. "Would you like to dance?"

"Please." She grabs his hand and stands. They leave the table.

Light in the Shadow

"Why are you so upset? He is a nice guy Rayen," Joshua says. "And, she is very much a woman. If I hadn't been with you, I would have taken a shot at her myself." He jokes, but Rayen is not amused.

"Not funny, Josh."

"You are not jealous are you?"

"Of course not."

"Angela is beautiful."

"I know, but she is like my little sister. I am afraid for her."

"You don't have to be."

"Men can be very…"

"Very what?"

"Never mind."

She tosses back her drink. "Look at them," he says as they turn their eyes to the dance floor. Angela and Sterling are looking deep into each other's eyes as they dance. It seems as if no one is watching them. They only see one another.

"Oh well," she shrugs.

She waves to the waiter for another drink. He moves his seat closer. She cuts her eyes at him. "What made you want to finally go out with me?" Josh asks.

"I don't know. I guess I miss talking to you," she replied nonchalantly.

"You sure?" he continues as she glances at him.

"Sure of what?"

"Talking is all you miss?" he whispers.

"Stop it, Josh. How can we communicate if your every reference is towards sex?" she questions.

He states, "I'm sorry. I… just can't stop. I will never forget what we had, even if it was brief." She stares at him. She pities him.

"I am so sorry I did that to you."

"Don't be. I'm not." He grabs her hand and stares into her eyes. "I will always be waiting in the wings. So, if he ever hurts you or if you ever tire of him, I am always here." He gently kisses her hand. She stares back at him again. He is very attractive. Not to mention, he provided her with her first orgasm. "You didn't stop me," he says.

"Stop you from what? A kiss on the hand?" she says confused. His breathing picks up. He slides his chair closer. When he is really close, he whispers in her ear.

"You smell so good tonight, Rayen." She closes her eyes.

"I have had too much to drink," she thinks. He leans toward her, places his hand on her thigh, and slides it up.

"Please, may I have one more night with you? That uptight cop can't please you like I can," he merely begs.

She closes her eyes and takes a deep breath, but before he reaches the apex of her high thighs she snaps, "No! Josh, stop." She shakes it off. He sits back. He is breathing hard. She pulls her dress down to her knee and wiggles into her seat. She scans the room to see if anyone was watching. Right then, the waitress brings her drink. She whispers, "We can't keep doing this. It is over. I love you as my friend. The impact you have had on my life will never be forgotten, but that's it," she says sympathetically.

Light in the Shadow

He slides his hands through his gorgeous glossy hair. "I get it, but I don't fucking care anymore. I have never wanted anything so much in my life. You were supposed to be mine. All I think about is you. I don't want anyone else," he remarks intensely as he drops his head on the table.

She sighs, "Maybe you should go work in New York." He lifts his head instantly.

"No, I won't! You are not sending me away. I am staying here." She takes her drink and gulps it. She then waves to the waitress for another refill. She arrives and takes their glasses.

"Same thing for you both?"

"Yes," Rayen answers. He stares at her for a while. "What am I going to do with you, Joshua?" She resounds as she places her hands on the table and intertwines them.

"Give me another chance," he pleads.

"I can't. I really love Blake. I am in love him," she retorts. He places his hands over hers.

"You could not have completely gotten over me! We shared something special!" It comes out as a gentle roar. She shakes her head. He leans over to kiss her. She turns away.

"Stop it, Josh." He plops back in his seat like a child who could not have his way.

"I'll just go. I will stay with my parents until after the holidays. I will return late January. Maybe if I don't have to see you, I will get over you. But, make no mistake, I am coming back." She smiles.

"Good. I really value your friendship. I need it."

"See, it is when you say things like that which makes me want to love you even more."

"I cannot apologize for appreciating what you did for me. I would not be in the place I'm in now if it wasn't for you, Joshua."

She leans over and kisses him on his cheek. "Enjoy the holidays with your parents."

"I am going to the airport early in the morning. I made the reservations weeks ago. But, when you invited me out, my hopes were up. I would have cancelled in a heartbeat, but I didn't because somehow I knew I would still be going."

He stands and slides his chair under the table. "Thank you, Rayen."

"For what?"

"For coming out with me tonight. I really appreciated it."

"Oh, no you don't! Don't thank me. We are still and will always be friends."

He leans over, lifts her hand, and with a long, lingering motion, kisses it. "I absolutely adore you, Rayen Vasu. Hopefully, one day someone else will fill the void left in my heart." She tilts her head and smiles.

"You are a great guy, Joshua. I hope some young woman steals your heart and soon." He lets her hand down gently, grabs his coat off of the back of the chair, and leaves. She watches him as he walks away, and her heart is feeling very heavy.

Chapter 12

Rayen's eyes search the crowded dance floor for Angela. It is getting very late, and she wants to go home so she can wrap the gifts she brought for everyone. She stands to get a better look. She doesn't see them anywhere. She glances at her watch. "It is 1:30. Where could they be?" She grabs her jacket and searches the lounge for them. She does not find them anywhere. She returns to the table and collects her purse and Angela's coat. She steps outside and asks the valet about the vehicle. It is still parked. "Will you please put these items in the black Escalade?" He nods, and she reenters the lounge. She searches everywhere. She checks the restrooms. "Where in the hell are these two?"

She marches toward the back and notices a door in the back that reads "Exit". It is slightly open. She walks up to the door and nudges it carefully. As it opens, she hears panting. Her eyes grow wide. "No!" She peeks outside the door and she spots Angela with her back pressed up against the building. Her legs are firmly planted around Sterling's waist. His slacks are at his ankles. He is thrusting in and out as she moans. Her arms are wrapped around his neck. He has one hand on her behind and the other on the wall. Rayen steps back inside the door. She places her hand over her mouth. "Oh my God!" She mouths. "What should I do? Someone may find them." She motions toward the door once more. But, she stops.

"Oh, Angie! I'm..." he screams. She slaps her hand over his mouth.

"Shhh, Sterling! Someone will hear you."

"I don't care. Oh! Oh!" he shouts in pleasure. Soon she follows.

Annetta Hobson

"Sterling, faster. Harder. Harder. Ah!" she says a little quieter. They collapse against the wall. He gently lets her legs down. She grabs her underwear and slides the other leg back into them. He pulls his slacks up and fastens them. She rushes, "Come on. Rayen is probably looking for us." They step toward the door. Rayen backs up. When they sling the door open she pretends to be startled.

"Oh, hey! I have been looking all over for you guys."

"Oh um, we just stepped out for some air." Angela says, looking at the floor as they pass Rayen.

She asks, "Are you guys ready?"

"Yes. Just let me get our Angela's coat," Sterling says nervously.

Rayen smirks as she speaks with sarcasm, "It is already in the car." He nods and hurries ahead of them. "Your back is wet Angela," she says amused. Angela stops walking.

"You saw us didn't you?" Rayen pretends to be in horror.

"Saw what?" She reaches up and smooths the back of her hair.

"Nevermind, Rye." They cut through the dance floor. When they reach the entrance Rayen turns to her.

"Oh, Angela, he has such a cute ass!"

"Rayen, stop!" she whines. She slaps her on the back and they laugh. Sterling pulls up and jumps out to open their door. He does not give Rayen eye contact. She smirks as he helps her in the car. Angela kisses his cheek as he holds her while she gets in.

"Wonderful night, wouldn't you say, Sterling?"

"Yes, ma'am."

Light in the Shadow

"Cut it out, Sterling. You staying over tonight? No use to sneaking anymore."

"I wanted to tell you, but Angela begged me not to. She can be very persuasive." He smirks as he peeks at her through the rear view mirror. She blushes.

"I'm sure she is," Rayen returns. They remain silent the rest of the ride home.

"I am leaving for the weekend. I will be back on Monday. Sterling, I guess you will be picking up Miss Margaret?" Rayen states, peeking into the kitchen.

"Yes of course," he replies in his professional tone. The doorbell buzzes.

She says, "You guys enjoy yourselves and Merry Christmas. Angie, walk me down." Angela slides her chair from the table and stands. They walk down the stairs. "Is he treating you right?"

"Yes, Rye. We are having so much fun. We like each other a lot."

"Nothing serious yet?"

"No, not yet. You will be the first to know, I promise."

They hug when they get to the bottom of the stairs. "Merry Christmas, Rayen." She opens the door, and Blake is standing there. He grabs her bags and goes to the trunk. Sterling appears behind Angela with the rest of Rayen's things.

"What is all of this, Rye?"

"Gifts. Yours and Margaret's are under the tree you insisted we put up."

"I have one for you guys under there too," Angela says. Blake returns and grabs the rest of her bags.

"Baby, are you moving in?" he laughs.

"They are gifts for your family, Mr. Smart guy," she scolds.

"Oh no. I was happy for a moment," he jokes.

"We have plenty of time for that my love," she speaks seductively. He smiles and kisses her lips. She hugs Angela once more and dashes to join Blake.

On the way to his house they converse. "So, you found out about Angie and Sterling?" Blake blurts out easily. Rayen snaps her head to look at him. "How did you know?"

"I have seen them together. It was so obvious."

"Why didn't you tell me?"

"It was none of our business."

"Wait! None of your business maybe, but it was definitely my business."

He reaches over and grabs her chin. "Stop, baby. You are happy, so let her be."

"I want her to be happy, but I should have been informed. I would have seen for myself if I wasn't so wrapped up in you."

"Stay wrapped in me. It is where you belong." He grabs her hand and places a wet kiss on it.

They arrive at Blake's house. "I can't wait until you see everything. I have a surprise for you" he resounds.

She asks, "What is it?"

"You'll see. Be patient." He pulls into the driveway, steps out of the car, and hurries around to open her door. He lifts the trunk to get her bags.

"You don't have to take the big ones out. Those are the gifts," she directs.

Light in the Shadow

"Okay." He grabs her overnight bag.

They enter in the house, and it is beautiful. There are Christmas decorations in the living area and a big wonderfully decorated tree. There are tons of presents underneath. There is a brown leather sofa set with oak coffee tables. Then in the dining area, it is an oak dining table and chairs. He leads her to the bedrooms. They are decorated with the finest furniture. One room is still empty. They get to his room. It has a very large four-post bed. The posts are very high. "Here is your surprise. He pulls her over to the dresser. She looks at the dresser.

"I don't see anything." She searches.

"This space is yours." He pulls her over to the closet. He drags her back to the dresser. She looks again and there are a set of keys on it.

"Are you giving me keys?"

"Yes, Rayen. I know we are taking things slow, but I want to share everything with you."

She turns to him. "You are too much for me, Blake Pierce." She grabs his face between her hands and kisses him deeply. "Wait," He stops her. "What?" she speaks with curiosity.

He pulls her down the stairs to the Christmas tree. "It's Christmas. Open your gifts." He hands her several boxes. She sits on the floor in front of the tree. He slides beside her and crosses his legs. She opens the first box. It is a diamond bracelet.

"Thank you." She kisses him on his lips. She rips through the other boxes. It is like she is a child. She has not been this excited about opening gifts in so long. The boxes contain earrings to match the bracelet and a diamond heart pendant necklace. There are about ten karats of diamonds all together.

Annetta Hobson

"Why did you do this? I don't need these things."

"I know you don't need me to buy you anything, but I wanted to give you diamonds. Diamonds say 'I love you' the best." He smiles.

"No, you say I love you the best." She leans over and kisses him. She opens several more boxes. "I am so happy right now." She stands and walks over to the door. She grabs one of the boxes she carried in. "Here you are." She gives him a gift. It is a tailored suit and a very expensive painting she purchased. They sit by the tree and talk for a while.

"Let's go break that bed in," Blake suggests. He pulls her off the floor. She smiles.

"Okay, if you insist." They precede hand-in-hand up the stairs to the room.

When Rayen opens her eyes, the sun is beating down onto her face. She turns to look at Blake sleeping peacefully. She stands and goes over to the dresser. She picks up the keys Blake gave her and admires them. She smiles at the thought of living with him one day. She sets them down and picks up her phone. She checks it for the time. It is 12:30 p.m. "Blake." She motions toward the bed. "Blake." He turns away as she approaches. She sits on the bed and leans over to kiss him. "Blake."

"Huh? Yes...baby...what is it?" he says as he stretches.

"What time is the Christmas party at your parents' house?" He rubs his eyes.

"Umm it starts at 3 p.m."

"Oh, okay. Maybe I can make us something to eat."

"I'm not hungry. I'll just sleep until then."

Light in the Shadow

"Okay." She goes downstairs to the kitchen. She opens the refrigerator and searches for something to snack on. She does not find anything. "Somebody needs to go grocery shopping," she says. She walks to the patio door and stares out of the glass. The water is still lovely to look at. It may be more beautiful with the islands of ice floating by. She walks over to the table and sits. She places her elbows on the table. She thinks about the road she has traveled in her relationships. She has had a lot of disappointing and deadly endings. She drifts into a deep daydream.

***

Rayen was selected to participate in the travel experience for the college's seniors. She won the spot out of 200 participating students. She was to spend ten days and nights in Zurich, Switzerland. Margaret was so happy that she was chosen, especially since she had been through so much. She was going to be there a week and a half during the summer of her senior year. She arrived in Zurich in mid-July. Her plane ride was long and tiring. She kept thinking what she would do besides study.

She took out her map and itinerary. She looked over her list of things to do. She hailed a cab in front of her hotel. The sites were lovely, but Rayen wasn't really interested. She arrived at her hotel and realized she was very hungry. She left her room and searched for a place to eat. She walked down the street. Occasionally, she glanced at the historic scenery. She finally arrived at a small, quaint restaurant and entered in to have a bite. The waitress approached her. She did not speak English. Rayen opened her translation book and ordered from it. She knew every place had some type of burger. The waitress brought a funny looking dish that she did not recognize. "What is this?" she asked as she gestured to the waitress. The waitress just shrugged her shoulders and repeated a word she could not make out.

"Hello, signorina. I take it you wanted a hamburger?" a handsome man said as he approached.

She carefully returned, "Yes I did." He turned and spoke to the waitress. She took the plate and left.

"I am Paolo, Paolo Fabbiani. I am here for your ordering pleasures." He smiled a nice smile. She scanned him over. He was kind of skinny but was about six feet tall. He had shoulder length, black oily looking hair. He had a very exotic and cute face. "Where are you from?" He asked through a heavy Italian accent. "American, No?"

"As a matter of fact, I am. I am from New York," she answered. The waitress returned with an American style Burger. She nods at the waitress for her approval as the waitress leaves. "Thank you Paolo," she said with a dry expression.

"May I ask your name?

"Rayen," she states, taking a sip of the water.

"Are you traveling alone, Rayen?" he questioned. She pursed her lips.

"How about I ask you a question?"

"Fire away, Ra-yen."

"Where are you from?"

"Milan."

"Oh, Italy. The accent gave that away." She takes a bite from her burger.

"Good?"

She nods.

Light in the Shadow

After finishing her meal, she took out her credit card and waved to the waitress.

"Do you have a tour guide, signorina? "

"No, I am winging it."

"How old are you, Ra-yen?"

"You sure have a lot of questions. How old are you?"

"26. Now you."

"21."

"Why are you here alone? "

"I am done with questions for today. I am tired and I want to get up early tomorrow."

"Okay, okay, Ra-yen. May I have your phone number so I may call you?"

"No. Give me your number, and I will contact you."

He smiled. "I will just be around, Ra-yen. See you, sweetheart."

He then left out of the restaurant. She wondered about this stranger but not for long. She received back her credit card and left herself. She walked to her hotel to retire for the night.

The next morning, Rayen woke up early to get started documenting her sightseeing. She had to record the educational monuments of the city. She got an early start. She found a tour bus that traveled to most of the frequented spots. She rode the tour bus all day. That evening, she disappeared into her room and did not emerge until the following morning.

Her cell phone rang. Margaret was calling to check on her. "Hi, Rayen."

"Hello, Miss Margaret."

"I am just calling to make sure you are okay."

"I am fine. Trust me, I know how to take care of myself."

Margaret sighs, "I know, Rayen. I am just worried."

"No need. I'll be fine."

"Okay, just watch your surroundings and trust no one."

"I never do."

"Goodbye, honey."

"Bye."

She shook her head and placed the phone in her pocket. Rayen left her hotel and began her day with breakfast. The food there was really good. After she had eaten, she searched for something to do.

"Well, hello again, Ra-yen!" She bumped into Paolo. "Are you enjoying Zurich?"

"I am," she lied.

"May I tag along? You will be much better with an escort," he offered.

"It really isn't necessary…" she started, but he interrupted.

"Come on. I will show you the fun places." She hesitated for a moment, but she felt he probably was not going away.

"I guess." She rolled her eyes. Paolo stuck to her like glue for the next couple of days. Every morning when she left her hotel, he was always there waiting.

By the end of the week, Rayen and Paolo had become as close as anyone could get to her. She did not show it, but she was becoming a bit smitten with him. "I have to leave in two days. This has been a very unique experience," she remarked.

Light in the Shadow

"Same here, Ra-yen. I have really enjoyed your company. I do not want it to end. May I return with you to your room for a drink?" he asked with a convincing demeanor. She hesitated because she felt uneasy, but agreed. She did not let people get close to her, but she figured maybe men were different there since she was half way around the world.

When they got to her room, Paolo looked around. "Why are you here in Zurich?" she questioned. He paced around her room not speaking. "Is everything alright?" Rayen continued now alerted.

When he noticed her alarm he spoke, "Well, my dear, I have been here for three years. I live alone. My family is still in Milan. I am a bit of an outcast."

"Oh ok. Well, I think I have enough information for school, thanks to you," she said as he chuckled. She hitched her eyebrow as he glanced her over.

"You are very beautiful, Ra-yen. Truly captivating." She walked over to her small refrigerator and poured herself a drink. Paolo finally made his way over to her when she gave no response. "May I please kiss you?"

"No, absolutely not!" Rayen snapped.

"I apologize. We are not in the same place tonight." He nervously fidgets as he walked over to the sofa.

"It's getting late. I think you should go." She walked over to the door and opened it. He followed her. When he got to the door, he closed it.

"Sorry, Ra-yen, but you are the longest target I have ever trailed. I do not know if it is worth it yet." He pulled out a handgun from his pocket. "All of your credit cards, jewelry, traveler's checks! Place them on the table if you please." Rayen did not flinch. She just stared at his gun. "I suppose you have

Annetta Hobson

spent half of your money. You filthy Americans spend money like running water," he insulted. She slowly walked over to the nightstand and emptied her bag. "I must decide what I will do with you since I have spent so much time with you." He tapped the gun against his chin. She stood there frozen and not speaking. He commanded, "Get undressed, now! Sorry, but this will be your last experience. I promise to make it good." She closed her eyes.

"Why? Am I a disaster magnet? Will it always be this way? Does any man have good intentions?" She became angry as she listened to him ramble.

"Okay, if you don't want to do it, then I will." He motioned toward her. He placed the gun to her temple. She kept her eyes closed as she remembered her training. "Open your eyes, American whore. You will witness all of what I am planning." He dug the gun in her head, making an impression. She stared in his eyes. "Oh you are a strong one. No tears. Good, I hate to make a woman cry," he laughed. He dragged her over to where the bed was as he kept the gun to her head. Then he tossed her on the bed. He ripped the sundress she was wearing off. She was on the bed with her bra and underwear on. He climbed on her and started to kiss her. His smell made her want to throw up. "Your taste is exquisite, you American slut. I wish I did not have to get rid of you." He sat the gun beside them on the bed. He then reached to unzip his pants. When he pulled his pants down a bit, she grabbed the gun and threw it across the room. "Oh, you little bitch! You will regret that!" He grabbed her by the throat. "I am going to have my way with you, then kill you!" She suddenly grabbed his hands and quickly bent them back until he loosened his grip. He shouted, "You bitch!" She then kicked him so hard that he soared across the room. He landed against the wall. She jumped to her feet, and he lunged at her. When he reached her, he attempted to grab her. She spun behind

Light in the Shadow

him and grabbed his face. She twisted really hard until she heard a snap in his neck. He fell to the floor, and his body went limp. She twisted his neck once more as hard as she could manage to make sure he was dead.

    Rayen scurried to clean her room. She wrapped his body in a sheet and dragged it to the door. She carefully cleaned the gun for any prints. She searched her bags for something to put on. She grabbed a t-shirt and some cotton shorts. She glanced at her clock. It was 2:30 a.m. She peeked out of her door. The halls were like a ghost town. She jogged down the hall to see how big the trash chute was. It was the right size for a large garbage bag. As she returned to her room, she scanned for cameras, and there were none. When she was back inside her room, she tried to bind his body. She took his legs, bent them into his chest, and tied them tightly with the sheet. She then folded his arms into his chest and secured them as well. She pulled the fitted sheet from the bed and slid it over his body. She checked the hall again. When she was sure it was clear, she dragged the sheet down the hall to the chute. She opened the chute and struggled as she picked his body up. She finally got it in the chute and she slammed the door shut. She listened as the body tumbled down floor by floor. She knew she had at least until the morning before anyone found him. She ran back to her room and began to pack. She took a moment to sit on the bed. She wondered how she would replace the bedding without getting caught. She contemplated as she went back into the hall. She did not see anyone as she searched for some type of linen closet. She started back towards her room, and one was not found. She then noticed a room door slightly cracked. She lightly knocked and no one answered. She quickly went in and pulled the sheets from the bed. She ran back to her room. She quickly made the bed but did not go to sleep.

Annetta Hobson

Rayen waited until 6 a.m. and checked out of the hotel. She hailed a cab to go to the airport. When she arrived there, she immediately approached the receptionists. "It's only one day, but I am just so home sick," she explained as she asked for a ticket back to the states. They gave her no issues about her early departure. She was seated her on the next flight that afternoon. When she got to the terminal, she turned and bade a good ridden to Zurich.

***

"Rayen?" Blake shakes her. "Baby, are you sleep?" She jumps.

"Oh, Blake, I must have dozed off."

"Were you dreaming?" he asks.

"I suppose I was," she says, trying to shake off the old memories.

"Good or bad?"

"I don't know." She rubs her hair.

"Rayen, you look troubled. What's wrong?"

"Blake…I love you so much."

"What is it?"

"It's just… there are some things you don't know about me. I want to share them with you, but…"

He pulls her from her chair. He embraces her. "Whatever it is, I am sure we can work it out." She shakes her head.

"No…it puts you at risk."

"Risk for what?" he questions with a look of concern upon his face. She looks over at the clock.

Light in the Shadow

"Nevermind. It's time for us to go. It is 2:15."

"I know. That's why I came looking for you." He grabs her hand and leads her upstairs.

Blake walks in the bathroom and turns the shower on. "You want to shower together?" She looks at him in amusement.

"That is probably not a good idea." He smirks.

"Probably not."

"I'll go to the other bathroom and bathe," she states.

"You are no kind of fun today," he jokes. They go their separate ways to get ready. When Rayen returns to the room with her towel on, Blake is getting dressed. He is sliding into his white dress shirt when she enters.

"Are you wearing a dinner jacket?"

"Are you telling me you are not satisfied with my choice of clothing?"

"No, I am not saying that. I just love you in blazers."

"Well, let me get a blazer. As a matter of fact, I will wear the suit you gave me."

"I was hoping you would."

He walks over to her and grabs her waist. "It is extremely hard for me to keep my hands off of you when you are half dressed."

"You must control yourself and focus. We have somewhere to be," she teases. He wraps his arms around her and pulls her closer.

"Come on. Let me remove this towel," he whispers through her hair into her ear. A shiver trickles down through her. She tingles deep inside. He grabs the back of the towel and yanks it from her grip.

"Blake! We have to go," she slightly protests.

"I do not care," he says softly each word caressing her. He gently pushes her back so he can look at her. "Rayen, why are you so damn gorgeous? Your every curve, your beautiful tone, you silky smooth skin is all so hypnotizing." She does not resist. He runs his knuckles lightly along her back. His other hand cups her behind. He rubs it in a circling motion. He leans in and kisses her neck. He sucks and licks it, tasting the fresh water lingering from her bath. He drops his shirt to the floor.

"You know, Blake, your body is also a treat I enjoy." She rubs his chest, skidding down his six pack and stopping short of his hairline. She steps onto the tips of her toes and kisses him. She leaps up and straddles him. He is staring at her hungrily. His breathing is increasing. She lifts her behind and positions herself to take him in. First, he rubs her center to see if she is ready. He inserts his finger and rolls it around. When he takes it out, it is dripping with her moistness. He rubs her wetness on his erection and rubs it around. "Oh, please, put it , Blake," she begs impatiently. He leans back to look at her and smiles.

"You want it?"

"I fucking need it!" she says throttled with passion. He tilts his hips, grabs her behind, and pushes himself in. She sighs with relief.

"Oh yes! I love this. I could never be without it!" He smiles as he thrusts over and over, in and out. She bucks back. She is holding on with her hands around his neck. He struggles to get to the bed and finally reaches it. Before he lays her down, she stops him.

Light in the Shadow

"I want to make love to you." He gently sits on the bed, and he lies back without breaking their connection. She snuggles him inside her deeper. She then winds her hips, bouncing and twirling them. She positions her hands on his stomach to gain leverage.

He moans, "Oh shit, Rayen! What are you doing to me?" He leans up for a kiss, and she returns it. They kiss so deeply that their tongues are dancing with one another. She begins to grind. She reaches back and rests her hand on his knee. He caresses her breast. She moans. She rides him as if he was a prized thoroughbred and they were trying to win a race. She slings her hair forward. She grabs his chest. She is so close.

"Oh shit! Oh…"

"Oh, Rayen! You are driving me…Ohh!

She releases in a whirlwind of pleasure as he follows. She collapses onto him. "I never knew sex could be so…I can't even describe how I feel," she says breathlessly.

"You feel so good. Your insides feel like soft suction cups massaging me while inside of you," he softly speaks barely audible. She smiles.

"Good, now let's shower again so we can go."

When they arrive at Blake's parents' house, there are a ton of cars. Blake finds a space on the street. "Rayen, you look stunning," he marvels as he assists her out of the car. She is wearing a red dress. It has jeweled straps, a beautiful sweetheart bodice, and it flares down to her knees. She has on silver closed in stiletto shoes, and she is wearing a white mink shawl. He grabs her hand, and they walk up to the Pierce house. Abagail opens the door.

"Merry Christmas!" She kisses Blake on the cheek and turns to Rayen. "Thank you for coming."

"I have been looking forward to it all week," she returns.

"Come in, sweetheart. I want everyone to meet you," his mom remarks as they walks in to the living room. It is filled with people. Abagail grabs her hand and introduces her to everyone. "This is Rayen. She is Blake's fiancée and the CEO of Vista Corp."

"She is introducing me to everyone as Blake's fiancée?" she thinks. When she makes it back to Blake, she grabs his hand. "So, everyone in town thinks we are engaged."

"Really?" He smiles. "Is that okay with you?"

"It's fine. I want to be your fiancée, but you haven't even asked yet," she states nonchalantly.

"You do, huh?" he questions. She goes on.

"Yes. I love you, and you said you would take me no matter what is in my past, even though you don't know what it is." "Well?" He drops to one knee. "Marry me, Rayen Vasu." She smiles. The whole room gets quiet as all witness the display.

"Yes, of course," she answers as she blushes. People start to whisper.

"Now she is my fiancée," he yells to his mother standing across the room. His mother laughs and blows a kiss to him. Emily starts to clap. And, the room follows. He picks her up and kisses her deeply in front of the whole room.

"Finally, brother, you got a yes," Daniel says as he slaps his back. Robert comes over.

"Son, congratulations. I hope you and Rayen are very happy together." He grabs Blake and hugs him.

"Thanks, Dad. I am extremely happy, happier than I ever have been in my life," he says, staring at Rayen. His eyes glisten

Light in the Shadow

as if there is a hint of a tear, but it never surfaces. He grabs her and holds her. "Thank you, baby." She holds his face between her hands.

"Thank you, Blake. I am a different person because of you." Soon, guests start to come and congratulate them.

"So, you weren't his fiancée, but you are now?" Trevor interrupts. Rayen is caught off guard.

"I've worn his ring for a while, but he just asked me today. Answer your question?"

Trevor boldly replies, "Yes. Feisty one you got here Blake and very, very beautiful."

"Thank you, Trevor. I am a very lucky man," Blake says as he kisses Rayen on her cheek. Trevor's eyes rake her over as if she is an exhibit in a museum. Emily runs over.

"Oh my goodness! I am so excited. Finally, a wedding. When, when!" Rayen looks to Blake and raises her eyebrows.

"When, Blake?"

"You are leaving this up to me? I would say tomorrow." "How about…my birthday? It was the most tragic day of my life. I would love to turn it around," she says with an encouraging tone.

Blake speaks sympathetically. "You don't even celebrate it and you are comfortable with getting married on that day?"

"I told you, Blake. I feel different about so many things. And, I want to be happy," she speaks sincerely.

"Well, May 12th it is!" Blake shouts. Abagail runs over and kisses Blake.

"Oh my. I can't wait!"

"Me either, Mom," Emily says. Blake leans over and whispers to Rayen.

"You don't feel pressured, do you?" She smiles.

"No one, I mean no one, can make me do anything I don't want to do." A man approaches them. Blake shakes his hand.

"Hello, Don."

"Hello, Blake. I came to do a story about your parents' party and take some pictures, but now I want to do your wedding announcement. Ms. Vasu is quite the catch, being a beautiful young exec and all. You never settle for less, Blake. Do you?" the man chuckles.

"Baby, this is Donald Mendelsohn, a reporter for the Bay City Times. He and my Dad are lifelong friends," Blake introduces. Rayen reaches to shake his hand.

"I would love for you to do our announcement."

"Great! Come and stand by this delightful tree. I'll get a picture," he directs. They walk holding hands to the Christmas tree. Blake grabs her from behind and pulls her close to him. She places her hand on top of his so that her ring is a clear view. Donald snaps several pictures as guests watch. They turn to face one another, and he places his hands on her hips, and she wraps her arms around his neck. She looks at the camera, and he kisses her cheek. Donald snaps the final shot. "I will use that one. It was so genuine. The smile on Rayen's face is priceless." Blake kisses her several more times before he releases her.

All evening, Blake is beaming. He works the room like a pro. Samuel and his wife arrive. He runs over to them and hugs them. Soon, they are hurrying over to Rayen. "Hi. I am Zaria, Sam's wife. Congratulations. I am so glad Blake has found a woman worthy of his big heart," she states with a polite smile.

Light in the Shadow

"Hello, Zaria. Thank you so much," Rayen states as they embrace.

"Watching him recover from Lauryn was so painful." Rayen scowls when she hears her name. "I know, I know. But anyway, I am so happy for him. Please continue to keep that smile on his face." She says and touches Rayen's arm.

"I will definitely do my best."

"Okay, everyone. It is time for presents!" Robert yells. The children come bursting through the crowd to the tree.

"Blake, can you go get our gifts?" She asks sweetly. He runs out to the car and Sam follows. They return with several wrapped boxes. Emily and Trevor's children are the only grandchildren. It is evident that Robert and Abagail adore them. Hayden and Hunter Huffman are eight-year-old twin boys. Hailey Huffman is the only girl and is three-years-old. Blake takes the gifts to the tree and starts handing them out.

"These are from Rayen, guys. Please bear with her. She doesn't do the gift thing, so this is her first time." They all smile politely as he passes his mom a box. She opens it.

"Oh, Rayen, thank you, honey!" She places a ruby and diamond pendant on her dress. Robert opens his next. It is a gold Rolex watch with several diamonds.

"Oh, looks like she is doing fine to me, son," he chuckles. He steps over to the children and calls Rayen over. He gently caresses her hand. She is a beam of light tonight. She cannot remember the last time she enjoyed Christmas. He hands the children their perfectly wrapped boxes. They rip the fine wrapping paper as if they were animals. The twins receive three different vintage model cars each.

"Say thank you, boys. Rayen, you shouldn't have. Those look very expensive," Emily says with surprise. Rayen nods.

"Thank you." They sing in unison. Blake walks over to his niece.

"Here is yours, Hailey," he says as he plants a sweet peck on her forehead. Emily takes it and opens it. It is a Beatrice Perini collectible doll. Her name is Isadora.

"Oh my goodness. This doll is 2000 dollars! You are too much." She walks over to Rayen and hugs her. She also has a guitar for Daniel, a sizeable check for Danielle's education, and a five-day all-expense paid trip to Paris for Emily and Trevor.

"Wow, Blake! She did a great job to be new at this," Daniel laughs. He approaches Rayen.

"Thank you, baby. You are unbelievable."

"I tried. It wasn't too much was it?" she questions nervously.

"You made me look crazy, but no." He jokes. Abagail motions to Rayen with a box that is not wrapped.

"We didn't know what to get you, so I went for a family heirloom. I talked it over with my girls, and they agreed that Blake deserves it more than anyone else. My grandmother passed this down to my mom and my mom to me. Emily turned it down for Danny, due to Trevor giving her his Mother's." She hands her an antique box. Rayen takes it and pops the clasp. It is a gorgeous antique band with diamonds completely around it. It is not very large, but it is absolutely beautiful. She takes it out and slides it on top of her engagement ring. She looks up at Abagail with tears welding under her eyes.

"Thank you so much. I will never take it off."

"Actually, you should let me slide that on your finger on our wedding day," Blake interjects.

"No, Blake, please? No one has ever given me anything like this," she protests.

Light in the Shadow

"Come on, baby. Let this be your wedding band. It would mean so much to me. This was my Nana's wedding band. My grandpa slid that on her hand at their wedding day. I would love to do the same," he pleads. She spreads her fingers out and looks at it again.

"Okay." She takes off the ring and places it back in the box. "Here, Mrs. Pierce. You keep it until our wedding day."

"I will." She hugs her tight.

Chapter 13

As the party guests disperse, they offer up another round of congratulations. "That announcement will be in the paper on Monday. Congrats again. Merry Christmas, everyone," Donald shouts as he leaves. Rayen walks into the kitchen.

"Abagail, would you like some help?"

"Sure, honey. You can load the dishwasher." She grabs the dishes off the counter and begins to put the dishes in. "Rayen, my son is so happy. He has been a mess for years, but now he is just alive. It is delightful to see," Abagail beams.

"You know, everyone is constantly raving about how happy he is. But, I assure you, he has made me a different person. You have a great son. He is so kind and such a gentleman," she reveals honestly. Abagail crosses her arms and smiles.

"Oh, Rayen, you love him so much. Don't you?"

"I really do, Mrs. Pierce," she says convincingly.

"I knew you were special when I met you at dad's party," Emily states, entering the kitchen. "Well, Mom, Trevor is ready to leave, and the children are very tired."

"Okay, honey. Let me kiss my babies before you go." She exits the kitchen to go say her goodbyes.

"Rayen, I heard about the Lauryn incident. No matter how hard she tries, do not let her win."

"I have no intention of giving Blake up. I will be his wife."

"Good because she can be very persistent. It is the reason he took so long to move on. As miserable as he had been, she kept him tied to her. She is here in the city, and she wants him back."

"I don't care what she wants. He is mine, Emily. I mean that."

"Good. He has really hit the jackpot with you."

"And, I have with him as well."

"I have to go, but let's get together. Our family is very close, and I would really like to get to know you."

"I look forward to it."

They hug, and Emily leaves. Rayen wipes the counter and daydreams about herself actually having a wedding day. She wishes her dad could be there. Blake sneaks up behind her, grabs her around the waist, and kisses her hair. She jumps. "You startled me, Blake."

"I'm sorry, baby. What were you thinking about?" He questions. She pauses a moment and then answers.

"I was just thinking how I wish my dad could be at our wedding...he would have been very proud to walk me down the aisle and into your arms."

"I am so sorry, Rayen," he reassures as he consoles her.

She returns, "No, it's okay. I just never thought about any of this, but now here I am."

He spins her around and speaks sincerely. "I promise I am going to take care of you from now on, and I will make your dad proud." She smiles and wraps her arms around his neck.

"You already have. Now I have to work hard to redeem myself."

"I can't imagine why he would not have been proud of you. You are a terrific person," he states. She turns away.

"My father was an honest man. He never hurt anyone."

"Nor you," He speaks with concern. She looks at him.

Light in the Shadow

"Oh, Blake, you have on rose colored glasses when it comes to me."

"I am a pretty good judge of character, Ms. Vasu."

"If you insist..."

"I do, my love."

He kisses her and dips her back. "Okay, you love birds, break it up," Robert interrupts.

"Dad, I want to love on my fiancée. She has made me the happiest man in the world," he says, pulling her back up.

"I know, son. I know," he smiles at Blake.

"Are you finished helping out so we can get back to my place?" Blake asks impatiently to Rayen. His dad interrupts.

"Blake, you are going to have her for the rest of your life. Let us have her for one day."

"No, Dad. She is mine," he says playfully as a kid that does not want to share the shiny new toy. Robert laughs.

"I am finished with everything. We can go," Rayen adds with a giggle.

"Good." He grabs her by the hand. "I am so damned happy."

"I am too Blake," she returns. They get their coats and leave.

"I am getting married! I can't believe it," she screams. "I never imagined I could be someone's wife." Her smile is so wide. He lifts the hand with the ring on it and kisses it softly.

"I was so afraid to ask you to be my wife."

"I have said to you time and time again I wanted to be with you."

"You have to understand, I have been humiliated, and that scarred me. I was so afraid you were just saying you would."

"Even though I accepted your ring? I thought that was the dead giveaway."

"Well…she took the ring too…"

"Blake, I am not her. Can you guys please leave her where the hell she belongs?"

"Where is that?"

"She is in the past, old news. I am your future, so let's get on with it. Unless, you like living in the past?"

He pumps the brakes. They both jerk forward. She places her hands on the dash board.

"I never want to go back there again, so enough about her."

"Oh, no! I have to tell Angie. She is going to kill me."

She changes the subject as she glances at her phone. It is 12:30 a.m. She dials her number.

"Hey, Rye. What's up?"

"Hello, Angie. I have something to tell you."

"What's wrong you? You sound so serious."

"Yes, umm, Blake asked me to marry him, and I said yes."

"Eek! Oh my goodness! When, when?" she screams.

"My birthday."

"What, wait, really? Why?"

"Well, I wanted that day to finally be positive. I want to make it a happy day."

"Oh, Rayen, you have changed so much. I love the new you, and I love Blake for finding you."

"Thanks."

"When are you telling mom?"

Light in the Shadow

"Monday when she gets here."

"I wanted you to know because there will be an announcement in the paper Monday."

"Thank you for sharing your special news tonight. I want details when you get home."

"How was your Christmas?"

"Great. We will talk," she says a little dryly.

"Okay, bye."

"Congrats. You deserve every bit of it this. Bye, Rye"

She presses end. "Happy now?" Blake asks. Rayen answers,

"Yes, Blake, I am."

"There are so many things we need to discuss. But, let's just enjoy each other," he says as he heads home.

Monday morning, December 27th at 7:30 a.m., Rayen opens her eyes. "Blake looks so majestic sleeping. He is not a morning person, especially since he works midnights." She stares at him for a moment. "He will be my husband. In five months, I will be a wife." He opens his eyes and smiles.

"Are you staring at me?"

"You are so cute asleep," she softly speaks.

He remarks, "Only sleep?"

"Of course not." She kisses him, and he sits up straight. He questions, "Do you have to go in today?"

"Yes, I am the boss, and I must be there. I have some problems I need to handle," she returns.

"Okay, if you must." he says and then slams his face into the pillow.

Rayen takes a shower and dresses for work. She is wearing a dark green blazer with a knee length pencil skirt to match. She has a charcoal camisole under the blazer. She slides on her black boots and grabs her jacket to leave. "Sterling is picking me up. Get lots of rest, Blake."

"When will I see you?" he asks from his pillow.

"Maybe tomorrow. I meet with Detective Shaw today," she says, running around the room to make sure she has everything. "Call me with the details. Maybe I can help."

"I will, my love. I want you to meet Margaret, okay?"

"I look forward to it."

She leans down to the bed and kisses him goodbye. The bell rings, and Blake slowly sits up.

"I want to walk you to the door," he states.

"Oh, this is new," she jokes.

He proclaims, "You are about to be my wife. I have to see you off."

"Okay, sleepy head," she says, shaking her head. He slides across the bed and hops up. He grabs her hand and leads her downstairs. He opens the door. "Hello, Sterling. Get my fiancée to work safely." He twirls her around, pulls her close, and kisses her. "Blake, go back to bed. You are in your underwear."

"Okay. I am just excited and upset that you have to leave me."

"I will see you tomorrow."

"Okay."

He gives her one more kiss, and she leaves. He closes the door and returns to his bed.

Light in the Shadow

"Angela, can you come in here, please?" She stands from her desk and enters the office.

"Yes, Rayen?"

"I am leaving at noon to meet with Ms. Shaw," Rayen states.

"I know. Sterling is picking them up," Angela assures.

She continues, "Margaret is going straight to the house. Will you go and help her get settled in?"

"I planned on it, but what about Evelyn's work?" she questions.

"Oh, that reminds me," Rayen picks up her phone and dials Mr. Drake. "Hello, Evan. I was calling to ask you about the extra work you are giving Ms. Taylor."

"Oh, yes, Rayen. Evelyn quit. She said she was not coming to New York. She left a ton of work, so I split it between our offices."

"So, she isn't there with you?"

"No. She's not there in Michigan?"

"I don't know. I haven't seen nor have I talked to her. I can just have someone go by her apartment, and I will call you when I hear something."

"I am sure she is fine. She is just very upset with me. This is one of her temper tantrums."

"Oh, okay. I will definitely call you, Evan."

"Thanks, Rayen. You are really making things happen down there. I am very proud of you, and I am sure your father is smiling down on you."

"Thank you. I appreciate that."

"Good bye."

"Bye."

Rayen hangs up the phone and gathers her belongings. "I'm leaving, Angie. I'll see you for dinner at the World Café at six."

"Okay, see you then," Angela replies. She dashes out of the door to get in Sterling's SUV.

On the way to the station, she is very uneasy. "Sterling, when you picked up Ms. Shaw how, was she?"

"Very reserved," he answers. They get to the station. Sterling gets out and opens her door.

"Hello, Ms. Vasu. How are you today?" an officer says as she enters the station.

"Fine, thanks. I am here to see Detective Shaw from New York." He offers small talk.

"Yes, of course. I see congratulations are in order. Pierce is a great guy."

"Thank you," she responds. He leads her back to the interview room.

She spots Ms. Shaw. She still looks exactly the same, except for the longer hair that she wears straight now. She stands when Rayen enters. "Ms. Vasu, you are quite the woman now." She shakes her hand. They sit.

"I want to get straight to business."

"Okay."

"Well, we have been going over some old cases. We have a new DNA system on tracking suspects. We are now running old DNA from most of our unsolved crime scenes."

Rayen nods.

"We were testing the DNA from your parents' case, and we got a hit. It was some blood that didn't match your mom or

Light in the Shadow

dad's. I was going to go over it with Margaret, but I wanted to tell you first in person. Margaret has contacted me over the years for updates on the case. I am positive this news will be enlightening for her as well as for you."

"Okay?" Rayen says as her emotions whirl.

"Do you know a man by the name of Matthew Brennan?"

She looks up in the air and thinks. "The name sounds familiar."

"He is an ex-Marine and a Las Vegas Cop. I am told he took care of you the night your grandfather died."

She thinks. "Oh my goodness! The officer that I went to for help. You think he killed my parents?"

"We are not sure. We found a couple drops of blood on the bathroom floor. We don't know much about him, except the fact that he is tied to a woman named Vera Stone. They were last seen together in Texas. When we went to question them, they fled. Is there anything you remember about them that could help us?"

"Vera, my grandfather's assistant and that officer?"

Tears begin to pool, and fury is building in the pit of her stomach.

"Grandfather had something to do with this?"

"We don't know. Do you remember any details or know where Vera would go?"

"How would I know?" she snaps.

"It's just that she took care of you for months. Did you guys develop any kind of relationship?" Rayen's eyes become dark. Her blood starts to boil.

"No. She was a horrible woman. I hated her."

"Okay, Rayen." Detective Shaw reaches out and touches her knee. "I am so sorry to dig up these old wounds, but I think we are really close to solving you parents' murder. Our future correspondence will be through your local police."

"Thank you," she says, holding back her rage.

"I will be in touch," the detective assures.

"Are you flying back to New York today?" she asks as she wipes way a single tear that managed to escape.

"Yes. I am just here to update you on the case and try to get some sort of answers. Before I leave, I will fill Margaret in." Detective Shaw shakes her hand as they stand. They exit the room. Rayen hurries to Sterling.

"I need to go to Blake's house, please."

Rayen cannot stop the tears from flowing. As if Vera hadn't done enough, she was involved in her parents' murder somehow. "Officer Brennan?" she thinks back. "I should have killed them both," she thinks to herself. She places her hand over her eyes. "That bitch is still hurting me. When I find her, I will kill her! But, I can't kill again. I don't want to ruin things for myself. I have to stop." Sterling glances in the rear view mirror.

"Are you alright, Rayen?" She just waves her hand. He continues to drive.

He reaches Blake's house. He jumps out and opens her door. She wipes her eyes. "I am so sorry, Sterling. Tell Angela I won't be home. I will call her and Miss Margaret later."

"I understand," he replies sympathetically. She touches his back and walks to the door. She searches for her keys, but she is so upset she can't find them. She gives up and rings the bell. She takes a peek at her watch. It is 1:27 p.m.

Light in the Shadow

"He is asleep." She rings it again. She waits a moment then she hears the door rattle. He opens the door with concern on his face.

"Rayen, what are you doing here? What happened? Oh no. You've been crying." She finally bursts into tears. "Oh, Rayen, come on." He embraces her as she walks in. They walk over to the couch and sit. He pulls her close to him so she can rest her face on him. She leans into his chest. She places her palm on his bare skin.

"What's wrong, Rayen? Is it your meeting with Shaw?"

"Yes, Blake. It is worse than I thought." She wipes her eyes and grabs a tissue from her purse for her nose. "Vera Stone," she pauses and looks in the air. "It has been literally ten years since I have mentioned her. She was my grandfather's personal assistant and girlfriend." Blake sits up straight. He sits back but grabs her hand to caress it. "When they ripped me away from Margaret, I was devastated. That woman was so cold. At first, I thought I would embrace my situation. I tried to think about meeting new people and getting to know my grandfather. The first week I was there…" She starts to cry again. "The first week I was there, she came into my room and beat me. She then dressed me in lingerie and presented me to him. He raped me, over and over. When he wasn't raping me, she was beating me for four months. The day he died was the happiest I had been since before my parents' murder." She stares at the ceiling. "That day I left that house. I was driven to the nearest police station where I met Officer Brennan. He gave me a place to sleep for the night and delivered me to Margaret the next morning…" She looks at Blake's hand resting on top of hers. She leans down and places her forehead on them. She then sits back up and continues. "They found Officer Brennan's DNA at the crime scene with new technology. They connected him with Vera. Grandfather may have had some type of plot that left my mom and dad murdered." The tears flow as she releases his hand and jumps up. "That fucking bastard stole my innocence and probably took away the only people that ever loved me. My parents were my everything!" Blake stands and walks to her. His heart is heavy. He feels sad for her.

"Is that what you thought would run me away? I would never…" She quickly spins towards him. Her eyes are wide with shock.

"I have never said any of that out loud ever. You were the first person I wanted and needed to share this with. You have to fix me."

"Baby, you are not broken," he encourages softly.

"I was, I mean, I am. Don't you understand? I wanted him to die, and it turns out he deserved it even more now. His fucking greed drove him to kill them! I hate his guts. I spit on his grave!" she screams. He grabs her and holds her tight.

"Rayen, it's okay. Let it out." He kisses her hair.

"I am going to do everything I can to help find them. I promise." She cries so hard and so long, time escapes them. He lies on the couch with her as she cries herself to sleep. "Oh my goodness." He kisses her hair over and over.

Blake calls Sam, and he is already aware of the visit. "I figured she would need you. Don't worry; nothing is going on here," he speaks reassuringly.

"Thanks, Sam. I really appreciate this." He ends his call, still holding Rayen in his arms. He lies there and watches her sleep. "She looks so serene. How could anyone hurt this beautiful creature?" He lies back and takes in everything she revealed to him. "No wonder she was so afraid to tell me. Her grandfather was a fucking monster. Why did this happen to her?" He

Light in the Shadow

caresses her shoulders and kisses her hair again. "She has me now. I will never let anyone hurt her ever again."

Rayen wakes. She sits up and notices that it is dark as she is lying in Blake's arms. She nudges him. "Blake." He turns and looks at her.

"Hey, baby. Are you okay?" he says as he stretches and as she leans.

"I am fine now. Why didn't you go to work?"

"I wouldn't dare leave you like this," he says seriously as she turns away.

"I am so sorry you had to see that. I can't believe I said those things out loud, but it felt so refreshing. I love you so much right now. I wish I met you long ago. I would have had followed a much different path," she says aloud. He wraps his arms around her and kisses her head.

"I love you too. I wish that I met you long ago. My heart would have been in much better care."

She remarks, "I agree." He kisses her lips, her cheeks, her forehead, and then her hair. They gaze at each other, smiling.

"I am such a lucky man!"

"No, I am the lucky one."

"Come on. You need to get out of those clothes. You can use a nice bath and some rest."

He stands and pulls her up from the coach. He sweeps her into his arms and cradles her. "Let me take care of you, Rayen. You have been strong for so long, but I want to be your hero." She smiles.

"Come on, Clark Kent. Fly me to my bath," she jokes. She lets her head fall on his chest as he whisks her upstairs.

Annetta Hobson

Blake places Rayen on the bed and removes her boots. He rubs her feet. She lies back and enjoys his touch. She attempts to remove her blazer. "I'm going to take care of that." She smiles and drops her hands beside her. He removes her jacket. He lies her back down and scurries to the bathroom. He goes to the closet and grabs some bubble bath. He starts the water and pours the bubble bath into the tub. He sticks his hand in to make sure the water is perfect. He returns to her. He continues her disrobing. When she is down to her bare skin, he grabs a towel and wraps it around her. "Come Lois," he chuckles. He pulls her into the bathroom and helps her in the tub. She sits in the bubbles.

"Oooo, this is perfect."

He picks up a loofa and drizzles the soapy water over her body. "Lift your leg." She does what he asks. He then drags it up and down her leg. He repeats it on the other leg. He washes her back. He sits on the floor by the bathtub while she soaks.

Blake wraps his arms around his knees. "Rayen, does Margaret know about your grandfather?"

"No. I would never tell her. She would be riddled with guilt," she remarks.

"I see. Did you tell her about the wedding?"

"Oh no! It totally slipped my mind." She sits up and stands to reach for her towel. "The announcement was in the paper today! I know Angie went out to get it."

"I want to see it myself. We look damn good, baby!" He stands and runs downstairs. While he is grabbing the paper, she steps out and dries off. She smiles, thinking about her life since she landed in Bay City. "Besides one hiccup, life has been perfect here."

"What are you smiling about?" He surprises her.

Light in the Shadow

"My wonderful fiancée," she happily states.

"Oh, are you engaged?" he says playfully as she smirks. He hands her his phone so she can call Margaret. She dials Angie.

"Hello?"

"Hi, Angie. It's me."

"Mom, it's her. What's going on? Sterling told me how upset you were. Are you still at Blake's?"

"Yes. Let me speak with your mom."

Margret grabs the phone. "Hi, Rayen. I wanted to talk to you. How did things go with Ms. Shaw?"

Rayen answers softly, "I really don't want to talk about that now."

"Okay?"

"She will fill you in later. It is just too much right now."

"Honey, I understand."

"I called to tell you that I'm getting married."

Margaret is silent for a moment.

"Aunt Margie?"

"I know, Rayen. Angie showed me the announcement by mistake. She thought you told me."

"Oh, good."

"You look so happy. It is a great picture. Is the wedding really going to be on your birthday?"

"Yes, I wanted that. I need it."

"That is wonderful. Congrats, sweetie!"

Just before she ends the call, the line beeps.

"Blake's line is ringing. I have to go, but we need to do lunch tomorrow."

"I am looking forward to it."

"See you tomorrow."

"Bye."

She hands the phone to Blake. He switches the lines. "Hello?" Blake says.

"Are you fucking kidding me, Blake?" the voice announces. He is confused.

"Lauryn?"

"Are you seriously marrying that bitch? A fucking wedding announcement, Blake! Really? My damn parents saw this shit! I am going to rip her fucking hair out!" Lauryn threatens.

"If you harm one hair on my fiancée's head, I will…" Rayen shakes her head towards him. He calms himself before he speaks again. "I am not going to do this with you, Lauryn. I am marrying Rayen." Lauryn screams.

"I couldn't have hurt you this bad, Blake! I have loved you for so long. My colleagues and family are calling me. They thought we were getting married."

"That's your fault, not mine." He returns as she screams again.

"Blake!" She tries to calm herself. "I moved here to show you I was ready. You sold our house and moved. Now you are marrying this new whore in five months, five months! I can't believe this! I won't accept it. I won't!"

"Lauryn, you really don't have a choice. Rayen loves me, and I love her. She wants to be my wife. So, if you don't mind, talking to you is taking time from her. Goodbye, and do not call

Light in the Shadow

me again, understood?" he warns. She shouts through tears, begging.

"I can't let go! You are my soul mate. Please...I won't give you up." He ends the call and turns the phone off.

"Rayen, I am so sorry." She grabs his face between her hands and kisses him.

"Why are you apologizing? She regrets letting you slip through her fingers. I don't blame her. That's why I am marrying you. You are the one, Blake Pierce."

"The one for you, Rayen Vasu." He smiles as they climb into the bed.

"Tonight, we are going to just hold each other, okay?"

She giggles feeling like a schoolgirl having her first intimate moment. "Okay."

He wraps her in his arms and closes his eyes.

Chapter 14

"Rayen, are you awake?" He nudges her. She moves a little. Just sleeping next to her naked body has been a task he cannot complete. He rubs her behind. She wiggles.

"Oh goodness." He nestles close to her body. He cannot stop himself. He tries to pull her legs apart. "Now, I know you told me you were just holding me tonight," she reminds him.

"I know, but how long can you dangle candy in front of a sugar fiend?" he questions playfully. She laughs.

"Go to sleep. We have plenty of time for that." He rolls his eyes.

"Alright, alright." He wraps his arms around her and snuggles in behind her. They lie there in silence. All they hear is one another's breathing rhythms.

"Rayen?"

"No, Blake."

He smiles. "You don't know what I was about to say."

"I'm sorry. What is it, my love?"

"I was just thinking. When will you move in here? I want you here with me."

She doesn't answer right away. "I don't know. I don't want to abandon Angie. She came here to stay with me."

"Maybe you should talk to her about it. I would like to live with my future wife eventually." She turns to him.

"Turn on the light so I can see your eyes." He releases her and turns the lamp on. "Blake, I am going to be your wife. I want to live with you. Just let me slowly ease out. I don't want to just abruptly leave her. You understand that, don't you?" she remarks.

He kisses her forehead. "I understand. I am just eager to start our new life together. This is your home too. "

"Just give me time to talk to her. I am positive she is expecting that next," she states.

Blake's home phone rings. He looks at the time. "I am not answering that. It is 3 a.m."

"Give it to me," Rayen snaps. "Hello?" There is silence, but she can hear sniffling.

"Hello!" she yells. "Why are you answering his phone?" Lauryn snaps back. Rayen drops her head.

"You have several degrees dealing with the mind, yet you won't or can't comprehend that you fucked yourself. You! Not me and not Blake. You had a man that loved you enough to buy you a house, which you didn't even move into. He waited two years after you humiliated him in front of everyone he cared about for an answer to his marriage proposal. You destroyed your whole wonderful life. You have the audacity to be angry, hurt, stunned, or whatever feeling you would like to convey. Bitch, get it together. You lose!" She hangs the phone up and kisses Blake. "Problem solved."

"Remind me to never get on your bad side," he says stunned.

"That would be impossible." She smirks and snuggles under the comforter as he follows.

Lauryn presses end on her cell phone. She stares at the phone for a very long time. When she finally tears her eyes from it, she scans the room. "I am all alone. How did I get here? Do I really lose the man because I wanted to pursue my career?" She sets the phone on her night stand. Tears stream down her face. "I lose. I lose. I have not been to work in weeks. All the work I, we put into the relationship is wasted. He was there for me through my every endeavor. And, I rewarded him with what?" she grabs her phone and dials. "Jim?"

"Fleming?" the male voice returns.

"Yes. I am going to need my condo back. I will not be staying here. I need to get back to work as soon as possible," she speaks in her professional tone.

"No problem, but I don't know how fast I will be able to move out."

"Don't worry. Take your time. I just have to come back. I can stay in the guest room. I will be there tomorrow."

"Are you alright, Fleming?"

"I will be. I just had an incredible wake up call."

"See you tomorrow."

"Thanks, Jim. See you then."

She presses end. She grabs her laptop and starts to compose an email.

December 28th, 4:26 a.m.

From: Lauryn Fleming

> *Blake, I don't know where to begin. So, let me start by expressing my sincerest apologies. I have been acting like a person that needs treatment. I realized something tonight. While I had you, I did not think of your feelings and how I hurt you. The only thing I cared about was getting to the next level. I started off as the assistant to the assistant. And now I am one of top the Criminal Psychologists for the state*

of Michigan. You helped me get to where I am. You continued to support me even though I hurt you. I am waving the white flag. Rayen is smart. She hit the ground running. I will never make this same mistake again. Rayen learned from my lesson. When he asks, say yes if you want him. I will try to get over you. It will be the hardest thing I ever had to do. You are going to make a wonderful husband. I just will not be the one to experience it. Tell your fiancée if she ever messes up, I will be there to pick up the pieces. I am so, so sorry for everything. I wish I would have been what you wanted, but I now accept defeat. I am leaving Bay City tomorrow to return home. I will not bother you unless it is work related.

I love you, Blake Pierce. Goodbye.

Blake runs downstairs. He searches his fridge for something they can eat for breakfast. "Nothing. I really need to start shopping." He closes the door and walks over to his laptop. He opens it and checks his emails. He scans through offers and old emails. Finally, he spots the email from Lauryn. He opens it and begins to read. After he reads it twice, he closes the computer. "Wow. That was…wow." Rayen enters the kitchen.

"What was wow?" He opens the laptop and points to the screen. She slowly walks over to the table and looks. She reads the email. She makes no expression and walks towards the refrigerator.

"Well?"

"Wow."

He stands and walks over to where she is standing. He grabs her around her waist.

Light in the Shadow

"Finally, she is out of my life."

"Yes, but only time will tell."

"Let's be done with that conversation. I am starving."

"Let's get dressed, and we can go to my house for breakfast."

"This is your house."

She smiles and kisses him. "Let's go."

Margaret dashes to the door when she hears the keys. "Hello, Rayen! You look wonderful, dear. This must be Blake." She walks over and embraces him with a squeeze.

"You must be Margaret," he returns. She releases him and scans him over.

"He is very attractive, Rayen. I couldn't have selected a better match." He smirks.

"Thanks. I love him so much, but it certainly doesn't hurt that he is absolutely delicious." She grabs him and kisses his cheek. "I know there is some food here. Blake's fridge is totally bare, and we would like a home cooked meal," Rayen says, looking helpless. Angela chimes in, "You guys are in luck. Mom is whipping up a giant breakfast for Sterling and I. Join us."

They all enter the kitchen, and Margret resumes constructing her masterpiece of recipes. "Angie, why are you not the one cooking for your mother?" Rayen questions.

She defensively answers, "I wanted to, but she insisted."

"I am so happy to see my baby. I wanted to make her breakfast." Margaret glances over at Angela and smiles.

"I have really missed your cooking, Mom."

"And, I have missed preparing it for you."

Sterling enters the kitchen. "Good morning, everyone." They stop talking to acknowledge his entry. He sits at the table. "How are you, Rayen?"

"I'm fine now. Thanks for asking," she replies. Margaret starts to pour juice in the glasses and place them in front of each person. She then begins to plate the food and serve it. Pancakes, sausage, bacon, eggs, and banana nut muffins are what she offers them.

"Oh wow! I haven't had breakfast like this since college. My mother would cook me breakfast every time I came home," Blake says, reminiscing.

Margaret adds, "Well enjoy. I love cooking. I can't wait for Rayen or Angie to give me grandchildren that I can for too." Blake lights up.

"Miss Margaret, we are on the same page." He touches Rayen's hand and forms a devilish smile on his face.

"Wait a minute! One life-changing event at a time, please?" She pleads. Margaret chuckles.

"I'm sorry. I know I am pushing it." During the conversation, Angie and Sterling scarf down their food without saying a word. When Rayen looks their way, Angie sinks her head and eats faster.

"Angie, what's up?"

"What do you mean?"

"You are way too quiet this morning."

"I really just don't have anything to say. I want you to enjoy the spotlight for a change. You totally deserve it, Rye."

"Thank you. I truly appreciate that."

Light in the Shadow

Margaret grabs a plate and joins them at the table. Blake's cell phone chimes. He pulls it out of the holster and glares at the screen. "Excuse me; I have to take this. He leaves the kitchen and steps into the foyer. Rayen continues to eat. The aroma of the food and the smile on Margaret's face reminds her of her childhood. She would send Rayen to school with muffins. She put love in those muffins every time she made them for her and her parents. Her dad would always remind Margaret to have him plenty in the morning, so he could take some to work. His associates begged for them. Those were haunting memories she had not allowed herself to visit in a very long time. Blake breaks through her reverie. "Baby, I have to go. Trevor has some information about the park murder."

"Oh, Mitchell Weaver?" Sterling notes. "We went to U of M together. He was known as the date rapist, but none of the girls would say anything. His family had so much influence that no one dared to speak of it publicly or even dared to report it to the authorities. It is a shame someone killed him in cold blood. That guy was a total slime ball, but he did not deserve to die and be tossed away like trash." Blake rubs his chin.

"We have an arrest, but I can't give all the details." Sterling displayed no contest.

"Sure, man, I understand."

"I know we did some investigating that led to some minor charges for assault down in Ann Arbor, but that was it. Would you like to accompany me, Rayen? Em usually meets Trevor for lunch. You guys can talk while you go over the information," he speaks quickly. Before Rayen answers, Angie jumps in.

"So are you playing hooky today boss?"

"You know, I forgot to call you last night. Send out a memo that the office will be closed until after New Year's Day. They may return on January 3rd."

"Rayen, that's great. I need a vacation. Will you be here or at Blake's?"

Rayen shoots a worried look towards him. She speaks slowly, "Actually, I need to talk to you about that." Angela stands.

"I already know. Should I look for a new place?" She reassures her.

"I am not leaving now, but I will be in and out for a while. The lease is paid for 6 months, and I have a two-year contract. After I am married you can move, but you are more than welcome to stay." Angie lets out a big sigh.

"Thanks, Rye. I was worried about that."

"Don't be. I will never leave you without making sure you are taken care of first. It's just that my husband to be is quite anxious to have me home," she says playfully. He raises his brows.

"I am dying without her, Angela. I need to wake up next to this woman. I need to go to sleep with the warmth of her in our bed," he jokes. Margaret grins.

"You two are absolutely adorable. I can't imagine what took you so long to enter her life."

"About seven hundred miles," she spits.

"I am just ecstatic that she arrived when she did. I might have made the biggest mistake of my life," he says, playfully wiping his forehead. Margaret glances at Angela in confusion.

Light in the Shadow

"Long story, Mom. Don't ask." Margaret begins to clean the table. "I'll get that for you, Mom. You cooked, now I will clean." Angie grabs all the plates and puts them in the dishwasher. She washes some in the sink. The others exit the kitchen to enter the living room.

"Rayen, do you need me this week?" Sterling asks.

She thinks before she answers, "Um I don't think I do, but if anything changes, I will call you." He motions toward her.

"My family is leaving tomorrow. We go to Hawaii every year before New Year's Day. I want to go, but I wanted to make sure you were taken care of."

"I am sure one of your employees will do, but I think we can manage either way. If we go out, we could drive or get a cab."

"No. Leslie can manage. She is my best driver. I use her for airport pickups, celebrities, and government officials."

"Leslie it is, but only on New Year's Eve. I can drive the rest of the week."

Angela emerges from the kitchen. "Hawaii? When were you going to inform me of this little trip?" Sterling turns to her nervously.

"Today. My father called this morning to tell me we were still going." Angela purses her lips.

"When do you leave?" He looks at the floor.

"Early tomorrow morning." She crosses her arms.

"Well, I guess I'll see you next week then." She storms out of the living area and up the stairs. He pauses and surveys the room. He does not follow her. He grabs his coat and walks out of the door.

"Wow! What was that about?" Blake inquires.

"I don't know, but I am going to find out." Rayen turns to go upstairs.

"Rayen, you cannot solve all her issues. She has to be a grown woman," Blake states.

"I understand that, but...she falls too fast and too hard for the wrong guys," she says with frustration as she stops on the stairs.

He sighs, "Go ahead, honey. I know you are just looking out for her." She views Margaret for a moment and thinks to herself as she comes back down the stairs.

"Does she know something I don't?"

"I know my daughter. And, I know her type," Margaret says as she catches Rayen's blank glare.

Rayen can't help herself as she asks, "Sterling is right for her?"

She says worried now, "No. That is why she wants him. I can see him from a mile away with his false shyness. He is no shyer than a veteran stripper." Blake bursts into laughter.

"I am totally confused." Margaret places her hand on Rayen's back.

"Honey, he was on the phone for hours last night in the bathroom down here. I heard him. He tried to convince her he was watching TV." Rayen stares in horror.

"Why didn't you tell her?"

"She won't listen. She never listens to her mother. Telling her will make her want him more," she reveals sadly. Rayen turns to Blake.

"I promise I won't be long. Don't leave." He peeks at his watch.

Light in the Shadow

"It's 12:37. I need to be at Trevor's office by 1:45," he remarks.

"Okay. I won't be long."

Rayen dashes up the stairs. She walks to Angela's door and knocks. "I don't want to hear it, Mom! Go entertain Rayen!"

"It's me, Angie. I just want to talk to you." She stands there a moment before she hears the door knob turn.

"Come in." She stomps over to her bed and flops across it. Rayen follows her and sits carefully on the bed.

"I know what you are going to say, Rye. I don't want to hear it."

"I came up here to listen, Angie."

She turns to Rayen with tears forming in the corner of her lids. "I don't know what is wrong with me. I always, always date douche bags. I thought since you came here and found true love that I would too."

"You have to be patient. I have always guarded my heart. No one has ever been granted access. I have been hurt several times. The way Blake slid in, it had to be fate."

"I know."

"Tell me what the issue is?"

Angela sighs. "I knew from day one Sterling was an ass. I was getting a ride from work, and he asked could he use the restroom." Rayen hitches her brow and then rolls her eyes.

"I know, Rye. But, he was so darn cute…after he finished in the restroom, he lingered, so I offered him a drink and a meal. Of course he accepted."

Rayen stares. Angela has her undivided attention.

"We got so drunk I didn't want him to drive home. At first, he fell asleep on the couch, and I went to bed. Later that night, he crept in my room. I woke to him kissing my belly. I wanted to so bad. It had been so long for me that I just let it happen."

Rayen turns her head to hide her disgust. "He took advantage of you, Angie!"

"No, Rayen, he didn't. I wanted him just as much as he wanted me." She shakes her head.

"The next morning, he got dressed and left. He didn't call me for days, so I called him. Our relationship has been based solely on sex, and he made it very clear that was how he wanted it to stay."

"Angie, you are not the kind of girl."

"I really care about him…and he doesn't know…I…"

"Tell me now, Angela!"

She hesitates. "I think I am pregnant." She bursts into tears.

"Oh my goodness, Angie! A baby?"

"I'm not sure, but my cycle hasn't been regular for months."

She hugs her. "That bastard will pay."

"No, Rayen! I knew he was not into me like that, but I let this happen. I just pretended it was more, and he played along for my mom's sake, but I don't think she is convinced."

"She's not."

"I figured as much. You have to tell her."

"I can't. She will be so disappointed."

"You need her."

"I have you, don't I?"

Light in the Shadow

"Of course you do. Just go to the doctor and make sure."

"I have an appointment January 5th."

"Good. I will keep my mouth shut until then."

Angela hugs her. "Thanks, Rayen. I really love you."

"And, I love you."

She turns her attention to the clock and she stands. "I have to go, but we will talk."

Angie stands to hug her once more before she leaves.

Blake pulls into the parking space. "There is Emily now." He hops out. "Em! Em!" She spots him.

"Hey, Blake. Trevor said you were coming, but I got tired of waiting," Emily says.

"Sorry, Rayen had something to handle," he offers.

"Oh, where is she?" She looks around. Rayen steps out of the car.

"Hello, Rayen."

"Hi, Emily. Are the children enjoying their gifts?"

"From afar. It will be a while before I will allow Hailey to touch that gorgeous and very expensive doll."

"I understand."

They leave the parking lot and enter the building. When they get onto the elevator, Blake selects the 6th floor. They exit the elevator and step directly into the DA's office. Blake walks up to the desk, and the receptionist spins around. Her face brightens when she notices it is Blake. "Hello, Officer Pierce. It's been a while," she says.

He returns, "Hello, Holly. How are you?"

"Very well, thank you," she politely replies. He reaches back and grabs Rayen around the waist.

"This is my fiancée, Ms. Rayen Vasu." She stands and extends her hand.

"Hi, I am Holly Rothschild."

"Hello, Ms. Rothschild. It is a pleasure."

"The pleasure is mine, Ms. Vasu. This way, please?"

She escorts them to Trevor's office. She sashays as she leads. She is obviously putting an extra sway in her walk for Blake to see. He notices the distaste in Rayen's expression and slides his hand inside of hers. She jerks a little as he grips her hand. He blows a kiss at her, and her expression loosens. They arrive at Trevor's door. The plaque reads Trevor Huffman District Attorney. She taps twice and turns the knob. She nods as they enter. "Mrs. Huffman, Ms. Vasu, and Blake Pierce." Her tongue caresses his name and it lingers. Blake places his hand on Rayen's back and leads her in. "Hello, Detective. It is so great of you to finally make it. My lovely wife has been waiting for you quite some time."

"Sorry, Trevor."

"Rayen, it is always such a breath of fresh air to see you." He extends his hand. She grips his hand and gently shakes it.

"Hello, Trevor."

"Please sit," he directs. They all take a seat.

"Emily, you and Rayen can stay in here and talk. I will take Blake in the other office." Trevor comes from his behind his desk. Blake gives Rayen another look and as they exit.

"What do you guys have planned for New Year's Eve?" Emily asks.

Light in the Shadow

Rayen states, "Nothing in particular. I was just going to find a party and go." Emily folds her hands in her lap and crosses her legs.

"We give our annual New Year's Eve bash at the boat club. I would be offended if you two didn't come."

"I would love to. Do you mind if I bring my little sister?"

"Angela? Please, she is family also."

"Okay, we will be there."

They start to chat. An hour passes, and the men have not returned. "Excuse me, Emily," a woman brushes past. Rayen does not look up right away but immediately recognizes the voice.

"Evelyn?" Her eyes shoot up.

"Rayen." She purses her lips. "What brings you here? Oh yes. You are engaged to the DA's brother in law."

"That explains my attendance, and yours is?" She asks. Evelyn laughs an evil wail.

"I work here, sweetie. Mr. Huffman was kind enough to give me a job as a financial advisor for the office. I make sure there are funds available for the trails."

"You two know each other?" Emily interjects.

"Yes, Mrs. Huffman. We were friends I thought, but that is neither here nor there. Have a great afternoon." She stacks the papers she carried in neatly on Trevor's desk and struts out of the office.

"What is with her? I thought she was a lovely young lady until now." Rayen fiddles with her fingers.

"Her ex is a very good friend of mine. Please don't ask the ugly details. I don't have the stomach for this today; I am so sorry."

"We have plenty of time for gossip." Emily reaches over and pats her hand. She lifts her head and manages a smile. They get back to their previous conversation. Soon, the men reenter the room.

"Are you ready, Rayen?"

"Emily, thanks for waiting with me. I am sorry about lunch. Maybe we can go another time," she says as she stands.

"It's not a problem, Rayen. I am just too darn happy for you and Blake. We must get together after the holidays and start planning for your wedding."

"I am looking forward to that."

Emily kisses her husband and walks out of the office. "We will get you all of the tapes and transcripts from the interview Trevor," Blake states.

"Good," Trevor returns as he motions toward Rayen. He leans in and hugs her. His lip brushes her ear. A foul sensation rides her back. "It is always nice to see you and again, welcome to the family. He straightens his blazer, walks to his desk, and nestles in his chair. He picks up his files and begins to work. She stares at him for a second. She does not like him. She turns to Blake. He is holding out his hand.

"Shall we?" She grabs his hand with both her hands, and they leave. On their way out, Evelyn passes them.

"Hello again, Detective Pierce. Rayen." Rayen does not speak back. They get to the elevator. The bell chimes. They step in and the door closes.

Chapter 15

Thursday, December 30th at 3:30 p.m.. Blake holds Rayen's hand as she steps into the car. "Did you know Evelyn was working for Trevor?" she asks.

"No I did not," he answers honestly. "Did you call her Father?"

"That was my intention, but it appears he may already know since I haven't heard anything from him."

"Is she still upset about Joshua ending things with her?"

"Did you not see how she looked at me?"

He shuts her door, scurries around, and hops in.

"No, I didn't, but I would think she might just be a little envious that you are marrying such a handsome devil."

She smiles. "I guess that could be a good reason."

"Are you bored since are not working this week?"

"No. I am having a ball. I just miss you while you are working."

"Oh, trust me, I count the minutes until I see you at 4 a.m."

"Don't forget, we need to pick Angela tomorrow before the party.

"What time do you think would be best to pick her up?"

"Seven or eight sounds great. This is going to be our first New Year together. I am going to relish each and every minute to make it enjoyable for you."

"Trust me, I plan on it too."

Annetta Hobson

He jumps in the car and drives to work. "I wish we could just lie in bed all day naked. I really want to spend all of my time with you. I love being around you, but it's not enough time in the day for us." She reaches over and grabs his thigh. She slowly slides her hand higher and higher. She says seductively,

"Maybe we should utilize our time that we do have more wisely." He glances at her and quickly returns his eyes to the road. "I mean, I feel I keep you from having more. Maybe I should give you something to hold you over until I see you again, so I can keep up my end as well as you do." The silky words slide off of her tongue. Her hand continues to inch upward.

"Rayen, what are you doing?" He says, mildly panting.

She leans over her hand still in his lap. He glances at her again. His eyes fill with anxiety. He eagerly awaits the point of contact. He tries to focus on the road. "Should I pull over?" He asks slowly while breathing more rapidly.

"No, keep driving." She takes her free hand and clicks the seatbelt so it flips off. Her hand finally reaches its destination and he is fully erect. She rubs it and moans.

"Rayen," he breathes. She massages it through his pants. He grinds matching her rhythm. "Oh, Rayen!" He rolls his eyes. She unzips his pants. Her other hand joins in. She uses it to free his erection. "You have become quite the seductress," he whispers. She stops, grabs his face, and kisses his lips.

"Rayen...I am going to crash," he resounds.

"Oh no, just focus," she utters softly. She leans down and places her lips around his exposure.

"Ohh!" he moans. She slurps and sucks. She starts at the tip and works her mouth down so that it is completely covered. She can feel the tip tickling the back of her throat. She releases it from her mouth. "Shit! Rayen, don't stop."

She smiles. She caresses it and slides her tongue around it. She begins to slurp and suck again. Up and down, in and out. She performs like a professional. He tries to keep his eyes on the road. He is gripping the wheel with both hands.

"Oh shit...ohh."

She picks up the rhythm faster, and the slurping sound fills the car. She keeps hold of him and matches his rhythm with her mouth. Soon, he explodes inside her mouth, letting out a loud cry. He turns the wheel and pulls over. "Whoa, Rayen! Are you trying to kill me?" he breathlessly speaks. He lifts his body to zip his pants.

"If I were trying to kill you, I probably wouldn't get you off first." She smirks.

"Oh, baby, you are becoming a very naughty girl."

"I want to be as naughty as I have to be. I am going to do any and everything for you, Blake."

He grabs her face and kisses her passionately.

"You are late for work, Blake."

"I don't care. You shouldn't have taken me in your mouth like that while I was driving."

Rayen leans back in the seat with satisfaction. He sits forward and gazes at her. "Can I return the favor?" She lifts her head and turns to him.

"How?" He puts the car in drive and takes off.

"Where are we going?"

"I am going to work, and you are going with me." She leans back then jumps forward.

"No, Blake!" He chuckles.

"Oh yes. It will be quick."

"You are insane, Detective."

"I am since the day I lay eyes on you. You make me want to live in the moment. I want to scrap all of my plans and start over."

"When you say things like that, it makes me think you love me."

He looks at her with a serious glare. "I do really, Rayen. I have never loved anyone more than I love you."

Blake pulls up to the station, gets out, and opens her door. "Come on." She steps out and he grabs her hand. They walk into the police station. He caresses her hand as they enter.

"Hello, Pierce." a chunky officer waves as they pass the desk.

"Hello, fiancée," he adds. She sends him a girly wave as he continues his work. Blake drags her along. They walk down the hall. He checks behind him and then carefully scans the hall.

"I am really going to enjoy this." He pulls her into a room in the back. Most of the officers use it to nap in. It has a cot and a 26" flat screen television. He closes the door and locks it. He sweeps her into his arms. He kisses her deeply, removes her dress, and undergarments. He lays her down and removes his blazer. He kisses her stomach.

"I cannot believe we are doing this," she says. He completely undresses and lies down beside her.

Light in the Shadow

"I need you, Rayen, every day, all day. That stunt you pulled on the way here only made me want to make love to you right here right now," he says in a deep husky voice. He grabs her hips and moves closer. He begins kissing her, and they make passionate love.

"I had a wonderful day. The guys kept asking me why in the hell was I smiling," he says as he drives home. Rayen yawns. She is dressed in sweat pants and a t-shirt underneath her coat. "What's wrong? Am I boring you, baby?" She slowly turns to him. "Blake, it is four in the morning. Maybe I need to start driving my car and letting you keep yours."

"I really like you dropping me off. I get to look at you for a few more minutes." She places her hand over her mouth and yawns again.

"I go back to work next week, so this is just temporary."

He returns, "I know, but I am really enjoying all this extra time with my beautiful fiancée." She smiles, straining to keep her eyes open. They reach the house and go inside.

When Blake steps in the door, he takes off Rayen's coat. Suddenly, his phone rings. He hangs her coat on the rack. 'Who could this be?' He slips out of his own coat and answers it. "Hello?"

Rayen waves at him and whispers, "Goodnight, Blake."

"Wait," he whispers back as he places his hand over the phone.

"I'll see you upstairs." She walks into the kitchen and up the stairs. He shakes his head and follows.

"Hello?" he states again walking through the kitchen.

"Hello, son."

"Dad, why are you calling so late? Is everything alright?"

"With us, yes. With you, not so much."

"What do you mean, Dad?"

"Well, I got a call from one of my buddies at the station and you seem to be slacking a bit. Can you tell me what's going on with you?"

Blake becomes agitated. "Dad, I don't need you checking up on me. I am a grown man."

His father pauses, "You are a man with a bright career in law enforcement. Don't screw this up, Blake. Rayen is gorgeous. We love her, but you are caught up, and it is affecting your work ethic. That stunt you pulled this afternoon…well it almost got you fired." Blake covers his mouth then he releases.

"Dad, I am in love with someone who loves me back. Do you want me unhappy? Better yet, alone? It seems to me that whether I am with Lauryn or whomever doesn't matter as long as I don't screw up my career?" His father speaks carefully but directly.

"Son, you know that is not the case. I love you, and I definitely want you happy. Focus and get back to the top detective I know you are. You are going to be chief of police one day. You are a very wise young man. Be in love and treat Rayen as good as I did your mother. Just don't be reckless, son. Please?" He sighs and drops his head.

"You are right, Dad. Rayen tried to tell me, too, but I want to be with her all the time. I have never felt this way about anyone. She makes me not give a damn about anything else. I can't help myself." His dad laughs.

Light in the Shadow

"Son, that's how you know it's true. But...stop missing days and no more stolen moments in the back room. You got it, Blake?"

"Yes, Dad, I got it. Must have been bothering you a lot for you to call me after four in the morning?"

"You are important and I know your career is important."

"But, Rayen is more important to me than anything. I hear you, Dad, and I will do better, but she is my life now. I don't care about anything those guys say at the station. Maybe after we are married, I won't be so desperate for her."

"After the wedding, you will be more desperate for her. Take it from me."

"Okay, Dad, I love you. Thanks."

"And, I love you, Blake. You kids are my whole reason for being. Take care, Blake."

"Bye, Dad."

He presses the end button and continues up the stairs. He gets to the room, and Rayen is sleeping soundly. He undresses and takes a hot shower. When he gets out, he tiptoes to the bed and slides behind her. She reaches for his hands and nestles in front of him.

"Who was that?"

"It was my Dad."

She turns toward him.

"Is everything alright?" she says with concern.

"Yes. He was calling to lecture me on my carefree behavior and on our little tryst at the station." She jumps up.

"No!"

"Yes, baby. I am so sorry. I didn't think anyone would notice."

"Are they watching every move you make?"

"Yes. My dad wants me to be in charge one day, but the new chief, Scott, wants his son Adam to take over. So, it would be a service to them if I keep missing days and acting like a lovesick puppy."

She smiles and caresses his face. "I am a lovesick puppy too, if that makes you feel any better."

"It doesn't, you aren't jeopardizing the career you love for me."

She slides up and presses her back against the headboard. "Just because you do not see me, doesn't mean I don't mess up."

"No... not you?" he says sarcastically.

"Okay, Mr. Grumpy. I am going to sleep now. I will talk to you when you are not upset about doing something I told you we should not do." She slams her body onto the bed and throws the covers over her head. He slides underneath the comforter behind her and wraps his arms around her. He kisses the back of her head.

"I'm sorry, baby. You didn't put me in your mouth on the way to work and make me want to put myself inside you at my job. I will never make that mistake again." He jokes.

"Oh, sir! You never have to worry about that happening again. Goodnight!" She says with anger then closes her eyes.

"Shit!" he says to himself. He snuggles in and falls asleep.

"Angie, what time do you want me to pick you up for the party?" Rayen asks.

"What time do you want me ready?" she returns.

Light in the Shadow

"8 p.m."

"I'll be waiting."

Rayen presses end. She stands and walks out of the bedroom. She walks downstairs and searches for Blake. She looks in the kitchen, but she does not find him. She turns and walks in the living room. When she does not find him there, she calls his name. "Blake! Where are you?"

"I'm here," he says softly.

"Where?" She looks around, trying to follow his voice.

"I'm in the foyer," he answers. She scans the area and spots him on the floor.

"What's wrong? Why are you on the floor Blake? What happened?" He does not look up.

"I was just sitting here thinking." She walks over to him and sits beside him. She places her arm around him and rubs his back. "I was going to the door to take a peek outside and I just sat down. I've been thinking for a while."

"Why are you thinking? What's the problem?" She turns her head to the side and glares at him.

He turns to her as if he is in pain.

"What is it, Blake!"

He turns back to the floor. "Are we rushing, Rayen? I feel as if I somehow bullied you in to this situation." Rayen stops rubbing his back.

"Are you kidding me, Blake?"

"No, Rayen, I am not. After talking to my father, it made me think. I have never behaved this way before. My father has never had to bring me back to reality." She snatches her arm from around him.

"Back to reality? What in the hell does that mean?" He searches her face with his eyes before he answers.

"I have been behaving irresponsibly. I've been jeopardizing my job and my upstanding reputation." Rayen's facial expression is ghastly. He drops his head. "I am so sorry. I am just…" She quickly stands.

"You know what? I am so sorry I gave you my heart and loved you like I have never loved anyone before. Let's not mention how I revealed my secrets, which I have never ever disclosed. And, you do this? I don't fucking understand. You love me. What is the fucking problem?"

"I am just…thinking, Rayen. I am…"

She throws her hand up. "Just do all the thinking you want. I am going home. Bring the New Year in alone. Is that enough thinking for you? Matter of fact, why don't I just give you some space for a while!"

"What does that mean? What are you saying?"

She storms through the kitchen and up the stairs. He tries and follows her. She bursts through the door and grabs her things. All the things she has in the closet and the dresser she throws them on the bed. "Wait Rayen," he sighs. "I'm sorry, I…" She turns and stares at him.

"Tell your Dad he doesn't have to worry anymore. I wouldn't dare ruin his wonderful son's future." He tries to grab her. She snatches from him and shoots him a death glance. "No. I get it. I really do, Blake. Daddy does not approve of the carefree exec. I need to be a stuffy bitch like Lauryn, or maybe it's because I don't have a law enforcement career." While she

Light in the Shadow

speaks, she packs her things in her overnight bag. Tears began to stream down her cheeks.

"Rayen, please don't cry."

"Fuck you, Blake Pierce!" She throws on some sweat pants over her boy shorts. She grabs her bags and stomps down the stairs. When she gets to the door, she grabs her coat from the rack. Slowly she turns to him. "I really thought you were better than this. We are not hurting anyone. I released myself to you. No one could take that from us as far as I was concerned. Your dad expresses a little distaste for your behavior, and now you are confused and bewildered. People in love behave recklessly sometimes. I have never been in love, but I have witnessed it." He tries to speak, but she stops him. "No! I have heard your inner voice, and it is having second thoughts. I'll save you the dilemma."

"No, Rayen! I do love you, baby, I do."

"Well, maybe love isn't enough." She says as she swings the door open and storms out.

"Rayen, don't go please."

She steps off the porch and begins walking.

"Rayen, at least let me drive you."

She turns toward him and yells, "Fuck you and your ride!" She storms down the block. Blake hurries upstairs, get dressed, grabs his car keys, and coat. He dashes out of the door and jumps in his car.

Rayen is marching down the block. "I can't believe he said we were rushing! I have given him all of me against my better judgment." Tears stream down her face. She struggles with her bag. She switches it from hand to hand. Blake pulls up beside her.

"Rayen, come on. I am so sorry. I just respect my dad's opinion." He puts the car in park and jumps out. She does not stop walking. "I'm sorry," he yells behind her as she picks up the pace. He jogs to try and keep up with her. "You are so far away from home. There aren't any cabs, and it's New Year's Eve." She pauses and drops her bag.

"Take me to my house, please." He grabs her bag and tosses it into the car. Before he can open her door, she grabs it and hops in. He closes it and scurries to his side and jumps in. He puts the car into drive and pulls off.

"Is there anyway I can convince you to come back to our house?" he questions. She sighs and turns to him.

"I have never been more serious about anything in my entire life."

He resounds, "What are you saying, Rayen? I am head over fucking heels in love with you. I won't live without you." She slams her head into the seat.

"We are just going to take a break from each other. When you are sure that you are making the right decision about marrying me, then and only then will I come back."

"I am sure. I promise," he admits. She looks at him with tears in her eyes.

"You didn't look sure. Actually, you were very unsure." He turns his eyes to the road. "See? Don't call or come by. I will see you when I feel you are absolutely positive you are ready for all of this," she demands. He scrunches his brow.

"I have been ready for this since I laid eyes on you. I don't know if I will survive not being able to talk to you or see you." She wipes her tears.

Light in the Shadow

"You will be fine. Spend time with your father. Be on time to work. Show him you are serious about your job and that you are serious about your future."

"My future is with you," he states softly. "Are we still getting married in May?" She sits forward as he approaches her condo.

"That all depends on you." She steps out before he can get to her side. She grabs her bag out of the back. She does not look back as she walks to the door and fumbles with her keys. He runs up to the door before she disappears inside.

"I am a fucking idiot. I shouldn't have said those things to you. I was just worried about what my dad said."

She pauses and rolls her eyes. "Everything you said is exactly what you were feeling. Maybe the reason you hate Lauryn so much is because she embarrassed you in front of your dad. Obviously his opinion of you means more than you think." He reaches for her hand but she pulls it away.

"Goodbye. I'll call you." He sighs. He looks as if he is going to cry.

"I do love you. I want to marry you. Please don't this."

"Goodbye, Blake."

She turns and closes her door. She leans against it for a while. The tears come faster and harder. She does not hear his footsteps nor does she hear his car pull off. She lifts herself from the door and start up the stairs. She turns to look out of the small window in the door. He is still standing there with his hands in his pocket. He just stands there and stares at the ground. She shakes her head and continues up the stairs. She gets to the top and opens the door. She steps inside and slams her bag on the floor. Angie meets her at the door.

"You're early. I wasn't expecting you for three more hours. Why aren't you dressed?" She looks around her and spots her bag. "Rayen, what happened?" When she opens her mouth to speak, Margaret enters the room from the kitchen.

"Hello, Rayen."

"Hey, Aunt Margie." She lifts her bag and heads up to her room.

"Wait, Rayen? What is going on? You look like you have been crying." She strains a smile.

"Can we talk tomorrow? I am so tired."

"Tomorrow? We're not going to the party?" Angie asks shocked.

"No. I am so sorry. I'm getting a drink and getting in my bed." She proceeds up to her room. "Bring me a bottle of something. Whatever I have in there, I'll take it."

Rayen opens the door to her room and turns the light on. She scans it then steps in. She tosses her bag in the closet and steps out of her sweat pants. She enters her bathroom and turns on the water. She undresses and steps in. Angela yells to her. "I found some white wine. Is that good enough, Rye?"

"Yes, it's fine." She washes and steps out. She grabs her towel and dries herself off. She goes over to her dresser and selects a long white silk nightgown. She opens her door and yells down the hall. Why don't you guys come in here? We can watch the ball drop. And have some girl talk." Angie peeks out of her room.

"Okay, I was hoping you asked." She laughs. Margaret makes her way to her room and Angela follows. Rayen slides in her bed and pours some wine in her glass.

"Umm, Rayen," Angie carefully speaks.

Light in the Shadow

"Yes?" she answers, sipping her wine.

"Why is Blake sitting in his car?" she asks as Rayen almost spits her wine out.

"He's not still out there?"

"Yes, he is," Angie says.

"What is going on, Rayen?" Margaret snaps. She sighs and places her glass beside her bed. She explains everything that has happened and what has led to her return.

"Did he actually say you guys were rushing?" Angie questions.

"Yes. I was mortified," she responds. Margaret shakes her head.

"Sometimes men stick their feet in their mouths, honey, but I know one thing: that man loves you. He adores you, Rayen. Don't write him off."

"I'm not. I am just giving him time to make sure it is what he wants," she says, trying to convince herself.

"Okay, let's just drink wine, enjoy this boring New Year's Eve, and the fact that neither of us have a man to kiss this year." Angie states before she gulps down wine. "I'll go and make sure there is plenty more where that came from." Angela dashes out to go to the kitchen. Margaret steps away also. They return about the same time.

"He finally left," Margaret informs.

"Good, maybe he will have a nice evening after all."

"Rayen, don't do that. You know he is going home to mope."

Rayen smiles. "I sure hope so."

They laugh and drink together for hours.

"Its 11:59! Let's count down, ladies." They watch the television and they sing in unison.

"10, 9, 8, 7, 6, 5, 4, 3, 2, 1, Happy New Year!" Margaret stands, and they begin to hug one another. Angela breaks away and speaks.

"I just want say although I had some tough times, last year was the best. Rayen, you finally opened yourself not only to us, but to love." She smiles.

"But, for how long?"

"Stop it! We got a wedding to plan. I am leaving Monday, but I will be trying to make wedding plans from New York."

"If there is still a wedding, Aunt Margie. His dad really got to him about his job."

"Oh, the hell with him! Blake will not let you go. Just wait and see. Now I am going to sleep."

"Me too. Mom, wait for me." Angela trails her mom out of Rayen's room and closes the door behind her.

Rayen checks her phone. It reads 12:01 a.m. Before she can set it on the nightstand, it buzzes. She looks at the number, and it is Blake. She does not answer. It rings and rings. She turns over and nestles under the comforter. The ringing stops. A few minutes pass, and she hears a single chime escape from her cell again. She turns over and grabs it. She glares at the screen.

Text Message.

She presses the button to open it.

January 1st, Saturday - 12:10 a.m.

From: Blake

Light in the Shadow

Happy New Year's, Baby! I wanted us to be kissing and enjoying each other as the year rang in. But, I see you are serious about this separation. I do not agree with it. I love you. I had a moment of doubt, and now you are punishing me. Don't do this, Rayen. I'm so, so sorry. It will never happen again. I swear it. I am going to put all my efforts into proving to you that I can love you completely and be responsible as far as work. I am not going to stop calling you, and I won't to stop trying to see you. Every moment I am not working, you will be all that I focus on. You will be Mrs. Blake Pierce. Start the plans because we are getting married May 12th.

I love you Rayen, and nothing or no one will ever change that.

Rayen deletes the message and does not respond. She lies in her bed and covers her head. Eventually, she falls asleep.

Chapter 16

Monday, January 3rd at 9:15 a.m., Rayen struts into her office. She and Angela drove in together. "Start the Lansing contracts. Organize them and get them to me before noon. Okay?" she directs. Angela takes her coat off, sits down at her desk, and immediately begins to work. Rayen takes her coat off and hangs it on the rack in her office. She sits in her chair and switches on the computer. She has several emails from clients and the corporate partners. She goes right to answering them. By noon, Angela peeks in.

"I am all done. You want lunch? Everyone is going out."

"No, Angela. I'm fine, just bring me back something. You know what I like."

"Will do. See you in an about an hour."

"Okay." She returns to her work.

Rayen focuses on her work. She tries not to think about Blake, but it is very hard when he continues to text her. She stops typing and places her elbows on the desk. She rests her chin on her clasped hands. "I don't blame his father. I never should have allowed him to get close to me. My secrets would destroy his career for good. If anyone found out his wife was a murderer, it would ruin him." She closes her eyes and sadness washes over her. "Maybe I should let him go for good. No, I can't! I love him, and I could never love anyone more." Her phone rings. It startles her from her thoughts. She does not look at the screen.

"Hello, Rayen Vasu."

At first there is silence.

Annetta Hobson

"Hello?"

"Hello Ms. Vasu."

"Yes? Who is this?"

"Let me see. Who should I say I am? Well, how about your step grandmother."

Rayen gasps. "No, it can't be!"

"Oh yeah, you little bitch! It's me!"

"Vera?"

She laughs. "Did you miss me, little girl?"

Rayen purses her lips. Anger, rage, and fear run through her.

"And, what the fuck do you want with me?"

"First of all, Happy New Year. We are practically family. Is that how you speak to your family?"

"You raggedy bitch! You are no relative of mine."

She pauses. "I'll just cut to the chase. I know you know about me. The fucking police are all over us. I need money and you, my dear, are going to give it to me."

Rayen laughs so loud her voice echoes through the office. "Why, you stupid, delirious whore. I wouldn't piss on you if you were on fire. Why would I give you money?" She mocks her.

Vera threatens, "Well one reason is if you don't...I won't give Margaret and Angela the courtesy of a quick and painless death. I will make them wish they never walked into that Manhattan high rise." Rayen clutches her chest.

"You wouldn't. You don't..." Vera interrupts.

"Oh, I do know where they live. I also know they are in Michigan with you. I have made it my job to always know

Light in the Shadow

where you are staying. Impressed?" Rayen is at a loss of words. She does not know how to respond.

"Cat got your tongue? What's it gonna be?"

"I am not giving you money, Vera."

"Fine, then say your goodbyes because those bitches are history. Matt is already close. He knows you haven't been at the condo lately. You've been occupied with that yummy cop. I understand. I have a weakness for law enforcement too."

"Look, stop threatening me. I am not afraid of you anymore. I am not that fifteen year old girl you tortured."

"Suit yourself."

"Look, bitch! Bring it on. I want to hurt you so bad. I will wait on you."

"Oh! Rayen, you are so confident. You think you can catch me?"

"If you come to Michigan, I will find you."

"We shall see."

Before Rayen can respond, Vera hangs up the phone.

"Vera? Vera? Shit!" She slams the phone down. She stands and begins to pace. "What am I going to do? Fuck! I should have offered her the damn money. Now, I don't know when she will come." She paces back and forth. Finally, she scurries back to her desk. Her heels click clack across the floor. She picks up the phone and dials.

"Hello," Margaret answers.

"Hi, Aunt Margie."

"Hi, dear. Sterling is loading my things into the car. What's wrong?"

"Don't go. Please stay a little longer."

"Rayen, my flight leaves in an hour. I am leaving as we speak."

Rayen panics. "Please, Miss Margaret, don't leave. I need you here. Please?"

"Rayen, what is it? Is everything alright?"

"No. I need you. Please stay?"

Margaret frowns. "What about my ticket?"

"I will take care of it, I promise. Just don't leave."

"Okay, but how long?"

"I don't know, but I will make sure you have everything you need."

"Okay, Rayen."

"Thanks. I'll see you later. Don't go anywhere and don't open the door for anyone."

"Okay?"

She hangs up.

"Rayen, I brought you a corned beef sandwich," Angie states.

"Good. Come in," she says shaking. She asks with concern,

"Rayen what's wrong?"

"Nothing really," she pauses. "I just asked Margaret to stay. She agreed." Angela's eyes grow wide.

"Why on earth would you do that?"

Light in the Shadow

"I am going to need to keep an eye on you guys, so for now we will be spending a ton of time together," she returns. Angela raises her brows.

"You are kidding, right?" Rayen stands and walks over to her.

"No, Angie. I am very serious."

"But, I didn't want Mom here for the baby situation."

"We can handle that. Don't worry. I have got other things we can occupy her with."

"Okay?"

Angela turns and looks at Rayen. She is rubbing her hands together nervously. She watches her and then returns to her desk.

Weeks pass, and Rayen's behavior becomes even stranger. She refuses to leave the house unless it is necessary. Margaret is getting worried, but Rayen will not answer any questions. Angela's relationship with Sterling is non-existent since the pregnancy scare. She informs him after she got confirmation of the false alarm. He is so upset about it that he has been avoiding her. When they ride to work, he is always very professional, too professional. Rayen will not let Angela go out. It is like they are under house arrest. Work then home is their routine and poor Margaret does not even get to go grocery shopping. She never goes anywhere alone. She fears Vera's threat is real, and she is somewhere waiting to strike.

Blake has been calling, and she will not respond. She refuses to put anyone else in danger. Blake has come by several times, but she will not let him inside. One day he decides he will just come to her office, but she closes her office door and refuses to see him. She deletes his texts. She would rather he forget her, but he cannot and will not give up. Blake decides to talk to his sister about it. His family has been questioning him about the wedding. A month has passed, and there are no plans being made.

"Hey, Blake, I have been trying to reach Rayen? She has not returned my calls," Emily asks with concern.

"Em, I messed up big time," he responds sadly.

"What happened, Blake?"

"Come to Dad's. I need to talk."

"Okay, when?"

"How about fifteen minutes?"

"I guess. I'll have to bring the kids."

"I'm leaving now."

Sunday, February 13th at 5:40 p.m., Blake enters his parents drive way. Emily pulls in behind him. She exits her red Lexus RX 350. She opens the doors, and the twins jump out. She walks around and unbuckles Hailey from her car seat. Blake gets out of his car and rushes to help her. He picks up his niece. "Hey, Hailey. I have missed you so much." He kisses her cheek and she giggles. They approach their parents' door. Daniel already has it open for them.

"Hello, siblings. What brings you guys here?" Emily kisses his cheek. Blake just passes him. Robert greets him.

"Hello, son. I have heard very good things around the station about you lately and about the case you assisted Trevor with." Blake stares at his dad for a moment.

"Dad, I am so glad you are satisfied because you know it is all about you," he states sarcastically.

"What's wrong, Blake?" his dad asks with concern.

Light in the Shadow

"Nothing, Dad. Don't worry about it. Come on, Em."

He grabs Emily's hand, and they walk into the guest room. The TV is on, but no one is watching it. He turns it off. "Emily, I fucked up major. I may have lost her forever."

"What happened?" she asks. He begins to explain the events that night, his behavior the next morning, and how she is avoiding him now.

"Blake, that is terrible. You have to fix it."

"Believe me, I have been busting my ass trying."

"I can't believe Dad. He has always encouraged family over career."

"I know, but he made me doubt everything. I don't blame him. I am a grown man. I shouldn't have reacted that way."

Robert overhears their conversation. He steps in the family room. "Blake. I am so sorry. I wasn't trying to…" He drops his head.

"No, Dad. I was the one who started having second thoughts."

"But, I put them there. Please let me make things right. Let me call her."

Blake stands. "Absolutely not! I am not a child. I'll fix it myself."

His father's face is riddled with sadness. He leaves and retires to his room.

"He means well, Blake."

"I know Em, but I am desperate. What can I do?" He plops back onto the couch.

"Just keep trying. She will come around."

Annetta Hobson

"I don't know. She has been hurt so much in her life."

He drops his head into his hands. He folds his arms and rests them on his knees. Emily rubs his back. "It will be alright. She was made for you and you for her. I know it."

He just keeps his head down. "Oh God. I hope she stills loves me. I don't know what I will do if she doesn't."

"I have to go, but keep trying, honey."

He continues to rest there, not moving. Emily stands, collects her children, and yells as she leaves. "I love you guys!" Blake sits up and grabs his phone out of its holster. He composes a text.

February 13th, Sunday – 7:05p.m.

From: Blake

> *I love you, Rayen. I have never loved anyone as much, and I never will. Please answer me. I haven't touched your skin in weeks. I haven't tasted your lips. I haven't smelled your scent. I am dying slowly each and every day. I know I have said it all, but how can I express to you that I fucking adore you? I cannot live and my life is nothing without you. I refuse to move on. Just respond and let me know if you still love me. I am going forward with wedding plans myself, starting today. I am going to pay a planner to do whatever she can to make it happen. So, please be there on May 12th. I am going to be the one in the tuxedo. I want you Rayen. Forever.*
>
> *I Love You!*

"Ha! I win! You two can't beat me if you were sharing one brain. I am a freaking genius," Angela gloats. Rayen slams her cards on the table.

Light in the Shadow

"Damn it! Where did you learn to play like this?"

"I am a prodigy." She jokes.

"That's it for me. I am going to my room." Margaret states. Rayen has remodeled her home office. It is now a bedroom for Margaret.

"Aww, mom, you are no fun," Angela says.

Rayen interjects, "Mr. Drake sent someone over to check on the house. He says everything is fine." Margaret stares at her.

"Rayen, I miss my home. When can I go?" Rayen twiddles her thumbs.

"I don't know?" Margaret stands and moves toward her.

"Does this have anything to do with Detective Shaw's visit?" She jerks her head away. She wants to avoid eye contact.

"Does it? Because I called her, and she said they think they have a couple of suspects. Do you know something we don't?"

Before she can answer, her phone chimes. She picks it up and opens the message that is flashing. She smiles and tears pool under her eyes. She plops her head on the table.

"From Blake?" Angela asks. She lifts her head and nods.

"Don't you think he has suffered enough? He loves you, Rye. Stop doing this. It has gone on too long. Don't you think?"

Tears start to fall from Rayen's eyes. They are spilling down her cheek. "Yes, yes! I miss him so much. Sometimes I feel as though I can't breathe. I find myself attempting to drive to his house, our house. I think I have let this go too far, but I wouldn't even know where to start."

"Start with I love you, too. Let this thing go," Margaret says.

"But, what about my issues, my past?"

"Relationships are built on the ability to love unconditionally. When someone really loves you, they love you no matter what."

Rayen stands and runs to Margaret. She hugs her tight. "Thank you so much. I am so glad you are here. What would I do without you?"

"You are going to find out eventually," she says through her teeth. Rayen smiles.

"I am going to call him."

"Oh thank goodness!" Angela says, throwing her hands in the air.

Margaret and Angela start up the stairs. Rayen watches them and waits until she hears the doors close. She takes a deep breath. She lifts her phone and starts to dial. The line rings three times. "Hello? Rayen?" Blake says, surprised.

"Hi, Blake."

"Baby, I am so glad to hear your voice." He is out of breath.

"I am glad to hear your voice also. I want to see you, Blake."

"I can be there to pick you up in ten minutes."

"No, I want you to come here so we can talk."

"That sounds wonderful, Rayen. I'm on my way!"

Before she can say anything else, he hangs up. She smiles and presses end. She runs up the stairs and takes a quick bath. She throws on a pair of gray sweat pants and a white tank. She slides into her black UGG boots and her jacket. When she gets to the bottom of the stairs, the doorbell buzzes. "I'll be right outside, Angie!" She yells up to her.

"Gotcha! Go get 'em tiger." She jokes.

Light in the Shadow

She bounces down the stairs and slings the door open. When she opens the door, he is standing there looking handsome as ever. He hasn't shaved in a while, but he still is a vision of hotness. He has on some jeans and a pea coat. "Hi, beautiful," he says as he lifts her off her feet. He embraces her. He holds her very close and very tight. They both inhale one another's scent. She wraps her arms around his neck and squeezes him. He hears her sniffle. He places her back on the ground. He stares into her eyes and witnesses the tears falling. He takes his thumbs and wipes a falling tear. He then kisses her face. She grabs him around the waist and squeezes him.

"I have missed you so much. I have been absolutely insane without you," she admits.

"I am so happy to hear that. I have been going out of my mind. I thought you were done with me, with us. I have been the toughest Detective to deal with since your abrupt exit," he shares. She glances at the ground.

"Blake, forgive me. I know you didn't mean the things you said. I am just full of angst."

"I don't want to dwell on the past. Let's talk about our future."

"I would love to, but first, let's get in your car out of this cold."

She grabs his hand and they run to his car.

"So, does this mean the wedding is still on?" Blake says. He turns toward Rayen, so he can look at her.

"Yes, sir, and that planner is off the hook. Margaret and Angela can take over," Rayen says.

"Emily would die if you leave her out."

"Okay then, the more the merrier."

He stares at her for a moment. "I miss being able to kiss those enticing lips. May I?"

"They belong to you. You don't have to ask."

He leans over and places his hands on her face. He slowly moves in and touches his lips to hers. The kiss starts slow. Then it deepens. She slides her fingers through his hair. She clutches it as she sucks his mouth into hers. He removes his hands from her face and moves them to her back. He rubs it and slides them down her back to her behind. Quickly she removes her coat. He stops and gazes at her for a moment. "Damn it! I really have missed you, Rayen. Don't ever leave me again." He grabs her hair, pulls her back to him, and kisses her again. He snatches his coat off, never leaving their lip lock. She reaches and grabs what belongs to her.

"Oh, baby, he misses you."

"I miss him."

When she unzips his jeans, someone taps on the window.

"Shit!" She pulls away and smiles. She wipes her mouth and straightens herself into her seat. He turns toward his door and slides his hand across the window to wipe away the steam. He does not see any one at first, so he slides his window down.

"Sorry to bother you, sir, but I am looking for East Center Street."

Rayen sits back and slides into her coat. Blake glances at her and whispers, "Wait, baby. Keep that off." She presses her hair down with her hand.

"You have to go back to Euclid, turn left and you will run right into it."

"Thanks, man."

Light in the Shadow

"No problem."

He begins to roll up the window. The man stops him. "Can you tell me where I can find that bitch, Rayen?" She springs forward.

"What?" When Blake looks up, the guy slaps him across the face with his gun. "Oh my God!" Rayen screams. The man snatches open the door and Blake partially falls out. He lifts him up and yells at her.

"Pull the seat up now!" She leans over and tries to grab it. The man scans the block. "Slide over here and do it or I am going to shoot him in his fucking head!" she peeks at Blake lying limp. Half of his body is on the ground and half in the car. She hops on her knees and pulls the seat forward. He pushes Blake into the back seat and pushes it in place. "Get out." He waves the gun at her. She steps out; he grabs her arm. He turns the gun on Blake. "Run, and I will kill him." He releases her arm and slides to the passenger side. He keeps the gun pointed at Blake. "Get in and drive." When she gets back in, he points the gun at her. Before she starts the car, she glances back at Blake. His face is bruising quickly and is turning bright red. She cringes at the sight. "Drive now, bitch! Or, you will die right here right now!" She starts the engine, puts the car in drive, and takes off. "Where are we going?" she asks. "How about his house?" he mumbles as he points to Blake.

"Why are you involving him, Matthew?"

He smiles. He appears very rugged. He has red hair. He has a black skullcap and a black ski coat. His eyes are a bright blue. He pierces her with them. It is like he is looking through her. "I was wondering if you recognized me. How do I look?"

She rolls her eyes and cuts them back to the road.

"Aw, don't be like that. You have grown up to be an exquisite beauty." His eyes scan her body. "I had to break you two up. I was getting bothered. Anyway, I've been watching you for years and you've had no idea."

"Cut the bull shit. What are you going to do with us?" He rubs the gun against her arm.

"I was hoping you would consider Vera's proposal. But if not, I am going to torture your boyfriend and make you watch. Then I will torture and kill you. I am hoping you refuse. I have so many things I can do to you." He stares at her with a disgusting look on his face. She watches the road and drives in silence.

When they reach Blake's house, she looks back at him. He turns and rubs his head. He tilts up and spots Rayen in the driver seat. "What happened?" Matthew peeks at Blake through the seats.

"Welcome to the party."

"Who in the fuck are you?"

"Let's get inside and we will start with the introductions."

"Rayen, are you ok?" Blake says as he sits up.

"I'm fine, Blake. Just take it easy."

"Step out. Stay where I can see you or I will kill him."

She steps out slowly and looks around. He slides out of the same side. "Let's go, Blake." Rayen pulls the seat up and helps him out. "Are you sure you are alright?"

"I'm fine." He grabs her arm and pulls her close.

"Get to the door and open it! Fast!"

They quickly walk to the door and open it. Blake switches on the lights. Matthew steps in and slams the door. "Nice place,"

Light in the Shadow

he says as he scans the room. "Now sit down." He points the gun toward the couch. Blake removes his coat and helps Rayen remove hers. He slides his arm around her shoulders and they move together.

"So, what's it gonna be, Rayen? You have had plenty of time to think. Let's have it."

"I will pay you. Tell me what to do."

"Okay. Come here."

Blake stands.

"Sit down! I was talking to her. Please don't try that cop shit with me because I was a one also and a marine."

Blake sits. "What a terrible waste."

He laughs. "You have no idea the money I have made being a criminal. You should try it." Blake is appalled.

"I would never. I enjoy enforcing the law."

"Oh really? Who fucking cares. Shut up! Now back to this divine creature." He begins to pace, but never taking his eyes off them. "I wanted to take you 11 years ago, but I am not really into children. Vera hates you. She warned me not to touch you, but I have been watching that fine ass too long not to touch." Blake stands again.

"If you lay one fucking finger on her…" He grabs Rayen and points the gun at her temple. "You will what? Watch her die, that's what. Now, Sit. Your. Ass. Down." Rayen nods at him. He sits.

"This is going to be fun." He yanks her closer and wraps his arm around her neck. She grabs his arm so he will not choke her. He switches his gun to the hand that is free. He slides his arm from her grip. He smells her hair. "Wow, Blake. She smells delicious." Blake motions as if he is going to stand. "Don't even think about it, hero. Move one more time, and it will be lights out." Blake rubs his fist. He wants to kill this man. Matthew smells her skin. "He is such a lucky guy," he whispers in her ear. When he closes his eyes he drops the hand with the gun slightly. Rayen grabs his hand with the gun, twists out of his grip, and kicks him between his legs. Blake jumps to his feet. When Matthew crouches to grab himself, he twists his arms behind his back and throws him to the floor.

"Go get something I can restrain him with."

"What do you have?"

He slams his knee into his back so he cannot move. Matthew just laughs. Rayen spots him laughing and grabs the gun from the floor and walks over to him.

"What are you going to do with that?" Blake looks up at her.

"Don't do it, Rayen."

She takes the gun, raises her hand with great force, and strikes him. She strikes him three times. "Okay, baby! he's out! Now hurry to the garage. I believe I have some cables."

She runs to the garage, searches, and finds two cables. She takes a quick look in the corner and there is a battery next to them on the shelf.

"Rayen!"

She shuffles back to him. "Here you are."

He takes the cables and ties his hands with one and legs with the other. "I need to call the station." He searches for a phone.

"Wait, Blake. If you call the police now, he will not tell where Vera is."

"That is not your decision, Rayen. Let me do my job."

Light in the Shadow

She runs to the sink and fills a glass with water. She runs back to him and splashes it in his face. Then she smacks him to wake him up.

"What are you doing, Rayen?"

"I need my family safe. I just want to persuade him to tell us where she is."

He shakes some of the water off. He lifts his head and gazes at the two of them. "Where is the police, cop?" He asks. Blake turns his head. Rayen crouches beside him.

"Where is Vera?" He smiles and lays his head on the floor.

"Wouldn't you love to know?" She leans closer.

"I am not the cop. He is," she whispers.

"Be careful Rayen. You sound a little dangerous. Besides, it doesn't matter. If I go to jail or if Vera gets caught, it won't end with us. The major player is..." He bursts into laughter. "This is deeper than you know. When the police take me in, my contact will find out. Well, let's just say it will be worse." She stands and looks at Blake.

"What are you saying?"

"I am just a player in the game. I am not the person pushing the buttons. They promised if I go to jail, you will suffer."

"He is lying, Rayen," Blake snaps.

"I assure you I am not. You will be looking over your shoulder."

"I am calling the station now!"

"No, Blake, wait."

He stops.

"If we send the money, then what?"

"Then all is well for a while. All you have to do is transfer the money to the account I have in my pocket."

"How much?"

"200,000 dollars."

She looks up at Blake and runs to get the lap top.

"Rayen, no! Please."

"Text your contact, and tell them okay."

"Money first, beautiful."

She logs into her online account.

"Reach right in here. He flips on his side and nods toward his pocket. She takes his phone and the piece of paper. She types in some transaction numbers. She waits a moment. "How will we know when they receive it?" His phone suddenly chimes. She looks at it. There is a text.

February 13th, Sunday - 11:05 p.m.

From: Vera

> *Got it! I'll send your half to your account now. When will you return?*

Rayen looks at him. She stands and walks away. She then texts back.

February 13th, Sunday - 11:08 p.m.

To: Vera

> *Good. I will lay low for a while. I had to do some dirty work. Call you in a few weeks.*

She hits send and the message is sent.

Light in the Shadow

February 13th, Sunday - 11:12 p.m.

From: Vera

Okay, until then. Good job. Get rid of the phone.

Rayen does not text back. She slams the phone shut and turns to him. "They will come after us if he is arrested. If we get rid of him, they will think he ran off with the money." Blake's mouth flies open.

"Rayen what are you asking me to do?"

"You bitch! Are you saying what I think you are?"

She turns to him and slowly walks over. "Obviously, you haven't been watching as closely as you think. You have no idea what I have become. Thanks to Vera."

He turns to Blake.

"Oh, don't look at him."

"Why aren't you calling the police, officer?"

She punches him. "Shut the fuck up! Scum."

"What the…"

"See, you thought you were getting poor little Rayen. No, officer, I have eaten low lives like you for lunch."

He looks at Blake confused. Blake stares at her with equal confusion. He walks over to her. "Rayen, what are you asking me to do?"

"I am asking you to help me protect the only family I have left: you, Angela, and Margaret."

"You want me to kill him?" He stares into her eyes and pain stretches across his face.

"No."

He sighs in relief and turns to Matthew.

"I want you to walk away while I kill him."

He spins back to face her. "What? How?"

She places her fingers over his lips. "The less you know, the better."

He removes her hand. "Have you done this before?"

While they are talking, Matthew slithers along the floor. She hears him, runs over to him, and kicks him in the throat. He gags and collapses. Blake is in disbelief. She walks away from him to the kitchen. She grabs a knife and sets it on the table. She runs to the garage and grabs the battery. She takes the lids off of it. She scurries around preparing. When she has everything she needs, she slides his body towards the garage. She glances at Blake. He sits on the couch. He runs his fingers through his hair. "Rayen, wait." She stops.

"How do you know I won't turn you in?"

"I don't, but I can't let him go back to Vera. I would rather this be her, but…"

She grabs his arms and slides him toward the garage.

"What did you do to him?"

"He is just unconscious."

"He will contact whomever he works for. I need to find out why they killed my parents and who is in the driver seat of this extortion, slash murder mess I call my life. I cannot do that if they kill you guys or me for that matter."

He circles the kitchen back and forth. "I can't believe you are doing this. I am law enforcement. It will destroy my life, my career."

Light in the Shadow

She drops Matthew and walks over to him. "I have never been caught. I would never jeopardize you. I love you."

He stares at her for a moment. "Exactly how many times have you done this?"

"I can't talk to you about this right now. Do you love and trust me?"

"Yes. I trust you, and I love you very much."

"Good." She picks his arms back up and slides him into the door way between the kitchen and the garage. She grabs some garbage bags and rips them in half. She spreads them out. When she has enough to cover the area she places several towels around his body. She carefully places two thick, fluffy towels in front and props his chin on them.

"Wait! I can't watch you do this."

She steps back. "Blake, It has to be done."

He rubs his face with his hands. He begins to speak very slowly. "I am going to be your husband. If anyone is going to do this, it's me. It's my job to protect you."

Her face brightens, but she does not smile. She goes over to the table and grabs the paring knife she laid out. She hands it to him. He lifts Matthew's head and takes a deep breath before he strikes. Matthew speaks, "Someone from your father's company…" Blake slices deep into his throat to stop him from talking. He drops his head and it lands on the towels. He tries to speak but gurgling sounds escape. He collapses, and the life leaves him.

"What did he say?"

"I don't know, but you need to go to that utility sink and wash your hands with bleach." She grabs some leather gloves she found. Blake is literally shaking. She begins to clean up. She lets the blood soak into the towels. She gathers them all around his head. He stumbles over to the sink and washes his hands. He starts to undress. Leave your clothes there. He strips down to his underwear. He stands there and stares. She works quickly, unbinding his hands and feet. She lifts the battery and releases the liquid onto his face. The skin begins to melt. She then dips each finger into the compartment of the battery. Blake just watches in horror. His face is disintegrating. The acid is causing his face and fingers to bubble. She grabs a comforter and rolls his body onto it. She runs outside and grabs a cinderblock and brings it in. She cleans everything that has blood on it. Luckily, the towels catch most of it. She drags him to the patio door and opens it. She ties the cinderblock to his ankle with his ripped t-shirt. She makes the tie strong by continuously ripping and tying knots. She drags the comforter to the end of the deck and dumps the cinderblock in first. There is a small splash. Then, she pushes his body in. It makes a splash also. She looks around to see if anyone hears, then grabs a bucket with soap in it and cleans the deck. She picks up the cover and towels. She takes them to the garage door. She places the bags into the sink and rinses them really well. She undresses herself. She dumps all of the towels, the comforter and all of their clothes into the washer. She pours a whole bottle of bleach in it along with soap. After that, she shreds the garments with scissors and places everything in a bag. Blake has not moved for about an hour. She gets on her knees in her underwear and searches for blood. When she doesn't find any, she runs upstairs and jumps in the shower. Quickly, she washes and gets out. She throws on a robe of Blake's. She takes the bag she put the things in and places it in Blake's trunk.

   Rayen grabs Blake's hand and leads him to the shower. She scrubs his body from head to toe. She grabs a towel and dries him off. "Are you going to be alright, Blake?" she questions softly. He shakes his head from side to side. She leads him into

Light in the Shadow

the bedroom, and he sits on the bed. "It's going to be alright. If it surfaces, no one will be able to identify him right away. His body will be thousands of miles away before it comes back up." Finally he speaks.

"I want to know how this started and every single time you have done this. You are a professional, and I want to know every detail starting now." Rayen gulps. She feared this day. She knew one day her secret would be discovered. She turns towards him, takes his hand, caresses it, and starts with the beginning of her story.

About the Author

Annetta is a Romance Novelist from Detroit Michigan. As a woman with a modern urban personality, Annetta has a firm grasp on the wiles of romance, dating and love. She shares these

Annetta Hobson

through her intimate characters who deliver naughty and nice tendencies with an extra dose of sugar and spice.

Her first title release, "Light in the Shadow" you've just read – future titles currently in development include:

- Chronicles of a Bethroved
- Love's Therapy
- Reverse Seduction 1
- Reverse Seduction 2
- The Flame
- Weather Vane

Currently, Ms. Hobson is attending college pursuing a criminal justice major.

She has been married for eleven years and shares seven children with her husband. She loves to read and write.

Connect With Annetta!

Social Media

FaceBook: https://www.facebook.com/AuthorAnnettaHobson

Twitter: http://www.twitter.com/AuthorAHobson

Blog and Websites

Wordpress Blog: http://annettahobson.wordpress.com

Website: authorannettahobson.org

You can purchase other titles by Annetta Hobson at:

DonnaInk Publications: http://www.donnaink.org

www.donnaink.com

Made in the USA
Charleston, SC
10 April 2013